A HOUSEFUL OF
GIRLS

I0617623

SARAH TYTLER

1ˢᵗ WORLD
LIBRARY
Literary Society

A Houseful of Girls

Sarah Tytler

© 1st World Library, 2007
PO Box 2211
Fairfield, IA 52556
www.1stworldlibrary.com
First Edition

LCCN: 2007901836

Softcover ISBN: 978-1-4218-4308-7
Hardcover ISBN: 978-1-4218-4210-3
eBook ISBN: 978-1-4218-4406-0

1st World Library is a literary, educational organization
dedicated to:

- Creating a free internet library of downloadable ebooks

  - Hosting writing competitions and offering book
    publishing scholarships.

1st World Library Literary Society

Giving Back to the World

"If you want to work on the core problem, it's early school literacy."

- James Barksdale, former CEO of Netscape

"No skill is more crucial to the future of a child, or to a democratic and prosperous society, than literacy."

- Los Angeles Times

Literacy... means far more than learning how to read and write... The aim is to transmit... knowledge and promote social participation."

- UNESCO

"Literacy is not a luxury, it is a right and a responsibility. If our world is to meet the challenges of the twenty-first century we must harness the energy and creativity of all our citizens."

- President Bill Clinton

"Parents should be encouraged to read to their children, and teachers should be equipped with all available techniques for teaching literacy, so the varying needs and capacities of individual kids can be taken into account."

- Hugh Mackay

CONTENTS

CHAPTER I

A FLUTTER IN THE DOVE-COT

Is there any sensation equal to that produced by the first lover and the first proposal coming to a girl in a large family of girls? It is delightfully sentimental, comical, complimentary, affronting, rousing, tiresome—all in one. It is a herald of lovers, proposals, and wonderful changes all round. It is the first thrill of real life in its strong passions, grave vicissitudes, and big joys and sorrows as they come in contact with idle fancies, hearts that have been light, simple experiences which have hitherto been carefully guarded from rude shocks.

It does not signify much whether the family of girls happen to be rich or poor, unless indeed that early and sharp poverty causes a precocity which deepens girls' characters betimes, and by making them sooner women, robs them of a certain amount of the thoughtlessness, fearlessness, and impracticability of girlhood. But girlhood, like many another natural condition, dies hard; and its sweet, bright illusions, its wisdom and its folly, survive tolerably severe pinches of adversity.

The younger members of such a sisterhood are politely supposed to be kept in safe ignorance of the great event which is befalling one of the seniors. It is thought at once a delicate and prudent precaution to prevent the veil which hides the future, with its casualties, from being lifted prematurely and abruptly, where juvenile minds are concerned, lest they become unhinged and unfit for the salutary discipline of schoolroom lessons, and the mild pleasure of schoolroom treats. The flower in the bud ought to be kept with its petals folded, in its innocent absence of self-consciousness, to the last moment.

But there is an electric sympathy in the air which defeats precautions. There is a freemasonry of dawning womanhood which starts into life everywhere. How do the young people pick up with such surprising quickness and acuteness the looks and whispers meant to pass over their heads, the merry glances, nervous shrugs, quick blushes, and indignant pouts, which have suddenly grown strangely prevalent in the blooming circle? The bystanders are understood to be engrossed with their music-lessons, their drawing-classes, their rudimentary Latin and Greek—if anybody is going in for the higher education of women—their pets, their games of lawn-tennis, their girl companions with whom these other girls are for ever making appointments to walk, to practise part-singing, to work or read together, to get up drawing-room *tableaux* or plays.

The general consciousness is not, in certain lights, favourable to a lover's pretensions. For human nature is perverse, and there is such a thing as *esprit-de-corps* running to excess. There may be a due amount of girlish pride in knowing that one of the sisters has inspired a grand passion. There may be a tremulous respect for the fact that she has passed the Rubicon, that, in place of girlish trifling, she has an affair which has to do with the happiness or misery of a fellow creature, not to say with her own happiness or misery, on her burdened mind. Why, if she does not take care, she may be plunged at once, first into the whirl of choosing her trousseau and the fascinating trial of being the principal figure at a wedding, and then involved in the tremendous responsibilities of house-keeping, butchers' bills, grocers' bills, cooks' delinquencies, with the heavy obligations—not only of ordering dinners for two, but of occasionally entertaining a room full of company, single-handed!

And this is only one side of the shield; there is a reverse side, at least equally prominent and alarming. The second side upholds maidenly claims, finds nothing good enough to match with them, and is tempted to scout and flout, laugh and mock at the rival claims of the lover upon trial. This is true even in the most innocent of dove-cots, where satire is still as playful and harmless as summer lightning.

"The idea of Tom Robinson's thinking of one of us!" cried Annie Millar. "What could possess him to imagine that we should ever get over the shop—granted that it is a Brobding-nagian shop, an imposing mart of linen-drapery, haberdashery, silk-mercery enough to serve the whole county?"

"To be sure it is only Dora, not you, Annie," burst in eighteen years' old Rose, who had just left school, and was fain to drop the pretence of being too young to notice the most interesting event in the world to a family of girls.

"Why do you say that, Rose? Dora may not be so pretty as Annie—I don't know, and I don't care—it is all a matter of taste; but she is as much one of us, father's daughter, brought up like the rest of us in the Old Doctor's House."

The speaker was May, between sixteen and seventeen. She was the tallest of the four sisters—let them call her "Little May" as long as they liked. She had so far forgotten herself as to follow Rose's lead.

"Hold your tongues, you two monkeys; what should you know about it?" Annie, who had a tendency to sit upon her younger sisters, tried to silence them. She had reached the advanced age of twenty-two, and by virtue of being the eldest, had been considered grown up for the last four years, when Rose and May were chits of fourteen and a little over twelve. Of course this gave Annie a vast advantage in womanly dignity and knowledge of the world. But at the present moment she was herself so interested in the discussion that she could not make up her mind to drop it till Rose and May were out of the way.

"I must say"—Annie started the subject again—"that I think it great presumption in Tom Robinson, though he is not so ugly as that comes to, and he's really well enough bred in spite of 'Robinson's.'"

"He is a college-bred man." Dora ventured shyly to put in a word for the dignity of her suitor, and for her own dignity as so far involved in his. "And so were his father and grandfather before him, father says."

"But the Robinsons had the silk-mill and the woollen-factory then as well as the big shop," corrected Annie. "And Tom might have gone into the Church or into some other profession if he had chosen, when things might have been a little different. Still, if you are pleased, Dora," with a peal of derisive laughter, "if you do not object to the—shop."

"Of course I object," cried Dora, tingling with mortification and shame. "That is, I should object to his having a shop, if I had ever thought of him for a single moment in that light. I cannot imagine what put me into his head—in that sense. Indeed I cannot believe it yet. I am sure it is just some nonsense on the part of the rest of you to tease me."

"No, no," Annie hastened to contradict her. "It is sober reality. He has said something to father; you know he has, mother owned it."

"He has been meeting us and throwing himself in our way everywhere," broke in the irrepressible Rose and May.

"He has been coming and coming here," resumed Annie, "where, as we don't happen to have a brother, there is not even another young man to form an excuse for his coming. We cannot so much as pretend, when people remark on his visits, that he has come ever since we remember, and is as familiar with us as we are with ourselves. No doubt, in a little town like this, everybody who has the least claim to be a gentleman or a lady, knows every other gentleman or lady—after a fashion.

But naturally father and mother were not intimate with the late Mr. and Mrs. Robinson; and we—that is, Tom and we girls—are not so near each other in age as to have been brought together by our respective nurses. We did not pick daisies in company, or else pull each other's hair, and slap each other's faces, according to our varying moods. Tom Robinson is four or five years older than I, not to speak of Dora."

"He stopped us this very morning," Rose again joined in the chorus, "when May and I were going with the Hewetts to gather primroses in Parson's Meadow. He asked if our sisters—that was you, Dora, with Annie thrown into the bargain—thought of going on the river this afternoon."

"He might be an inch or two taller, I don't suppose he is above five feet six or seven," suggested Annie, maliciously recalling a detail in the description of Dora's future husband, that be he who or what he might, he should certainly not be under six feet in height. Dora, who was herself considerably below the middle size, would never yield her freedom to a man who had to admit a lower scale of inches.

"And his hair might be a little less—chestnut, shall we say, Dora?" put in Rose with exasperating sprightliness, referring to a former well-known prejudice of Dora's against "*Judas-tinted hair.*"

"Would you call his nose Roman or Grecian?" asked May naively, of a very nondescript feature.

"And he has so little to say for himself," recommended Annie, "though when he does speak there is no great fault to be found with what he says; still it would be dreadfully dull and tiresome to have to do all the speaking for a silent partner."

"Oh, hold your tongues, you wretched girls," cried Dora, standing at bay, stamping one small foot in a slipper with a preposterously large rosette. "What does it signify? The man, like his words, is well enough—better than any of us, I dare say," speaking indignantly; "but what does it matter, when I could never look at him, never dream of him, as anything more than a mere acquaintance? I don't wish for a lover or a husband—at least not yet," with a gasp; "I don't wish to leave home, and go away from all of you, though you are so unkind and teasing—not for a long, long time, till I am quite a middle-aged woman. I don't see why I should be plagued about it when Annie here, who is two years older than I am, and ever so much prettier, as everybody knows, has escaped such persecution."

"My dear," said Annie demurely, "it is because you have the opportunity of presenting me with a pair of green garters. If it should occur again, and you choose to avail yourself of it, I mean to accept the garters with the best grace in the world. Isn't that good of me when you have been coolly telling me that I have been overlooked as the eldest, and the belle of the family—flattering my conceit with one breath and taking it down with another? But it is not a case of Leah and Rachel. We are not in the East, and in the West the elder sister does not necessarily take precedence in marriage. You are quite welcome to marry first, Dora; you are all welcome to marry before me, girls," with a sweeping curtsey to her audience all round. "I am perfectly resigned to your leaving your poor worthy elder sister to end her days as a solitary spinster, a meek and useful maiden-aunt."

The Millars were the daughters of Dr. Millar of Redcross, an old-fashioned country town in the Midlands. They were happy in having a good father and mother still spared to them. The girls were what is called "a fine family," in a stronger sense than that in which Jane Austen has used the term. Their ages ranged from twenty-two to midway between sixteen and seventeen. They were all good-looking girls, with a family likeness. Annie, the eldest, was very pretty, with delicate, regular features, a soft warm brunette colour, dark eyes, and a small brown head and graceful throat, like the head and throat of a greyhound.

Dora, the first wooed, was, at a hasty glance, a mere shadow of Annie. She was pale, though it was a healthy paleness. Her hair was lighter in tint, her eyes, too, were considerably lighter— granted that they were clear as crystal. It was difficult to think of Dora as preferred before Annie, if one did not take into account that there are people who will turn away from June roses to gather a cluster of honeysuckle, or pick a sweet pea— people to whom there is an ineffable charm in simple maiden- liness and sweetness. Dora's modest unhesitating acceptance of the second part in the family and social circle, and her perfect content to play it, would be a crowning attraction in such people's eyes. So would her gentle girlish diffidence, which moved her rather to meet and reflect the tastes and opinions of others than to exercise her own, though she was by no means without individual capacity and character.

Rose was the least handsome of the family at this stage of her existence. The family features in her had taken a slightly bizarre cast, and she had a bad habit of wrinkling her smooth low forehead and crumpling up her sharpish nose, in a manner which accentuated the peculiarity. But Annie, who was an authority on the subject of looks, maintained, behind Rose's back, that there was something *piquante* and *recherchee* about Rose's face and figure. Not one of the Millars was tall—not even May, though she came nearest to it; but Rose's slight pliant figure had a natural grace and elegance which its quick, careless movements did not dispel. When she held herself up, uncreased her forehead and nose, showed to advantage her very fine, true chestnut hair, and was full of animation—as to do Rose justice she generally was—giving fair play to her dimples and little white teeth, Annie said Rose had a style of her own which did no discredit to the family reputation for more than a fair share of beauty. In addition to Annie's high spirit and ready tongue, Rose had a decided turn for art, which her father had taken pride in cultivating.

"Little May" was like Annie, and promised to be as pretty; but she was a rose in the bud still, with the unfilled out outlines and crude angularities of a girl not done growing. She was very much of a child in many things, and she had Dora's soft clinging nature, yet under it all she was the born scholar of the family, with a simple aptitude and taste for learning which surprised and delighted her father still more than Rose's achievements in pastilles and water-colours pleased him. It was seeing May at her books, when she was a very different May from the girl who ran about with Rose, and was kept in her proper place by Annie, which revived in Doctor Millar the old regret that Providence had not blessed him with a son. He could not exactly make a son of May, since from her early childhood she was a little sensitive woman all over, but he did what he could. He had her taught Latin, Greek, and mathematics just to afford her the chance of being a scholar. He never told himself, and nobody else did, in the meantime, what she was to do with her scholarship when she was a little older. Whether it was merely to grace her womanhood, or whether the youngest of the family, her father and mother's last pet, was to summon up courage, tear herself away from familiar and dear surroundings, and carry her gifts and acquirements out into the world, in order to win for them the best distinction of usefulness.

Dora's lightly held suitor was the head of "Robinson's." "Robinson's" was a great and time-honoured institution in Redcross, while it and its masters were somewhat of anomalies. The first Robinson whom the town troubled to remember was as good as anybody in it, the proprietor of a silk-mill, and latterly of a wool-factory in the neighbourhood. As a mere convenient adjunct to the mill and the factory he had started a shop in the town, and kept it going by means of a manager. Even in that light it was a handsome old shop. The walls were lined with polished oak, so was the low ceiling, and there was an oak staircase leading from one storey to another which a connoisseur in staircases might have coveted. "Robinson's" was a positive feature in Redcross, and if it had been anything else than a good shop of its kind would have been greatly admired. The son of the founder of the shop was also reckoned, to begin with, as good as his professional neighbours. He was college-bred, like his father, as Dora in her jealousy for the dignity of her first lover had stated. This was "all to begin with." Whether because it was advisable, or from mere grovelling instincts, he dropped in turn both the mill and the factory, neither of which did more than pay its way, and retained the shop, which was understood to be a lucrative concern. He did worse; though Redcross continued to acknowledge him— somewhat dubiously to be sure—as a gentleman, because of the fine presence which Tom had not inherited, and the perfect good breeding which had descended to the son. In spite of the magnanimity which forgave frostily the second Robinson for so far forgetting himself as to take the management of his great shop into his own hands, walk up and down and receive customers, and be seen working at his books in the glass office if he did not go behind the counter, he went and married for his second wife a farmer's daughter. She was an honest, sensible, comely young woman, but she had no pretensions to be a lady, and no more inclination to enter the society of the Redcross upper class than the upper class had a mind to receive her as an equal. Charles Robinson's first wife had been all very well, though she was penniless. She had been a curate's daughter, educated to fill the post of governess in high families. She had died young, without children, and he had filled her place with the farmer's daughter, who was the mother of Tom. Thenceforth the Robinson's house, a good, old-fashioned house, though not so handsome as the shop in an adjacent street, was effaced, nominally, from the visiting-lists of those who had visiting-lists in Redcross. The family were ostracised, and left to their own devices, receiving their sentence, in the case of the farmer's daughter and her husband, with apparent equanimity.

But there was an exception made in favour of Tom. He went to the Grammar School along with the other better-class boys in the town and neighbourhood, and was accepted as their companion and playfellow. He was sent to college according to the traditions of his family, just as Cyril Carey, of Carey's Bank, and Ned Hewett, of the Rectory, were sent according to the traditions of theirs. Presumably the three young men were on one footing at Cambridge, unless, indeed, Tom had the advantage. He was slightly the elder of the three, and he took his degree with a fair amount of honour; while, sad to say, for the credit of Redcross, neither Cyril nor Ned made their last pass. It was confidently believed that Tom Robinson would cut the shop, so far as any active management of it was concerned, and enter either a gallant or a learned profession. If he had ever entertained the intention, it was put a stop to in the first place by the death of his father, followed within three months by that of his mother, shortly after Tom had completed his course at the university. He stayed at home for a time, to put his house in order it was supposed. Then all at once, in the most cold-blooded fashion, he told those who asked him that "Robinson's" was a good business, which he did not see himself justified in throwing up in these hard times. He was not such a conceited ass as to believe he must necessarily succeed in the crowded ranks of the professions, for none of which had he any particular bent, while he had, he added, with a certain manliness and doggedness for a pacific fellow like Robinson, a considerable interest in the great old shop. It had been in the family for three generations; he had known it from childhood; many of his father's old trusted servants still served in it. In short, he meant to keep it in his own hands, and not to let it go to sticks and staves, possibly, in the hands of others. He did not, for his part, see any mark of gentle breeding and fine feeling in devolving his responsibilities on others, and only reserving that tie to the shop which had to do with pecuniary profits. As for his university training and academic degree, if they did not benefit him in all circumstances they were not much worth. The town of Redcross was caught in a trap. The gentle-folks of the place had already received him as a man and a brother, and they could not refuse to know him any longer because he stuck to the paternal shop, though they might exercise their discretion in looking coldly on him in future. For that matter, there was another opinion among the older professional men—the Rector, whose tithes were only quarter paid; Dr. Millar, whose paying patients were no longer able to call him in on all occasions; Carey, the banker, whose private bank, it was whispered darkly, was struggling in deep waters; Colonel

Russell, who had come home from India on half-pay and his savings, which every year he found more inadequate for the expenses of an increasing family. All these gray-headed men, growing haggard and careworn, agreed that in the present depressed state of the commercial world, young Robinson was showing himself a sensible fellow and ought to be commended for his decision. They declared that they were the more inclined to take him up because of it. It was their wives, where they had wives, and especially their daughters, with the young men who had not known the brunt of the battle, and felt inclined to clutch their professional dignities and privileges, that were of a different mind. Girls like the Millars turned up their saucy little noses at the shop. They thought it was mean-spirited and vulgar-minded, "low" of Tom Robinson to sit down with such a calling. They held it audacious of him to lift his eyes to Dora, and to follow his eyes with his voice, silent fellow though he was generally, in asking her from her father.

Certainly it did not help to redeem Tom Robinson's draw-backs in the judgment of a rash young world that he lacked his late father's fine presence. Though gentleman-like enough, he was insignificant in person, and he had little to say for himself. Probably it would have struck his critics as little short of profane to make the comparison, otherwise there is a great example that might have stood him and all men not giants and glib of tongue in good stead. It is written of an apostle, and he not the least of the apostles, that he might have been termed in bodily presence mean, and in speech contemptible. But boys and girls are not wont to take up such examples and ponder their meaning in foolish young hearts.

The Millars, as one of the girls had said, were brought up in the Old Doctor's House at Redcross. It would seem that professions and trades were hereditary in the old-fashioned, stationary town. Dr. Millar's father had not only been a doctor before him, he had been *the* doctor in Redcross, with a practice extending from an aristocratic county to a parish-poor class of patients. His pretty sister Penny, whom Annie was not unlike, had married into the county, General Beauchamp of

Wayland's younger son. The marriage, with all its consequences, was a thing of the long past, leaving little trace in the
present. For young Beauchamp, though he was a squire's son,
had not been able to get on at the bar, and had emigrated with
his wife while emigration was still comparatively untried in
Australia, where it was to be hoped his county extraction had
served him in the Bush at least as well as Tom Robinson's
university education would avail him in the shop. It had all
happened an age before the young Millars could remember,
still the tradition of a marriage of a member of a former
generation of the Millars into the squirearchy had its effect on
her collateral descendants. It did not signify that the reigning
Beauchamps of Waylands had almost ceased to remember the
ancient alliance in their dealings with their doctor. That dim
and distant distinction established the superior position of the
Millars in their native town, to the girls' entire satisfaction.
Dora to marry Robinson, of "Robinson's," a farthing candle of
a man, when her Grand-aunt Penny had married a Beauchamp
of Waylands, by all accounts the handsomest, most dashing
member of the Hunt in his day, was a descent not to be
thought of for a moment.

Sarah Tytler

CHAPTER II

THE "COUP DE GRACE."

The crisis had come. Dr. Millar had granted a final formal interview, not without some agitation on the father's part, to the still more agitated suitor; and after assuring him of the paternal good-will, had turned him over to the daughter—the whole being done with a sorrowful prescience, shared by the unfortunate young man, of what the answer would be.

Poor Dora was hardly less to be pitied, for she had to be brought up to the supreme effort of dealing the *coup de grace*. Nobody could do it for her, even her mother told her that severely, in order to brace the girlish nerves, when Dora gave way to the first cowardly instinct of seeking to shirk the ordeal. If a girl was old enough to receive an offer of marriage, she was old enough to answer it for herself in person. It was the least return she could make for the high compliment which had been paid to her, to see the man and tell him with her own lips that she would have nothing to say to the honest heart and liberal hand, for he had hinted at generous settlements, which he had been only too eager to lay at her feet.

It was little use even for mild Dora to protest that she had not wished for such a compliment, and had done nothing to provoke it, so that the reckless compliment-payer was but receiving his deserts in an unconditional refusal. It did not make the step easier for her. It was no joke to her, whatever it might be to her hard-hearted young sisters.

To tell the truth, Rose and May, aye, even Annie, took much lively diversion, as Dora guessed, in secretly watching the entire proceeding. The sisters found out the hour of the compulsory interview. They covertly looked out for the arrival of the commonplace wooer—anything save their idea of a lover and hero. They keenly took note of him from an upper window as he walked with a certain studied composure, yet with a blankness of aspect, through the shrubbery. They even deigned—Annie as well as Rose and May—surreptitiously to inspect the poor wretch between the bannisters of the staircase, as he ran desperately up the stairs, thrusting one hand through his foxy hair and carrying his hat in the other, and vanished into the drawing-room.

After this brutal behaviour on the part of a trio of English girls, one must show a little moderation in condemning the cruel conduct of the Roman dames, who contemplated with zest the deadly contests of the gladiators in the arena; at least the gladiators were strangers and barbarians, not fellow-townsmen and near relations.

As for the present victim, he was happily unconscious of any spectator beyond Bella the house-maid, but he felt relieved to be delivered from her compassionate stare. He had an instinctive sense that she knew as well as he did what he had come there for, and was pitying him—an inference in which he was quite correct. For Bella was older than the unseen "chorus" on the landing, who did not think of pitying him. She had seen more of the world, and was better acquainted with its cares and troubles. She called him in her own mind "the poor young gent!" It occurred to her as it did not occur to the others, that he might take to bad ways and be a lost man, like Jem Wade the carpenter, after her pretty, flighty sister Lotty had given him the sack. Nothing less than that might be the end of this day's work.

But such a way of looking on a lover and his woes was far from the thoughts of Bella's young mistresses. On the contrary, they had difficulty in restraining merry little titters, though Annie did take herself to task and murmur "For shame!" when Rose made a solemn, stupid face like what she considered Tom Robinson's on this occasion.

To do the girls justice, however, they did not laugh when Dora, who had been with her mother, came slowly across the lobby and followed the visitor into the drawing-room in order to administer the *coup de grace*. It might have been a veritable dagger-thrust to be dealt by a weak little shrinking hand, with the owner's head turned and face averted—such a white, grieved, frightened girl's face it was.

Her companions' eyes were opened, for the instant a fellow-feeling smote them. This was no light jest or piece of child's play; it might be their turn next. Oh! who would not be sorry for Dora to have to inflict real pain and bitter disappointment, to be condemned to kill a man's faith in woman, perhaps, certainly to murder his peace and happiness for the present, to extinguish the sweetest, brightest dream of his early manhood, for he would never have another quite so tender and radiant? Would Dora ever be quite the same again after she had done so hard a thing?

Annie pulled herself up and accused herself of getting absolutely maudlin. The idea of Tom Robinson of "Robinson's," with his middle size, matter-of-fact air, and foxy hair and moustache, entertaining such a dream and relinquishing it with a pang of mortal anguish that would leave a long sickening heart-ache behind! It was the infection of all the silly love stories she had ever read which had received a kind of spurious galvanic life from the very ordinary circumstance, the feather in her cap, as so many girls would have regarded it, of Dora, having to receive and refuse an offer of marriage. Why, she—Annie—and her sisters, including Dora herself, had been much diverted by it, as well as interested in it, until the dramatic crisis had somehow taken their breath away also, and startled them by a glimpse of the other side of the question. But though Annie strove to recover her equanimity, and Rose tried to hum a tune softly as the girls still loitered behind the bannisters, to see the end of the play, they said nothing more to each other; a sort of shyness and shame had stolen over them. It was not enough to make them run away, especially as each did not realize that what she felt was common to all. Only their lips were chained simultaneously, and they were disposed to turn aside their heads and avert their eyes, like Dora when she killed her man.

The deed did not take long—not more than was necessary for him to plead once or twice with small variation on the words, "Will you not think of it, Dora? Can you not give it a little consideration? Perhaps if I were to wait, and you were to try—"

And for Dora to answer with drooping head, panting breast, and still less variety in her phrases, "Oh, no, no, Mr. Tom. Of course, I am very much obliged to you for thinking a great deal more of me than I deserve. But, indeed, indeed, it cannot be—you must give it up—this foolish fancy. It is a great pity that you have wasted time on such an absurd idea."

"Wasted time!" he repeated, with a little irony and a little pathos. "Well, I don't think it wasted even at this moment—and—and the idea does not seem so absurd to me; but I will not distress you by forcing my wishes upon you when you are so averse to them. You will allow me to continue your friend, Miss Dora?"

"Yes, oh yes," sighed Dora, who would have said anything, short of agreeing to marry him, to get him to go away, "if you like, after what has happened. I know I don't deserve your friendship; but, indeed, I could not help it, Mr. Robinson. I never guessed till lately that you thought of anything else, and then I would have stopped you, but I could not."

"Don't blame yourself," he said with a faint smile, "I am not blaming you. I shall count it a favour, an honour, if you will let me do anything for you that I can."

Sarah Tytler

"Thank you very much," she murmured humbly.

"Then you will accept a little mark of my friendly feelings?" He took a small case from his waistcoat pocket, opened it, and drew from it a valuable ring, holding it out to her.

They were the most beautiful rubies and sapphires she had ever seen. But she would not touch it; she even put her hands behind her back in her confusion and dismay. "I could not; I ought not. It is far too costly a thing, I can see that at a glance. You must keep it; you will find some far fitter girl to give it to."

He shook his head, hesitated, and then took an old-fashioned little vinaigrette case, shaped like a tiny gold box, from the watch-chain at which he wore it. "Will you accept this from me, then? It was my mother's, and I should like you to have it."

"It's so good of you," the girl faltered. "I don't like to deprive you of what was your mother's, but if you care that I should have it—"

"I do care," he said.

That last little episode was entirely between themselves. When she quitted the room, not crying, but paler than before, she had the vinaigrette case clasped tightly in her hand, while nobody except Tom Robinson knew of the gift.

He let her go, and then he left the house. When he did so there was that in his face which caused Rose Millar to cry under her breath, "Come away. It is not fair to spy upon him. I'll never want to see anybody refused again." As for "little May," she burst into tears, though the principals had shed no tears.

"Hold your tongue, you little goose," remonstrated the disturbed Annie. "He may hear you. School-girls like you and

Rose should not meddle in grown-up people's affairs."

"I thought I had left school after the Christmas holidays," said Rose, interrogating the world in an abstract fashion. She was herself again on the instant, carrying her funny little crumpled nose well in the air.

"It is dreadful," said May, with a half-suppressed sob, "and he was so good-natured. He promised only last week to get Rose and me a fox-terrier puppy."

"Oh, you selfish little creature! It is over the failure of the prospective puppy and not over the sorrows of the rejected man you are lamenting. Never mind, Maisie, I doubt if mother would have allowed us to keep the puppy. As for Mr. Tom Robinson, he is cut up just now, of course; but he will soon get over it. How long does it take a man to forget, Annie? Anyhow, presently he will be busily directing his attentions in another quarter, until the day may come, after he is successful and triumphant, well pleased with himself and his choice, when he will heartily thank Dora there for having administered to him the cold bath of a rejection, so nipping his first raw aspirations in the bud."

"No, no," insisted May; "you are so cynical, Rose, like everybody else now-a-days, and I hate it. He can never be glad to have lost Dora."

"Don't you agree with me, Annie?" Rose maintained her point.

"Really, you seem to be so well informed on the subject yourself—though I cannot think where you have got your experience, any more than your slang, unless at second-hand"—said Annie sarcastically, "that my opinion is of no importance."

"Now, don't be nasty and elder-sisterish," was Rose's quick rejoinder.

Though Dora shed no tears of contrition in public, Annie, who shared her sister's room, heard her in the night crying softly.

"What ails you, Dora dear?" Annie sat up and asked sleepily. "What is the matter? It can't be, no," rousing herself, "it can *not* be—you don't mean that you repent what you've done, and would swallow the shop, foxy hair, and everything?"

"Oh, no," denied Dora, "but I didn't think a man would care like that; such a queer, gray shade came over his face, though I durst hardly look at him; and his hands which were—well, were holding mine for a second, you know—"

"No, I don't know," interrupted Annie, smiling to herself; "but go on, what about the hands?"

"They were as cold as ice."

"Very likely, it is only the month of April."

"And it is not above a year since he lost both his father and mother—all the near relations he had."

"Poor man!" admitted Annie. "But you could not help that, and many men, young men especially, seem to get on quite well without near relations."

There was a strain of hardness about pretty Annie, whether bred of that cynicism in the air of which May had complained, whether it was an integral part of Annie, or whether, as in the case of some valuable kinds of timber, it was merely an indication of the closer grain, the slower ripening, and the greater power of endurance of the moral fibre.

"Men are not like women." Annie was continuing her lecture. "I dare say Tom Robinson will do very well—all the better, perhaps, because he has no ambition, and is content to make money in the most humdrum way as a tradesman."

Dora sat up in turn, like a white ghost in her place in her little bed, seen by the dim light. She had the instinct which causes women to look back upon the men who have made love or proposed to them, even though the women have rejected the men—as in a sense their property, if not their prey, so as not by any means to relish the men's depreciation at the hands of other women. Then it becomes a point of honour alike with the proudest and the meekest of her sex to stand up in his absence in defence of the discarded swain.

"I don't know about ambition," began Dora hesitatingly, "but father says Tom Robinson is not at all stupid; he took his degree with credit at Cambridge, and was not plucked like poor Ned Hewett, or that fop, Cyril Carey. Father says when he worked with Mr. Robinson in getting up the bill to lay before Parliament for closing the old churchyard, he could not have desired a more intelligent, diligent fellow-worker. All the salesmen and women at 'Robinson's' have been well looked after, and are superior to the other shop-people in the town, don't you know? There is Miss Franklin at the head of both the millinery and mantua-making departments; I am sure she looks and speaks, as well as dresses, like a lady?"

"Yes, and everybody is civil to her, but nobody thinks of making her acquaintance out of the shop, and she is wise enough to keep to her proper sphere. They say she is a distant relation of Tom Robinson's—you see he is not altogether destitute of kindred. Why does the man not marry her? That would be a suitable match."

"Annie!" protested Dora, in nearly speechless indignation, and then she recovered breath and words. "She's forty if she's a day; and she's as fat as a pin-cushion, with her cheeks a mottled red all over."

"How can you make such unkind remarks on your neighbours' looks? *He* is not an Adonis, I may be allowed to say; and I have noticed that shopkeepers are apt to marry women older than themselves, women who have been in the trade—to keep the business together, I suppose."

"At least, his father did not marry like that either in his first or in his second marriage," retorted Dora; "for the first Mrs. Robinson was the daughter of a curate, and the second of a farmer, and she was not half his age, though she did not survive him long."

"As you please. What's Hecuba to me, or what am I to Hecuba?" demanded Annie airily.

"Besides," Dora returned laboriously to the charge, "there are shopkeepers and shopkeepers, as you must be aware, Annie. Father says old Mr. Robinson was a man of independent ideas and original mind, and had his own theories of trade."

"I have nothing to say against it, especially at this hour of the night, or morning," said Annie, professing to strangle a yawn; "only that I do not think a linen-draper's business, however large and well-conducted, is exactly the career of a gentleman, a man of fair ability and education. He might leave it to any respectable well-disposed tradesman. However, if you are going to exalt Tom Robinson, with his shop, into a patriot and philanthropist cherishing a noble scheme for the public good, and all that kind of thing, do it if you like, nobody will hinder you. Call him back if you care to, I dare say it is still possible if you are willing to make the concession. But oh, Dora!" appealed Annie, who had talked herself wide awake by this time, "don't forget the loss of position involved in really keeping a shop, however eccentric and meritorious a man's intentions may be. Why, he had better become a stonemason or a ploughman, if he is to do the thing at all; far better a gamekeeper or a soldier in time of war, the plunge would be deeper but more picturesque. Think of the entire breaking with the county with which we have a right to hold ourselves connected, not merely because father's patients are willing to take us up and make quite a fuss about us sometimes, but because his Aunt Penny married and was welcomed into that set. You have not yourself alone to consider, remember, Dora;

you might not mind, but you have the rest of us to think of, some of whom would mind very much."

"You need have no anxiety about the matter," said poor Dora hotly and huffily. "I am not going to marry Tom Robinson; you know I have refused him this very afternoon."

But Annie was determined to empty out her whole budget of warnings. "Even professional people like father, all our friends and acquaintances, our relations on both sides of the house would begin to drop us, and fight shy of us. What people that had any pretensions to being gentle-folks would care to be mixed up with our brother-in-law the linen-draper? And it is not as if the temptation were great; I cannot see wherein the attraction lies; but instead of letting it beset you, please don't lose sight of the three hundred and sixty-five days to be spent every year in Tom Robinson's silent company. Think of the three hundred and sixty-five breakfasts, dinners, and suppers to be eaten opposite his mute figure."

"Stop, Annie," Dora cried energetically: "you know as well as I do that I could never face such a thing, that I never dreamt of it. Only loving a man could make it possible for a girl to give up her family in order to belong to him; and even if there had been no 'Robinson's' to shock you, I do not care the least little bit for poor Tom Robinson; yet surely for that very reason," protested Dora with a sudden revulsion of feeling, "I am at liberty to pity him."

"If you will take my advice, Dora," said shrewd Annie, sinking back on her pillow as a sign that the untimely discussion ought to come to an end, "you will get rid of your pity as quickly as you can. It is not your pity which he seeks—very likely he would rage like a bear, for as quiet as he can look, at the mere mention of it. But it strikes me that it is not safe for either of you."

Sarah Tytler

CHAPTER III

THE HEADS OF THE HOUSE LOOK GRAVE

"It is a thousand pities," said Dr. Millar, holding a consultation with his wife, while he sipped his glass of sherry and ate his biscuit, before retiring for the night, after his last round among the patients in greatest need of his visits.

In spite of his daughter Dora's preference for tall men, the Doctor was short and rather stout. He ought to have looked comfortable, he had the physique and air of a comfortable man, but a certain harassed, careworn expression was beginning to settle down on the spectacled face which had once been round, rosy, and very comely. He was at least twenty years older than his wife. The old-fashioned practice had prevailed in the old-fashioned town, of elderly men, whether bachelors or widowers, ending by marrying for the first or the second time women a score or more years their juniors. Indeed, Dr. Millar was hard upon seventy, though he had till recent bad times carried his years so well that he had looked ten years younger than his actual age.

Mrs. Millar also began to look worried as a rule, though she had more of the woman's faculty of putting the best face on things, both in public and in private. She was a tall woman, who had enjoyed the advantages of what was called "an elegant figure" in her youth. Now she was large and heavy, with a mixture of unconscious stateliness and wistful motherliness in her gait and gestures. Like Dr. Millar, she ought to have seemed at least easy-minded, but circumstances were becoming more and more against the happy condition, of which a pervading atmosphere of content and cheerfulness should have been the outward expression.

The man and woman were not cut out, so to speak, for adversity. They had not been seasoned to it in their younger days. On the contrary, they had been cradled for many years in the lap—if not of luxury, of fair middle-class prosperity. It was a few tolerably rough jolts which had shaken them from their cradle. Still the trouble was more in apprehension than in reality. As yet it had not caused the sufferers to change any one of the domestic habits which had grown second nature to them. It had not induced them to darken the sunny sky over their young daughters' heads with a shadow of the clouds which were already looming black on the parents' horizon. It may be said at once, that Dr. and Mrs. Millar, though they were reckoned clever, sensible people enough by their contemporaries, had softer hearts than they had hard heads. They had not been used to painful self-denial and stern discipline, either where they themselves or their children were concerned.

The couple were sitting now together in the dining-room with its solidly handsome furniture, Russian leather and walnut wood, bits of family plate on the sideboard, bronze chimney-piece ornaments, and good engravings on the walls. Husband and wife had spent the last part of the evening there, for four-and-twenty years, every night they were in Redcross, when the Doctor was not kept out late, or when the couple were not abroad in company, or seeing company at home. Dr. Millar, in his slightly old-fashioned professional black coat and white tie, was leaning back in his easy-chair sipping his sherry, and occasionally drumming lightly on the table near him with these fine long sensitive fingers which were a born doctor's fingers.

Mrs. Millar wore a demi-toilet in the shape of an expensive cashmere and silk gown—not an evening dress, but an approach to it, as became the wife of one of the leading professional men in Redcross, connected with the county to boot. Her lace cap was a costly trifle of its kind, but it had an awkward habit—the odder in a woman who was neat to formality in the other details of her dress—of slipping to one side, or tilting forwards or backwards on the brown hair, still abundant and just streaked with gray; so that one or other of her daughters was constantly calling Mrs. Millar's cap to order and setting it right. She was sitting in an arm-chair, opposite her husband. Mechanically she put one daintily slippered, very neat foot, considering the weight it helped to carry, beyond her skirts, and stretched it towards the fire. There was still a good fire blazing in the steel grate, though the spring was well advanced, the weather was not more than chilly, and the hour was late. It was as if coals were not a marketable commodity and a serious item in the expenses of an embarrassed house-hold. She held up a Japanese fan between her face and the fire, from mere custom, for she had ceased to pay much heed to the exigencies of a florid complexion.

"It's a thousand pities," repeated the little Doctor, looking quite portentously regretful and oppressed. "It is not only that Tom Robinson is an excellent fellow and would have made Dora the best of husbands—given her a safe and happy home, and all that sort of thing; but in case of anything happening, I am convinced he would have been as good as a brother to the other girls, and a son to you. A man like him is a stay and support to a household of helpless women."

"But nothing is going to happen, Jonathan," said Mrs. Millar, with an involuntary nervous quiver which sent her cap hovering over one eyebrow. "At least nothing worse than we know. Your practice is not so lucrative as it used to be; how can it, in these bad times, with so many poor young fellows of doctors settling here and there and everywhere in Redcross and the villages around, starving themselves out, while they impoverish their seniors? Nothing more than that, except the little trouble at Carey's Bank."

"Quite enough too, Maria, quite enough," commented the

Doctor deep down in his throat, prolonging the words a little as if he were chanting the refrain of a dismal song; "and when a man is my age and has plenty of the young rivals you refer to, it is high time he should be looking out for something happening. A family of girls, too. God help me! If they had been four boys, who might have made their own way in the world, and provided for you among them, I could have faced it better." He struck the table again, with spasmodic force this time.

"Now, Jonathan, you will wake up the house. This is not like you," remonstrated his wife—all the more energetically that her heart sank while she spoke. "I should not have expected you to give way in this manner." She gave a quick push back to her unruly cap. "I am sure there is no occasion for it. We are in no worse position than we were last year, even the year before that."

"Save that I am growing older every year," he said grimly, "and the affairs of the bank are not mending, as I hoped they might."

"Can't you sell out?" she suggested breathlessly, as she clasped her hands on her knees.

"I have put it off too long, supposing I had the conscience to transfer my liabilities to some simpleton who might not draw half a dozen of the dividends of which I have drawn scores. Besides, the thing is impossible, as I am telling you. Between you and me, the shares are far below par."

"What is par, Jonathan?" interrupted Mrs. Millar in a praiseworthy attempt to understand her husband.

"Oh, bother," he cried, running his hand in mild exasperation through his white hair; "the standard value, or the original value, whichever you like best. I should not dare to propose to sell out at such a loss; it would not only be to impoverish myself at once in order to avoid the risk of greater ruin, it would draw attention. It would have a most suspicious look, and might bring the rotten affair down about our ears instantly, while I should get the blame of the downfall."

"But some of the large foreign investments might be realized any day—you told me the last time you spoke of business—with the first good turn of trade," she reminded him anxiously.

"I trust so still, and I believe old Carey is an honest man and a perfect gentleman—that is one comfort; but I cannot help thinking he has got into bad hands. I tell you, Maria, I don't like that brother-in-law of his who comes down from London to attend the Redcross meetings, and tries to blarney us all round. And I cannot approve of the bolstering up of Carey's cousins, the Carters, in their chemical works at Stokeleigh, which it strikes me will never do much good. It—the bolstering up—has been going on for a long time now, to what extent I am not prepared to show. Unfortunately I have a bad head for figures," he shrugged his shoulders as if anticipating a reproach, "the less reason why I should have laid out my savings on bank shares, you will say? No doubt, no doubt, but there had been fewer troubles with banks in my day. When I made the first investment everything appeared right, and the dividends announced were tempting."

"I am not finding fault with what you did, Jonathan; I never thought of such a thing," the perturbed woman found voice to reassure her husband. "I know you did it for the best; and for that matter, I am convinced it will all come right in the end," she ended with a little sigh.

"It is very good and pretty of you to say so, Maria," he said with a certain old-fashioned, stiff gallantry which, while it complimented her, treated her as a much younger and more irresponsible being than he was. As he spoke he took up the hand which lay in her lap and held it for a moment clasped in his. "And I can say you have been all that I could have wished as a wife and mother, you have never once failed me during the whole of our married life."

"Oh! thank you, thank you, Jonathan." She acknowledged his praise with a momentary choke in her voice, and a bend of her head which was not without a docile dignity.

"We are all in the same boat," resumed the Doctor in the deep tones which somehow sounded like bass recitative; "the Rector, Colonel Russell, and I—not to say Carey himself. We all wished to increase our incomes with as little trouble and risk as possible—so it seemed then, but if the bank comes to smash, all the old Redcross gentle-folks, as we were pleased to call ourselves, will go with it."

"Don't mention such a thing, don't think of it," cried Mrs. Millar in her dismay.

He went on without noticing her. "The Bishop won't let the Rector come down, and Russell is twenty years younger than I. He is no older than you are, though a foreign climate has told a good deal on him; still, he is patched up, and with care ought to have lasted as long as the rest of us. He may exert his interest, and get a post in India again, though I should be afraid it would finish him in six months."

The poor middle-aged lady who sat listening with dry lips apart, and pleasant hazel eyes distended with fright and distress, though she was no older than the unfortunate colonel, had not been exposed to a foreign climate, and had hardly suffered from a serious illness in her life, did not look much like such an arduous undertaking as going out to India to redeem a wrecked fortune. She pulled herself together, however, and set herself to the good woman's business of comforting and encouraging her husband. "I am certain it is right to go on hoping. You often say that in your profession you have no such helpful allies as hope and courage; you must practice what you've preached, Doctor," and the faithful soul actually contrived to impart a playful ring to her unsteady voice. "The Rector has not preached the duty more strenuously than you have; and you are not going to be the first to break down, especially when there is no real occasion. Depend upon it, Carey's Bank will pull through like some of your most doubtful patients, with time and care."

"With all my heart," he said, absently taking off his spectacles, polishing, and replacing them. Then he resumed his former line of thought. "Tom Robinson is out of the mess. He, and his father before him, found other ways of disposing of their capital where it was more under their own inspection and control. If that foolish girl of ours, Maria, could only have brought herself to listen to Robinson," he worked himself up into a fresh access of vexation, "the liking would have come in good time. I did not expect her to have a fancy for him on the spot, for quiet, steady young fellows like him are not apt to take girls' fancies—the worse for the girls."

"But, father"—remonstrated Mrs. Millar, involuntarily bestowing on her husband the title the girls gave him—she drew herself up as she spoke, and again destroyed the equilibrium of her cap—"you cannot surely think that Tom Robinson would have been a fit match for Dora, or any of her sisters. He is well enough in himself, I say nothing against him, but he has not gone into a profession, instead he has identified himself with 'Robinson's'—that shop;" a shade of ineffable disgust stole into her ordinarily good-humoured voice.

"Showed his good sense and manliness," said the Doctor gruffly. "I wish every one else had been as wise. I wish all of us had big paying shops at our backs instead of Carey's shaky bank. I for one would swallow the indignity cheerfully. Why, my father kept on his dispensary in the days when the practice was at its best. The greater fool I to give it up. I tell you England will never be what it was till it gets rid of this rubbish of despising trades and shops. Don't you help to put it into these silly girls' heads. It makes me sick to think how they may live to wish they were connected with an honest, solvent shop."

"My dear, I think you are going a little too far." Mrs. Millar fired up in defence of her young like a ruffled mother-pigeon.

"I should be very sorry to teach the girls to look down on anybody; but that there are different sorts and conditions of men, they may learn from their very Bibles and prayer-books. There are such things as education and culture—not to speak of good birth. You yourself, Dr. Millar, are fairly well born and well connected for a professional man." She instanced this with an imperceptible bridle and toss of her matronly head, which hinted broadly, "If it had not been so, Jonathan, I should never have been Mrs. Millar." The movement threatened to deposit her cap on the carpet behind her, but she recovered it in time, and took up the thread of her discourse by quoting the much-prized family distinction—"There was your Aunt Penny, who married into the county."

"Oh! are you at that humbug?" he cried, with a man's disrespectful impatience. "I thought it had seen its day, and was long over and done with. I could not have conceived that you—" ("were such a fool," he was going to say, when he caught himself up.) He was quick-tempered and impulsive, but he was also suave by nature, and his long habit of courteous indulgence to his wife caused him to alter the phrase. "I did not know that you had so lively an imagination as to persist in believing that old myth, Maria."

"But your Aunt Penny did marry one of the Beauchamps of Waylands," insisted Mrs. Millar.

"Certainly; and she made the poorest marriage of anybody that I have ever had to do with, though I have always understood that he was not a bad sort, beyond being as thick-headed as his brother the squire or an officer of dragoons. He get on at the bar! I dare say not. And he was no quicker-witted or longer-sighted in Australia. You must have heard me say how grieved I was once when I came across a fellow from Sydney who had been up the country, and remembered something of the Beauchamps and their straits. They were regularly hard up, and went through no end of trouble. Poor Aunt Penny seldom had a woman-servant—women-servants were more difficult to get out there in those days. She had to wash, cook, and scour for the men at the station."

"Why didn't they come home?" inquired Mrs. Millar rather weakly.

"Come home! They had nothing to come home with, or to. You don't suppose his brother, the squire, with a wife and family of his own, would have kept them, though the Beauchamps had received her civilly enough at the time of the marriage! She had to milk the cows when the cow-man was otherwise wanted. I do not say that many a better born woman than she was has not done as much and thought little of it, only it was not in Aunt Penny's line. I can just remember her when I was a small boy, a pretty creature who read Italian, sang to her guitar, and made bread seals for her amusement. She had such a mortal terror where cows were concerned that she would run like a lapwing when she heard one come lowing up the lane behind the house. Paton, the man from Sydney who remembered them, thought they did a little better towards the end, when they got a store, and Mrs. Beauchamp kept it. Do you hear that, Maria?" cried the Doctor, with a half-humorous, half-indignant emphasis.

"Yes, I hear," replied Mrs. Millar, with an obstinate inflection of her voice which said, "I am of my own opinion still." She illustrated this by adding, in an undertone, "They were in Australia."

"A store," continued the Doctor, "is the rudest, most uncouth kind of shop; and Beauchamp was not fit to keep it, he had to turn it over to his wife, who was thankful to serve shepherds and bush-rangers for aught I know. She lost one child in the bush, God help her! The little thing wandered away and was never heard of again; and her other child, a boy, who grew up, did not turn out well. I tell you, I never like to think or speak of the mother."

"Poor Aunt Penny!" said Mrs. Millar hastily. "But there is one thing"—with a sudden accent of triumph in the perception that she had the advantage of her husband at last—"your Aunt Penny married the man she cared for; she got her choice, and in that light she had no reason to complain, though she had to abide by it."

The Doctor was a little taken aback. "I do not know that she complained—at least her people at home heard nothing of it. And you must do me the justice of owning that I have done nothing to force Dora's inclinations. Indeed, I am not clear that I have done my duty. I ought to have reasoned with the girl. Robinson is not only a good man, he is also a gentleman, every inch of him, so was his father before him."

"In the choice of Jenny Coppock, of Coppock's Farm, for a wife!" exclaimed Mrs. Millar, still rebellious, even satirical and disdainful.

"He was entitled to choose whom he would, I suppose, so long as she was an honest woman, and Jenny Coppock was that quite as much as her husband was a gentleman. She made him happy, I believe, strange as it may sound to some people, as ladies do not always make their husbands happy—you know I mean nothing personal, Maria. Whether she was quite happy herself is a different question, of which I have had no means of judging. But I have heard you yourself say that she never presumed on her rise in rank, or sought to thrust her comely, kindly face where it was not wanted. Her son has a look of her, without her good looks. Poor Mrs. Robinson! I was with her in her first and last illness, as you are aware, and a more courageous, self-forgetful soul I had never the privilege to attend."

Mrs. Millar turned back in the conversation, and took to dogmatizing. "People who are well-informed and well-bred will never descend to a lower level without great discomfort and serious loss. I for one, though I have not profited by the advantages the girls have commanded, and I daresay have not their brains"—she made the frank admission with womanly, motherly humility—"though I could not to save my life make one of Rose's beautiful water-colour sketches, or read Greek and Latin like 'little May,' or even talk to the point on every subject under the sun like Annie, still I should not be happy if I had to keep company with Wilkins the butcher's or Ord the baker's wife, and they would not be happy either. It would not matter, in one sense, though I knew they were respectable, worthy women, and were ever so much better off as to money than I. That would not keep me from feeling thoroughly out of place and having hardly an idea in common with my neighbours in their plush-trimmed gowns and fur-lined mantles. I could not stand such degradation for my girls," she protested, with rising agitation. "I had far rather that they and I should be the poorest ladies in the land, should have to pinch and deny ourselves all round."

"It is little you know of it," muttered Dr. Millar, shaking his white head, and pensively contemplating his finger-nails.

"While we still retained the position to which we were born, and the associations among which we were reared," ended Mrs. Millar, with a gasp.

"Bless the woman, what does she mean?" cried Dr. Millar after his lively fashion, with an air of injured innocence. "Does she pretend that Tom Robinson has not been educated—stamped, for that matter, with the last university brand, to which he does credit, I must say? Stay, there goes the night-bell. I am wanted for somebody."

"You'll never go out again to-night, Jonathan," pleaded Mrs. Millar, "after all your worry, when you have not had more than a couple of hours' rest." She was already reproaching herself keenly for having contradicted and argued with him. She had never been able to comprehend, for her comfort, that to a man like him an argument is both rousing and refreshing. In the middle of her remorse she instinctively held up her head, and balanced her cap as a Dutchwoman of the last century balanced her milk-pail, or a girl of the Roman Campagna her sheaf of grass and wild flowers. "It is a shame," she reflected indignantly; "it is very likely nothing of any consequence, just one of those inconsiderate people who think that a professional man ought to be always at their beck and call."

"There, Maria, you're scoring another point for trade," said the little doctor, getting on his feet, and buttoning up his coat as a preliminary to obeying the call. "I'll warrant Wilkins and Ord will be toasting their toes, and retiring to bed with the comfortable conviction that their night's rest will not be disturbed; since Wilkins's head-man attends to the slaughter-house, and the eldest journeyman baker sees to the setting of the sponge. Why don't you say, *noblesse oblige*, Maria? But I think I know the name of the inconsiderate individual who has interrupted our conversation, and I assure you he would not if he could. It is little Johnny Fleming—Fleming the grocer's son—whose case is critical, I fear. I told his mother if he got worse to send for me at once. When I am out, at any rate, I'll just look in on old Todd, in Skinners' Buildings. He appeared in a dying state this morning; but as the family have not sent to let me know of the death, if he has hung on so long, the chance is he will rally and come round this bout. I'll be some time; don't sit up for me, my dear."

"It is too bad," Mrs. Millar fretted. "They ought to send at night for Newton or Capes from Woodleigh—it is only a step for any of the young doctors, instead of disturbing a man of your age."

"Good heavens! don't breathe such a thing. I could not afford it. I thought of taking a young partner twenty years ago, but I put it off till it was too late. Perhaps it was a mistake; we all make mistakes," he sighed. "An active young practitioner, well up to date, might have kept the business better together."

"Nonsense!" cried his wife energetically. "Nobody would have looked at him when they could have had your skill and experience."

"Then be thankful I'm still fit for work—one must take the

bad with the good. It is the fortune of war, Maria," said the gallant old doctor as he departed.

CHAPTER IV

THE CRASH

Within a month Carey's Bank broke, not altogether unexpectedly. The breaking carried dismay and desolation into not a few households in Redcross, and administered a sharp shock—productive of much startled speculation, and roused distrust, even in those quarters which had not suffered financially by the bankruptcy. The stoppage of a bank, with little hope of its resuming its functions, is like the stoppage of a heart which will never beat again. It may have been dreaded as a possible calamity, and occasionally hinted at in awed whispers; but when the blow falls it does so with a stunning, crushing force because of its irreparable nature and far-reaching ruin.

There was just a little preparation to herald the catastrophe. Poor Carey, an honest, weak tool of dishonest speculators and birds of prey in the shape of needy, unscrupulous relations, when the appalling tidings reached him which could only betoken immediate wreck, did all that there was left to him to do. He called a meeting of the Redcross shareholders. These were the leading professional men in the town who had invested their savings, and a small proportion of the neighbouring country gentlemen who had put a little capital—not often to spare in those days—in a concern once regarded as sound and incapable of collapse as the Bank of England itself. With a faltering tongue and a hanging head the nominal head of the firm told to those nearly concerned what was coming on them. Nobody reproached him; either no man had the heart, or all felt the uselessness of reproaches. Certainly these share-holders' silence was his heaviest punishment.

They made a hasty examination, as far as they could, for themselves, and then the meeting broke up. Its members did not even linger to consult, being well assured that consultation, like reproaches, would be of no avail; the failure was so much more extensive and complete than their worst fears had led them to anticipate. The men looked blankly in each other's whitening faces and sought the refuge of their own houses at first. There would be time enough for outcry, for desperate plans and schemes a little later.

Poor Dr. Millar had not even this breathing space. It happened to be a particularly busy day with him. Various neutral individuals, in no way concerned with Carey's Bank, even when its misfortunes should be made public, took that inconvenient time for falling ill, and their medical man had to attend upon them with spasmodic promptitude and mecha-nical attention—projected, as it were, against the dazed and confused background of his brain. After all he was glad of his profession with its outward and immediate calls, taking him out of himself in the hour when he had heard the worst. He preferred to be about the town doing battle with this man's attack of paralysis and that woman's symptoms of typhoid, even though his ears were ringing with clamorous questions which no one else could hear or answer. How was he to pay up the liabilities of his bank shares from his dwindling practice? What about inexperienced young girls driven out to make their own way in the world, and the gentlewoman (in every sense of the word) whom he had loved and cherished for four-and-twenty years, soon to be left a desolate, all but unprovided for widow? But better a thousand times to be dragged in different directions than to be sitting like Russell, locked in his room, his little children and their young mother shut out, holding between his hands the erect head of a soldier who had come out of many a hard battle, but none so hard as this ambuscade which had been sprung upon him after he had been invalided a dozen years before, and returned home to spend his declining years in peace. Better than to have to write sermons and read prayers, like the Rector, and pause between every sentence to take himself sternly to task. Was it common forethought and prudence, with the necessity of providing for the wants of a household, which even the apostle Paul had commended, or was it worldly-mindedness and greed which had brought him, a beneficed clergyman, a priest in holy orders, the vowed servant of a King whose kingdom was not of this world, to this lamentable pass? Yes; he would be dishonoured in the eyes of men, a debtor who could not pay his debts, and even with the support of his bishop would be scarcely able to weather the storm, while he must make up his mind, as he was an honest man, that he and his should endure the pinch of poverty for the rest of his days.

Annie and Dora had been out on a shopping expedition, and were coming in talking and laughing as usual, when they were startled by the apparition of their mother standing in the doorway of her room, and motioning to them to come in directly and speak with her. The poor lady really looked like a ghost, as she stood there with her fine colour gone, beckoning to her daughters with her hand, as if the power of speech had suddenly forsaken her.

"What is it, mother?" cried the alarmed girls in one breath, hurrying towards her. "Has anything happened? Is anybody ill?"

"Hush! hush, my dears," said Mrs. Millar in a low tone, carefully shutting the door of her room behind the girls, as if she were ready to guard her secret with her life—at the same time painfully sensible that the bad news would be all over Redcross the next day, or the next after that. "I thought it would be better to tell you myself; nobody in the house knows anything of it yet, except your father and me."

"But what is it, mother; you have not told us?" Annie urged; while Mrs. Millar sank down in a low wicker chair, and her daughter Dora instinctively stooped over her, and began to set her vagrant cap right.

"Never mind my cap, my love," said Mrs. Millar hurriedly, and then she grew incoherent. "What does it matter, when perhaps I may not long have a cap to wear."

Annie and Dora stared at each other in consternation. Was their mother going out of her senses?

"It is the bank, Carey's Bank," said Mrs. Millar, recovering herself, "Oh dear! I am afraid it is in a very bad way."

"Is that it?" cried Annie vaguely but gravely, opening wide her brown eyes. "Is it going to fail?" She, too, spoke of the bank as if it were a responsible being.

"Annie, Annie, take care what you say. Girls are so heedless. I tell you it is very dangerous to make such broad statements. You do not know what harm you may do by a single word when you are so childishly outspoken." Mrs. Millar felt bound even yet to give her own words the timid qualification, though she was forced to add the next moment, "Your father has suspected things were going wrong for some time, and spoken of his suspicions to me repeatedly. He has just come back from a private meeting of the Redcross shareholders. He says in consequence of some additional losses in South America, I think, and inability to realize capital there, the bank cannot meet two or three heavy calls at home. I daresay I am not telling you rightly, for I don't understand business, and I don't suppose you do."

"I understand so far, that if this is not failure, I don't know what is," said Annie.

"Don't, Annie," said Dora; "let mother tell us in her own way; it is not easy for her, it is a dreadful misfortune."

"You may say that, Dora," exclaimed her mother. "Your father does not believe the bank can hold out for another week; it may stop payment to-morrow, since there are rumours afloat which will destroy what credit it has left."

"Will no other bank help it?" cried Annie shrewdly.

"I believe not," said Mrs. Millar dolefully.

"Then there will be a run, like what one has read of in similar circumstances—a rush of the people, and a riot in the town," suggested Annie, getting excited over the idea. "The police may have to guard the bank and the Bank house—soldiers may have to come from Nenthorn!"

"Oh, surely not," cried Dora; "the poor Careys—who could treat them so cruelly?"

"No, no," said Mrs. Millar; "there is one good thing, your father does not think there will be much ill-feeling, or anything like an angry mob, or tumult—not even when the people see the closed doors. There has always been such confidence in Carey's Bank, the Careys have been respected for generations; even now it is James Carey's misfortune and not his fault, though he may have been misled and imposed upon; and, after all, the depositors are tolerably sure of their money in time. But your father is afraid," she ended, her voice sinking, "that it will go hard with the shareholders."

"And poor father is one of them," said Annie quickly.

"Poor father!" echoed Dora piteously; "and you, poor, poor mother, to have to think of us, and break it to us, while your heart is with father."

"And he has not even been left in peace for a single afternoon, to make up his mind what we shall do," lamented his sympathetic wife. "As usual, so many tiresome people have fallen ill—as if they did it on purpose, and sent for him."

"I daresay they could not help it," said Annie, "and I don't think it would quite suit father if they were never ill."

"Don't speak so unfeelingly, child," remonstrated her mother; "well, I suppose I gave you a bad example," she corrected herself immediately, "but I have been in such trouble since lunch time."

"Poor mother!" repeated Dora in a voice that was only more soft and caressing because of its sorrowfulness. She was very fond of her mother, who reciprocated the special fondness, while Dr. Millar was rather inclined to favour Annie and Rose, and both father and mother petted May.

"Will it ruin us, mother?" inquired Annie directly, but before her mother could answer her, Annie's practical mind took a sudden flight. It went straight back to the purchases which she and Rose had been making that afternoon. They had been at "Robinson's," of all places. But Tom Robinson was only to be seen in the glass office, or walking about the place in the morning, at hours which these two customers had carefully avoided. Dora's heart had quaked all the same, in dread of an event which, bad enough when it was confined to a passing bow, or a limp hand-shake and half a dozen words exchanged in the street, would have been intolerable in "Robinson's," under the eyes of his satellites. Yet for the Millars to have refrained altogether from going to the one great shop in the town, where women oft did congregate, would have been to expose an event, the participators in which devoutly hoped was buried in oblivion. They had been in Miss Franklin's department without anything untoward happening; but it was neither "Robinson's" nor the person who served them there that flashed like lightning across Annie's thoughts at this crisis. It was the articles the girls had been buying, the Tussore silk and Torchon lace for frocks that Annie and Dora had meant to wear at a garden-party—for which the Dyers, the new people who had come to Redcross Manor-house, had sent out invitations. If the Millars were ruined, they were not likely to go to many more garden-parties, and though the sisters might still want frocks, yet frocks of Tussore silk trimmed with

Torchon lace—granted that the materials had appeared a modest and becoming wear for a doctor's daughters an hour before—might not be quite an appropriate selection in the family's altered circumstances.

"It depends upon what you call ruin," Mrs. Millar was saying falteringly, "and of course the bank's assets may turn out better than is thought just now, though your father is far from hopeful. He says all his savings will go, and he may count on having to pay bank 'calls' on his income till the business is wound up, which may not be in his lifetime. No doubt he is taking the darkest view of things at present." Then she yielded to the relief of pouring forth some of the coming woes in detail. "Oh, my dears, your father says, though nothing can be settled in a moment, there is one thing certain—this house must be given up."

"Our house!" cried both of the girls in dismay.

"Where we were all born, where father himself was born," pleaded Dora, still hanging about her mother.

"The Old Doctor's House—why, it seems to belong to the practice," protested Annie, sitting down, taking off her hat and tossing it on the bed as if the better to realize the situation.

"No, I don't think it would hurt the practice—not in a town the size of Redcross, where everybody would know where your father was to be found, though he were to change his house again and again. Still it does seem hard," she admitted, as she covertly wiped away a tear, "particularly when the fault has not been ours—we have always lived within your father's income, even though his practice has been falling off in these bad times, what with his getting up in years, and what with these young doctors trying to get in their hands everywhere. He tells me that he has never had to find fault with me for extravagance," she finished wistfully.

"I should think not," said Annie emphatically. "Why you have always been as simple as simple could be in your own tastes and habits, not a woman in your circle dresses more quietly. You have hardly even driven in the brougham when father was not wanting it, in case you should over-work the horse—you have always said, but I really believe that you chose to walk for the simple reason that many of your acquaintances had no choice. Nobody can ever reflect upon you, mother, for having wasted either father's means or other people's," said Annie, with a bright glance which became her infinitely.

"Thank you, my love, for saying so," replied her mother gratefully; "and you see it is as well that I did not accustom myself to driving, among other indulgences, for another of the retrenchments which your father mentioned was putting down the brougham. Yet how he is to manage his more distant patients on foot, at his age, I cannot imagine," she broke off in helpless distress, clasping her hands tightly together, according to a way she had. "It seems downright madness to propose it."

"Then you may be sure it will be prevented," said Dora with earnest trustfulness, as she gently patted her mother's cap. "Nobody can ask a sacrifice from him which he is unable to make. Mother, do you know what I was thinking? that the only occasions on which you and father were regardless of expense have been where the profit or pleasure of us girls was concerned. You have given us every advantage you could get for us in the shape of education. You sent Annie and me to London to take these costly music-lessons;—Annie, I wish we had made more of them. You arranged that we should go on that foreign tour with the Ludlows."

"We did our best for you—your father and I. I think I may say that," admitted Mrs. Millar simply.

Dora went on eagerly with her generous catalogue. "There was the young artist who exhibits at the Academy and the Gros-venor, who was sketching at Nenthorn, you had him over at a high price once a week, and he condescended to help Rose with her drawing and painting. Then there was Mr. Blake, the university man whom father considered so far in advance of any classical master Miss Burridge could afford, he was induced so long as he was staying at Woodleigh to bring on May with her Latin and Greek."

"So far so good," said Mrs. Millar, in her excitement borrowing one of her husband's brisk, cut and dry phrases. "I hope you will reap the benefit of any effort we made, dears, because"—she hesitated, and nearly broke down—"well, I don't think you need mind so much your father's giving up this house and going into a smaller one; I'm sure I don't mind it at all when I think what other people will have to suffer; and as for you, why, you may not be here—not always, at least. We are afraid, your father and I, that you'll need to go and do something to keep yourselves."

"To be sure," said Annie promptly. "Don't trouble about that, mother; we'll be only too glad to be of use!"

"We'll be too thankful to relieve you and father as much as we can," said Dora in a voice soft and fervent, but less assured.

"That will be the least trial," asserted Annie fearlessly.

"Oh, you don't know what you're saying!" cried Mrs. Millar, fairly giving way and permitting herself to sob for a minute or two behind her handkerchief. "You are dear, good girls! I knew you would be, and so brave that I ought to take courage; but young people are so hopeful and inexperienced. I don't wish you to be unhopeful, of course, still you cannot tell what it is for your father and me to send our girls—our own girls whom we have been so proud and fond of, that have been making the old house brighter and brighter ever since they were born—out into a cold world, to have to struggle for a pittance, to lose their youth and its privileges, to be knocked about, and perhaps ill-treated, and looked down upon by people in every way their inferiors."

"Don't, mother," interrupted Annie with decision; "you're

conjuring up bogies which have ceased to exist now-a-days. Think of the women who go out into the world by no compulsion, simply for the honour and pleasure of the thing, because they will not stay at home to lead idle, useless lives, when there is needful work to be done abroad. I don't question that they have difficulties to encounter, but I have yet to learn that staying at home will keep away crosses. Brave women can bear whatever trouble comes. I have often thought of such workers, if you will believe me"—the girl was in a glow of animation—"with both shame and envy. It is true I have not proposed to join them," she added in a lower tone, "because I knew I was young for such work and not half good enough or clever enough, and because we were all so happy at home— you and father made us so," and Annie turned away her head, and forthwith came tumbling down a few steps from the exalted position she had taken up.

"No, don't tell me, Annie Millar," said her mother with something like passionate resistance, "that any good father or mother can be glad to send their young daughters out into the wide world to fight and suffer by themselves. It is not natural and it is not true. It is an altogether different thing to give them to good men who will take care of them and make them happy."

"But if the good men are not forthcoming, or if they happen to be the wrong men," protested Annie. There was an irresistible twinkle in her dark eyes, in spite of the care and trouble that had come upon the household, which she was too sensible and warm-hearted a girl not to share fully.

Dora stood conscience-stricken and guilty-looking, until, as she stroked her mother's locked hands, she at last found words to put in her humble petition, "We shan't all go away, mother dear. Father and you must let one of us stay to take care of you and cheer you?"

"Oh, my dear, we are not old enough, at least I am not old enough to accept such a boon, supposing we are very poor," said Mrs. Millar sadly, "and in that case it might be sacrificing one of you, and spoiling your prospects in life."

"No, no," cried Dora vehemently.

"Dora means that one of us ought to stay at home to set your cap right," said Annie brusquely.

It sounded an inopportune jest, positively unfeeling. The truth was Annie still laboured under the common youthful necessity to hide her deeper feelings, an obligation made up of a touch of hysterical excitement, pride, shyness, and possibly the unsubdued buoyance of two-and-twenty years. The last is apt to rebound swiftly, with a mixture of cheerfulness and defiance from any sorrow, short of the one sorrow which cannot be trampled down or made light of, that has its root in a grave. Annie must find something to laugh at, to get fun out of, in the tribulation which she nevertheless felt in every nerve of her body, to the core of her heart.

"I ought to be able to keep my cap straight," said poor Mrs. Millar very literally and meekly, looking a little puzzled by Annie's ill-timed nonsense, and apparent hardness. "I daresay I should pin it, but the pins drag my hair so and hurt me."

"Never think of it, mother," said mild Dora indignantly, looking daggers at Annie.

"Of course I did not mean that, mother. I was not in earnest," Annie made the penitent amendment.

"You are right to make the best of things," said Mrs. Millar, giving a little shivering sigh on her own account. "It is the will of Providence. We are in God's hands, poor Mr. Carey and all of us, as we were a year ago—twenty years ago when you two were babies."

They were simple truisms which she uttered, but they were honest words, which meant a great deal to her. They borrowed impressiveness from the truthfulness of the speaker, in addition to the truth of the sayings, and by force of sympathy told on the listening girls, quieting and controlling them.

"Poor Mr. Carey as you say, mother," Annie caught up the words. "Well, I suppose the Careys will be in a far worse plight than we can be, and Cyril has been such a fool, though I don't suppose he meant much harm, with his dandyisms and idleness and his college airs—all that he has brought back from college."

"Hush! child," exclaimed the elder, more tolerant woman. "He has been a silly, selfish lad, but as he will know it now, to his cost, I do not like to hear you casting it in his teeth to-day. Perhaps it will steady him, and then this misfortune will be a blessing so far as he is concerned."

"Rather hard that we should all be sacrificed to prop up Cyril's weak moral nature," muttered Annie.

"And the Russells," suggested Dora. "I have heard Colonel Russell speaking to father, as if he and the Rector also had to do with the bank. Oh! there is Ned Hewett, who has not passed his Cambridge examination any more than Cyril Carey. Not that it has been Ned's fault, or that he goes in for nothing save amusement, only he is so slow over his books, poor fellow! He will grudge his father's having spent money over him to no purpose more than ever now; and Lucy and Bell will be sorry for him—they are so fond of Ned."

CHAPTER V

PROMOTION

At that moment a rush was heard on the stairs, and Rose and May burst into their mother's room, Rose at the last moment bethinking herself that she had left school, accordingly she must be grown up, or on the brink of it, if Annie would but allow it, and therefore trying to moderate the headlong pace, which would have better become a troop of boys than a pair of girls.

"Little May," who, in spite of her height, was still in frocks an inch from the ground, was not troubled by any such scruples. She scampered up to her mother, and hailed her breathlessly— "Mother, we want you to let us—Rose and me—go with Ella and Phyllis Carey a walk to the Beeches. Ella says she saw some periwinkles and young ferns there, and we need, oh! ever so many fresh roots for the rockery. We should have gone without coming home to tell you, because you wouldn't mind, but we might have kept tea waiting, and we'll be horribly late. Besides, we are not coming home for tea; Ella and Phyllis say we must go up with them to the Bank House."

"No, no, my dears, you can't do that," said Mrs. Millar, hurriedly but decidedly. "I am sorry that you should be disappointed, but you must not think of such a thing. Ella and Phyllis don't understand—don't know—that their mother is particularly engaged this afternoon. She will not wish to have people in the house, not even in the schoolroom."

Rose and May looked in wonder at their mother, discomposed enough in her own person, sitting leaning back in her chair doing nothing; she whose motherly hands were wont to be busy with some little bit of sewing or knitting.

Annie, too, was sitting idle at a short distance, with her hat thrown on the bed, but still wearing her jacket; and Dora, in her walking dress, was standing like a lady-in-waiting, or a sentry, behind Mrs. Millar's chair.

Annie and Dora remained silent, looking at the intruders in a peculiar manner. At the same time the first pair did not tell the second more or less curtly, as the elder girls had been in the habit of doing not so very long ago, to go away and leave grown-up people to finish important discussions in peace.

What other new thing could have come about? Was there a fresh wooer in the field, a second offer of marriage to be laid at reluctant feet? Was it Annie, their beauty, who was in request this time? Who was the lover? not Cyril Carey, with his plush waistcoat and gold chains and odious snuff-box? He had no means of keeping a wife, unless his father took him into partnership in the bank, and their father would not hear of Cyril; besides, Annie held him in supreme disdain. She had more patience with Tom Robinson and "the shop" than with the nineteenth century dandy, whom she pronounced a mistaken revival of one of the many curiosities of Queen Anne's reign.

But Rose and May had no certainty that Annie was the object of pursuit. She was pretty enough, they had all pinned their faith to her beauty, yet already Dora had been preferred before her, though it was only by the head of "Robinson's." Was it possible that now it might be Rose, unsuspecting, uncon- sulted? Could her own mother and sisters be so unfair as to arrogate to themselves the settlement of her affairs without her consent or knowledge, without so much as admitting her into the conclave?

Annie took the initiative, she was sufficiently quick to see both behind and before her. She had a head for directing and managing which her mother did not possess.

"Mother, don't you see they had better be told at once?" she said, with the aplomb of a girl who, however young and irresponsible, is capable of arriving at independent conclusions and reversing existing conditions. "They are, as Rose says, all but grown up; indeed not so very much younger than Dora and I. I think Rose and May are entitled to be told."

Annie was proceeding to act upon the permission implied in her mother's nod. She was not without some small sense of personal importance in being the mouthpiece which was to announce the calamity to her younger sisters. She did it in a very different fashion from that in which their mother had broken the news to her and Dora.

"What we are going to speak to you about is not a thing that can be long concealed. It will not be a secret for more than a few days, if for so long. But that does not mean that you are not to shut this room door which you have left wide open. Thanks, May. Don't bang it! You are not to show that you know what is going to happen. And, after it has happened, you are not to chatter about it before the servants or to your companions. We are trusting you because you have almost come to the years of discretion, and ought to have a notion how to behave under the circumstances."

"Well, this is too bad of you, Annie!" cried Rose, showing instant symptoms of revolt. "What have May and I done that we should be spoken to as if we were a pair of tell-tales, or babies—and geese into the bargain? Dora and you are not so much older, as you confess; neither are you so much wiser with all your pretensions. If something of so much consequence to everybody is on the eve of happening, I think we might have been told before. Surely mother is not afraid that we should repeat anything which we ought not to mention," and she glanced with burning reproach at her mother.

Rose was both high-spirited and touchy. She was not disposed to play the second part without a murmur like Dora. She was not content, with her art as a balance to Annie's beauty and May's budding scholarship. Rose desired everybody to acknowledge her mother-wit and trustworthiness.

Dora and Mrs. Millar spoke together in reply. "Mother only told Annie and me this afternoon," said the general peacemaker.

"It was not such a pleasant piece of information for me to give, or you to receive, child, that you and May should grudge my keeping it from you as long as I could, as I dared," was the mother's weary reply. "Besides, your father did not wish it spoken about before; it would have been wrong, a great risk to many others as well as to ourselves, to have mentioned such a thing."

"Then don't tell us now if you don't care to, mother, and if father disapproves of our hearing it," said Rose magnanimously, for she was dying to be at the bottom of the mystery.

"No, don't, mother dear, please don't, if it will hurt you," said May affectionately, with something of a childish ring in her voice. Her mother took her hand at the words and clasped it tightly.

"Mother has made up her mind and father has given her leave to speak," said Annie with determination, "because you must hear soon anyhow. There is something wrong with the bank, Mr. Carey's bank. We have all, even May, read and heard of bank failures, and have some idea how disastrous they are."

"The Carey's bank!" cried Rose, with sufficient intelligence in her astonishment. "I understand now why we were not to go home with Ella and Phyllis."

"Then somebody must run over and tell them that we are not coming," interrupted May. "Do let Bella take the message, mother, in case I should look as if I knew something. Poor Mr. Carey! he was always so kind to us. I am so sorry; but the bank has not anything to do with us; father is not the banker, he is just a doctor like grandfather," ended May composedly.

"O May, you are a baby, though you read the Greek Testament and have something to say to Tacitus in the original," exclaimed Annie indignantly.

"Your father has shares in the bank, my dear," explained her mother with patient reiteration. "He bought them with his savings, and he will get nothing for them. Nobody will buy them from him again, they will be no better than waste paper. But that is not the worst. The shares make him responsible for the bank's debts—I am sure I cannot tell you how far; he told me, I daresay, but I was so grieved for him and for all of you, and so confused, I could not take it in. But he says that what he will have to pay up will be as much as he can do, with a hard fight, for the rest of his days."

"I am so sorry for father," murmured May in an awed tone, but with a little of a parrot note, just as she had pitied Mr. Carey, who was only an old acquaintance and the father of her friends. The fact was that the young girl, brought away suddenly from her girlish interests and her whole past experience, and plunged into the cares of older people, was thoroughly staggered and bewildered, in spite of a small head which was capable of construing Latin and conjugating Greek.

There was a moment's pause. "Will it make a great difference to father and the rest of us?" asked Rose, in spite of her quickness, and in spite of what her mother had said.

"Certainly," Annie took it upon her to answer, with a mixture of fire and conviction, "we'll all have to earn our living."

"Oh, don't make such sweeping statements, Annie, frightening your sisters," said their mother reproachfully; and unquestionably May looked scared, and dropped her gloves without noticing it. "You must do what you can to help your poor dear father, and I am sure you'll do that willingly, but so long as he is spared to work for all of us—" She stopped short, unable to say any more.

Then her daughters closed round her, from the youngest to the eldest, and told her in concert that she was not to be concerned for them. They were ready for the occasion and equal to it, and they would not mind in the very least.

"Mind!" declared Rose, with her eyes beginning to shine and her cheeks to flush like Annie's. "Why, it is the one great comfort that we'll have to make our way in the world, and push our fortunes like boys. We'll have plenty of adventures and rise triumphant over them all, and be such a help to you and father. Think of that, May, you little coward," appealing to her younger sister who, in spite of her small dabbling in masculine acquirements, did not look as if the prospect of pushing her fortune like a boy was full of unmixed charm for her. But she brightened up at the visionary honour and delight of being a great help to their father and mother, and cried, "Yes, yes, Rose," with subdued enthusiasm.

Dora also echoed the "yes" with a quiet intensity.

Annie, on her part, graciously approved of her juniors, and rewarded them by patronizing them tremendously.

"That is right. I don't very well know yet what Dora and I can do, but we'll find something. However, you two young ones are the geniuses of the family, and we'll look to you. I suspect Dora and I will have to march under your wings. You, Rose, must be quick and paint Academy pictures, get them hung on the line, and have them sold before the opening day. May must pass all her examinations in no time, gain a scholarship, and be appointed classical mistress to a Girls' Day-school, of which she will eventually become the head. Fancy 'little May' a full-blown school ma'am."

"Dear! what creatures girls are! They are jesting and laughing already over their own and other people's misfortunes. It is little they know of life, it is little they guess what will befall them," sighed Mrs. Millar to herself. Nevertheless, in the middle of her anxiety and sorrow, she was in some respects a happy woman, and she had a dim but consoling perception of the truth.

CHAPTER VI

THE CLOUD DEEPENS

The storm burst, but the cloud did not disperse, it only closed in more darkly over Redcross. At the same time, as the bank authorities had foreseen, there was little or nothing of the wild, panic-stricken run on the capital which heralds and intensifies many a bank's fall. The losers went about their ordinary occupations. The Rector preached, presided over meetings of the vestry and Christian Associations, and attended to his sick. Doctor Millar looked after his sick. Colonel Russell even went to the Literary Institute and read the newspapers as usual. Every one of them wore his customary face, however abnormal the working of his heart. The Redcross victims, and many another innocent man besides, behaved like gentlemen, Englishmen, and Christians. There was neither outward fuss nor fury.

The individual who came nearest to breaking down was naturally Mr. Carey. The very forbearance with which he was treated cut to the quick the honest man who had been the tool of fools and knaves, brazening out their share of the business and contriving to escape with the least damage of anybody. They had been impecunious, trading upon other people's funds to begin with, and Carey's Bank's failure only left them where they were originally, under circumstances in which no reasonable person would expect redress from them. But poor James Carey, who had been credulous and weak, was made of other stuff.

"I'm not easy about Carey," the little doctor confided to his wife. "He was talking quite in a stupid, dazed way to Russell and me this morning. Do you observe his eyes? Have you noticed the veins on his forehead and his throat? I'm far from comfortable about him." (As if he felt comfortable about anything at this period!) "I question much whether he'll ever get over it."

The public of Redcross, who could remark the glassy look of the eyes, though they might not be qualified to speak of the condition of the veins, were still more struck by the immediate and melancholy effect the bank's failure had on Mr. Carey, when their attention was drawn to Mrs. Carey's behaviour. She was a woman who had seldom left her house save for her daily drive, now she walked out with her husband every fine afternoon. Her arm was drawn through his; but it was evident at the merest glance that she was supporting his failing steps and not he hers. She was a little, thin, somewhat wizened woman, but she looked equal to the task she had set herself, if a strong will would do it. There was a peculiarity to be seen in her eyes too, by those who could read the sign. It was a fixed desperate determination to keep her husband and the father of her children by sustaining his weakness with her strength, to fight and vanquish the enemy whose icy touch was already on his heart and brain.

But although there was little outward demonstration in Redcross, much inner ferment and growing concern prevailed beneath the surface in what had been considered the principal houses in Redcross—houses safe and sure as they were honourable in their ascendancy in the past. After the affairs of the bank were in the hands of liquidators, and it became clear that the ruin was great and complete, hope had hardly a hole or corner left to linger in, even in the hearts of the most simple and sanguine. The impending changes which must follow became the talk of the town, extending to circles far beyond that on which the blow had fallen. Within the narrower limits, the anxious question what was to be done became the one engrossing, breathless subject of the hour.

Sarah Tytler

Some of the reforms and retrenchments were marked by the spasmodic haste and severity which are apt to defeat themselves. These formed pendants to the spurts of grovelling distrust and quaking care for one's own welfare which caused Wilkins the butcher to send in his quarter's bill before it was due to Colonel Russell, and have the debt discharged within the hour. In like manner, Honeyman the grocer felt bound delicately to intimate to the Careys that he declined to give the family more than a week's credit. He was answered in a formally polite note from Mrs. Carey to the effect that she had not intended to ask for any longer credit thenceforth, but from that date she would pay ready money. These offensively defensive acts and vulgar tokens that times were changed got wind, and were discussed in awed, indignant whispers by the mass of Wilkins's and Honeyman's fellow-townsmen.

There was little need to remind the poor Careys of their altered circumstances, since it was in the Bank House that some of the spasmodic sweeping reforms referred to had at once been practised by Mrs. Carey. She had always been the ruling spirit in the house, and people now said openly that it would have been well for everybody if she had been the ruling spirit in the bank also. She was a woman with locally aristocratic connections, of a more tangible kind than what constituted the Millars' shadowy link with the county. Her brother was Sir Charles Luxmore of Headley Grange, and her nephew had allied himself to the peerage by marrying an Honourable Victoria Brackenridge. All the greater the glaring recklessness and insolence of Honeyman to take the word into his own mouth and refuse the Careys credit. At the same time Sir Charles's place was nearer the town of Nenthorn than that of Redcross, and he did not deal with Redcross tradesmen unless at election times. As for his daughter-in-law, the Honourable Victoria, she came so seldom to see her aunt-in-law that her face could not be said to be known in Redcross streets, where she never entered even the "fancy shop" which the other county ladies patronized occasionally in search of missing shades of silks or wools.

Mrs. Carey had stooped considerably when she became the wife of Mr. Carey of the bank, though the bank was nominally his own, and the Careys were a highly respectable family of old standing in Redcross. When it came to that, there had only been two generations of the Luxmores at Headley Grange, and the original baronet's rise to the honours of knighthood and a baronetage was due to his success and favour in high places as a fashionable physician. Mrs. Carey had not been very young at the date of her marriage, and her fortune was moderate enough, for the moneyed strength of her grandfather and father had gone to found a family and support a baronetage. Still, she had been accustomed to carry herself, after she became Mrs. Carey, not in an obtrusive and offensive manner, but in a quiet, well-bred way, as one who had been undeniably better born and bred than her neighbours. Indeed, under any circumstances she would have been a reserved woman, who would, in homely parlance, have kept herself to herself.

This was the woman who, with an absence of any sense of proportion, and an equal lack of humour, sometimes to be found in women of her class and character, together with an excess of mingled fiery zeal and feverish apprehension, hidden under a quiet exterior, took her measures on the very day after the bank's failure. These measures made a thorough exposure of the conclusion which she had arrived at, and subjected herself and the whole family to immediate privations, for which they were unprepared. They were injurious as well as useless and uncalled for, and had a ludicrous side. Acting for Mr. Carey, she dismissed the coachman and the gardener, paying them their month's wages which were unearned. She let the valuable horses take their chance of casual grooming and feeding, till they were sold off. She left the garden at the most critical time of the year, as the old gardener said with tears in his eyes, when the young vegetables were only coming into use, and the whole fruit would be lost unless it were properly seen to. The wood pigeons would have all the later seeds springing in the beds, and the place on which he had bestowed so much time and labour would lie waste, instead of providing a considerable part of the food of the household in summer and autumn. "But there was never no sense in them ladies like missus, no more in their sparing than in their spending." At one fell swoop she dismissed her own maid, the cook, and the parlour-maid, retaining only a young table-maid to "do" for the family.

Mrs. Carey had hitherto been an indulgent mother, but all at once she told the scandalized university dandy and failure, Cyril, that he must brush his own boots and help his schoolboy brothers to clean the knives, if he were not satisfied with what a maid-of-all-work could accomplish in these departments.

As for Ella and Phyllis, looking on aghast at the wholesale destruction of what they had been accustomed to consider the ordinary comforts—not to say the luxuries and refinements of their home—the girls were informed that they were not to go back to Miss Burridge's, where their quarters were paid in advance. The younger brothers might continue at the Grammar School, because the fees were low; they would be kept out of harm, and they could do nothing else to speak of. But Ella and Phyllis had better lose no time in learning to make beds, sweep floors, and lay tables. "For myself, I have your father to see to," said Mrs. Carey in her somewhat deep and strong voice, the measured steadiness of which had acquired a ringing vibration. "I do not mean to conceal from you that Dr. Millar is apprehensive on your father's account, and I intend to devote myself to him. We must pull him through and save him at any cost, though his health and nerves may be shattered from this date, and he may never be able to retrieve his losses and those of other people, which, of course, press most heavily upon him. We can try at least for the credit as well as the life which is so dear to us, and never have it said for his sake, still more than for ours, that he was blind and imposed upon, and then let himself slip out of the misery which he had helped to bring about, while others who were not accountable were condemned to pay the penalty."

Mrs. Carey would fain not have touched a farthing of the

income allowed the family till the bank's affairs were wound up—that winding-up which Dr. Millar said might last throughout his life. She would willingly have resigned the bulk of her small fortune in favour of the bank's creditors, but marriage settlements and trustees are stubborn facts to deal with. All she could do was to stint and punish herself and her family in the manner described, and inasmuch as the stinting and punishment were done in good faith, doubtless they would serve their purpose and have their reward.

The Rector was a widower. Hitherto he had kept an efficient housekeeper and chaperon for his daughters, the elder of whom must now take the housekeeper's place. He, too, put down what had served him for a carriage. It was remarkable how uniformly the first idea of retrenchment took this form in Redcross, but it was natural under the circumstances. It was difficult to say at once what was to be cut down from a not very extensive list of supernumeraries, unless one was prepared to make a clean sweep like Mrs. Carey. The Rector had been simple enough in his tastes and habits. He was a member of the Church of England Temperance Society, and so had no valuable cellar of wine to dispose of. He did not possess more silver plate than was wanted for the Rectory table. His library contained no rare and costly books. The very carriage in question was no more than one of those pony-phaetons with regard to which Bishop Pattison appealed, in one of his letters from Melanesia to his brethren in peaceful, pleasant country rectories and vicarages at home, asking the astonished clergymen, with their clergywomen in the background, if they really considered the clerical equipage, with its modest expense, equivalent to a divine institution? The Rector proved his freedom from the superstition by doing away with the phaeton and its pair, and falling back, as he was a spare man, on an old pony which the children had ridden by turns. Though he was not a book fancier, he had entertained a fondness for art, and since he could not indulge in much picture buying, had dabbled in old prints, of which he had rather a fine collection. This all at once vanished along with the phaeton.

Sarah Tytler

Bell Hewett, the second daughter, who was several years younger than her sister Lucy, but had left Miss Burridge's some time before, and was as far removed from a school-girl as Annie Millar herself, unexpectedly appeared again on the familiar benches. She was not there as a junior governess, she was not sufficiently clever or educated, since Miss Burridge sought to work up to the new standards. Poor Bell was in her old place, in her old classes, as a pupil once more, only she sat looking deeply affronted, and nervously trying to make up for lost time, among a set of young girls like May Millar.

There was not much difference made in Colonel Russell's establishment. But this was caused by one of two things. There was the probability of the establishment's soon being broken up, if its master succeeded in getting a post which should enable him to return to India. On the other hand, the second Mrs. Russell was too foolish and self-willed to comprehend without a prolonged struggle how she and her babies could get along unless they were fortified by every imaginable aid in the shape of an expensive table, fine clothes, a couple of under nurses, and a boy in buttons. Fanny Russell, the Colonel's grown-up daughter by his first wife, looked sad enough over the prospect of her father's departure at his age, with his shattered constitution, and over what was to become of herself, left behind with the frivolous, unreasonable young stepmother with whom Fanny had never been able to agree.

The Millars were still in the old quaintly spacious house with its great bowery garden, for the plausible reason that Dr. Millar could not, on the spur of the moment, find a purchaser or an available tenant. He took some credit to himself for having more breadth of view and controlling common sense than poor Mrs. Carey, otherwise he might have rushed off and crammed his family into a small inconvenient house, for which, at the same time, he would have had to pay rent, that was not called for, unless in the form of rates and taxes, where his old house was concerned. There might be something to say on the other side of the question, but as yet that had not occurred to Dr. and Mrs. Millar. However, the Doctor's brougham, like the Rector's phaeton, was a thing of the past. He trudged manfully on foot to his patients. There are few evils which do not offer some compensations. It really seemed as if the Doctor's deprivation, which weighed heavily on his wife's mind, served to divert it from other trials, by the degree to which it was occupied in looking after her husband's changes of coats and boots, in order to ward off evil consequences to his health.

The four girls were so engrossed with what had happened and was going to happen to them from the failure of Mr. Carey's bank, that they had largely lost sight of the first wooer in the family. This was strong evidence of the extent to which their minds were filled by the rapid descent of what they called poverty on themselves and their neighbours. Rose and May ceased to have qualms of conscience when they caught sight of Tom Robinson fishing in the Dewes, not knowing what desperate promptings of despair might not suddenly lay hold of a rejected and forlorn lover. They left off glancing covertly at him in his pew at church, for the purpose of detecting the earliest symptoms of a broken heart and a galloping consumption. Instead they speculated on whether Bell Hewett would have had a new hat if it had not been for the bank's failure; and whether her brother's absence from home was owing to his having gone to London for the first look at the columns of the advertising newspapers, and that he might be on the spot to apply in person at the addresses given, and to haunt the agency offices, as young men are represented doing in novels.

Inevitably Tom Robinson's recent intercourse with the family had been confined to a formal call or two, awkward and unpleasant to all concerned. Only Dr. Millar brought him into the conversation occasionally, dealing with his name in the spirit of a faithful partisan. "That good fellow Robinson did not draw out a farthing of his deposit at the bank after disquieting rumours must have reached him. Carey tells me that Robinson, in place of seeking to be reassured, did his best to reassure him, Carey; told him never to mind him, he could lie out of the money; he was willing to let others who had more need be paid first. Ah! well, it is good to have it in your power to be both just and generous, and it is still better to have a heart to use the power. Robinson has acted handsomely throughout, in short, like the gentleman he is. I wonder if his behaviour on this occasion will weigh with snobs against the iniquity of his having a shop. I thought Thackeray had done something to demolish similar rubbish when he described the young cads who gave the schoolboy Dobbin the nickname 'Figs.'"

The speaker was guilty of glaring rather fiercely at his daughters, assembled for afternoon tea. They became eminently innocent and meek-looking on the instant, but when the sisterhood were left to themselves Annie delivered her opinion with admirable fairness and candour.

"I am sure I am glad that Tom Robinson should behave himself like a gentleman, but that does not make his trade a profession fit for a gentleman, neither does it render the man, with his lack of ambition and his commonplaceness and dulness, an interesting specimen of humanity."

"Not a man that a woman would care to die for," said Rose, wrinkling her forehead and crumpling up her nose till her face was half its natural length. "Oh, I say, think of any woman being so infatuated as to be willing to die for an insignificant, foxy-headed, well-bred shopkeeper!"

"Don't be slangy, Rose," Annie rebuked her sister.

"Still I am very glad," said Dora's soft voice quite distinctly, and while she blushed furiously she reared her little neck with an unconscious gesture. It said plainly, "Yes, I am glad that the man who sought me for his wife has shown himself liberal and merciful, so that I can always think of him and his wishes with respect and gratitude."

"And so am I glad," agreed May warmly. "It is so nice that 'Robinson's' has not made its master grasping and greedy."

"I don't know that rapacity is confined to trade," admitted Annie. "You ought to know, May, for you have a good deal of intercourse with royalty in your reading; but I have a notion that it has been the distinguishing characteristic of a good many kings and emperors."

Annie and Rose had grown more and more eager to take up their burdens from the first day they were aware that there were burdens for them to take up. They were becoming positively enamoured of pushing their fortunes and encountering adventures—not in the least understanding, in spite of their bright wits, what the burdens, fortunes, adventures might mean. The two sisters' enthusiasm was just kept within bounds by two drags on its quicksilver quality. These laggard spirits, Dora and May, weighed upon their more enterprising companions. Neither could Annie and Rose quite shut their eyes to the increase of wrinkles on their father's face, and to their mother's red eyes when she came down of a morning. If it had not been for these small drawbacks, it is to be feared that Annie and Rose would have arrived at such a height of *tete exaltee* that they would have begun to rejoice in their own and their neighbours' misfortunes. There was something so fresh and exciting in looking about for openings and careers, in calculating how they were to earn their bread—which would taste so sweet to those who earned it—and at the same time save money. They were not quite so insane as to propose to amass fortunes and fling them into the gulf caused by the crumbling away of the late bank in order to redeem their father's pledge as a shareholder. But surely in the course of a year or two they might help him, and generally assist in keeping the old folks at home in state and bounty.

Annie and Rose looked on working for themselves in a very different light from that in which they regarded Tom Robinson's sticking to his father's and grandfather's shop. To be sure, they did not start with any intention of keeping shops. Even if they had done so, the descent might have been redeemed by a dash of sentiment and romance which did not apply in the least to a man with only himself to look to, a man of independent means to boot, who had forgotten what was expected from a gentleman.

There was no danger of Dora or May's being infected with their sisters' frame of mind. Dora and May were mortally ashamed of themselves. They feared they were not of the stuff of which heroines—not to say martyrs—were made. They looked back almost as fondly and sadly as their mother looked on the old state of matters. They dreaded with a shrinking terror going away from home, leaving their people, facing the cold, critical world, being left to their own slender resources. It was bad enough in Dora, but it was really dreadfully disappointing in May, with her youthful learning, to have so little spirit and courage; still so it was, and in the meantime there was no help for it. Dora might have been glad for purely personal reasons to get away from Redcross for a time; but she was not thrown into Tom Robinson's company, and the fact of his refusal had been kept so quiet by the Millars that, unless he himself betrayed it, which was not likely, the greatest gossip in the place could only suspect the truth.

It was a small comfort to the unheroic pair, and perhaps to Annie and Rose also, though they did not consciously take it into account, that all the older professional men in the town, the leaders and those who were on most intimate terms, were "in the same boat," as Dr. Millar had said. But there was a family named Dyer lately settled at Redcross, a semi-retired stockbroker, with his wife and daughters, who had come from London to occupy Redcross Manor-house—naturally they had nothing to do with Carey's Bank, and were still supposed to be rolling in wealth, as they had been reported from the first. However, there was a notion that the Dyers' riches had not been acquired in any very refined fashion. Cyril Carey had always insisted, as he settled his collar and twirled his cane, that stockbroker was simply pawnbroker writ large. Anyhow the Dyers were not so distinguished in mind and manners as they were wealthy. Old conservative folks sighed at the idea of Redcross Manor-house, which had belonged to the Cliftons from time immemorial, till the last Clifton fell into the hands of the Jews before he was twenty, and was driven to break the entail by the time he was forty, passing to a family of Dyers. The best that could be said of them was, that the old people were comparatively inoffensive and the young were presentable. They were inclined to be friendly with the town—it might be till they could secure a footing with the county people, if that were possible. They dressed well, thanks to their milliners and dressmakers, kept a good table, a good stable, and a good staff of domestics, and furnished Redcross—especially young Redcross—with country-house hospitalities and gay gatherings, which they would otherwise have lacked. Yet fanatics of young people like Annie and Rose Millar, who were persuaded that they were now well acquainted with a reverse of fortune, began to behave as if they considered it was no longer the *creme de la creme* of human experience to amass and retain a fortune. They began to pity the rampantly prosperous family for the lack on their part of any knowledge of life's vicissitudes, with their trumpet call to earnest effort and supreme self-devotion—all that makes man or woman worthy of the name. As for the younger Dyers, they were content to echo the sentiments of their mouthpiece, the head of their house. He spoke in the privacy of his family with a half-affable, half-contemptuous concern for those unfortunate beggars of uppish Redcross townspeople who had all come to smash by the failure of one paltry twopenny-halfpenny local bank.

The Millars were constantly hearing of fresh examples of hardship, and courage to meet the hardship, piquing and inciting them to enterprise and self-sacrifice on their own account. Now it would be May, who would come in from Miss Burridge's with a blanched face, crying, "Oh! you girls, do you know Ella Carey has gone and is not coming back again? Phyllis is crying her eyes out, because she and Ella were never separated before. No, Ella has not gone to be a lady-help, as she thought she might do, after she had got a little more practice in washing dishes and peeling potatoes. It is nothing bad, except that she is gone for good and all, and it has been so sudden. And Mrs. Carey says Ella is not to come back. One of her sisters, the one without children, Mrs. Tyrrel, wrote and offered to take either of the girls. And what do you think Mrs. Carey said? That Ella must go, because if she went there would be a mouth less to feed. She was sorry, because she said it was giving up Ella, and she told her she must not expect to have much more to do with Phyllis and the rest of them at home, for it would be out of the question, in the different circumstances of the Tyrrels and Careys, for them to carry on frequent or intimate intercourse. Ella would have refused if she had dared, for she is so fond of Phyllis and all of them, even of her mother, though she has grown very hard since the bank failed. She used to let the girls have their own way. Don't you remember, Rose, she allowed us to dress up for charades out of her wardrobe? Why, you once wore her wedding-gown pinned up round you. But Mrs. Carey would not give Ella any choice. She repeated that there would be one mouth the less to feed. She said Ella was the elder, and it was her duty to her father and his creditors to go. So all poor Ella's things were sought out and packed up last night—the letter only came yesterday. She has had no time to bid Rose and me, or any of her other friends, good-bye. She started with Cyril early this morning, and I don't know what Phyllis will do without her."

"She must do the best she can," said Annie promptly, "and occupy herself with something better than gossiping with you when she chances to meet you coming from school. I suppose that was the manner in which you heard all this; I don't think Mrs. Carey will approve of such a waste of time."

"But, Annie," pled May, with her dark eyes ready to brim over, "poor Phyllis has only me now, and she has a great many messages to go, because their single servant has so much work to do in the house that she cannot get out marketing. Mrs. Carey is always walking or sitting with Mr. Carey. If it were not so, Phyllis is sure that her mother would go out and not mind taking the market-basket herself—a rough, heavy market-basket. The Careys' servants used to complain because one of them was expected to carry it in the mornings. Phyllis is glad to let me have it sometimes, her arms get tired and ache so. You see Jack and Dick are not often home from school in time, and then they have the boots and knives to clean. Cyril would carry it for her after it was dark, but Mrs. Carey won't let her go out then, and sends her off to bed that she may get up earlier for what she has to do in the morning."

That rough market-basket over which the Careys' former servants had grumbled, was like a badge of honour in certain shining eyes—far more so than Thirza Dyer's thoroughbred, or Camilla and Gussy Dyer's exquisite hats and dainty parasols. Even Annie Millar was not too old or too wise to refrain from wishing that Mrs. Millar, who still would not let her daughters soil their fingers if she could help it, had sent them out marketing in their native town, each in her turn flourishing a market-basket.

At another time it would be Rose who would arrive flushed and breathless with the great piece of news that Ned Hewett had taken the post of station-master at a small station some-where on the Yorkshire moors. He had done it when nothing else turned up, without waiting to consult his father. But the Rector had not forbidden him when he heard. Steadiness and punctuality had always been Ned's strong points, so that, though he had not taken his degree at the university, and his old masters had said they were not surprised to hear it, he might be trusted not to wreck trains, slay their passengers, and find himself tried for manslaughter. The difficulty was to fancy a big, slow fellow like Ned rushing here and there in a noisy, fussy little station. After all, it would only be noisy and fussy at long intervals, and on rare occasions, "somewhere on the Yorkshire moors." Ned might have time and space to walk about in. But what of the uniform? Would the poor boy—they had all known him as a boy—who had once cherished the notion of going into the army, have to wear a railway company's coat and a station-master's cap? How funny it sounded! Well, not altogether funny. There were Dora and May crying at the bare anticipation. If they were ever on the Yorkshire moors, and had to greet Ned in this extraordinary guise, it would be awkward for all parties, to say the least.

Sarah Tytler

What were they thinking of? Of course they would be proud to greet him when he was twice the man that he had ever been. No doubt Cyril Carey would be glad to have Ned's chance; Cyril, who had renounced his delicate plush vests and Indian gold chains and charms, his loitering and dawdling, and taken to a shabby shooting-suit and spade-husbandry. He was getting rid of his time and keeping out of his mother's way by digging aimlessly in the garden. He was inquiring, in a desultory fashion, all over Redcross for any opening in an office which he could fill. He was not likely to find such an opening unless it were made for him out of charity. He had not been trained to office work, and he was far from having Ned Hewett's reputation for steadiness and punctuality. If Tom Robinson should be the charitable man and ask Cyril, a schoolfellow and college chum, to help him with his accounts, the head of "Robinson's" would have to be at the trouble of running up every column of figures over again. Cyril might ride to hounds and row in a boat-race with the best; he might even have some elegant acquaintance with the renaissance and old French, and be capable of distinguishing himself in stately Latin verse, though that sounded more than doubtful when he had been plucked at his university— the inhabitants of Redcross did not, as a rule, pretend to be judges in such matters. What they did know, because it had oozed out some time before, was that Cyril Carey, though a banker's son, was lamentably weak in arithmetic, and his handwriting would have been held a disgrace to any shop-boy.

Money was required to start lads in the world in the humblest fashion. Ned Hewett wanted an outfit, and if possible furniture for his station-house, that he might not begin on credit. Even girls, though they had been a good deal set aside in such consideration, could not enter on an independent career without money any more than boys could. The Millars were therefore thankful that Mrs. Millar had a little money of her own, not above a hundred and fifty pounds a year, settled upon her from the first, by one of those marriage contracts which are so hard to break, and she could use it to supply what was needed for the girls, who were going into the world with such dauntless spirits and light hearts.

CHAPTER VII

ROSE GOES WEST AND ANNIE GOES EAST

In the end it was settled, to Annie and Rose's great satisfaction, and no less to the temporary relief of Dora and May's quaking hearts, that the two former were to take the first plunge into unknown waters. If things had been as they were formerly, and there had been leisure to spare from rougher rubs for highly delicate considerations, it might, as has been hinted, have been held that Dora should have been the sister selected to go away from Redcross—at least for a time.

But a great deal had happened since Tom Robinson's unsuccessful suit and all connected with it had been in honour hushed up. People had too many weighty matters to think of to keep in mind that small sentimental episode between a couple of young people.

Rose's fate was chalked out from the first. She was to be an artist—that went without saying. She had certainly artistic talent, she might have genius. But though she had been tolerably well trained so far, by a good drawing-master at Miss Burridge's, and by the lessons she had received from the wandering exhibitor at the Academy and the Grosvenor, neither she nor her family could be sufficiently infatuated to imagine she wanted no more teaching. Their conceptions of art might be crude, and their faith in Rose unbounded, but they did not suppose that she had only to open her portfolio and sell its contents as often as it was full. Dr. and Mrs. Millar made up their minds, Rose agreeing with them, that she should have at least a year in a London studio.

All the three considered it very fortunate when the artist who had given her lessons at Redcross, hearing of her intention, and of what had rendered it incumbent on her to work for her living, not only recommended a studio in which art classes were held, but good-naturedly gave her a testimonial and helped her to a post as assistant drawing-mistress in a ladies' school, a situation which she could fill on two days of the week, while she attended the art classes on the remaining four. The salary thus obtained was of the smallest, but it would supplement Mrs. Millar's allowance to Rose, and help to pay her board in some quiet, respectable family living midway between the school and the studio. Rose was a lucky girl, and she thought herself so. Indeed that minimum salary raised her to such a giddy pinnacle in her own estimation that it nearly turned her head. It was only her sisters, the wise Annie among them, who regarded the assistant drawing-mistress-ship with impatience as a waste of Rose's valuable time and remarkable talents.

A qualification came soon to Rose's exultation and to her pride in being the first of her father's daughters—and she the third in point of age—who had just left school, and had hardly been reckoned grown-up by Annie till quite lately—to earn real tangible money, gold guineas, however few. For something better still befell Annie. If Rose was lucky, Annie was luckier. True, she would never be a great artist, she would never get hundreds and thousands for a picture. At the utmost she would only be at the head of a charitable institution. She might save the greater part of her income then, and hand it over to her father, but that was a very different prospect from the other. Still, from the beginning Annie would be, so to speak, self-supporting; she need not cost her mother or anybody else a penny, her very dress would be provided for her. Above all Annie was going to do a great deal of good, to be a comfort and blessing, not only to her people, but to multitudes besides. She was, please God, to help to lessen the great crushing mass of pain and misery in the world, not by passive, sentimental sympathy, not by little fitful, desultory doles of practical aid, but by the constant daily work of her life. Young as Rose was, and enamoured of art in her way, she was able to comprehend that if Annie could do that worthy deed, her life would be greater in a sense, fuller in its humanity, perhaps also sweeter than that of the most famous and successful painter.

Annie had always taken a lively interest in her father's profession, and he had liked her to do so. He had been fond of talking to her about it, and enlightening her on some of its leading principles. He had even pressed her into his service in little things, and been gratified by the hereditary firmness and lightness of grasp and touch, the control over her own nerves and power of holding those of others in check, the quick and correct faculty of observation she had displayed. But with all his loyal allegiance to the calling which had been his father's before it was his, which he would have liked to see his son fill, if a son had been born to him, he was taken aback and well-nigh dismayed, as her mother was, when Annie came and told them quietly that she had made up her mind, if they would consent, to go into an hospital and be trained for a nurse. He laid before her as calmly and clearly as he could the conditions of the undertaking, and reminded her that it could not be gone into by halves, while he thought, as he spoke, that Annie was not the style of young woman to go into anything by halves.

Mrs. Millar followed with a trembling recital of the painfulness, the absolute horror to a young girl of many of the details of the office. But Annie was not shaken in the least. "I should not mind that," she asserted with conviction. "I know there must be strict discipline and hard trying work, with no respite or relaxation to speak of; but I am young and strong, fitter to stand such an ordeal than most girls of my age are qualified. I am too young, you say? Yes, I admit that; it is a pity—at least I know I have always reckoned myself too young when the thought crossed my mind six months—a year ago, of leaving home and becoming trained for a nurse."

"You don't mean to say, Annie, that you ever thought of going out into the world before our misfortunes in connection with the bank?" cried both father and mother in one breath.

Annie hung her shapely head a little, then held it up, and confessed frankly, "Yes, I have. Oh, you must forgive me. It was not from any failure of kindness on your part, or, I trust, any failure on mine to appreciate your kindness, for I believe you are the best, dearest father and mother in the world," she cried, carried out of herself, and betrayed into enthusiasm. "But what were you to do with a houseful of girls, when one would have served to give you all the help you need, mother, in your housekeeping and the company you see? I *have* hated the idea of being of no use in the world, unless I chanced to marry," ended Annie, with a quick, impatient sigh.

"My dear, you are talking exaggerated nonsense." Mrs. Millar reproved her daughter with unusual severity, dislodging her cap by the energy of her remonstrance, so that Annie had to step forward promptly, arrest it on its downward path, and set it straight before the conversation went any further. "Nobody said such things when I was young. I was one of a household of girls, far enough scattered now, poor dears!"—parenthetically apostrophizing herself and her youthful companions with unconscious pathos—"I would have liked to hear any one say to us, or to our father and mother, that we were no good in the world. I call it a positive sin in the young people of this generation to be so restless and dissatisfied, and so ready to take responsibilities upon themselves. It is a temptation of Providence to send such calamities as the one we are suffering from. You will know more about life when you are forced to work for yourself, and do not set about it out of pure presumption and self-will, with a good home to fall back upon when you are tired of your fad."

Mrs. Millar had been hurt and mortified by Annie's avowal. She had been further nettled by the slighting reflection on a houseful of girls, made by one of themselves, while she, their mother, the author of their being, poor unsophisticated woman! had always been proud of her band of bright, fair young daughters, and felt consoled by their very number for the lack of a son.

"Come, come, mother," said Dr. Millar, "you must make allowance for the march of ideas."

"I cannot help it," said Annie, with another quick sigh. "I suppose girls are not so easily satisfied as they once were, or they have been taken so far, and not far enough, out of their place. I could not have remained content with tennis-playing and skating, or *rechauffe* school music, French and German, or fancy work, however artistic—not even with teaching once a week in the Rector's Sunday-school—for my object in life. But after the way in which things have turned out, there is no need to discuss former views. Mother dear, it is surely well that I had not a hankering after idleness, after lying in bed half the forenoon, as people say the Dyers do, getting up only to read the silliest and fastest of novels, with secret aspirations after diamonds and a carriage and pair, if not a coach and six. Of course I should not have been contented with a one-horse shay, a mere doctor's pill-box, such as you have put down, father, which Rose and May are determined to set up for you again before they are many year's older."

"Good little chits!" exclaimed the little Doctor, blowing his nose suspiciously. "Tell them, Annie, that I like walking above all things. I find it a great improvement on driving. I have been troubled with—let me see, oh! yes, cold feet—a deficiency in the circulation, not at all uncommon when one gets up in years, and after walking a bit I feel my toes all tingling and as warm as a toast."

"I should prefer nursing to any other mode of earning my living," said Annie, keeping to her point. "I may be presumptuous, like the girls of my day, as mother says, but I really think that I have a natural turn for nursing, derived from you father, and grandfather, no doubt, which might have made me also a good doctor supposing I had been a man, or supposing I had sought from the first to be a medical woman and had been educated accordingly. If I am wrong, you will set me right, won't you?"

In place of contradicting her, he simply nodded in acquiescence, while he linked his hands across the small of his back.

"Mother, I do not think I should shrink from dressing wounds, if I only knew the best thing to do to avoid danger and give relief. You remember when Bella burnt her arm badly from the elbow to the wrist, I tied it up to keep out the air, before father came in, and he said it was rightly done, and would not change the dressing. And when poor Tim, who has lost his place with the putting down of the brougham, gave his hand the terrible hack with the axe in breaking wood for cook, I was able to stop the loss of blood, and did not get in the least faint myself. Yes, I know it would be very pitiful to see a human creature die whom we could not save," she added, in a lower tone, "and very sad to prepare such a one for the grave. But, dear mother, somebody has to do it at some time, and I may be the somebody one day, anyhow I shall have to be indebted to my neighbour to do the last charitable offices for me. It might be all the easier to look forward to in my own case if I had done it for other people, not merely because they were my own, just because they were God's creatures, and He had set me, among other women, to do the sorrowful work, and would lend me strength for the task."

"I believe it, Annie," said Dr. Millar firmly, as he looked at the reverently bent head, and listened to the faltering yet faithful words.

Mrs. Millar said no more, though the poor lady still shivered, as she looked at the girl in her brilliant youthful bloom. It was too terrible to think of her associated with disease and death, she whom her father and mother would have sheltered from every rough wind. Yet what was pretty Annie in the ranks of humanity, in the march of history? The frivolous product of a heathen world, the feminine counterpart of some

"Idle singer of an empty day"?

or—

"A creature breathing thoughtful breath,
A traveller 'twixt life and death"—

a Christian girl who with all true Christians had the Lord
Christ, who went about doing good, for an everlasting
example? And had there not all along been something fine in
Annie, under her superficial hardness and inclination to
conceal her feelings, something which her family had not
suspected, brought to light by their troubles? something of
which everybody connected with her would be prouder in all
humility, with reason, in the days to come, than they had ever
been proud of her supreme prettiness and lively tongue in
times past.

"It is a pity about my age," went on Annie ingenuously,
lamenting over her deficiency in years as other people lament
over their superfluity in that respect, "but it is a fault which
will mend every day. I have found out that there are two
hospitals which make twenty-three—just a year older than I
am—the age of admission for probationers, and there is one
hospital that admits them at twenty. Would not the fact of my
being a doctor's daughter go for something? Have you not
interest, father, if you care to exert it, to get the hospital
authorities to stretch a point where I am concerned? You
might tell them that I am the eldest of the family," drawing up
her not very tall figure, "that I have been treated as grown-up
for years and years, and that I have several younger sisters
whom I have tried to keep in order." There was a returning
twinkle in Annie's brown eyes and a comical curve of her rosy
lips.

But she relapsed into extreme gravity the next moment;
indeed, she was more agitated than she had yet been, and for
Annie to betray an approach to tearfulness was a rare spectacle.

"There is something worse than my age. I am afraid I am not half good enough. I have a hasty temper; you have frequently said so, mother. I often speak sharply, and am not always aware when I am doing it. I hurt people, as I hurt myself, without being able to help it—something seems to come over me and impel me to do it. Often I cannot resist making game of people. I am so silly and fond of fun, like a child, a great deal worse than 'little May' ever is, when the fit is upon me. Now, if I could think that I should lose patience with poor sick people, and wound instead of comforting them, or that I should find them food for my love of the ridiculous, and forget and neglect their wants in following my own amusement, I should hate myself—I would die sooner than so disgrace a nurse's calling."

"You would not do it, my dear," said Dr. Millar, with calm conviction.

"Why, what treason is this you are speaking against yourself?" cried Mrs. Millar, bristling up in her daughter's defence, the assailant being that daughter. "You unkind or unfeeling when there was any call for kindness—whoever heard of such a thing? I should as soon suspect Dora of harshness or levity in the same circumstances. Don't you remember my bad eyes last winter, when I had to get that tincture dropped into them so often that your father could not always be at home to do it? You dropped the tincture as well as your father could, and though I know I must have made faces wry enough to frighten a cat, you never vouchsafed a remark, and I did not hear the ghost of a laugh. Poor Dora was ready to read to me by the hour, and to fetch and carry for me all day long, but when she tried to drop the tincture her hand shook so that she sent the liquid down my cheeks; and she was so frightened for giving me pain that I could see when I opened my eyes she was as white as a sheet, and fit to faint herself."

"Dora's hand will get steadier and her heart harder by and by," said Dr. Millar, laughing. "Not that she has the knack of the operator, any more than you have, Maria. I don't think one of you has it, except Annie here."

"That was nothing," said Annie quickly. She added in a lower tone, "And oh, mother, how could you imagine that I should laugh at your pain?"

"It was only for a moment, and I daresay it was not agonizing, as I was tempted to call it; very likely your father and you would not have so much as winced at it. Then there was Miss Sill, poor old Miss Sill. Annie, I am afraid you girls laughed at her. Girls will be girls, and she does dress outrageously. You all said her mantles were worse than my cap," tenderly touching that untrustworthy piece of head-gear. "When she sent for your father all of a sudden, just when he had been summoned to Dr. Hewett's brother, who was very ill, as we knew, while we thought Miss Sill had only one of her maiden-lady fancies, your father told you to go over and say he would be with her in the course of the day. But you found her nearly choking with bronchitis. How you were not frightened out of your senses, I, who am a great deal more than twice your age, and the mother of a family, cannot tell. You propped her up in exactly the right position, saw to the temperature of the room, and caused her cook to bring in the kitchen boiler and set it to steam on the hob, before another doctor could be found. Miss Sill told me all about it afterwards; she believes she owes her life to you."

"Oh, nonsense," protested Annie, "I was a little better than her two servants, who stood looking at her, and beginning to sob and cry; but I made several gross mistakes. You told me about them afterwards, father; it was a great mercy that I did not cause her death."

"So far from that," continued Mrs. Millar, in triumphant defiance, "she calls you her young doctor to this day, and says she will send for you in preference to your father or any other doctor the next time she has an attack."

"Infatuated woman!" declared Annie.

"I have not needed to talk to you in order to get you to go with your sisters and see her since then. You have gone of your own accord twice as often, and I am sure you have not laughed at her half so much. In fact, I believe you are becoming quite attached to her."

"I suppose I am grateful to her for not dying in my unskilled hands. I am afraid I still think her rather fantastic and foolish; but it does make a difference in one's judgment of a person to have really rendered him or her a service. I ought to be fond of Miss Sill, after all, if she is to rank as my first patient."

Mrs. Millar sank into silence on the instant. She stood convicted in her own eyes. What had she been doing? Proving to her daughter's satisfaction that she had the special talents of a nurse!

"I am very glad that mother and you think me—not by any means good enough, of course, not that, but not too impatient, sarcastic, and trifling to be a nurse," said Annie brightly, addressing her father, who simply acquiesced in an absent-minded fashion.

After that there was no serious objection made to Annie's wish, great as the wonder was at first—a shock to her relations no less than to her acquaintances. The former reconciled themselves sooner to it than did the latter, with an entire faith in Annie and an affectionate admiration which was genuine homage. It swelled Dora's heart well-nigh to bursting with sister-worship. How good Annie was showing herself, how capable of great acts of self-denial and self-consecration, while she was prettier than ever with her graceful head, her merry brown eyes, and that soft, warm colour of hers!

Only Mrs. Millar lay awake at night and cried quietly over what lay before her young daughter, her first-born, the flower of the flock, as people had called her in reference to her beauty. Annie's pretty Grand-aunt Penny had at least enjoyed her day; she had had her triumph, however short-lived, in marrying the

Sarah Tytler

man of her heart, who was also a Beauchamp of Waylands, and in being raised for even a brief space to the charmed circle of the county. What she had to go through—whether she would or not—in the end, was not worse than Annie was proposing to encounter in the beginning, to live in an hospital, to spend her blooming life amidst frightful accidents, raging fevers, the spasm of agony replaced by the chill silence and stillness of death. Annie's father's time and strength had been given in much the same cause, ever since he was a young man passing his examinations and taking his diploma. But he was a man, which changed the whole aspect of affairs; besides he had always had a cheerful home to come back to, with the command of all the social advantages which Redcross, his native town, could afford. He had not lived among his patients with no life to speak of separate from theirs.

At the same time Mrs. Millar felt herself powerless. She dared no more interfere to keep back Annie from her calling than a good Roman Catholic mother would forbid her daughter's "vocation."

CHAPTER VIII

STANDING AND WAITING

It was all over in its earlier stages, that dividing and dispersing of the goodly young group of sisters, that bereaving and impoverishing of the abandoned home to which Dora and May had looked forward with such fear and pain, for which all Dr. Millar's fortitude and all his wife's meekness had been wanted to enable them to bear it with tolerable calmness. It was only Annie and Rose doing what every young man, with few exceptions, has to do. It was only their going away to work out their bents in London. They had often gone from home and followed various impulses and promptings before. But this was different. All who were left behind had a sure intuition that this was the beginning of the end, the sifting and scattering which every large family must undergo if their time is to be long on earth. Annie and Rose might often come back on visits. Rose might even set up a studio in Redcross and work there, but it would not be the same. She would be an independent member of society, with her own interests to think of—however faithfully and affectionately she might still be concerned for the interests of others—and her individual career to follow. Her separate existence would no longer be merged in that of a band of sisters; it would stand out clearly and distinctly far apart from the old state of tutelage and subserviency of each unit to the mass. The lament of the tender old Scotch song over the departing bride applied equally to Annie and Rose, though there were no gallant "Jamies" to accuse of taking them "awa', awa'." In the same manner it was not so much over the cause of their going that Dora and May lamented, or the father and mother's hearts were sorrowful, as

"Just that they'd aye be awa', awa'."

One day as May was coming back from school she met Tom Robinson, and he stopped her to ask how the family were, and to tell her something. There had always been less restraint in his and May's greetings than there had been in those of the others since his dismissal as a suitor. There was something in May's mingled studiousness and simplicity, and in the strong dash of the child in her, which dissipated his shyness and tickled his fancy. If matters had turned out otherwise than they had done, he told himself vaguely, he and "little May" would have been a pair of friends. He had no sister, and she had no brother, and he would have liked to play the brother to this most artless of learned ladies. "Look here, Miss May," he said, after the usual formulas, while he turned and walked a few paces by her side, "do you remember the fox-terrier puppy I was to have got for you and your sister Rose, in the spring? Well, he died of distemper, poor little brute; but I have heard of another of the same kind that has had the complaint. I could get him for you if you cared to have him."

"Oh! I am so much obliged to you, Mr. Robinson, so very much obliged," cried May, beaming with gratitude and pleasure. "Rose and I did so wish to have that dear little puppy which you brought down to show to us once—don't you remember? and so it is dead, poor little pet; and Rose has gone away to London to be regularly trained as an artist, just as Annie is in St. Ebbe's learning to be a nurse. I suppose you have heard," she ended a little solemnly.

"Yes, I have heard—let me carry these books for you a bit— what is there of Redcross news that one does not hear?" Then he paused abruptly, while there darted simultaneously across his mind and May's whether his speech did not sound as if he thought that Dora Millar's refusal of him must be public property? "For that very reason," he went on with a momentary shade of awkwardness, "I mean, because two of your sisters are gone, I fancied you might like this other little dog to keep you company."

"I have Dora," said May simply, and then she dashed on in an unhappy consciousness that she ought not to have mentioned Dora's name to him on any account. "I should like it immensely though—thank you a hundred thousand times, it was so good of you to think of me. But Rose could not have it now, could she? and she wished it quite as much as I did. It does not seem nice to have it when she is not here to share it," finished May, with wistful jealousy for Rose's rights in the matter.

"I do not see the force of that objection," said Tom Robinson, cheerfully. "Rose has something else instead. She has all London to occupy her. I am certain she would like you to make the best of Redcross without her."

"Yes, and of course the little dog would be half hers, the same as if Rose were here. She would see it every time she came home. She might have her turn of it at her studio, when she gets a studio. In the meantime I could write full particulars of it, how it grew and what it learnt. Oh, Mr. Robinson, has it white boots like the other you brought?"

"I am afraid I did not attend to his boots, or to his stockings either for that matter," said Tom with a laugh; "but he has a coal-black muzzle, his teeth are in perfect order, and I believe he has the correct tan spots."

"If mother would let us," said May longingly. "You know Rose and I had not spoken to her about it; we were waiting for a good opportunity to ask her, when you were so kind as to give us the chance of having the other little dog. Mother seldom refuses us anything which she can let us have, still Rose was not sure that mother would give her consent. You see she is troubled about the stair-carpets and the drawing-room rugs, and the garden-beds, and we were afraid she would think we should have the dog with us everywhere."

"Then it rested with yourself, I should say, to show her that you could keep a dog in his proper place."

"But I doubt if I could," said May candidly, shaking her head, with the brown hair which had till recently hung loose on her shoulders, now combed smoothly back, and twisted into as "grown-up" a twist as she could accomplish the feat; while to keep the tucked-up hair in company, her skirt was let down to the regulation length for young ladies. "Indeed, I am almost certain I could not refuse anything to a dear little dog coming to me and sitting up and begging for what he wanted. What is more, if I could Dora couldn't." She could have bitten out her tongue the next instant. What was she doing always speaking of Dora? What would he think? That she was wilfully dragging her sister's name into the conversation? And what had tempted her to say that Dora could not refuse anything to a dog, when she had refused her heart in exchange for his to the man walking beside May?

He made no remark. If his mouth twitched a little in reproach or sarcasm, she could not see it under his red moustache; besides, she dared not look at him.

"I wonder," continued Miss Malapropos, "how I could let you know what mother thought." She never once suggested his bringing the dog for inspection, as he had brought the other, or calling for her answer.

"You might drop me a note," he said, stopping to give her back her books, "and I hope for your sake that it may be favourable, for this is a nice little dog, and I think you would like him."

May went home more nearly on the wings of the wind than she had done since Rose's departure, and presented her petition. Mrs. Millar could not find it in her heart to refuse it, though the stair-carpet, the drawing-room rugs, and the garden-beds were all to be sacrificed.

"Poor little May! she misses Rose, though Dora and May have become great friends of late. Dora is very good, and puts herself on an equality with May, as Annie could not have done. Still, she does not rouse the child as Rose roused her. What do you think, Jonathan? Would a little dog be in your way? Would its barking disturb you?" Mrs. Millar appealed to her husband.

"Not in reason, Maria; not if it does not take to baying at the moon, or yelping beyond bounds. Dora gives in too much to May, in place of taking the child from her books, on which naturally she is inclined to fall back. Dora has become her audience, and listens to her performances—even aids and abets them. I caught them at it yesterday. First May actually declaimed several paragraphs from a speech of Cicero's, and next she got Dora to repeat after her the most crabbed of the Greek verbs. I shall have a couple of blue-stockings, and what is worse, one of them spurious, in the room of the single real production I reckoned upon among my daughters. By all means let May have a howling monster. She is not too old for a game of romps; and I must say, though I have never opposed the higher education of women, I don't want her cultivated into a gossamer, a woman all nerves and sensations, before she is out of her teens."

"Do you suppose Tom Robinson can still be thinking of Dora?" suggested Mrs. Millar dubiously.

"I wish he were," said the little Doctor, ruefully. "I wish he were. Yes, Mrs. Millar, I am sufficiently mercenary or sordid, or whatever you like to call it, where one of my daughters is concerned, to give expression to that sentiment. But I should say he is not, unfortunately. Robinson is a shy man, and, no doubt, proud after his fashion. It must have taken a great effort—premature, therefore mistaken, according to my judgment—for him to screw himself up to the pitch of proposing for a girl of whose answering regard he was uncertain. Having made the blunder and paid the penalty, he is not at all likely to put his fate to the touch again, so far as Dora is concerned. He is not the style of pertinacious, overbearing fellow who would persecute a woman with his attentions and ask her twice. Poor Dora has lost her chance, I take it."

"I cannot say that I think it any great loss, to this day," answered Mrs. Millar, stubbornly. She gave a toss of her head, of such unusual spirit, that it so nearly dislodged her cap. Dr. Millar involuntarily put out a finger and thumb to lay hold of the truant. "We have our worldly losses, to be sure, and the other poor dear girls have gone out into the world very cheerfully. I must say I could not have done what they have done with so good a grace—so heroic a grace, not to save my life, Jonathan. But that is not to say that they are to be in haste to marry—tradesmen. Indeed, when I come to think of it, the fact of their being so independent and able to provide for themselves, ought to be like having so many fortunes. It should entitle them to be more particular, and free to pick and choose the husbands who exactly suit them. Another thing, if our daughters are not worthy of being wooed and wooed, and asked—not twice, but half a dozen times, before they are persuaded to say yes, I don't know who is. The idea of their jumping at any man!—you have drawn me into vulgar language, Jonathan,—the moment he makes his bow is too bad or too good, I do not know which to say. You do not mean that I ever accustomed you to such forward behaviour?"

"No, no, Maria," the gentleman assured her with a smile, "far from it. There was a bad epidemic raging at the time our little business came off, don't you remember? I forget now whether it was small-pox or scarlet fever, but I know I was not only tremendously busy, I dared not go to your father's house. Then I heard that another swain—an officer fellow from the barracks at Craigton was hanging about either you or your poor sister Dolly, nobody could tell which, and I dared not delay longer. I was driven to the supreme rashness of committing my suit to paper, and what do you think you wrote back? Have you forgotten? You thanked me very prettily for the compliment I had paid you, and you promised to give the substance of my letter your best consideration. Literally that was all—to a man worn off his feet with work and hungering for a word of assurance."

"Go away with you, sir," exclaimed his wife, restored to high good humour, and tapping him on the shoulder. "You understood me perfectly—you had wit enough for that. You went off directly and ordered new drawing-room furniture, what we have to this day, on the strength of that letter—you know you did."

"Showed how far gone, and what a confiding simpleton I was," he said, and then he tried again to set her right with regard to Tom Robinson. "You don't understand Robinson, Maria. It is not that he was not in earnest, or that he is fickle or anything of the kind. It is rather a case of the better man being beaten, and fools rushing in where angels fear to tread. Such men as he is accept a sentence without disputing it, because they do not think too much of themselves while they think a great deal of other people. It is not a flaw in their sensitive manliness, it is part and parcel of it, to know when they are dismissed, and take the dismissal as final. They are not the most light-hearted and sanguine of mortals, but they are constant enough, and brave enough to boot, and a brave man is not without his compensations—

"'For sudden the worst turns the best to the brave,'

"some poet has written."

"So much the better," said Mrs. Millar, again with a suspicion of hauteur in her voice. "It is lucky for all parties, since I have not the slightest reason to suppose that Dora would change her mind."

"Then why find fault with poor Tom Robinson?" Dr. Millar remonstrated in vain.

The appearance of the dog on the scene with his fine pointed nose, alert eyes, incessantly vibrating little tail, and miniver black and white coat picked out with tan, caused May as much excitement and delight as if she did not know one Greek letter from another, and were innocent of Latin quantities. She was so wrapped up in her acquisition, so devoted to his tastes in food, the state of his appetite, his sleeping place, the collar he was to have, that for the first time in her life she had to be reminded of her books. It needed her great superiority to her companions in any approach to scholarly intellect and attainment to enable her to retain the first place in Miss Burridge's classical department.

"What shall we call him, Dora?" she earnestly consulted her sister, hanging breathless on the important answer.

"Call him whatever you like, May. You know he is your dog," said Dora with decision.

"Mine and Rose's," the faithful May made the amendment. "Of course Rose must agree to any name we think of, or it cannot stand. Perhaps she would like to choose the name as she is away. Don't you think it ought to be put in her power— that she ought to have the compliment?" suggested May quite seriously and anxiously. "I shall write to her this very minute."

But Rose, like Dora, left the name to May.

"It was so kind of Tom Robinson to remember and offer him to me," said May meditatively. "O Dora! do you think I might call him 'Tom'?"

"Certainly not," said Dora, with still greater decision. "What are you thinking of, May? I don't suppose Mr. Robinson would relish having a dog named for him. Besides, other people might wonder. 'Tom' is not an ordinary name for a dog, though it is common enough for a man."

"Nobody, not even the person most concerned, would know if

I were to call him 'Son,' the termination of 'Robinson,' you know," explained May, after a moment spent in concocting this subtle amendment, and in fondling the unconscious recipient of a title which was to distinguish him from the mass of dogs.

"Are you out of your senses, May?" was the sole comment Dora deigned to deliver with some energy.

"'Friend,'" speculated May; "there is nothing very distinctive about 'Friend,' and I am sure it was the act of a friend to get him for me."

"'Foe' would be shorter and more easily said," was Dora's provoking comment; "or why not 'Fox,' since he is a fox-terrier? You might also desire to commemorate the donor's complexion, which you all used to call foxy," said Dora, half reproachfully, half dryly.

"I don't like *doubles entendres*," said May with dignity, "and if I ever said anything unkind of Tom Robinson I don't wish to be reminded of it now; anyhow, I could never give a sneer in return for a kindness."

"No, I don't believe you could, May," said Dora, penitently.

May continued a little nettled in spite of her natural good temper.

"What are Shakespeare's names for little dogs?" she asked. "'Blanche,' 'Tray,' and 'Sweetheart.' You could not be 'Blanche,' could you, pet, unless you were '*Blanche et Noir*'? and that is too long and reminds one of a gaming-table. You could not be 'Sweetheart,'" went on May, revenging herself with great coolness and deliberation in view of the red that flew into Dora's cheeks; "no, of course not, because Mr. Tom Robinson is not, never has been, and never will be *my* sweetheart. There is only 'Tray' left. Well, I think it is rather a good name," considered May, critically. "'Old dog Tray' is an

English classic. It is not altogether appropriate, because my Tray is just a baby terrier yet, but we trust, he and I, that he will live to see a venerable age."

CHAPTER IX

A WILFUL DOG WILL HAVE HIS WAY

Dora and May walked out together regularly, a practice enforced by their father as a provision for their health. To have Tray to form a third person in their somewhat formal promenades certainly robbed them of their formality, and introduced such an element of lively excitement into them as to bear out Dora's comparison of their progresses thenceforth to a succession of fox-hunts. For Tray was still in the later stages of his puppyhood. He was frequently inspired by a demon of mischief or haunted by a variety of vagabond instincts which such training as he had received, without the support of prolonged discipline and practical experience, failed to extinguish.

May was very particular about his education in theory, but in practice she fell considerably short of her excellent intentions. She always carried a whip with a whistle in the handle; and the sight of the instrument of punishment ought to have been enough for Tray, since there was no farther application of it. In reality, the sharp-sighted little animal no more obeyed the veritable whistle than he winced under the supposititious lash of the whip. He took his own way and did very much what he liked in spite of the animated protests of his mistress. Dora and May went out walking with Tray instead of Tray going on a walk with them, and not infrequently the walk degenerated into an agitated scamper at his heels. The scamper was diversified by a number of ineffectual attempts to reclaim him from forcing his way into back-yards and returning triumphantly with a bone or a crust between his teeth, "as if we starved him, as if his dish at home was not generally half full, though we've tried so hard to find out what he likes," said May plaintively. If otherwise engaged it would be in chasing cats, running down fowls, barking at message boys—to whom he had the greatest antipathy—or, most serious foible of all, threatening to engage in single combat with dogs twice his size and three times his age.

There is no accounting for tastes, seeing that these tumultuous walks were the delight of May's days, and that even Dora, with her inveterate sympathy, enjoyed them, though they deranged somewhat her sense of maidenly dignity and decorum. It was to be hoped that as Tray grew in years he would grow in discretion, and would show a little forbearance to the friends who were so forbearing to him.

Tray, Dora, and May had gone on their customary expedition. The human beings of the party were inclined to direct their steps as quickly as possible to one of the country roads. Tray's eccentricities at the present stage of his development were hardly calculated for the comfortable traversing of a succession of streets and lanes. But the canine leader of the party decided for the main street, and Dora and May gave up their own inclinations, and followed in his erratic track with their wonted cheerful submission.

It was a fine October afternoon, when Redcross was looking its best. It was rather a dull town, with little trade and few manufactories, but its worst enemy could not deny it the corresponding virtues of cleanliness and freedom from smoke. Here and there there was a grand old tree wedged between the houses. In one or two instances, where the under part of the house was brick, and the upper—an afterthought—was a projecting storey of wood, the latter was built round the tree, with its branches sheltering the roof in a picturesque, half foreign fashion. Here and there were massive old houses and shops, with some approach to the size and the substantial— even costly—fittings of "Robinson's." A side street led down to a little sluggish canal which joined the Dewes, a river of considerable size on which Redcross had originally been built. This canal was crossed by a short solid stone bridge, bearing a quaint enough bridge-house, still used as a dwelling-place.

The sun was bright and warm without any oppressive heat. The leaves, where leaves were to be seen, had yellow, russet, and red streaks and stains, suggestive of brown nuts and scarlet berries in the hedges.

The flowers in the many window-boxes in which Redcross indulged were still, for the most part, gay with the deeper tints of autumn, the purple of asters and the orange of chrysanthemums setting off the geraniums blossoming on till the frost shrivelled them, and the seeded green and straw-coloured spikes of the still fragrant mignonette.

It was market-day, which gave but a slight agreeable stir to the drowsy town. The ruddy faces and burly figures of farmers, whose imposing bulk somehow did not decrease in keeping with the attenuated profits of long-continued agricultural depression, were prominent on the pavement. Little market carts, which closely shawled and bonneted elderly women, laden with their market baskets, still found themselves disengaged enough to drive, rattled over the cobble stones. An occasional farm labourer in a well-nigh exploded smock frock, who had come in with a bullock or two, or a small flock of sheep, to the slaughter-house, trudging home with a straw between his teeth, and his faithful collie at his heels, made a variety in the town population.

The latter consisted, at this hour, of shop boys and girls, boys from the grammar school, a file of boarders from Miss Burridge's, who walked as if "eyes right" and "eyes left" were the only motion permitted to them, notwithstanding May's frantic signs to them to behold and admire Tray's gambols; a professional man, or a tradesman, leisurely doing a business errand; one or two ladies carrying the latest fashion in card-cases, suggestive of afternoon calls.

Tray's devious path took him in the direction of "Robinson's," in the windows of which the golden brown of sable furs, the silver gray of rare foxes', and the commoner dim blue of long-haired goats', were beginning to enrich the usual display of silk and woollen goods.

Following his own sweet will, Tray, considerably in advance of his companions, darted into the shop.

"Oh, what shall we do, May?" cried Dora in dismay; "you ought really to put that dog in a leash when he *will* go into the town."

"Better say a chain at once," answered May indignantly, vexed by the imputation on her pet. "I am sure he has been as good as gold to-day. He has not chased a single thing, and he has only once run away from us. Couldn't I go in and fetch him out? I should not stay above a minute."

"And I am to wait at the door while you hunt him round all the counters and through the showrooms? I had much rather go in with you; but neither do I care to enter the shop when I do not wish to buy anything. Really Tray is too troublesome!"

"Oh! don't say that," exclaimed May in distress. "Don't reflect on him in case anything should happen to him," as if Dora's speech were likely to bring down the vengeance of Heaven on the heads of all three. "He soon finds out all he wants when he goes on private expeditions, and then he runs back and looks for us. I think if we walked *very* slowly his dear bright face, with one ear cocked up, would appear in the doorway by the time we reached it."

"Or some shop-lad may ask him what his business is, and turn him out. It will be a lesson for him in future," said Dora, severely.

Accordingly the sisters had to slacken their steps to a snail's pace as they approached the great shop. They had a full view of the interior, though it was a little dark, unless to the most modern taste. There was an air of old-fashioned substantiality, comfort, and something like modest dignity about the long-lasting, glossy brown roof and walls, in harmony with the heavy counters and shelves, not too heavy for the bales of every description, which with the contents of the innumerable boxes had an established reputation of being "all of the best quality," not figuratively but literally. The famous oak staircase, with the broad shallow steps and the twisted balustrade, which would not have disgraced a manor house, ran up right in the centre and terminated in a gallery—like a musician's gallery—hung with Turkey carpets, Moorish rugs, and "muslin from the Indies," and from the gallery various work and show rooms opened. It was evident that "Robinson's" was considerably older than the lifetime of the first Robinson—the silk-weaver and wool-stapler who had used it as a mart for his wares. Though it was only the product of a country town, it bore a resemblance to old London city places of business. These were wont to have a Dutch atmosphere of industry and sobriety, together with a fair share of the learning and refinement of the times hanging about them, so that their masters figured as honoured and influential citizens of the metropolis. Belonging to the category were the linen shop of a certain Alexander Pope's father, and the law-stationer's shop, from which issued, in his day, a beautiful youth known as "Master John Milton."

There was the customary bustle of a market day at "Robinson's." Miss Franklin was moving about in the women's department, seeing that everybody there was served, and giving an occasional direction to the women who served. She was, as Dora Millar had once described her, as "fat as a pin-cushion," with what had been originally a fair pink-and-white complexion, degenerated into the mottled "red all over," into which such complexions occasionally pass in middle life. But she looked like a lady by many small traits—by her quiet, easy movements; by the clear enunciation and pleasant tones, which could be ringing when necessary, of a cultivated voice that reached the ears of the bystanders. She did not wear the conventional black silk or cashmere of a shop-woman. There might be a lingering protest or a lurking vanity in the myrtle-green gown and the little lace cap, with its tiny *noeuds* of dark green riband, which she wore instead. One might guess by their dainty decorum and becomingness that Miss Franklin had thought a good deal, and to purpose, about dress, in her day—had made a study of it, and taken pleasure in its finer effects. In that light she was the right woman in the right place—presiding over the shop-women in a linen-draper's shop. At the same time she belonged as clearly to the upper middle class as did the two girls advancing towards the shop, who, in place of being studiously well and handsomely dressed, were just a little shabby, and careless how they looked in their last year's gray velveteens, with hats to match, which Dora in her conscientious economy had re-trimmed not very nicely.

Lag as the girls might, they could not delay their progress much longer, and their bosoms were torn with conflicting emotions. What were they to do? Leave the truant Tray to his fate? Boldly halt before the next shop window, and trust to his seeing and joining them there? Still more boldly, enter and request "the body of the culprit" to be delivered up to his owner? Before they could come to a decision, Tom Robinson himself appeared in the foreground. He was speaking, or rather listening to a giant of a farmer in a light overcoat and streaming cravat, who, in place of treating the master of "Robinson's" as "a whipper-snapper of a counter-jumper," was behaving to him with the most unsophisticated deference. Yet Tom's under size and pale complexion looked more insignificant than ever beside the mighty thews and sinews and perennial bloom of his customer. In spite of that, Tom Robinson was as undeniably a gentleman in the surroundings, as Miss Franklin was a lady, and the big honest farmer recognized and accepted the fact. While the pair stood there, and the farmer made an elaborate explanation of the matter in hand—broadcloth or blankets probably—to which Tom attended courteously, as courteously as he would have heard the deliverances of the member of the county or the bishop, Tray flashed out of the mellow obscurity of the background and sniffed vigorously at the trowser ankles of the master of "Robinson's."

"Hallo!" cried Tom, looking down at his feet.

"A bit fine terrier-dawg, Mister Robinson, sir," remarked the farmer; "but I'm thinking he's strayed."

At the same instant both Tray and Tom caught sight of May's anxious face peering in at the shop door. Tray rushed to his mistress with a boisterously gracious greeting, which did not include the slightest self-consciousness or sense of wrongdoing in its affability. Tom took a couple of steps after him.

"I'm afraid, Miss May, you're spoiling that dog," he said, in friendly remonstrance, before he observed who was with May, and stopped and bowed with some constraint.

"Oh! Mr. Robinson," replied May, in her volubility effacing any shy attempt at greeting on Dora's part, "I am so sorry for Tray's rudeness in going into your shop without being invited; but I do think he knew you again, I am almost sure of it," she said eagerly, as if the assurance were sufficient propitiation for any trifling lack of ceremony where a reasonable human being was concerned.

"It might have been better if I had known a little more of him," said Tom musingly, biting his moustache, as he took leave of the three.

Tray meandered down the street, followed hurriedly by his mistress and Dora. Tom looked after them, and speculated into how many more scrapes the brute would get the girls, wondered too if one of them would think she had him to thank for the infliction, and that it was an odd instance of the friendship which he had pressed her to give him in lieu of a warmer feeling. That friendship was not progressing very rapidly, though the world might consider the Millars more in need of friends than when he had begged to make one of the number. But Tom Robinson knew better. These girls were enough for themselves in any emergency. They would never fall back on friends or depend upon them. Even Dora, who had stayed at home with May, would suffer in silence and bear anything with and for her family, before she would complain or ask help.

Tray's errant fancy finally took him down a lane leading to the Dewes and to a sheltered walk between rows of yellowing elms by the side of the river. The girls were at last able to enjoy themselves. They sauntered along, talking at their ease, watching the bars of sunlight on the water, and the crowds of flies in the golden mist which the approach of sunset was drawing down over everything, and listening to a robin singing on a bough, when their misadventures for one day culminated and their worst apprehensions were fulfilled. A mongrel collie advancing in the opposite direction, with no better qualified guardian than a young servant girl, who had also a perambulator containing a couple of small children to look after, aroused the warlike spirit of Tray. He growled defiance and bristled in every hair, while Dora caught nervously at his elegant morocco collar, which burst asunder in her grasp, and May shrieked agitated soothing endearments to no purpose. What unmagnanimous cur could resist such a challenge? In another instant the inequal combat was raging furiously. The two dogs first stood on their hind legs, grappled together, and glared at each other for a second, like two pugilists trying a preliminary fall, or a couple of duellists pointing their pistols. The next moment the dogs were rolling over and over each other on the narrow path, worrying each other with the horrible snarling noise that accompanies such a performance.

May danced a frantic dance round the combatants, screamed shrilly, and made dangerous, ineffectual darts at Tray. The servant girl neither danced, nor screamed, nor made darts; she stood stolidly still, with something between a gape and a grin on her broad red face. She had not the passion for dog-fights entertained by the *gamins* of the streets, such fights were simply immaterial trifles to her amidst the weightier concerns of her life; and she had seen her master's dog get too many kicks in the ribs—a discipline from which he rose up howling but not greatly injured—to be troubled with any sensitive fears as to his safety. Besides his enemy was a small beast, a lady's dog, whom Growler could dispose of in a twinkling, if his temper were up.

"Oh! can you not call off your dog?" wailed May in her agony. "He will kill Tray. Oh! my Tray, my Tray," and she made another rush to rescue her pet.

"Don't, May, you'll be bitten," implored Dora.

"He don't mind me, miss, not one bit, our Growler don't," said the composed damsel, as if Growler's indifference were rather a feather in his cap.

Alas! for any attention that the victim paid to May's desperate remonstrances. She had in fact no right to reproach the enemy's temporary proprietress for her lack of authority over her four-footed companion. But poor May in her misery was neither logical nor just. She turned on the other with a passionate challenge, "What business have you to bring out a horrid brute like that, which you cannot master, to kill other people's dear little pets?"

"Hush, hush, May," besought Dora, "I think they are leaving off." There was a slight cessation in the hostilities. "The noise you are making may set them on again."

"It were your dog as begun it." Growler's sponsor defended both herself and Growler defiantly.

"Oh!" screamed May, "they're at it again. Tray is down and the cruel monster is at his throat. Will nobody help us? Will nobody save my poor little dog?"

The girls were carrying neither sunshades nor umbrellas. They could not reach the lower boughs of the trees to pull down a switch, but just as May was springing forward to dare the worst herself, sooner than see Tray perish unaided before her eyes, Dora caught sight of a large half-loose stone in the path. "Stand back, May," she gasped, as she tore it up. Dora's face was as white as paper; she was sick with fright and distress; she would fain have shut her eyes if she had not known that she needed every advantage which sight could give her to prevent her hitting Tray, instead of his foe, as the two rolled over each other in the struggle which was growing deadlier every second.

"Stop," cried a voice of command behind her, "you'll have the dog turn upon you as soon as he has finished his present job," and a welcome deliverer ran forward just in time. He seized the first tail he could grasp—luckily for him it was Tray's and not Growler's—and hung on to it like a vice. The "redder" of the combatants, regardless of "the redder's lick," which was likely to be his portion, continued to hold the tail of the now yelling Tray, and at the same time seized him by the scruff of the neck with the other hand, and dragged both animals, still locked together, with his whole force nearer and nearer to the edge of the bank by the river.

A new terror beset May. "Take care, you'll have them in the water."

No sooner said than done. With a plunge the two dogs fell heavily into the Dewes, while the man who had brought them to this pass kept his own footing with difficulty.

"They'll both be drowned," cried May, clasping her hands in the last depths of anguish.

"Not at all," said Tom Robinson, panting a little from his exertions and wiping his hands with his handkerchief. "I did it on purpose—don't you see? It was the only way to make the beggars lose their grip. Look there, they are swimming like brothers down the stream—that small spitfire of yours is not badly hurt. I told you that you were spoiling him—you ought to make him obey and come to heel, or he will become the torment of your life. The bank shelves a little a few yards further down; you will find that he will come to shore shaking himself nothing the worse. It may be a lesson to him; if not, I should like to give him a bit of my mind."

True enough, Tray scrambled up the bank presently, bearing no more alarming traces of the fray than were to be found in his limping on three legs, and halting every other minute that he might ruefully attend to the fourth.

Growler also landed, and after glancing askance at his antagonist and at the champion who had suddenly interposed between Tray and his deserts, wisely agreed with the small maid-servant on the judiciousness of immediately taking themselves off, in company with the perambulator and the babies, to avoid any chance of awkward inquiries.

May ran to Tray, clasped him all dripping in her arms, and prepared to carry him tenderly home. But in spite of the injuries, for which he was exceedingly sorry, he asserted his spirit of independence, and declined to be made a baby of.

"I am afraid we have given you a great deal of trouble, Mr. Tom," said Dora, while May was still devoting herself to her rescued treasure. Dora spoke shyly, and inadvertently used the old familiar name, which he had borne when his father was alive.

"Don't mention it," he said gravely, as shy as she was; "I feel answerable for inflicting that wretched dog on you—that is, on your sister. I was sure he would lead you a pretty dance after he was in the shop this afternoon."

"Oh! Mr. Robinson," cried May, tearing herself away from the contemplation of her darling in order to pour forth her sense of relief and the depth of her gratitude, "what a good thing it was you came up to us! What should we have done without you? Oh! you don't think dear little Tray is lamed for life—do you? Of course that is ever so much better than having him killed outright in our sight; still if he would only let me pick him up and rest his poor hurt leg it might help him," protested May wistfully.

"Let him alone, he is all right," he said in his short stiff way. Then he made a bantering amendment on his speech, because he was quick to see that his want of sympathy vexed the young girl, perhaps rendered her burden of gratitude more difficult to bear.

"At the worst, you know he would be as well off as Horatius Cocles, and he is likely to escape the beating which he richly deserves."

"Oh! Mr. Robinson, beat him! when he meant no harm, when he has been all but drowned or worried to death by that great, coarse, rough creature," cried May, opening large brown eyes of astonishment and indignation.

"I wonder what *he* would call Tray if he could speak—an insolent little rascal, who had no proper respect for his superiors."

Dora did not join in the conversation. Her colour came and went, and she kept glancing at the handkerchief which Tom Robinson was fluttering about in his hand.

It was May who stopped short and cried in fresh dismay, "There is blood on your handkerchief; I believe you have been bitten. What shall we do?"

"What should you do, Miss May?" he answered with a laugh. "It is only a minute impression left by the fine teeth of your friend. You would have it that he knew me a little while ago, and it seems we were destined to be more intimately acquainted."

"Come home with us this minute," cried May, so dead in earnest, that she grasped his arm, and made as if she would have dragged him forward. "Father will dress it and heal it. I am so sorry, so ashamed, though Tray did not know what he was doing."

He laughed again quite merrily, as it sounded. "If Tray did not know, he did his small best to get rid of me. I daresay I was not treating him with much ceremony. I am afraid I gave his tail as sharp a pinch as I could administer before I could get at his neck. No, I am not going home with you; thanks for the invitation. Do you wish Dr. Millar to think me crazy? Do you apply to your father for medical assistance when you give yourself a pin-prick?"

"But the bite of a dog is very different, though Tray is the dog," moaned May.

"Tray is in excellent health and spirits; I can vouch for that," said Tom. "I have not the slightest apprehension of hydrophobia."

"O—h!" said May, with a deeper moan.

Dora had continued silent; indeed she could hardly speak, and her face had grown more like ashes than paper.

He was standing still, and raising his hat a little awkwardly with his left hand, in lieu of shaking hands with his right, as they came to the point where their roads parted.

Dora made a great effort and uttered her remonstrance: "I wish you would come home with us, and let father look at your hand."

"You too, Miss Dora—nonsense," he said sharply as it sounded.

"If Annie had been here," she persisted, "she would have been of a hundred times more use than I, but if you'll let me I'll try to tie it up for you."

She spoke so humbly that he answered her with quick kindness, "And pain you by exposing a scratch to your notice? No, indeed, all that I'll ask of you is never to fling stones at strange dogs, though they should be tearing that unlucky imp of mischief limb from limb."

"It was very unkind of him to speak so rudely of poor Tray," sighed May, as the sisters hurried home; "although it was Tom Robinson who gave him to me, I don't think the man has ever put a proper value on the dog. But I daresay he will call to-morrow though he has not come with us just now, to ask for Tray, and to see how we are after our fright."

"No, he won't come," said Dora with conviction, and she walked on silently thinking to herself, "How strong and resolute he was, though he is not a big man, and how little he minded being bitten. Men are different from women. Of course, he is nothing to me, but I may be permitted to admire his courage and coolness. No, he will not come, I am sure of that, he is the last man to take advantage of an accident and of his coming to our assistance. Even if he did, and I had ever cared for him, and there had been no 'Robinson's,' it would be too late and too bad to change one's mind after we had grown poor and had to work for ourselves."

Dora was right. Tom Robinson did not come. He contented himself with intercepting Dr. Millar on his rounds, learning that Dora and May were no worse for their misadventure, and giving their father a piece of information.

In consequence of that hint, and under the pretence of having Tray's wounded leg properly seen to, he was, to May's intense chagrin and disgust, despatched to a veterinary surgeon's, where he remained for some time, returning at last a sadder and a wiser dog.

CHAPTER X

LIFE IN AN HOSPITAL WARD

St. Ebbe's was a model hospital, with every enlightened improvement in the treatment of the sick poor, and every humane ordinance which the highly developed skill and the strongly stimulated benevolence of the nineteenth century could enforce.

Annie Millar was one of six lady probationers, including a bishop's daughter, two daughters of squires, and three doctor's daughters like herself. The matron was the widow of a doctor, who had been eminent alike for professional talent and philanthropy. She was like-minded. If she had not her late husband's knowledge and acumen as a medical man, she had much of his experience, and was full of energy and determination to better the world, the sick, and the poor, almost whether they would or not. Very few people could look Mrs. Hull in the face and contradict her high motives and determined will.

Fortunately, Annie's beauty had not worked the scathing destruction which Mrs. Millar had anticipated with fear and trembling. An inflammable medical student or two might have been just singed by the fire of her charms; an older member of the fraternity might have neglected for an instant to look up at the card above a bed in order to turn his head and cast a second admiring glance after the new recruit in the hospital uniform; but no man forgot his duty or was false to earlier vows through her allurements.

Mrs. Hull had cast a sharp glance at the dainty figure and flower-like face under the nurse's linen gown and close cap. Annie's sister probationers, four of them considerably older than herself, had telegraphed to each other emphatic—perhaps pardonable enough—signals that the last accession to their number was so very ornamental they could hardly expect her to be useful. They must look out for defects, and prepare to atone for failures by their surpassing attainments. But the mistake was soon rectified, and fresh light dawned on the doubtful question. Mrs. Hull was the first to recognize and testify that nothing was to be feared from Annie Millar's youth and beauty, while something might be gained by them, because she was far more than pretty—she was a bright, clever girl, very obedient to orders, and exceedingly anxious to learn her business. In her St. Ebbe's had secured an auxiliary of the highest promise. The elder sister probationers soon found that instead of wanting indulgence, forbearance, and pity, the newcomer was more in danger of awakening their envy as well as their respect by her quickness in mastering details, her mental grasp of principles, her inexhaustible spirit.

Yet poor Annie had no light apprenticeship to serve. The programme, which extends from making poultices and making beds to receiving doctors' instructions, understanding them, remembering them, and acting on them, is neither short nor easy, though a fairly good and trained intellect and an unswerving devotion to duty will get through it triumphantly in time. Annie underwent the entire ordeal, while she doubtless brought a little additional intelligence and capacity and a few more grains of experience to the task than would have existed if she had not been Dr. Millar's daughter. In spite of the warm woollen jacket and cuffs which she wore under her linen gown, her little hands were covered with the chaps and chilblains which are the scourge of maids-of-all-work, because of their early rising, hard scrubbing, and the frequency with which their fingers are wet and dried on chill winter mornings. Her legs ached, as they had never ached after a night's dancing, with being on her feet all day long, and day after day, waiting on her patients and attending on the sisters who were placed over the respective wards. Her mind, too, was kept on the stretch with the serious charge of pulses and temperatures, with the grave responsibility of shelves on shelves of medicine bottles, with acquiring the best modes of bandaging, fomenting, bleeding, stopping the flow of blood, so that during the little leisure she had she could not turn to a book for relief; she fell asleep with sheer fatigue more frequently.

Annie was too high-spirited and independent to feel the loneliness of her position among strangers, whom she soon converted into friendly acquaintances, if nothing more, as many a girl—as Dora, for instance—would have done. But, accustomed as Annie had been all her life to much closer and warmer relations, she clung to the presence of Rose in London; and it was a proof of how much the elder sister was used up, when, even on her days and hours for getting out, it was often with difficulty that she could bring herself to go and see Rose, or to meet and walk a portion of the way with her on Rose's progress from Mrs. Jennings's boarding-house to the Misses Stone's school, where she taught drawing, or to Mr. St. Foy's art classes, where she learned it.

Annie had suffered considerably from what is known as hospital or infirmary sore throat, because it is understood to be caused by inhaling the fumes from the carbolic acid used in the wards. Her rich colour had to Rose's dismay grown poor and pale for a time. She had laboured under the still more trying and more dangerous infliction, when the senses morbidly excited become morbidly acute, and she seemed still to smell the peculiar air of the wards wherever she went. Then Mrs. Hull insisted on Annie's leaving for a few days, and bundled her off, without the power of resistance, to a sister of the matron's, who kindly consented, as her part of the work, to receive and recruit the temporarily overdone servants of St. Ebbe's Hospital.

In spite of the strength of Annie's nerves, and her power of controlling them, she sickened once or twice with a deadly sickness at sights and sounds worse than her most vivid imagination could have conceived possible. She had to summon all her courage, together with the conviction that if she did not overcome the weakness speedily, she would be compelled to own that she had mistaken her calling, in order to vanquish the insidious foe.

Sometimes, while she was ready to thank God that it was rather the exception than the rule, she had to witness the lowest moral degradation in addition to the sharpest human suffering, and this at an age and with a nature when the feeling of extreme repulsion, amounting to positive loathing, is in danger of prevailing. It needed all her faith to do battle with this worst temptation, and force pity to conquer disgust, to recognize humbly the frailty of the best and wisest men and women, to acknowledge willingly, even thankfully, the propriety, if one may so use the word, of what a preacher has called each Christian's suffering, "the just for the unjust."

No wonder poor Annie's bright face took frequently a worn and harassed look in those early days of hospital work.

Yet so great is the elasticity of youth, and so brave and cheerful was the girl's temperament for the most part, that within an hour of such prostrating attacks and violent revolts, she would be on her way with her own little tea-pot to the retiring-room, where the lady probationers and sisters assembled in order to profit by the great boiler steaming on the hob for their women's refreshment of tea. It was about the only servile act which they were required to do for themselves, while they were the servants of others, and they all enjoyed doing it with true housewifely relish. Annie, especially, was an adept at such tea-making, and would propound her theories and circulate specimens of her performance among her companions who profited by her skill, with a glee not far removed from the mirth of the Millar girls on many a happy family gathering in the old nursery or the drawing-room at Redcross.

The whole circumstances of one of the bad days in her lot

Annie could never quite forget. It was a raw, gray winter's day, cheerless above and below, and all went wrong on it, from the moment Annie opened her sleepy eyes, leapt shivering out of bed, washed in cold water by her own choice, in order to rouse herself, dressed by gaslight, swallowed her coffee scalding hot, and hastened to her particular ward. The sister and the house-surgeon were, as if affected by the day, a little sour and surly, and every patient seemed more or less out of tune, dismal, grumbling, delirious, or in a state of collapse.

It was one of Annie's out-days, and as a matter of duty, but by no means of enjoyment, she braced herself to change her hospital dress for a walking dress. After she felt chilled to the bone, she started for a walk, either to be jostled and forced along in a crowded thoroughfare, where she too might have said—

"Although so many surround me,
I know not one I meet"—

or to creep the length of the cleanest side of the pavement in a depressingly empty street, where the varying arrangement of the shabby window curtains and the cards in the dingy windows, offering an endless supply of rooms to the absent lodging hunter, furnished the sole entertainment to the listless passer-by.

Annie had been afraid that she would miss Rose on her way to her classes, and the fear was amply fulfilled—not the most distant glimpse of Rose was forthcoming. Instead, at a crossing, Ella Carey, in her Aunt Tyrrel's carriage, whirled by the pedestrian and administered a slight spattering of mud to her dress. "It ought to have been the other way," said Annie bitterly to herself, while she stood still to wipe the sleeve of her jacket. Yet she knew very well all the time that Ella's offence had been quite involuntary, and that she had not for a moment recognized Annie. If it had been so, Ella's round girlish face under its smart hat, leaning back among the soft cushions not discontentedly, would have brightened immensely. She would have stopped the carriage and been down in the street at Annie's side in a moment, for the girl was as warm-hearted as she had been docile. There was nothing she would have liked better than to hail a Redcross face, and hear the last news about Phyllis and May, and Ella's father and mother.

When Annie re-entered the hospital colder and more unrefreshed than she had left it, she thought that she was at last going to be compensated for life's rubs—beyond her deserts, she told herself a little remorsefully. She had been longing all the morning for a letter from Redcross, small reason as she had to complain of the negligence of her correspondents there, and a letter with the Redcross post-mark was awaiting her. She saw before she opened it that it was not from any of her family. None of them used such creamily smooth and thick note-paper, or exhibited such a cunningly contrived, elegantly designed monogram. But even a slight communication from the merest acquaintance was welcome as a flower in spring, when the acquaintance dwelt in dear old Redcross. Annie had been thinking fondly of it all day as a place of human well-being and geniality, free from continual sights and sounds of pain and sorrow, where everybody got up and sat down, went out and came in, worked and read, even dawdled and dreamt at will, subject to a few simple household rules. There was no unyielding iron discipline at Redcross. There was no hard and fast routine entering through the flesh and penetrating into the very soul. It was just, dear, deliberate, mannerly, yet comfortable and kindly Redcross. The writer was Thirza Dyer, and the reason why one of the Dyers, who had hesitated about shaking hands with one of the Millars after she was guilty of proposing to earn her livelihood, wrote a letter to a nurse probationer and addressed it to a public hospital, calls for an explanation. The Dyers, in their unceasing efforts to gain by their wealth and its liberal expenditure a footing in the county circle, had got one foot within the coveted precincts, and there Thirza found to her own and her sisters' amazement that nursing, not the rich and great, but common poor people, was a curious fashion of the day. Lady

Luxmore had a cousin who was a nurse. General Wentworth's wife had a friend professionally engaged in a London hospital for nine months out of the twelve, who was visiting the Wentworths this winter. Of course it had begun with the Crimean War, and the *eclat* with which lady nurses went out to attend on the wounded soldiers in the exceptional hospital at Scutari. But whatever was its origin, the rule was established that nursing even day-labourers and mechanics with their wives and children, was something very different from being a drudging governess or broken-down companion. It was like being a member of the Kyrle Society, with which one of the princes had to do, or like singing in an East of London concert-room, quite *chic*, perfectly good form, anybody might take it up and gain rather than lose caste by the act.

Accordingly, it became an obvious obligation on the Dyers to cultivate and not to cut the only nurse on their visiting list. With unblushing, well-nigh naive suddenness, Thirza Dyer, to Annie Millar's bewildered astonishment, proceeded to start and maintain a correspondence with her. Two are required for a bargain-making, and Annie was not altogether disinterested in scribbling the few lines occasionally which warranted the continuance of the correspondence on Thirza's part. For if Thirza had lived anywhere else than where she did live, near Redcross, the answer to her first letter might have been different. Therefore Annie did not perhaps deserve much solace from these letters, and certainly this one did not contribute to her exaltation of spirit. It was chiefly occupied with an account of several *recherchee* afternoon teas which the Dyers had held lately at the Manor-house, together with a full description of the tea-gowns of salmon, canary, and cherry-coloured plush, lined with *eau-de-nil* satin, which the Miss Dyers had worn on these occasions.

Now poor Annie was rather above hankering unduly after tea-gowns, or for that matter "smart" or "swell" dress of any kind. She liked pretty things, and things which became her charming person, at their proper time and season, well enough, but she was not greatly discomposed by the lack of such adornment, and hardly at all troubled when her neighbours displayed what she did not possess.

It was because the foolishly exultant gorgeous description, which ought to have been set to a fashion-plate, carried Annie back with a flash to one winter's day last year, that it made her heart sore. On the day in question Annie and Dora, and for that matter Rose and May, acting as deeply interested assistants, had been tremendously busy and merry in the old nursery, travestying national and historic costumes in calico. It was all on behalf of a certain scenic entertainment given in the Town-hall for the delectation of the scholars in the Rector's Sunday-school and night classes. It had been a very simple and intentionally inexpensive affair, and the principal charm to the performers had lain in the contriving of their costumes. Annie and Dora had appeared in magnificent chintz sacques—which might have represented tea-gowns—and mob caps, and had been declared by Cyril Carey, who was supposed to be no mean judge, a most satisfactory eighteenth century pair. Cyril himself had broken the rule as to material, and had figured in the black satin trunk hose, velvet doublet, and lace collar of a Spanish grandee. But Ned Hewett had stuck to Turkey-red cotton for a Venetian senator or a Roman cardinal, nobody had been quite certain which. And Tom Robinson had been a Scotch beggarman, Sir Walter Scott's immortal Edie Ochiltree, in a blue cotton gown and a goatskin beard, which she (Annie) had wickedly pretended must have been manufactured out of tufts purloined from the stock of boas at "Robinson's." Lucy Hewett had been shrouded in white cotton wool, to represent the Empress Matilda escaping from Oxford, "through the lines of King Stephen's soldiers," under shelter of a snowstorm. Fanny Russell had never looked better than she looked that night as a Norman peasant girl. It was all very well for Cyril Carey to condescend to the deceit of praising Annie and Dora up to the skies, when everybody knew whom he admired most, with reason. That was Fanny Russell, with her splendid black eyes and hair, and the Norman strength and fineness of her profile.

What was Nurse Annie, in her holland gown, apron, and cap, recalling and revelling in? The silly vanities and child's play of the past. Well, what harm was there in them? These had been blithe moments while they lasted, which had set young hearts bounding, young feet skipping, and young voices laughing and singing in a manner which was natural, and not to be forbidden lest worse came of it.

Annie was roused from her pleasant reverie and plunged into another of a totally different description. The last was made up of garbled reality, but with what truth was in it tending to a false, doleful vision. It would represent St. Ebbe's as a gloomy, ghastly prison-house of suffering and death, and she in her tender youth and sweet beauty immured in it by an error of judgment, a fatal mistake incidental to rash enthusiasm and total inexperience. If Annie ever arrived at that rueful conclusion, how could she bear the penalty she must pay?

Annie had heard and read of young women on whom the world did not cry shame, who turned from the decay and death they had not gone to seek, which Providence had brought to their doors, in paroxysms of repugnance and rebellion. They could not bear that their perfection of health and life should come into contact with something so chillingly, gruesomely different, that their glowing youth should be wasted in the dim shadows of sick-rooms or amidst the dank vapours hovering over the dark river which all must ford when their time comes. Those standing round who heard or read the outcry called it natural, piteous, well-nigh praiseworthy, it was so sincere. How could Annie realize for herself in a moment that such heroines(!) are the daughters in spirit of the women who, in outbreaks of mediaeval pestilence and latter-day cholera, have literally abandoned their nearest and dearest, fleeing from spectacles of anguish and risks of infection? How could she guess that such women are the spiritual sisters of poor heathen and savage Hottentot and Malay mothers and daughters, who, sooner than be burdened with the wailing helplessness of infancy and the mumbling fatuity of age, will expose the children dependent on these murderesses, and the hoary heads that once planned and prayed for the welfare of their slayers, to perish of cold and hunger?

It was Annie's hour for resuming work, and it was well for her, though she went but languidly into the spotlessly white and clean ward, among its rows of beds with the flower-stand, illuminated texts and oleographs, which generous supporters of the hospital sent to brighten its cold bareness and soften and cheer what was harsh and subdued in its atmosphere. Annie was not even greatly affected by the greeting of one of her patients, an elderly man recovering from an operation, and still slightly off his head when the fever rose on him. She went to him with a cooling, soothing application, and he told her incoherently to come again and give him his dinner and his tea. He liked a young lass or lady, be she which she liked, with red cheeks and shining eyes to wait upon him. It minded him of a bit wench of a daughter of his he had lost when she was twelve years—the age of the little wench in the Bible, for parson had preached about her the Sunday after his lass's funeral. It broke her mother's heart for all that, and he buried her too within three months. Then the place got lonesome, and he took what was not good for him, till he had come to this; though whether it were the House or just an hospital he was lying in he could not clearly say.

Then there happened what Annie was wont to describe as a miracle of mercy to bring her to a better mind. A young boy whose leg had been crushed by a waggon was carried into the operating theatre for an immediate operation. It was the lecture hour, and a great professor of surgery with his class of students, together with several of the other doctors connected with St. Ebbe's, was in attendance. But it was also customary, especially where a female patient or a patient so young as the boy in question was concerned, for a nurse, generally the sister of the ward, to be present to hold the sufferer's hand if it were wished, or when it was possible to support the poor head against her breast. It so chanced that the sister was out, and other available nurses were engaged, so in circumstances which would admit of no delay Annie was for the first time called to the front and summoned to undertake the responsibility of the situation. Already she had lost sight of herself, and was standing looking so calm, firm, and prepared for every emergency, that the operating surgeon, with a glance at her, put her youth and position as a probationer aside, and accepted what help she could give.

It was a critical case, and for some medical reason no anaesthetic could be administered. The boy was past the unconsciousness of childhood, and though nearly fainting with fright, pain, and weakness, remained quite sensible of the further ordeal he had to undergo. He was keenly alive to the humane motive which induced the surgeon to turn his back upon him in selecting his instruments. He even heard, with ears morbidly acute, the low words addressed to the interested spectators, "Now, gentlemen, I am about to begin."

With a stifled sob the poor little fellow suddenly managed to raise himself from the table on which he was stretched. He looked round wildly on the circle of men's faces, controlled and expectant, with a certain every-day expression in anticipation of what, in its blind terror and life and death importance to him, was a familiar occurrence to them, and on the one woman's face, controlled too, but with an indescribable wistfulness under the control. Then he made his childish appeal, shrill with misery, "Oh, gentlemen, will you not stop till I say my prayers?"

There was an instant pause of surprise, commiseration, constraint—the peculiar awkwardness which in Englishmen waits on any provocation to betray feeling. Nobody liked to look at his neighbour to see how he looked, lest there should be the most distant sign of emotion in his own face. Some strong men there had ceased to pray or to believe in prayer, yet all were more or less touched by the lad's implicit faith.

As for Annie she had been praying at that very moment, praying fervently in the silence of her heart, that she might be saved from breaking down and allowed to be of some service to the boy.

"Certainly, certainly, my little chap; but you must be quick about it," said the great surgeon a little hoarsely.

"Our-Father-which-art-in-Heaven," began the boy, running the words together and speaking with a parrot-like monotony in an unnaturally high-pitched key. Then his voice began to quaver a little till he stopped short with a cry of despair—"I cannot mind the words, I cannot say my prayers. Oh! will nobody say them for me? If mother, as is not in Lon'on, were here, she would do it fast," he ended, flinging out one thin arm and clutching convulsively at the air in a kind of panic-stricken terror.

There was another second's dead silence. It was broken by a woman's voice. Annie had taken a step forward close to the boy's elbow, so that her voice was in his ear. She could not kneel, but instinctively she clasped her hands and bent her head reverently as she said in low but clear tones which were carried throughout the length and breadth of the room, and thrilled in every ear, the Lord's Prayer. At its close she went on without hesitation in the same wonderfully audible voice: "God bless this little boy. Forgive him every wrong he has ever done. Keep him safe, and raise him up again, for Jesus Christ's sake. Amen."

Another voice—a deeper one—responded to the "Amen." It was said by the famous operator's enemies that he was lax in his religious opinions, and that he rarely found time to go to church. Nevertheless it was he who with grave heartiness repeated the Amen.

The little lad had sunk back when she began to speak, and there he lay without giving her a word or sign of thanks—his best acknowledgment of her compliance with what might be his last wish being his quaking submission. He could not keep still his quivering flesh, or hold back altogether his piercing cries and piteous moans, but he bit his tongue in seeking to stifle them. For he was not fighting with his Maker and his fate; he was trying in his boyish way, with his small fortitude and resignation, to endure, in the might of the support which had been asked for him.

Annie too clenched her teeth, while she opened her eyes to take in everything that passed before them, as a mirror may be turned to receive the minutest impression from the scene it reflects. But she did not hear a single shriek or wail, because her ears were filled with the higher harmonies which she had called forth. She clasped one of the boy's trembling hands in her own warm one, which did not grow cold in the contact. She was on the alert to meet his only half-seeing gaze, and to give back a glance of tender sympathy and protection—the true mother's look that is to be found when occasion calls for it in every good woman's face,—ay, it may even be seen in the precociously earnest, kindly eyes of many a loving woman-child.

There were plenty of other helpers to render the surgeon all the assistance he needed in his work, with far more celerity and ability than Annie could have supplied. But while sense lingered in the little patient's eyes, it was to the woman he turned for the pity and aid which did not fail him; it was through her that he drew from One mightier than all, the spiritual strength for his terrible bodily conflict. In a sense Annie and he were both on their trial, they served their novitiate together, and helped each other to bear and overcome. When the operation was over he lay, with the sweat drops of agony which Annie was gently wiping off, not gone from his forehead, but also with the reflection still lingering on his white face of the courage and patience with which he had been ready to meet death.

"You have behaved remarkably well, and shown no want of pluck, my lad," said the surgeon as a parting word of encouragement and cheer. "Lie still and you'll be able to see your friends by and by. I believe you'll do famously, and we'll see whether a substitute cannot be found for the limb you

Sarah Tytler

have lost."

He turned to Annie who had done all, and more than all, that was required of her, probably because she had entirely forgotten herself. She was not even then sensible of a swift reaction, an overwhelming tide of embarrassment. She continued more than half unconscious of the number of eyes which, now that the operation was over, were fixed upon her, marvelling, admiring, condemning, or ridiculing. For what act is there, let it be ever so disinterested or self-sacrificing, against which no voice will rise in condemnation or in mockery?

But it was not the operating surgeon who either condemned or scoffed at Annie's conduct. He drew her aside, not speaking to her on the religious side of the episode, which he did not conceive that he had the smallest right or title to do, but addressing her on the purely medical aspect of the incident, on which he considered that he was entitled, nay, even bound to speak. His manner was a little blunt and brusque rather than suave, like that of a man who had no time to waste in paying compliments or making soft speeches, but it was thoroughly approving.

"You did quite right, nurse; I'm much obliged to you. That poor boy wanted all the comfort he could get. If he had gone on and worked himself into a frenzy before I had taken up the knife, I do not know that I could have done my work, and certainly the probability of his recovery would have been greatly lessened."

"I am glad," said Annie simply, with a little gasp of returning consciousness. "It is good of you to say so, doctor," but it was doubtful whether she knew what she was saying. She was penetrated through and through with thankfulness, yet thanks to herself seemed so irrelevant that she did not care to hear them.

There was more than Annie who thought that thanks to her were out of place and superfluous. This was specially so with one among the group of younger men, who at the moment of entering the ward had been fully alive to the circumstance that "the pretty nurse," as she was known to them, was on active duty. They had speculated on whether she would stand an operation, and what a disturbance and nice mess there would be if she fell flat on the small of her back on the floor, or went off in a fit of hysterics in the middle of it; and how their "boss" would endure such a disconcerting interruption to the proceedings. As it happened, the speculators were in their turn startled, abashed, or irritated, according to their respective temperaments and frames of mind, by what followed.

But there was a young giant, with a blonde beard, who let his blue eyes fall on the floor, drew back till he leant against the wall, and thrusting his hands into his pockets, asked himself in a dazed, humbled way, if an angel had come down among them, and where was the good of presuming to thank an angel? It was a thousand times more officious and audacious than to disregard the hackneyed quotation about the folly of painting a lily and perfuming a rose.

Annie, the moment she could be spared, went to her own room, fell down on her knees, and cried as if her heart would break. Yet they were not unhappy, but blissful tears, though they were as much for her own unworthiness as for God's unmerited goodness.

Then she snatched up a sheet of paper and wrote home. "I was so discontented—such a peevish wretch, this morning, but I have had a tonic, and now I am so unspeakably satisfied with my lot in life that I believe I am the happiest girl in England to-night. I would not change places with a hundred old Aunt Pennys, only I know, alas! that I am not half good enough to be a nurse. Yet I would rather be a nurse than any other character in the world, and I would not go back for a permanency to dear old Redcross, after which I was hankering this very morning, and live at home with you all again, leading the aimless, self-seeking life I led, not though Mr. Carey's bank were to rise out of its ashes and flourish to an extent that its greatest upholders never dreamt of—not though I were to get a pension or an earl's ransom, or whatever else people count magnificent compensations and rewards. But you must not think that it is because I do not love you all as well and a thousand times better than I ever loved you, for that would be a great mistake, since I am just beginning to know your true value. But don't you understand it would break my heart to think that I should no longer be a nurse and never have such another experience as I have had this afternoon." And then she told them in a very few words what had happened and what the surgeon had said to her. How the sister of the ward, and the matron, and everybody she knew in St. Ebbe's had congratulated her. They had all united in promising that the poor little fellow should be her patient in future; they had begun already to call him "Miss Millar's boy."

The little Doctor not only wiped his spectacles, he held his head higher. Mrs. Millar read the letter again and again, appropriating it and carrying it in her pocket till it was worn to fragments. These were still religiously preserved and portions read to select and sympathetic audiences. And every time she read the lines herself with a full heart, she called on God to bless her good Annie, and thought she was honoured among mothers in having such a daughter.

As for Dora and May they were long of ceasing to talk with bated breath and the height of loving enthusiasm of how Annie had mastered herself, and what a stay she had been in the hour of need to the lad. They planned and carried out their plans at every spare moment, in the manufacture of knitted socks and cravats for his benefit. But their great achievement was a quilted dressing-gown which Dora contrived to cut out, and May, in spite of her bad sewing, to help to sew together, that in his convalescence he might sit up in bed like a little sick prince.

CHAPTER XI

MRS. JENNINGS AND HER DAUGHTER HESTER

Rose Millar had made up her mind to like everything, if possible, in her new surroundings, and when she came up to town it was not only by a piece of good fortune, it was to the girl's credit, that she found so much she could appreciate, and so little, comparatively, that it was difficult to put up with.

In the first place, and as of primary consequence to Rose's well-being, Mrs. Jennings, the lady with whom Rose was boarded, turned out an excellently-disposed gentlewoman. She had a well-ordered house, pervaded with the spirit of a gentlewoman. The whole establishment was full of the self-respect which showed itself in a scrupulous consideration for the rights and claims, the doings and feelings, of others.

Rose did not complain because Mrs. Jennings and her house alike were also antiquated and formal. But the lady was not merely formal; it was a point of honour and an inveterate weakness with her to refuse to own that she had anything to do with such small but welcome boons to her as boarders. There she sat, serenely disclaiming the slightest knowledge of what had taken place, and attributing every attention to her old servant Susan, who had been with Mrs. Jennings since her marriage five-and-thirty years before. Or, if it was not Susan, it was her coadjutor, Marianne, in her housemaid's neat dress, whom Susan, in her working housekeeper's black cap and gold-rimmed spectacles, had trained to all fit and proper service in a gentlewoman's house.

In person Mrs. Jennings was tall and thin, sallow, and slightly hook-nosed, but still handsome. Her upright, broad-shoul-dered, and, by comparison, slender waisted figure was conventionally good; but it was hard to say how far it was her own, or how much it was made up. For she was one of those women who consider that it is a duty which they owe to the world not only to show themselves to the best advantage in bodily presence to the last, but so to conceal and atone for the ravages of time as to preserve a semblance of their maturity after it is long past. The performance is not altogether successful. For one thing, it is apt to call forth a spirit of contemptuous pity in the youthful spectator who is still a long way from needing to employ such laborious, self-denying arts.

Mrs. Jennings added to her natural air of dignity by a filmy shawl of black lace in summer, and of white Shetland wool in winter, draped round her without so much as a fold out of order, and by a somewhat elaborate modification of a widow's cap which added half an inch to her height. As Rose wrote in an early letter home, Mrs. Jennings's cap looked as if she had been born with it on her coal black hair, or as if it were glued and gummed there beyond any possibility of being displaced. Mother ought to see it, take an example, and abandon her flighty, waggling head-gear. No, on second thoughts, Rose would not like to see mother with a cap fitted on her head like the bowl of a helmet, and giving the idea of such stony stability that it might have been fastened with invisible nails hammered into her skull.

Hester Jennings, Mrs. Jennings's daughter, was the young art student like Rose's self, to whom she and her friends had naturally looked for congenial companionship where the girl was concerned; and if she did not find it with Hester, she was not likely to discover it in any of the other residents at No. 12 Welby Square. Naturally Rose did not greatly affect the remaining members of that elderly society, on which Mrs. Jennings professed to set store. She could not help liking Mrs.

Jennings, though, alas! Rose scarcely believed in her so much as she would have been justified in doing.

In Mrs. Jennings's daughter, who had been from the first thought of as a friend for Rose, she believed entirely. Yet Rose had been in the beginning both startled by Hester Jennings and disappointed in her.

Hester Jennings looked considerably older than she was, which was about Annie Millar's age; in fact, she was prematurely worn with study and work. She was like her mother on a larger scale, with advantages of a fair paleness and remarkable violet-blue eyes, which Mrs. Jennings had never possessed. Hester might have passed for a lovely young woman if she had cared in the least to do it. But never was girl more indifferent to such claims or more capable of doing her worst to qualify them and render them the next thing to null and void. When Annie Millar made Hester Jennings's acquaintance, Annie maintained that there was something left out in Hester's composition, the part which makes a woman desire to look well in the eyes of her neighbours, and win admiration, though the admiration be as skin deep as the beauty which creates it.

To think that a daughter of Mrs. Jennings, an artist in her own right, could dress so badly, with such a careless contempt for patterns and colours, in such ill-fitting frocks and dowdy or grotesque hats! Her preference for strident aniline dyes and gigantic stripes and checks in the different articles of her costume looked very like perversity; especially when it was shown that with reference to other persons, in arranging to paint a portrait, for instance, no one, not Mrs. Jennings, displayed such a fine sense of fitness and harmony as Hester exhibited. Dress was to her, in her private character, mere necessary clothing, warm or cool as the season required. It was not worth the waste of thought implied by turning it over in her mind. Her mother dressed for the family; or, if she did not, Hester understood that her married sisters and sisters-in-law devoted, with success, a great deal of time which they did not value in other respects, to the subject in question.

Speak of Rose Millar's professional notions as to the human figure being left easy and untrammelled! Rose was a pattern of decorous neatness and trimness compared to Hester; indeed, Rose was appalled by the total absence of order and ceremony, not to say of embellishment, in her friend's toilet. Hester abandoned herself permanently to deshabilles. She appeared in a jacket indoors as well as out. She dispensed with collars in morning and lace in evening wear. She did her hair once when she got up, and regarded passing her hand over her head when she took off her hat as all that was incumbent upon her afterwards. Without intending it, and without dreaming of copying the bushes of hair in Rossetti's pictures, Hester Jennings's sandy-coloured locks, not a good point in her personal appearance, were, as her great-grandmother would have cried in horror, more like a dish-mop than anything else. She stopped short of dirt in her slovenliness because of her purity of soul, her deep respect for the laws of health, and because of the traditions of her class, from which she could not altogether escape. But between her bondage to work, and her scornful neglect of other claims which she had known over-exalted and exaggerated, she had accomplished marvels.

Hester Jennings had attained such eminence in her recklessness of consequences, that, in place of being a nearly lovely woman, in accordance with her profile, complexion, and glorious eyes, she was barely good-looking because of them, in a style which repulsed many more people than it attracted others. The sight of Hester was one of the numerous lessons which she was destined to give to Rose Millar. It frightened Rose into becoming tamely conventional and elaborately tidy in dress, to the surprise and edification of her sister Annie, for it was just at the time when Annie was most spent by her new life and labours, and least inclined to put off her hospital gown and cap.

CHAPTER XII

A YOUNG ARTIST'S EXPERIENCE

Rose respected Hester Jennings. She could not help respecting her—a creature so much in earnest, so indefatigably industrious, so indifferent to all the distractions of the outer world which might have taken her out of herself and away from her work, while she was not above three or four years Rose's senior. If Hester would have let her, the respect would have deepened to reverence, when Rose discovered what the elder girl neither hid nor boasted of, that she was not only paying for her art lessons at the art school, and in other respects freeing her mother from the burden of her maintenance,—she was steadily earning a small independent income by working incessantly at every spare moment snatched from her studies. She worked at all sorts of designs for the most insignificant and obscure cheaply illustrated books and periodicals which cannot exist entirely on old plates excavated from forgotten stores, bought by the thousand at trade sales, procured by transfer from America, or even—now that national costumes are dying out—from France and Germany. These attempts at art were intended to pass into the hands of children—not the favoured children reared on the charming fancies of Caldecott and Kate Greenaway; but homelier, more stolid, and easily satisfied children. Such art was also for the masses of the people who cannot pay for original art, save in its first uncertain developments, when the stagier it is, the blacker, the bolder, the more meretriciously pretty or fantastically horrible, the better it is relished by its public. Even the stereotyped representations of the coarser fashion-plates, and the eccentric symbols and arbitrary groups employed in the humbler trade advertisements which the magnates in such advertising have left far behind, were food for Hester's unresting pencil. She might have injured herself irreparably by such illegitimate practice had she not studied as faithfully as she designed, with something of a stern, merciless severity, hunting out and correcting in her studies the errors of her crude work.

Stress of circumstances had lent what the French would have called a brutal side to Hester's natural candour and sincerity. It was one comfort that she was still more brutal to herself than to the rest of the world.

When Rose Millar showed her sister-artist some of Rose's sketches, Hester gave them a glance and a toss aside one after the other.

"There is nothing in that," she said coolly, "though I can see you have taken some trouble with it. This is not so bad. No, don't show that thing to anybody else—it will do you harm." Her highest praise was the "not bad" of mildest negative approval. "When you go to the class to-morrow morning," predicted the slashing critic, "you may depend upon it you will be turned back to a course of free-hand, or to copying from the round again. I don't mean that Mr. St. Foy will be as plain-spoken as I have been; he is a great deal too much afraid of hurting your feelings and his own, and of losing a pupil, though he is not what I should call either a bad man or a bad teacher. He is just like the rest; but wait and see if he does not politely turn you back to very nearly the beginning."

"I have had good teachers before," said Rose, crumpling up her nose and her forehead tightly, and swelling a little with wounded self-respect as well as wounded vanity. "It is queer, to say the least, if all my teachers were in a conspiracy to push me on to what I was not fit for, and to give me work altogether beyond my powers."

"You asked my opinion," said Hester Jennings, with inflexible calmness, "and I am not surprised that you do not like it when you have got it—few people do. The truth is not generally palatable. Not that I go in for infallibility of judgment. Wait and see what Mr. St. Foy does—not says—to-morrow."

"But why were the others—one of them an exhibitor at the Academy and the Grosvenor—so much mistaken?" inquired Rose, with natural indignation.

"How can I tell? But I hope you do not imagine that exhibitors are necessarily geniuses, or not as other men, or that they must be able to do a little bit of tolerable teaching when it pays them to condescend to it? Mr. St. Foy never exhibits—very likely for the good reason that his pictures are not accepted; but it does not follow on that account that he cannot paint a fairly good picture—better even than some which are hung on the line—and teach very tolerably to boot."

This was a new, bewildering doctrine, and a thoroughly disheartening state of matters, to which Rose, extinguished as she was on her own merits, did not make any reply.

"What I think, if you care to hear further what I think," said Hester, with a dry smile, "is that in not taking time and in being wild to paint a complete picture—something which everybody could recognize as a picture, and your friends admire—as if such a thing can be done to any good purpose for years and years—you have fallen into the disastrous habit of forgetting, or of only half remembering, what you learnt before, as you went on learning more. At least, that is the only way in which I can account for the wretchedness of some of your drawing, and the badness of your perspective, when you have got so far as to have a feeling for a scale of colour and the tone of a picture."

"Well, I suppose I can learn it all over again," said Rose, with a mixture of spirit and doggedness, forcing herself not to betray further resentment, and to swallow a little girlish weakness at the uncompromising treatment she was receiving. What would May and Dora say? But she durst not trust herself to think of them.

"Of course," answered Hester, opening widely a pair of singularly clear keen eyes. "Do you think I should have taken the trouble to say as much if I had thought otherwise?"

It was the one dubious compliment which Rose extracted, without meaning it, from the fault-finder.

Hester's openly expressed desire was to be an artist out and out, to live like an artist, not to be troubled with the hindrances and petty restrictions of an ordinary woman's life, which she was tempted to despise, to which, if she yielded at all in her mother's house, it was with scarcely concealed reluctance and aversion. Very likely she had only the most one-sided conception of the life she would have chosen. Certainly her notions of Bohemianism were about as ingenuous as "little May's" might have been; to go where art called her, to do what art demanded of her, to be art's humble, diligent, faithful servant all her days, without being held back and fettered on every hand by set meals, obtrusive servants, changes of dress, the obligation to pay and receive visits. The dream of her life was to get to Paris and have lessons in one of the French studios, where she was led to believe women have as good a chance of being well taught as men possess. She would prefer to live with some young women students like herself *en fille*—a modified—much modified version of *en garcon*. They would hire an *etage* in some cheap, convenient quarter, get the wife or daughter of the *conciergerie* to prepare breakfast and supper for them, dine at one of Duval's restaurants work all day, and sleep the sleep of the labouring woman at night. She said she knew quite well how such artists were considered in Paris, that they were regarded as *vauriennes*, to whom there was no occasion to pay the respect and consideration which were reserved for the potent *mesdames* and the *jeunes filles ingenues* of society. But what had she to do with society? She belonged to the great republic of art, and had infinitely more to occupy her than to listen for what society would say. As to not being able to take care of herself and behave so that the slightest indignity to her would never be ventured upon, the bare mention of such a possibility was received by Hester with a wrath which bordered on fierceness, and for the most part silenced her opponents effectually. Any displeasure which Annie Millar had displayed on a similar supposition was mild by comparison.

Hester was not an only child. Mrs. Jennings had sons, all in the army or navy, the mother was proud to say; but none of them in those days of competitive examinations and expensive living was high enough up in the service to be able to help his mother. On the contrary, grown men, with men's callings, as they were, they found themselves under the necessity of taking help from her. There were also other daughters besides Hester married to men in professions as unexceptionable as those of their brothers-in-law, but neither were they in circumstances which could make them feel justified in granting the smallest subsidy to Mrs. Jennings. Only Hester toiled for her mother at every moment which she could take from her studies and her natural rest. Yet the two women, who had dwelt under the same roof since Hester's babyhood, who were united by the strongest and most sacred tie, were without one taste in common, were irreconcilably different in every mode of thought and impulse of feeling, were only alike in each being well-intentioned and desirous of fulfilling her intuitions and justifying her beliefs. Being wise, the pair agreed to differ. But oh! the pity of it where aims, ideals and standards, hopes and fears, were all equally wide apart.

Mrs. Jennings did not interfere with Hester's freedom farther than she could help. Hester had her own engagements, her own circle of friends.

It may not surprise those who are acquainted with the various versions of Hester Jennings to be met with in this generation, that she was a red-hot radical in contrast to her mother's conservatism—well-nigh a *communiste*, to whom woman's rights and wrongs meant a burning question of the day, which, next to her love of art, came very near to her heart. She was almost powerless to assist her sister women, so overworked was she on her own account, but whenever she could snatch a moment half a dozen clubs and societies claimed her for their own. She had really a wide personal knowledge of the working-women of London, employed and unemployed.

CHAPTER XIII

MR. ST. FOY'S AND THE MISSES STONE'S

There was a second and large portion of Rose's life which belonged to her art classes, and to the classes in which she was one of the teachers and not one of the taught. In the art classes Hester Jennings's influence still dominated over Rose. In spite of Mr. St. Foy's professional qualifications, for which Hester had vouched, he had not so potent a personality as that possessed by one of his favourite pupils. He was tall, thin, gentleman-like, and delicate-looking, with a habit of languidly winking his eyes every second or two, as if they were weary of the trying sights of this world. He was kind to Rose in his courteous way, but she would not have been certain either of his ability to judge her work or of his honest opinion of it, if it had not been for what Hester told her.

There were fifty pupils among whom she and Hester ranked. These occupied the desks, worked at the easels, copied from copies, from the round or—height of promotion—from well-known models attached to the institution. There was the old market woman who obligingly sat alike for wicked old hags and doting grandmothers. There was the athletic young porter, off duty, who was a brigand or a pilot as occasion served.

The pupils were of various styles, idle and chattering, picturesque and sentimental, industrious, commonplace, but the most of them were variations on that last accepted version of the lady artist—the individual girl who aims at being independent and natural to the verge of harmless lawlessness and Philistinism—strange reaction from aestheticism. There were many Hester Jennings's though none so pronounced as Hester.

The Misses Stone's select boarding-school carried Rose twice a week into another region, where the wind did not blow so freely and the air was a trifle stifling. Sometimes she wondered if the Misses Stone knew the tone of a large proportion of the young lady artists at Mr. St. Foy's classes—not that Rose herself could see anything absolutely wrong in it—whether they would care to have an assistant drawing-mistress from those half-emancipated, more than half insubordinate ranks. However, Rose's appointment was not in any great danger of being cancelled. She had involuntarily become doubly careful in her dress and demeanour lately, and she discovered that the Misses Stone were old and intimate friends of Mrs. Jennings, whom they pitied sincerely for having so troublesome a daughter.

At first Rose did not dislike the office of teacher, which brought her in a little income before she was out of her teens. The whole place reminded her pleasantly of Miss Burridge's school which she had quitted but recently, only instead of having a metropolitan superiority in enlightenment and progress, strange to say, the Misses Stone's establishment, as if drawing within itself and shrinking back from the constantly moving, restlessly advancing world around, was really older-fashioned, less in the van of public opinion than the school at Redcross. The Misses Stone, their teachers and pupils, were well-bred, and what might have been called in past days "prettily behaved," though the behaviour was a little formal. Women and girls were elegantly accomplished, in place of being solidly informed or scientifically crammed, in accordance with the fashion of the nineteenth century. Above all, they declined with a gentle unconquerable doggedness to be turned from the even tenor of their ways. Italian was still largely taught in the school, while only a fraction of the pupils learnt German. Latin had no standing ground save in the derivation of words, Greek was unknown. The word mathematics was not mentioned. The voice of the drill-sergeant was not heard, but the dancing-master with his kit attended twice a week, like Rose, all the year round. The harp was played by the pupils instead of the violin. Withal there was much careful learning and repeating of Sunday Collects and the Church Catechism.

The school found ample support. What it attempted to do was in the main well done. Undoubtedly there was an attraction, half-graceful, half-quaint, in all connected with it, from the gentle manners of the elderly Misses Stone, who were only bitter against what was bold, impertinent, and eccentric, to the most dainty of their small pupils. Strictly conservative people felt that their daughters were safe in such an atmosphere, and patronized it accordingly. Undoubtedly they learnt a good deal which was worth learning.

Rose began by receiving nothing save the most considerate kindness and approval in that house. It was a libel on its forms and ceremonies to imagine that they contained anything tyrannical and harsh in their essence. The very law of their being was amiability, combined with mild steadfastness in withstanding the subversive attitude of the time. The most highly-born, richly-endowed girl within the precincts—and the school was rather aristocratic—would no more have ventured on being rude to Miss Rose Millar, the junior drawing-mistress, than the girl would have presumed to stamp her foot at one of the Misses Stone. If Rose had dropped her pencil in the course of her work, the highly-born pupil, by force of example, if for no other reason, would immediately have risen and picked it up, though she might not have made the speech about a Titian being worthy to be served by a Caesar. In fact Rose was in danger of being killed with kindness. Soon she was conscious of something choking, crushing, dwarfing in this artificial system. This was made more conspicuous to her by the choice of art subjects for the girls' study. There was no end of flower and fruit pieces. There were the stereotyped noble ruins, and cottages, either embowered in roses or half-buried in snow. There were the

Dutch and Venetian boats which had never sailed on familiar waters. Stags abounded, and Rose ceased to ask why so many of them stood at bay. The sleeping baby, which might have been a dead baby or a stone baby, was there; so was the long-nosed, wooden-legged collie, watching the shepherd's plaid. With what a lively hatred Rose grew to hate that collie!

Rose felt herself "cribbed, cabined, and confined" when she came from the comparative open air and robust life of Mr. St. Foy's classes. Yet even these were not the world of art. She got nervous in the fear of unworthily committing solecisms against the silken softness and steely rigidity of the Misses Stone's shrine. She thought if she caught up and reproduced any of Hester's vagabond notes—the Misses Stone were necessarily slightly acquainted with Hester, of whom, however, they never spoke—it would be like throwing a bombshell among these quiet, unalterable proprieties. She came to have a morbid, feverish craving to do it, or to see some other person do it. For instance, if young Lady Maud Devereux would but bid Rose tie her shoe, or even if she would contradict Miss Stone, or Miss Lucilla, or Miss Charlotte, without prefacing the contradiction by "I beg your pardon!"

At last these two days a week of giving lessons at the Misses Stone's, from being merely the agreeable lucrative variety in her life which they had promised to be, became gray days of penance to Rose Millar, when she felt she was under a spell, and did her duty badly. She ceased to refer to them in her letters home.

Rose arrived one morning at the Misses Stone's in a peculiarly excitable and yet depressed frame of mind. She had not been to Mr. St. Foy's classes that day; but Hester Jennings had known, the afternoon before, a piece of unwelcome news which she thought fit to communicate to Rose in the course of their morning walk, that ran so far in the same direction. A group of peasants, with which Rose Millar had been taking a great deal of pains, had been summarily condemned and dismissed by the master. Rose waxed hot and restive under the sentence, and began to dispute it vehemently, Hester defending it with equal vehemence, in what she considered justice to Mr. St. Foy, on the ground of a lack of dignity and repose in the central peasant. Hester was at that moment tearing along a thoroughfare, and showing so little dignity and repose not only in her gait, but in her "loud," ill-assorted garments, that, as frequently happened, to Rose's vexation, several people among the passers-by turned and looked after them. Hester to talk of a want of dignity and repose! It was like Satan reproving sin.

At the same time, while it is hard to admit the justness of a criticism unaffected by the inconsistency of the person who utters it and of the circumstances under which it is uttered, Rose was perfectly well aware that Hester Jennings was as excellent a judge of dignity and repose, apart from her personal proceedings, as any artist could be.

Rose did not retaliate, save in self-defence. Hester was her senior in art-knowledge still more than in years. She was not her sister to be treated without ceremony, and pretty deep down in Rose's girlish heart there was a respectful tolerance, an approach to tender reverence, for the turbulent-minded, chaotic, gifted creature beside her. Still Rose's equanimity was considerably disturbed.

The unruffled serenity of the Misses Stone's domain, far from restoring Rose's composure, seemed to smite her by contrast with an intolerable sense of personal reproach, and to goad her into rebellion. Rose was conscious of her variable spirits—the heritage of her years—getting more and more uncertain, and of being wrought up to a perilously high-strung pitch. She felt as if she were panting for liberty to breathe, to express her discordant mood in some unconventional manner.

As it happened, the principal drawing-mistress, a highly decorous, self-controlled young woman, ten years Rose's senior, was absent, and her assistant was alone at her post, with the whole class in and on her hands. Rose had already taken off her hat and gloves, and she tried to compose her ruffled feelings before she began her round of the drawing-boards, as Mr. St. Foy inspected his easels. The analogy with its disproportion struck her, and moved her to silent, unsteady laughter, which she could not restrain, so that it broke out into a ringing peal at the first enormity in drawing which she came across.

Nobody laughed like that at the Misses Stone's—certainly no low-voiced, quietly conducted teacher. Rose was further aggrieved and tormented by the astonished heads privily raised, and the wondering eyes covertly looking at her. She laughed no more. She went on examining, commending, correcting, till she was tired out. Surely the morning hours were endless that day. She was exhausted, not merely by the "smart walk" from Welby Square, which, taken at Hester Jennings's pace, was always tiring, as Rose knew to her cost, but also by the turmoil of spirit she had been in. All the toils, disappointments, and drudgery of the life which lay before her seemed suddenly to press upon her and overwhelm her, and before she knew what she was doing she was sobbing behind her handkerchief. She had one grain of sense left, she turned her back; but her heaving shoulders and the muffled sound of a "good cry" were not hidden from the electrified class.

Nobody cried like that at the Misses Stone's, unless it might be to somebody's pillow in the darkness of the night. For any teacher to cry in her class was unheard of. Rose conquered herself in less time than it has taken to recount her weakness, and resumed the lesson with moist eyes, a reddened nose, and her whole girlish body tingling and smarting with girlish mortification. All the rest of the morning she seemed to hear two startling statements repeated alternately and without pause.

"Miss Rose Millar laughed loudly in the middle of her teaching;" and oh! shame of shames, for the womanly dignity of the last year of Rose's teens—"Miss Rose Millar cried before the whole class."

Rose had once joined in a girls' play, full of girlish cleverness and girlish points and hits. No less a personage than Queen Elizabeth was introduced into it. In the course of the plot great stress was laid on the fact that the Queen had laughed at Lord Essex's expense, behind his back. This was done in order to pique the proud, spoilt young courtier to resent the laughter, and, in homely parlance, to give Her Majesty more to laugh at. The phrase "*and the Queen laughed*," had been emphatically repeated again and again in Lord Essex's hearing, with much malicious meaning and effect.

That mocking quotation was resounding in Rose's ears with a characteristic variation. It was no longer "*and the Queen laughed*," it was "and Miss Rose Millar laughed," then alas! alas! as a fit pendant, "and Miss Rose Millar cried."

What a big baby she had shown herself, without the decent reticence of a gentlewoman's good breeding, or the proper pride of a girl who respected herself. How these school-girls must despise her! What was she to do? Wait for the girls to whisper and chatter as all girls will, however trained? Or go at once to the Miss Stone with whom she had most to do, tell her the solecism of which she, Rose, had been guilty in the best behaved of schools, and abide by Miss Stone's decision, though it should be that she and her sisters would in future dispense with the services of Miss Rose Millar as assistant drawing-mistress.

Rose had the courage and honesty to adopt the latter course, and she tried to think that the fresh affront it brought her, was part of the penalty which she was bound to pay for her disgraceful childishness.

Miss Lucilla Stone listened with a little personal discomfiture, for she was, like Mrs. Jennings, so thoroughly mistress of herself and the situation, that any *gaucherie* or boisterous indiscretion was positive pain to her. Besides, the bad example to the girls for whom Miss Lucilla and her sisters were responsible, made a matter which people who did not understand might wrongly consider a trifle, really a serious affair. "No doubt," acquiesced Miss Lucilla, "something had put you out, as you tell me," in low-voiced rebuke, which yet sunk Rose in the dust, deeper than she had been, when she was making her impulsive confession. "You were tired with your walk, of course, but, my dear Miss Rose Millar, it is necessary to learn to practise self-control, especially in the presence of young people. They are so quick to notice and to encroach on their elders and those placed in authority over them, when the necessary distance of perfect self-control on the one side—if possible on both sides—is not preserved between them. Perhaps," added Miss Lucilla meditatively, and beginning to brighten a little, for she hated to give the lecture well-nigh as much as Rose hated to receive it, "if you had swallowed just a teaspoonful of *sel-volatile* or something of that kind, when you came in, the little scene would have been avoided. I shall speak to my sister Charlotte, who has the key of our medicine chest, and get her to administer a tiny dose to you every drawing day; you will step into the study the first thing, and it will be ready for you."

"Oh, no, thank you, Miss Lucilla," exclaimed Rose hastily, "I never took *sel-volatile* in my life. Father says not one of us is hysterical, or is likely to faint on an emergency, not even Dora or May. He is quite proud of Annie—my sister Annie—for her nerve, and she needs it all, since she is in training for a nurse."

Miss Lucilla shook her head dubiously, whether at the modern institution of lady nurses, or at the superiority in nerve of any family to which Miss Rose Millar belonged.

"You may not have been hysterical before," said Miss Lucilla with mild obstinacy; "but that is no reason why you should not be so now. If you dislike *sel-volatile*, you ought to try red lavender drops. I know they have gone out of fashion, but my dear mother still used them and found much benefit from them till she was seventy-seven years of age."

Rose longed to say that there was a great gulf between

seventy-seven and nineteen and two months. She was stopped by the quiet determination and self-satisfaction visible in Miss Lucilla's face and manner, as she rose and graciously but summarily dismissed the trespasser on her valuable time.

"Yes, I hope this will meet the case. You have been overdoing yourself—that explains itself to everybody. Dear Mrs. Jennings must forbid you tea and coffee and limit you to cocoa in the meantime; indeed, my sisters and I take that precaution before any mischief appears. Don't forget Miss Stone's study the first thing on drawing mornings. I trust a little sedative and stimulant in one will prepare you nicely for the drawing lessons."

To Rose's disgust she was compelled to make wry faces and choke over so many doses of *sel-volatile* and red lavender to the end of the term. She made secret unfulfilled threats to write to her father and get him to say that he would not permit her constitution to be tampered with, he would himself order her what she required, if she needed to be quieted like an incipient mad woman or a weak emotional fool.

Rose was not sure that Annie ought not to have come to her help. The younger sister did not see what advantage there was to the family in the elder sister's being a nurse if she was not to interfere on occasions of this kind. But Annie had the bad taste to take the story as a good joke against Rose; and as for Hester Jennings, it was an instance of "*the Queen laughed*" with a vengeance. However, Hester stepped in so far. She would not let the soothing regimen, on which Rose was put, go the length of depriving her of her tea and coffee in Welby Square.

Within the next few weeks Hester did Rose a still better turn. She (Hester) came to her friend with an order for decorative designs in scroll-work, which had reached the elder girl from a decorator of some repute.

"I think you could do it, Rose," said Hester. "It would not take much time, and if your work satisfied the great tradesman who has given such an impetus to this kind of art, it might be a perfect windfall to art students wishing to keep themselves. You need not despise it in the light of house-painting. If you read your Ruskin, you will find him as good as calling Titian and Veronese house-painters, though to be sure frescoes are rather an extension of scroll-work."

"Indeed, I should never dream of despising it. I should be only too thankful for any kind of copying or pattern-drawing, or designing for Christmas-cards—like poor Fanny Russell—if it were the beginning of the least little bit of an order," said Rose meekly, with a stifled sigh given to her and May's old magnificent ideas of commissions. "But why don't you keep the work for yourself, Hester?" the young girl inquired. "You could do it so well and so easily, and it would be no pain to you; it would be a pleasure, for it is graceful and true work so far as it goes—not like these cruel illustrations."

But Hester waived aside the undertaking. "You have been more accustomed to this kind of thing than I have. No, I mean to stick to my illustrations, cruel or kind. There is a new man in the publisher's office who is giving me more of my own way, and I feel it would not be fair to leave him in the lurch. Who knows that we may not, between us, lead the way to a revolution in the style of the cheapest original English wood-cut. Besides, I do not want any more diversions from my main business. I am already on four different committees for women's trade unions, the female franchise, and all the rest of it. I must crib a little more time for my hand and foot. Don't you know?—Drawing my own hand and foot from their reflection in a looking-glass till I can put them in any position, and foreshorten them to my mind."

Rose competed for the scroll-work order, and did it so well that she got the order, and along with it a note of commendation, a tolerably large extension of the commission, and the first instalment of a liberal payment for the kind of work. Her elation knew no bounds—

"Oh! Hester, I should never, never even have heard of this delightful job but for you. What can I ever do for you?"

"Don't hug me," said Hester, retreating in veritable terror, for she had a peculiar genuine aversion to caresses, still more than to thanks. "Don't knock off my hat, for I cannot spare another minute to put it straight again."

The next thing Hester heard was a half-impetuous, half-shamefaced admission from Rose that she had resigned her post as assistant drawing-mistress at the Misses Stone's school.

Hester looked grave on the instant. "What did you do that for?" she demanded gruffly. "Did you mention it to your sister? Have you told them at home?"

"No," Rose was forced to own—at least not till the deed was done. She had acted on her own responsibility. "But indeed, Hester, it is the best plan," she argued volubly. "Annie and all of them will say so when they know how I mean to cultivate this scroll-work, which is paying me twice as well already. I put it to you if I could do two things at once, and if it would be wise to sacrifice the more profitable for the less remunerative. Why it would be quite shortsighted and cowardly."

"Humph," said Hester, without the smallest disguise, "much experience you have had of it! Do you know, Rose Millar, these decorators' fads are constantly changing? Perhaps in three months they will all be for mosaic, or tiles, or peacocks' feathers again. If I had thought you were such a rash idiotic little goose, I should never have breathed a word to you of this man and his scroll-work."

"Oh! but, Hester," pled Rose, determined not to be offended, "I was only relieving the poor Misses Stone of a painful necessity. I am sure they have never put any dependence on me since the day I broke down—I grant you idiotically. I cannot stand the repression—suppression—whatever you like to call it. Now that there is a way out of it, I have felt like a wild beast in the school—the girls are so very tame—so much tamer than we were at Miss Burridge's—where I was not a black sheep— May will tell you if you care to ask her," protested Rose with wounded feeling. "But I am so tired of the rosy and snowy cottages and the ruins, and of that long-nosed collie. Sometimes I feel as if I would give the world for him to wag his tail one day, just to give me an excuse for crying out and flinging my india-rubber at him. I wish May saw him; it might stop her ecstasies over her new acquisition—the brute at home. I feel that this other brute, and the rest of the Misses Stone's copies and models, are injuring my drawing—I know they are making it cramped; while the scrolls help my freedom of touch like Hogarth's line of beauty or Giotto's O. And it is such humbug, and so horrid to have to swallow these doses of *sel-volatile*—a great healthy girl like me!"

"Humph!" said Hester again, "I hope you may not repent what you have done—if so, you need not blame me."

CHAPTER XIV

THE OLD TOWN, WITH ITS AIR STAGNANT YET TROUBLED. IS MAY TO BECOME A SCHOLAR OR A SHOP-GIRL?

The spring found Redcross still staggering under the failure of Carey's Bank. Hardly a week passed yet without some painful result of the disaster coming to light. These results had ceased to startle, there had been so many of them; but they still held plenty of interest for the fellow-sufferers, and Dora and May's letters were full of the details.

Bell Hewett had left Miss Burridge's; she had got a situation, or rather, she had been appointed to a junior form in the Girls' Day School at Deweshurst, going in the morning and returning in the afternoon by train. It was a good thing for Bell on the whole. She was more independent, had a recognized position as a public school-mistress, which she would not have had as a private governess; and if she continued to study, and passed various examinations, she might rise to higher and higher forms until she blossomed into a head-mistress—fancy Bell a head-mistress! She had quite a handsome salary, more than poor Ned's according to the chroniclers, Dora and May. That was the bright side of it. Unluckily for Bell, as most people thought, there was another. The daily journeys, together with the school-work, constituted a heavy task for a girl. Bell, toiling up from the railway station on a rainy day, with her umbrella ready to turn inside out, and her waterproof flying open, because her left hand, cramped and numb, was laden with a great bundle of exercises to correct at home, presented a dejected figure, tired out and three-fourths beaten. So the Miss Dyers thought as they rolled past her in their carriage, and debated whether they should not stop to pick her up and save her walking the rest of the road. But she was such a fright, positively bedraggled with mud enough to soil the cushions, and she could speak of nothing now save the Deweshurst Girls' Day School and her duties there. It was too tiresome to be borne with. Poor Bell was not clever, she was one-idea'd and slow at work like Ned, and she had also his conscientiousness. Probably promotion was not for her; she must drudge on as best she might. Her great encouragement at this time, next to her father's and sister's approbation and sympathy, was, as she told Dora, the prospect of spending her Easter holidays with Ned at his station-house. What did she care for its being only a station-house? after the fagging school-work it would be great fun to put Ned's small house in order, and play at housekeeping with him for a fortnight. She was bent on making him comfortable, and cheering him as well as herself. If the weather would but be fine they might have glorious rambles on the Yorkshire moors when no trains were due.

Colonel Russell was sailing once more for India, to lay his bones there without fail, the little Doctor prophesied sadly. In the meantime he had got, and been glad to get, a subordinate post in his old field. At the last moment, after he had established Mrs. Russell and her children in a cheerful house in Bath, he made up his mind to take his grown-up daughter out with him. But she was not to stay in his bungalow, for he was going to a small out-of-the-way station where there would be no accommodation or society in the barrack circle for a solitary young lady. Fanny was to be left with a cousin of her father's, in the Bombay Presidency. The lady had offered to take charge of her, and have her for a long visit.

Did Annie and Rose know what that meant? Could they form an indignant, affronted guess? "Father said," Dora quoted, "that if Colonel Russell, an honourable gentleman and gallant officer, had not lived in the old days and had his feelings blunted to the situation, he would never have consented to such an arrangement for his daughter. But he had seen his sisters come out to India for the well-understood purpose of getting married to any eligible man in want of a wife, so why should not Fanny do the same thing, when his pecuniary losses rendered it particularly desirable and the opportunity offered itself? It was not in Colonel Russell's eyes an unworthy resource. Of course Fanny was going out to be married and creditably disposed of within a given time, else her father would not have felt justified in paying her outfit and passage-money. Certainly he had no intention of paying her passage-money home as a single woman."

What would the Millars have done in Fanny's case? For was it not dreadful—particularly when all the young people interested in the subject remembered quite well that there had been "something" between Cyril Carey and Fanny Russell for more than a year back? Annie had always wondered what Fanny could see in a silly, trifling fop like Cyril. Rose had not been without a corresponding sense of wonder as to what Cyril could find in Fanny, who, in spite of her grand Norman peasant's carriage and profile, was dawdling and discontented with things in general, and though she pretended to a little knowledge of art, did not in the least understand what she was talking about. However, Annie's and Rose's opinions were of very little consequence when the matter concerned—not them—but Cyril and Fanny. There had been "something" between them which had changed the whole world to them last summer. They would never entirely outlive and forget it—not though Fanny went to far Cathay and married, not one, but half a dozen of Nabobs. For she was going to obey her father, and give herself to the first eligible bidder for her hand. No doubt she would do it with set lips, blanched face, and great black eyes looking not only twice as large as their natural size, but hollow and worn in the young face, because of the dark rings round them. These were produced by the sleepless nights which she pretended were occasioned by the hurry of her preparations, and of her having to say good-bye to all her old friends. But she would do it all the same.

Dora had only once caught Fanny Russell alone, and ventured on a timid, heart-felt expostulation.

"Must you go to India, Fanny? We shall all miss you so much, and it is not as if you were to be with your father, but just to stay with a distant relative whom you have never seen; it does appear such a sacrifice."

"And what should I do if I stayed behind papa, Dora?" asked Fanny, turning upon her with those great burning eyes and parched lips. "The house here is to be given up and the furniture sold immediately—of course you know that. It will take all that he can spare after discharging his share of the bank debts to keep Mrs. Russell and the children. I am a useless sort of person—a blank in the world. I could not nurse like Annie, or paint like Rose. I could not even be a school-mistress like Bell Hewett. Supposing I were qualified I should break down in a month. I was born in India, and spent the first five years of my life there, so that I am idle and languid, without stamina or moral courage; I am like the poor Bengalees, whom I can just remember. There is nobody who will undertake to keep me in England," ended Fanny, with a short, hard laugh.

And Dora, thinking of Cyril Carey—still one of the unemployed, with his old supercilious airs lost in the gait that was getting slouching, in keeping with the clothes becoming shabbier and shabbier, and the downcast, moody looks—could not find words with which to contradict her.

Indeed, when Dora was betrayed into giving her mother a hint of that "something," unsuspected by the seniors of the circle, which had been between Cyril Carey and Fanny Russell, and rendered Fanny's destination still more heartless and hateful, Mrs. Millar took an entirely different view of the circumstances from that taken by her daughters, and was both indignant and intolerant. "What presumption in Cyril Carey!" broke out the gentle mother of marriageable daughters, full of righteous wrath. "To dream of making up to a girl and perhaps engaging her simple affections, with the danger of breaking her heart and spoiling her prospects, when he had just failed to pass at college, and had not so much as a calling—not to say an income, with which to keep a wife! I shall think worse of him than I did before, after hearing this."

"But you forget, mother," remonstrated Dora, "that the bank was in existence then. His father might have been able to do something for Cyril."

"He was not going to live on the bank's capital and credit. There was too much of that going on already with poor James Carey's encroaching, dishonest relations and their friends. And I beg to tell you, Dora, that a man who cannot help himself, but has to wait for his father to do something for him, is a very poor match for any girl. Fanny Russell is well rid of him. I have no doubt she will think so before she is many years older—that is, if this is not all a piece of foolish nonsense such as girls are apt to take into their heads about their companions. If there was anything in it, and she had not been going away, her father ought to have been warned, and Cyril Carey spoken to in the way he deserved—selfish scapegrace! As it is, the bare suspicion is enough to reconcile one to Fanny Russell's going out to India, though that custom for girls has fallen into disrepute, and I never had any liking for it. Still I hope that Fanny will soon make an excellent marriage, and will learn to laugh at Cyril Carey and his unwarrantable presumption, together with any girlish folly of which she may have been guilty."

Mrs. Millar spoke in another fashion to the little Doctor. She had happened to be at the railway station on the raw, chill morning when Fanny Russell, in her smart new gray travelling suit—part of her outfit—was put into a railway carriage by her father and left there alone, while he went to look after the luggage and find a smoking-carriage for himself.

Fanny sat like a statue. She did not even raise her veil when she was bidding farewell to Lucy Hewett and Dora, who were seeing her off—not to take a last look at Redcross, where she had spent her youth.

Mrs. Millar understood it better when she stumbled against Cyril Carey half hidden by a lamp-post, watching the vanishing train. She might have taken the opportunity to rebuke him for his unprincipled recklessness; instead of doing so—after one glance at the young fellow's haggard face—the ordinary words of greeting died away on the kind woman's lips. She turned aside in another direction, making as if she had not seen him, without breathing a word of the encounter until she had her husband's ear all to herself in the privacy of the dining-room.

"O Jonathan!" she said, "I am so glad, so thankful that you did not interfere and use any influence, any pressure on Dora about Tom Robinson. I think it would have broken my heart to see any daughter of mine going off as Fanny Russell went to-day, leaving the look I declare I beheld on that poor lad's face. I should not wonder though she has given him the last push on the road to destruction."

"Oh, come now; it is not so bad as that," protested Dr. Millar, and then he was guilty of a most audacious paraphrase of a piece of schoolboy slang, for which he had some excuse in the habits of his wife—"Keep your cap on, Maria. In the first place, I see no analogy between the cases. Dora had not a private love affair—at least I was never told of it."

"Father, what are you thinking of? A private love affair in this house! It was very different with poor Fanny Russell, who had only her silly, selfish young stepmother between her and her father. I dare say she would never have looked at an empty coxcomb like Cyril Carey if she had been happy at home."

"And did I not hear you say," asked the gentleman, who had before now been made the recipient of the disastrous compli-cation of the story, "that the girl was well quit of the jackanapes, for she could not have a worse bargain made for her than she had nearly blundered into on her own account?"

"Yes, I did say so," the lady admitted, when thus brought to book; "and I'd say it again, if I had not seen that miserable, desperate expression on his face, and he so young, and such a light-hearted, foolish dandy only the other day. I may be sorry for him, I suppose, though I have no son of my own. And I am grieved for poor James Carey, who is breaking up so fast, and for poor, poor Mrs. Carey."

It was a positive relief when Dr. Millar came in one day and announced that he had a piece of good news for the family, by far the best where the Careys were concerned that he had heard for many a day. Cyril had got an appointment at last; he had been offered the command of the mounted police at Deweshurst.

"A policeman. Oh! what a downfall," cried Mrs. Millar and Dora. But when the Doctor reminded them that there were policemen and policemen, insisted on the fact that the practice of placing gentlemen at the head of the constabulary was gaining ground, and asked them what they had been in the habit of calling Colonel Shaw and Sir Edmund Henderson when they were the chiefs of the London police, his womankind gave in.

Mrs. Carey did not say there would be another mouth less for her to feed, but she remarked, with the same sardonic calmness, that Cyril's clothes would be provided for him, which would be one good thing. Cyril himself was only too glad to get away. He would have something to do, however unpalatable in itself, instead of digging in the garden, and going through the form of helping Robinson, his clerks, and cashier, with their books. He would have a good horse under him once more, if he were only to ride it to police drill.

Dora could not be sure whether he experienced a throb of thankfulness at the thought that this had not happened till

Fanny Russell was gone. Where was constancy to draw the line? A man was not less a man because he was also a mounted policeman. He might even be grandiloquently styled, by those who were particular about the names of things, the soldier of peace. Still Dora had an irresistible conception of the pained disdain, the latent superciliousness, which would have sprung into full force in Fanny's dark eyes, if she had ever seen the once magnificent Cyril in the most careful modification of a *bobby's* braided tunic and helmet.

Bell Hewett would not look so, if she, in her school-mistress character, met Cyril at Deweshurst. Bell, like Dora, would feel her heart soften and warm to Cyril in his misfortunes. She would think of Ned, and hurry up to Ned's old playfellow and chum, to tell him the last news from Yorkshire, and ask what message from him she should send to Ned in her next letter. Dora was tempted to go on and wonder whether Cyril's heart would not be touched in turn by the cordial recognition of his Rector's daughter, who had, on the whole, kept her position better than he, with his advantages, had kept his, whose frank greeting had become a kind of credential of gentle birth and breeding afforded to him in full sight of the natives of Deweshurst. If he felt all that, he must recognize how womanly and sweet Bell was, though she was not pretty and not one bit clever, and be full of gratitude to her. And gratitude combined with considerable isolation on the one hand, and on the other the constantly present possibility of agreeable encounters with a loyal old friend, might lead to anything—to a good deal more than Dora cared to say even to herself, feeling frightened at the length to which she had gone on the spur of the moment in this most recklessly unworldly match-making. Yet was it reckless, when Bell would be such a good poor man's wife, and when marriage with a woman like Bell might make another man of Cyril Carey?

However, the Careys' adversity, with its reaction on their old associates, approached a climax shortly after Cyril left. His father grew so much more helpless an invalid that it was found absolutely necessary to have a resident nurse for him. Then

Mrs. Carey, though she continued the nurse-in-chief, stated clearly and dispassionately that she was now sufficiently disengaged to look after her house and give her single servant what assistance she required. Therefore, as it was high time that Phyllis should be doing something for herself, Mrs. Carey proposed to put her at once into "Robinson's," under Miss Franklin, if Mr. Robinson would receive Phyllis for an apprentice.

It was in vain that Phyllis cried and implored her mother to take back her resolution, and that all her friends apprised of the proposed step remonstrated; Dr. Millar even called expressly to enter his protest.

Mrs. Carey would hear of no objections. Phyllis must do something for herself, and she was not clever or qualified in any way to be a governess. Mrs. Carey had every confidence in "Robinson's" as an excellent shop, conducted on the best principles. She had a great respect for both Mr. Robinson and Miss Franklin—she would never find a more desirable place for Phyllis. As to cutting her off from all her connections and the circumstances of her birth and education, that had been done already pretty effectually. The sooner everybody found his or her level the better for the world in general. If Mrs. Carey was not much mistaken, more girls than Phyllis would have to learn that lesson before these hard times were over. No, it was not Phyllis who was to be cut off from her connec-tions—from those who ought to be nearest and dearest to her. It was poor Ella who was separated from the rest of the family, and condemned to gilded exile. Mrs. Carey was doing her best to keep Phyllis, not only for her mother and her poor father, but for her brothers, who must all start in life in a humble way, by putting the girl into "Robinson's," since Mr. Robinson had reluctantly consented to have her.

Dr. Millar retired from the field beaten.

The unheard-of destination of her friend Phyllis played the most extraordinary pranks with May Millar's mind. The fact was, there were two Mays dwelling side by side in one goodly young tabernacle of flesh. There was the May with the exceptional scholarly proclivities. She had a life of her own into which none of the family except her father possessed so much as the tools to penetrate. She cherished dreams of Greece and Rome, with the mighty music of the undying voices of their sages and poets, and the rich treasures of learning, among which a poor little English girl, far far down in the centuries, could only walk with reverend foot and bated breath.

And there was the other May, hanging about her mother, running to bring her father's slippers, sitting on his knee to this day, taking possession of Dora, ordering her about like a young tyrant, adoring Tray—the most guileless, helpless, petted simpleton of a child-woman that ever existed. The second May was at the present date the more prominent and prevailing of the two, so much so that all the sharp-tongued, practical-minded ladies in Redcross made a unanimous remark. Dr. and Mrs. Millar's youngest daughter was the most disgracefully spoilt, badly brought-up, childish creature for her years whom the critics knew. It was a poor preparation in view of her having to work to maintain herself. They could not tell what was to become of her.

At first May lamented, day and night, over the fate of Phyllis Carey, to have to stand behind counters, sort drawers full of ribands, tape, and reels of cotton, and wait on her towns-women! May could think of no fitting parallel unless the pathetic one of that miserable young princess apprenticed to the button-maker, dying with her cheek on an open Bible, at the text, "Come unto Me, all ye that labour and are heavy laden, and I will give you rest."

Then, as Phyllis accommodated herself to the new yoke, and found it not so galling as she had expected it to be, her friend May altered her tone with sympathetic quickness, and reflected Phyllis's change of mood almost before the mood was established. Phyllis was in mental constitution like her father, single-hearted and submissive—not bright any more than Bell

Hewett was bright, but contented and trustful as long as she was suffered to be so. She had been enduring harder and harder lines at home. She found existence actually brightening instead of darkening round her when she was transferred to "Robinson's." For everybody, knowing all about her and her father and mother, with their altered circumstances, began, at least, by treating her with kindly respect and forbearance, in spite of Mrs. Carey's austere request that she should be dealt with exactly like the other shop-girls.

Shop-work, in which Phyllis was to be gradually trained, felt comparatively easy to a girl who had been taken from school and launched into the coarsest drudgery of house-work under an inexperienced, flurried, over-burdened maid-of-all-work. Mrs. Carey was sufficiently just to exact no more home-work from Phyllis, and to arrange that she should have her time to herself, like other shop-girls, after "Robinson's" was closed, while the master of "Robinson's" was inflexible in setting his face against late hours, except for the elder hands on one evening in the week. Everybody was good to Phyllis, who, in truth, just because she was enough of a little lady to be free from arrogance and assumption, while she was willing to do her best to oblige her neighbours, provoked no harsh treatment. Above all Tom Robinson for one person could not be too considerate to her.

Miss Franklin looked on Phyllis Carey as a godsend, a harbinger of other better-class girls going into trade. The woman not only took the girl under her wing, she fell back instinctively and inevitably on Phyllis for companionship, with a selection flattering in a woman to a girl.

Then a complete revolution was wrought in May's opinions and wishes. Nothing would serve her but that she too must go as a shop-girl to "Robinson's," and share the fortunes of her friend.

May did not yet confide her purpose to her father and mother, but she poured it in daily and nightly outbursts into the startled ears of Dora, to whom the hallucination sounded like a mocking retribution on the young Millars' old scornful estimate of shopkeepers and shops. May stuck to her point with a tenacity which, touching as it did a tender, trembling chord in Dora's heart, threatened also to subvert her judgment, that was at once sounder and more matured than May's.

The vibrating chord lay in the knowledge that May too was destined to quit Redcross at no distant day, with the aching reluctance of Dora to give her up, and to find herself in the position that domineering, selfish girls sometimes covet—that of being the only girl at home, having none to share with her in the rights and privileges of the daughter of the house.

A sort of feverish anxiety, which was in itself ominous, had taken hold of Dr. Millar to see all he had projected accomplished in so far as it was still possible. That is, he would fain set in motion, at least, the wheels which would carry out his purpose. Perhaps he had reason to distrust his health and life; perhaps it was simply that he was not insensible to the fact, that money had a trick of running through his fingers and those of Mrs. Millar like water, though they did their best to catch it up and arrest it in its rapid course. Mrs. Millar's little private income was still in part free, and not engulfed in the needs of the household at Redcross, as it might not long continue. Rose had only sixty pounds of it, and Annie fifteen for pocket-money till she should have passed her probation and be in a position to receive her nurse's salary, which would be as soon as she had completed her first year in the hospital. There were seventy-five pounds remaining, which might serve to keep May at Thirlwall Hall in St. Ambrose's with the chance of her gaining a scholarship and partly maintaining herself for the rest of her stay in college. "Little May's" maintaining herself in any degree was a notion half to laugh at, half to cry over, while it took possession of Dr. Millar's imagination just as serving in "Robinson's" along with Phyllis Carey had hold of May's.

Another year (who knew?) it might not be in the Millars'

power to afford May the opportunity of growing up a scholar, on which her father had set his heart. That consciousness, and the sense of the value which her husband put on May's abilities and their culture, brought round Mrs. Millar. She began to contemplate with something like composure what she would otherwise have strongly objected to, the sending forth of her youngest darling—the child who so clung to her and to home—into an indifferent or hostile world.

Truth to tell, it was May herself who was the great obstacle. She was not cast in the heroic mould of Annie and Rose. It was like tearing up her heart-strings to drag her away from her father and mother, Dora, Tray, the Old Doctor's House, Redcross itself. She had enough perception of what was due to everybody concerned—herself included—and just sufficient self-control not to disgrace herself and vex her father by openly opposing and actively fighting against his plans for her welfare. But she threw all the discouraging weight of a passive resistance and dumb protest into the scale.

Sarah Tytler

CHAPTER XV

TOM ROBINSON TAKEN INTO COUNSEL

At last May, in the innocence of her heart, took a rash step. She heard her father say it was good, showery, fishing weather, and she was aware Tom Robinson often fished in the Dewes; what was to hinder her from making a detour by the river on her way home from school, and if she saw Tom near the old bridge—the pools below were specially patronized by fishers— she might go up to him and ask him frankly if he had an opening for her services, along with those of Phyllis Carey, in his shop? If he had, would he do her the great favour to speak to her father and mother, and ask them not to send her away to be a scholar at St. Ambrose, but to let her stay and be a shop-woman in Redcross?

Tom Robinson, at the first word of her appeal, put up his fishing-rod, slung his basket, in which there were only a couple of fish, on his back, shouldered her books, and turned and walked back with her, as if it was he who was seeking her company and not she his. How else was he to make the little girl who might have been his pet sister see that there was any harm in the irregular course she had pursued? How, otherwise, was she to understand that she was big enough—nearly a head taller than her sister Dora—and old enough with her seventeen years, though she was still the child of the family, to render it indecorous for her to come, out of her own head, without the knowledge of anybody, to have a private interview with him on the banks of the Dewes?

"'Robinson's' is highly honoured," he told her, in a tone partly bantering, partly serious, and wholly friendly, "and I too should, and do, thank you for the trust in me which your proposal implies, but I am afraid it would not do, Miss May."

May's fair young face fell.

"Oh! I am so sorry," she said simply; "but, please, may I know why you have Phyllis and will not have me?"

"The case is altogether different. Mrs. Carey made up her mind that Miss Phyllis should go into a shop—mine or another's. Phyllis was not happy at home; she is not a clever, studious girl, though she is your friend and is very nice—of course all young ladies are nice. There is no comparison between you and her."

"But why shouldn't clever people go and work in shops?" persisted May, in her half-childish way—"not that I mean I am clever; that would be too conceited. But I am sure it would be a great deal better for shops if they had the very cleverest people to work in them."

"It depends on the kind of cleverness," he told her. "With regard to one sort you are right, of course; with respect to another it would not answer, and it would be horrible waste."

She opened her brown eyes wide. "Why do you waste your abilities and college education?" she asked him naively—"not that everybody calls it a waste; some people say 'Robinson's' is the high-class shop it is, because its masters have not only been respectable people, they have always been educated men and gentlemen."

"I ought to say for myself and my predecessors that I am much obliged to 'some people' for acknowledging that," he remarked coolly.

"I beg your pardon, Mr. Robinson," said May humbly. "I

know I have been very rude—I am constantly saying stupid things."

"Not at all; and though you did, never mind—say them to me if you like," he gave her *carte blanche* to comfort her. "But look here, Miss May, I don't wish you to make mistakes. Indeed it is my duty, since I am a great deal older than you—old enough to be, well, your uncle I should say—to prevent it if I can."

"I don't see how you could be my uncle," said May bluntly, "when you are not more than five or six years older than Annie—I have heard her say so—you are more like my brother."

The instant she mentioned the relationship to which he had aspired in vain, she felt the blood tingling to her finger-tips, and she could see him redden under the shade of his soft felt hat.

May groaned inwardly. "Oh! I am a blundering goose; I wonder anybody can be so infatuated as to think me clever."

"I have not said what I wished to say," he resumed, for somehow, in spite of her forgetfulness and lack of tact, he could talk well enough to May. "I must set you right. I have not a grain of the scholar in me such as you have, neither do I believe that those who went before me had; we could never have been more than fair students. We did not go out of our way to get learning. We did what our associates and contemporaries did, that was all. I fancy I may take the small credit to us of saying that we had no objection to learn what the ancients thought, saw, and did, after we had been lugged through the Latin grammar and caned into familiarity with Greek verbs. We were like other men who had the same advantages. I honestly believe if we had anything special and individual about us it was a turn for trade. That is the only manner in which I can account for our sticking to the shop, unless we were mere money-grubbers. But all that signifies very little; what does signify is that you are not quite like other girls.

What, May, do you pretend that you do not prize the roll of a sonorous passage, or the trip of an exquisite phrase in Latin or Greek? That it does not tickle your ears, cling to your memory, and haunt you as a theme in music haunts a composer? Do you not care to go any deeper in Plato or in the dramatists? Is it a fact that you can bear to have heard the last of Antigone, and Alcestis, and Electra?"

May hung her head like one accused of gross unfaithfulness, with some show of reason.

"No, I cannot say that, Mr. Robinson," she owned, "I shall think and dream of them all my life. They are so grand and persecuted and sad. But there—if I do not turn my back on them and my books, I must go to St. Ambrose's, there is no choice," ended May disconsolately.

"But why not go to St. Ambrose's?"

"Oh! you do not know, Mr. Robinson," protested May with fresh energy. "In the first place you are a man and cannot understand. In the second, I suppose it is because I am so silly and childish and cowardly," she went on incoherently. "Annie always said it was cowardly; she and Rose went away quite bravely and cheerfully, keeping up their own and everybody's spirits to the last. But Dora and I could not do it, yet I do not know that anybody ever thought of calling our Dora cowardly exactly, or silly, and childish. She was not a bit cowardly with the horrid big dog and dear little Tray, you remember?—she would not let me interfere, but she would have stoned the dog herself."

"Which would have been very foolish of her," said Tom Robinson with decision. "I should say she was timid, not cowardly—there is a broad distinction between the two conditions."

"It is just that we cannot leave home for any length of time, Dora and I," said May piteously.

"So you and your sister Dora cannot leave home—that is the objection, is it?" he repeated, slowly pulling his red moustache. "What do you call home? The Old Doctor's House or Redcross?"

"Both," cried May quickly; "where father and mother and the rest of us are, of course."

"But the rest of you are gone, and what if your father and mother were to go too?"

"They won't, they never will," insisted May—"not until they come to die. You were not meaning that? Oh! you could not be so cruel, so barbarous," cried May, passionately, "when death is such a long way off, I trust. I know that God is good whether we live or die, and that we shall meet again in a better world. But we are not parted yet, and it is not wrong to pray that we may be a long time together here on this very earth, which we know so well, where we have been so happy. Why, father and mother are not more than middle-aged—mother is not, and if father is older, he is as strong and hale as anybody. Think how he was able to give up his carriage and attend his patients on foot last autumn without feeling it," urged the girl defiantly, in her passion of love and roused dread, which she would not admit.

"Certainly," he strove to reassure her, feeling himself a savage for frightening her by his inadvertence, "I never saw anybody wear so well as Dr. Millar. He might be sixty or fifty—he may live to be a hundred—I hope with all my heart he will; and I shall not be astonished if I live to see it. As for Mrs. Millar, it is an insult to call her middle-aged. It is something quite out of keeping to come across her with such a tall daughter as you are."

"Yes, I am the tallest of the four," exclaimed May complacently, diverted from the main topic, as he had intended her to be. "And I have not done growing yet; my last summer's frock had to be let down half an inch."

"Is it possible? What are we all coming to? You will soon have to stoop to take my arm—if you ever condescend to take my arm."

"No," she denied encouragingly, "I am not so far above your shoulder now," measuring the distance with a critical eye. "I shall not grow so much as that comes to. You are bigger than father, and you would not call him a little man; you are hardly even short."

"Thanks, you are too kind," said Tom Robinson, with the utmost gravity. "But I say, Miss May, if I were you, I don't think I should do anything to vex and thwart Dr. Millar, though he is so strong and active—long may he continue so. You know how disappointed he would be if you were to close your books."

"I am afraid he would," said May reluctantly. "I had almost forgotten all about it for the last minute or two. But don't you think if you spoke to him as I came to ask if you would," she continued unblushingly and coaxingly, "if you were to try and show him—it would be so kind of you—how comfortable and happy I should be with Phyllis Carey in your shop—doing my best—indeed, I should try hard to please you and Miss Franklin, all day—and getting home every evening—he might change his mind?"

"No, he would not," said Tom with conviction; "and what is more, he ought not. He would never cease to regret his shattered hopes for you—which, remember, you would have shattered—and your spoilt life."

"But your life is not spoilt?" she said wistfully, unable to resign her last hope.

"How can you tell?" he said, with a slight sharpness in his accent. Then he added quickly, "No, for I am a born shopkeeper in another sense than because I am one of a nation of shopkeepers."

He gave himself a reassuring shake, and resumed briskly—"I crave leave to say, Miss May, that I actually enjoy making up accounts, turning over samples, and giving orders. Sometimes I hit on a good idea which the commercial world acknowledges, and then I am as proud as if I had unearthed an ancient manuscript, or found the philosopher's stone. I pulled a fellow through a difficulty the other day, and it felt like taking part in an exciting fight. I have speculated occasionally when I was fishing—paying myself a huge compliment, no doubt—whether old Izaak Walton felt like me about trade."

"Was he in trade?" inquired May, with some surprise. "I know he wrote *The Complete Angler*, and was a friend of Dr. Donne's and George Herbert's, and is very much thought of to this day."

"Deservedly," said Tom Robinson emphatically. "Yes, I am proud to say, he was a hosier to begin with, and a linen-draper to end with—well-to-do in both lines. They say his first wife, whom he married while he was still in business, was a niece of the Archbishop of Canterbury of the day, and his second wife, whom he married after he had retired to live on his earnings, was a half-sister of good Bishop Ken's; but I do not pretend to vouch for the truth of these statements. Now, about your father. I cannot do what you ask—I cannot in conscience. Will you ever forgive me, 'little May'—that is what your father and mother and your sisters call you sometimes to this day, ain't it? and it is what I should have called you if I had been—your uncle say? Shall we be no longer friends?" he demanded ruefully.

"Of course we shall," said May, with a suspicion of petulance. "You are not bound to do what I bid you—I never thought that; and you are father and mother's friend—how could I help being your friend?"

"Don't try to help it," he charged her.

Tom Robinson went farther than not feeling bound to do

what May begged of him, he was constrained to remonstrate in another quarter to prevent trouble and disappointment to all concerned. He screwed up his courage, and everybody knows he was a modest man, and called at the Old Doctor's House for the express purpose. He had called seldom during the past year—just often enough to keep up the form of visiting—to show that he was not the surly boor, without self-respect or consideration for the Millars, which he would have been if he had dropped all intercourse with the family because one of them had refused to marry him. But though he had begged for Dora's friendship when he could not have her love, and had meant what he said, the wound was too recent for him to act as if nothing had happened. In addition to the pain and self-consciousness, there was a traditional atmosphere of agitation and alarm, a kind of conventional awkwardness, together with an anxious countenance, and protection sedulously afforded by the initiated and interested spectators to Tom and Dora, which, like many other instances of countenance and protection, went far towards doing the mischief they were intended to prevent.

Tom saw through the punctilious feints and solemn stratagems clearly; Dora did the same as plainly. Indeed the two would have been idiots if they could have escaped from the discomfiting perception of the care which was taken of them and their feelings, and the fact that every eye was upon them.

The sole result was to render the couple more wretchedly uncomfortable than if they had been set aside and sentenced to the company of each other and of no one else for a bad five minutes every day of their lives.

Another unhappy consequence of their being thus elaborately spared and shielded was, that when by some unfortunate chance the tactics failed, the couple felt as flurried and guilty as if they had contrived the fruitless accident to serve their own nefarious ends.

Tom Robinson called on the Millars between four and five the day after May had made her raid upon him, expecting to find what was left of the family gathering together for afternoon tea. He had the ulterior design of drawing May's father and mother apart, and letting them judge for themselves the advisability of her going up at once to St. Ambrose's, before her whole heart and mind were disastrously set against her natural and honourable destiny. He was distinctly put out by finding Dora alone. As for Dora, she told a faltering tale of her father's having been called away to a poor patient who was a pensioner of her mother's, and of Mrs. Millar's having walked over to Stokeleigh with him to see what she could do for old Hannah Lightfoot; while May was spending the afternoon with the Hewetts at the Rectory.

He hesitated whether to go or stay under the circumstances, but he hated to beat an ignominious retreat, as if *he* thought that *she* thought he could not be beside her for a quarter of an hour without making an ass of himself again and pestering her. Why should he not accept the cup of tea which she faintly offered from the hands that visibly trembled with nervousness? When he came to consider it, why should he not transact his business with Dora? She was as deeply interested as anybody, unless the culprit herself; she probably knew better what May was foolishly planning than either their father or mother did, and would convey to them the necessary information.

As for Dora, she was thinking in a restless fever, "I hope—I hope he does not see how much I mind being alone with him. It is just because I am not used to it. How I wish somebody would come in,—not mother, perhaps, for she would start and look put out herself, and sit down without so much as getting rid of her sunshade; and, oh dear, not May, for she would stare, and I do not know what on earth she would think— some wild absurdity, I dare say; anyhow, she would look exactly what she thought."

"Look here, Miss Dora," he said abruptly; "you don't think your sister May ought to renounce the object of her education hitherto, and your father's views for her, in order to do like

Miss Phyllis Carey? You are aware that May has become enamoured of Phyllis Carey's example, and is bent on following in her footsteps; but it won't do, and I have told her so. I trust nobody suspects me of encouraging young ladies to become shop-women," he added, with a slightly foolish laugh, "as old actors used to be accused of decoying young men of rank and fashion into going on the stage, and recruiting sergeants of beguiling country bumpkins into taking the king's shilling."

"Has May spoken to you about it?" cried Dora, startled out of her engrossing private reflections. "What a child she is! I am sorry she has troubled you; she ought not to have done that. I hope you will excuse her."

"Don't speak of it," he said a little stiffly, as he put down his cup and signified he would have no more tea.

"And you said no," remarked Dora, with an involuntary fall of her voice reflecting the sinking of her heart. "Of course you could not do otherwise. It was a foolish notion. I am afraid Phyllis Carey is enough of a nuisance to Miss Franklin—and other people. It is hard that you should be bothered by these girls. Only I suspect poor 'little May' will be most dreadfully, unreasonably disappointed;" and there was an attempt to smile and a quiver of the soft lips which she could not hide.

"I am not bothered, and I hate to disappoint your sister,—I trust you understand that," he said quickly and earnestly. "But it would be sacrificing her and overturning your father's arrangements for her—disappointing what I am sure are among his dearest wishes."

She did not ask, like May, why he did not count himself sacrificed. She only said shyly and wistfully, "I knew it was out of the question, but if it had not been so, or if there had been any other way, it would have been such a boon to poor May not to be torn from home." At the harrowing picture thus conjured up her voice fairly shook, and the tears started into her dovelike eyes.

"Home," he said impatiently, "is not everything; at least, not the home from which every boy must go, as a matter of course. 'Torn from home' in order to go to school! Surely the first part of the sentence is tall language."

"It is neither too tall nor too strong where May is concerned," said Dora, rousing herself to plead May's cause. "She has not been away from home and from father—especially from mother, and one or other of the rest of us, for longer than a week since she was born."

"Then the sooner she begins the better for her," he said brutally, as it sounded to himself, to the loving, shrinking girl he was addressing.

"She has always been the little one, the pet," urged Dora; "she will not know what to do without some of us to take care of her and be good to her."

"But she must go away some day," he continued his remonstrance. "How old is your sister?"

"She was seventeen last Christmas," Dora answered shamefacedly.

"Why, many a woman is married before she is May's age," he protested. "Many a woman has left her native country, gone among strangers, and had to maintain her independence and dignity unaided, by the time she was seventeen. Queen Charlotte was not more than sixteen when she landed in England and married George the Third."

Dora could not help laughing, as he meant her to do. "May and Queen Charlotte! they are as far removed as fire and water. But," she answered meekly, "I know the Princess Royal was no older when she went to Berlin; and poor Marie Antoinette was a great deal younger, as May would have reminded me if she had been here, in the old days when she travelled from Vienna to Paris. But there—it is all so different. They were princesses from whom a great deal is expected, and the Princess Royal was the eldest instead of the youngest of the Queen's children."

"Does seniority make so great a difference?" he said, with an inflection of his voice which she noticed, though he hastened to make her forget it by speaking again gravely the next minute. "Should May not learn to stand alone? Would it not be dwarfing and cramping her, all her life probably, to give way to her now. Can it ever be too early to acquire self-reliance, and is it not one of the most necessary lessons for a responsible human being to learn? Besides, '*ce n'est que le premier pas qui coute.*' It is only the first wrench which will hurt her. She will find plenty of fresh interests and congenial occupations at St. Ambrose's. In a week, a fortnight, she will not miss you too much."

Dora shook her head incredulously. It was little he knew of May, with her fond family attachments, and her helplessness when left to herself in common things.

"Follow my advice, Miss Dora," he said, rising to take his leave, "don't aid and abet Miss May in seeking to shirk her obligations. Unquestionably the one nearest to her at present is that she should go to St. Ambrose's. Don't prevent her from beginning to think and act for herself—not like a charming child, but in the light of her dawning womanhood."

He gave a swift glance round him as he spoke, and a recollection which had been in the background of both their thoughts during the whole of the interview, flashed into the foreground. It was of that day a year ago, a breezy spring day like this, when, as it seemed, there were the same jonquils in the jar on the chimney-piece, and the same cherry-blossom seen through the window against the blue sky, and he had asked her with his heart on his lips, and the happiness of his life at stake, to be his wife, and she had told him, with agitation and distress almost equal to his, that he could never be anything to her. He caught her half-averted eyes, and felt the whole scene was present with her as with him once more, and the consciousness brought back all his old shyness and reserve, and hurried his leave-taking. The slightest touch to her hand, and he had bowed himself out and was gone.

"How silly he must think me," Dora reflected, walking up and down the empty room in perturbation, "both about poor 'little May,' and about remembering the last time we were alone together. I dare say he is right about May, though men never do understand what girls feel. If she should fall ill, and break her heart, and die of home-sickness—such things have happened before now—I wonder what he would say then about her learning to stand alone? Very likely he would assert that St. Ambrose's is not St. Petersburg, or even Shetland or the Scilly Isles. It is not far away, and if she were not well or happy, she could come back in half a day, as the other girls could come down from London. But then he would despise her, for as quiet and good-natured as he is, and though people have said that he himself had no proper pride in consenting to have a shop. And I don't think May could bear contempt from anybody whom she had ever looked on as a friend. Men are hard—the best of them are, and they don't understand. He is kind—I am sure he means it all in kindness; but he is not yielding; he is as masterful as when he dragged the dogs to the edge of the bank and let them drop into the Dewes for their good. He will never be turned from what he thinks right. I wish he had not guessed what I could not help remembering— he was quick enough in doing that; and I could not tell him that I did not imagine for a moment—I was not so foolish— that he was under the same delusion he suffered from twelve months ago. If he had been oftener here in the interval, and we had met and been together naturally as we used to be, sometimes, I should have forgotten all about it, and so would he, no doubt. But how could I help thinking of it when there has always been such a point made of mother or some one else being present when he called? I am certain it is quite unnecessary and a great mistake. He will not speak to me again as he spoke that day. There is no danger of his running away with me," Dora told herself with an unsteady laugh. "I hope he is not under the impression that I did not think and act for myself when I was forced to do it. Because, although they all knew about it, and of course Annie and the others teased me about 'Robinson's,' and the colour of his hair, and his size, father and mother told me to decide for myself, and I did not hesitate for a moment. I could no more have borne to leave them all of my own free will than May could. Surely it was proof positive I did not like him in that way," Dora represented to herself with the greatest emphasis.

Tom Robinson was marching home with his hands in his pockets and his hat drawn over his eyes. "How hard she must think me—little short of a pragmatical, supercilious brute—not to do my best to keep 'little May' at home, where the child wants to be. I asked her to let me call myself her friend, and this is the first specimen of my friendship! she will take precious good care not to ask for another. She will be horribly dull left by herself without one girl companion, only the old people. These sisters were so happy together—I liked to see them, perhaps all the more because I had neither brothers nor sisters of my own—I thought it was an assurance of what they might be in other relations of life. I suppose she will tackle that little spitfire of a dog which I inflicted on them. May will lay her parting injunctions on Dora to plague herself perpetually with the monster, and these will be like dying words to Dora, she will sooner die herself than intermit a single harassing attention. And it will be impossible for her to avoid many deprivations. There are more partings to be faced in the future. Millar is an old man, even if he could hope to pay up the bank's calls and make some provision for his widow and daughters. It was a pity poor Dora could not care for me, when there need have been no partings where we two were concerned, save that material separation of death which is quoted in the marriage service. She would not have believed, nor I either, that it could touch the spiritual side of the question and the love which is worth having, that is God-like and belongs to immortality. I might have done what I could if

Dora had married me, so far as the other girls would have let me, to serve as a buffer between the family and the adversity which I am afraid not all their high spirit and gallant fight will hold entirely at bay. It was not to be, and there is an end on't. I wonder where I found the heart, and the cheek too for that matter, to bully Dora about May, though, Heaven knows, I spoke no more than the truth. Well, she has her revenge, and I am punished for it. It cut me up at the time to hurt her, and the recollection of having contradicted and pained so sweet and gentle a creature is very much as if I had dealt a lamb a blow or wrung a pigeon's neck—on principle."

Half an hour afterwards Mrs. Millar bustled into her drawing-room with an expression of mingled annoyance and excited expectation on her still comely face.

"My dear Dora, I am so sorry; he gave his name to Jane, and she has told me who has been calling in my absence. I wish I had not left you by yourself. But who was to guess that Tom Robinson would call this afternoon? It must have been exceedingly disagreeable for you."

"I don't know," said Dora, vaguely and desperately; "we must meet sometimes when there is nobody by, if we continue to live in the same town. I wish you would not mind it for me, mother, and keep on trying to avoid such accidents, for I really think it makes them worse when they do happen."

"Very well, my dear, you know your own feelings best," said Mrs. Millar, a little puzzled. In her day it was reckoned no more than what was due to maidenly delicacy and social propriety to preserve a respectful distance between a rejected man and his rejector. As if the gentleman might, as Dora had said, carry off the lady by force, or shoot her or himself with the pistol hidden in his breast!

CHAPTER XVI

ROSE'S FOLLY AND ANNIE'S WISDOM

Annie Millar not only warmed to her work in St. Ebbe's, she recovered her full glow of health and spirits. She not only liked her nursing, she enjoyed her holiday hours intensely with the peculiarly keen enjoyment of busy women doing excellent service in the world. If any one wishes to know what such enjoyment is like let him have recourse to a great authority. "*In the few hours of holiday that—only now and then—they (a nursing sisterhood) allow themselves, they show none of the weariness that sometimes follows the industry of toiling after self-amusement. Reaction, after great strain on the powers of self-sacrifice and endurance that they have to exert, may be thought to account in some part for the happy result; but, whatever the cause, their society has in it all that can best and most surely attract—grace, freshness, and natural charm.*"[1]

[Footnote 1: Kinglake in his *History of the Crimean War*, vol. vi. p. 436.]

Rose felt as if she had never sufficiently appreciated Annie before. She was very proud of her sister now when she came to Welby Square, and everybody, whether in Mrs. Jennings's set or in Hester's, was struck with Annie's beauty and brightness.

Even Hester Jennings saw nothing to find fault with on the ornamental side of a girl who had gone in so heartily for the serious business of life, nine-tenths of whose hours were occupied with grave tasks, to which Hester owned honestly that she with all her public spirit was not equal.

Annie's face was not only the most unclouded, her laugh the merriest of all the faces and laughs which appeared and were heard in Welby Square. She became almost as much of a peacemaker, a smoother-down of rough interludes, an allayer of irritating ebullitions, as Dora was wont to be at home.

"Annie is so much improved," Rose wrote to May, "I never saw her looking prettier. She is just splendid when she comes out of St. Ebbe's for an afternoon and evening. Everybody is delighted to see her, and wants to have her for his or her particular friend. She and I have such jolly walks and talks; she hardly ever calls me back or puts me down now."

After pronouncing this high encomium it was rather a shock to Rose not only to incur Annie's righteous displeasure, but to discover that on occasions Annie could be as severe and relentless in her sentences as ever.

Rose, like most middle-class girls not fairly out of their teens, and committed to their own discretion in the huge motley world of London, had been solemnly charged to behave with the greatest wariness. She was to treat every man or woman she encountered well-nigh as a dangerous enemy in disguise till her suspicions were proved to be misplaced, and the stranger shown to Rose's satisfaction and that of her seniors and guardians to be a harmless friend.

To do Rose justice, she remembered for the most part what had been told her, and was careful not to expose herself to the slightest chance of misapprehension—not to say rudeness, such as would have frightened her mother and incensed her father. Rose would not be tempted by the fearless independence of Hester Jennings and her cronies. They maintained, in theory at least, that though there might be dens of vice and dark places of cruelty in the great city, for those whose feet trod the downward path, yet its crowded thoroughfares, to those who honestly went about their own business, or to the messengers of divine charity and mercy, were as safe, and safer, than any quiet country road. Womanhood in the strength and confidence of its purity and fearlessness might traverse them alone at any hour of the day or night.

But Rose submitted to the ordinary if antiquated code, which implies the timidity and defencelessness of young women whenever and wherever assailed. She had not gone far enough in her emancipation to reckon as part of it, immunity from apprehension of every kind, including the strife of evil tongues.

However, one day in the beginning of May, Rose went to Covent Garden in pursuit of a pot of tulips, which she suddenly felt she must have, without delay, as an accessory in one of her sketches. She was coming home laden with her spoil by way of Burnet's, where there was an equal necessity for her to procure, on the instant, a yard or two of gauzy stuff of a certain uncertain hue, when a thunder-storm unexpectedly broke over the haunt of artists. Torrents of rain followed, enough to wash away whole pyramids of flowers and piles of art-materials. If the downpour did nothing else it cleared the crowded street, with the celerity of magic only seen in such circumstances, and left Rose cowering in a doorway, alone as it seemed to her, but for a cab-driver who took refuge in his cab, drawn up before one of the opposite houses. The rain looked as if it meant to continue, while, laden as Rose was, she could not have held up an umbrella even if she had found one ready to her hand.

Her slender funds did not set her up in cabs, as she had told herself on many a weary trudge in fog and drizzle between Mr. Foy's class-rooms and Welby Square. Besides she would like to see Hester Jennings's face when she (Rose Millar) proposed to indulge in such a luxury. But there would be more lost than gained if she stood shivering in that doorway till her best spring frock was ruined, waiting for an omnibus which was sure to arrive with every available inch of space occupied. She would catch a chill or an influenza with no kind father near to save her a doctor's bill, and cure her simply for the pleasure of doing it. She would brave Hester's eagle eye, supposing it could scan Rose's misdeeds from some coigne of vantage commanding this end of the street. She signalled to the cab-driver opposite, who put his head out of the cab window and signalled back that he had a fare besides himself at present ensconced in one of the inhospitable-looking houses.

Should she bid the thunder, lightning, and rain do their worst, and set out to walk home in defiance of them? While she still paused irresolute, peeping out disconsolately at the inky sky from which the downpour fell, a young man in the conscious superiority of a waterproof and an ample umbrella, walked leisurely along the sloppy, deserted pavement. He looked at her, seemed arrested by something which struck him in her appearance, hesitated a little undecidedly, stopped short, and addressed her, colouring up to his frank, honest blue eyes as he did so.

"I am afraid you have been caught in this tremendous shower. Can I do nothing to help you—call a cab, for instance?"

"Oh! thank you very much," she said gratefully, forgetting all about the cunning enemy in disguise for whom she was to be always looking out. Indeed she had felt so lonely a minute before that she was rather disposed to welcome a comrade in misfortune. "The cabman in the cab opposite tells me he is engaged, and I do not remember any cab-stand near this."

"There is one round the corner, which I passed a minute ago, but it was vacant; all the world is wanting cabs in such weather. However, I can shelter you a little, if you will allow me," and he held the umbrella in front of her.

"No, please; I am keeping you here in the wet, and you are exposing yourself to the rain," protested Rose, remorsefully. "I was just thinking of walking on, sooner than stand any longer getting gradually soaked," she confided to him with pleasant inconsiderateness.

"Then will you take the use of my umbrella?" he asked promptly; "and perhaps you will let me carry your parcels for you," he suggested in the humblest manner possible, eyeing covetously her flower-pot, and the paper wisp from "Burnet's."

"Oh dear, no," said Rose, pulling herself together when it was too late, and with an adorable frankness, which was another mistake so far as an unauthorized acquaintance's being nipped in the bud went. "I should be taking you out of your way; you must want your own umbrella, and I can manage perfectly well. I am accustomed to go about by myself"—the last piece of information given with a proud inflection of the voice which told its own tale.

"In storm and shine?" he took it upon him to question her, with the slightest rallying tone, and a twinkle in his blue eyes, but still with the greatest respect in his attitude and manner— "not in storm, surely. I shall not be going out of my way. I am only taking a stroll—that is, I generally do take a stroll in some direction on my way back to my lodgings. You may not think the weather nice for strolling, but I don't mind it. I am as strong as a horse, and I certainly don't want an umbrella. I have this waterproof affair, which, like the umbrella, is rather a nuisance than otherwise."

She could see at a glance that he was a broad-shouldered young fellow, over six feet, and that his kindly, deferential face, seen through the steaming atmosphere, was as ruddy as youth and a vigorous constitution could make it. He was evidently speaking the truth, and she could not resist the temptation of the friendly aid arriving thus opportunely, and so obligingly pressed upon her.

"Only for a little way," she bargained cheerfully. "The rain may stop in a minute, though I must say it does not look like it, or we may come on a return cab; anyhow, it cannot be long till an omnibus overtakes us."

She would have demurred at his ridding her of her flowers and parcel, which he disposed of easily under his arm and in his disengaged hand, as if he were well accustomed to being cumbered with such small impediments, had not a comical idea crossed her mind. He might think that she did not trust his honesty, and was beset by a fear that he would rush down a side street and disappear with her goods before she could cry, "Stop, thief!" and arouse the scanty passers-by.

Then Rose felt impelled to explain why she walked about London burdened with flower-pots and rolls of gauze. "I have just been to Covent Garden," she said. "I wished to get this pot of tulips—parrot tulips—yellow and scarlet, you know, to harmonize with a Chinese screen in a little picture I am painting. Then I had to go into 'Burnet's,' for 'Liberty's' is too far away, for some blue stuff of the right shade which I could drape into a frock for the little girl who is my model."

"Are you fond of painting?" he caught her up, being to the full as willing to speak as she was. "So is my sister, and she also goes to 'Liberty's' for queer rags and tags. I suppose they are part of the amateur's stock-in-trade."

"I am going to be a professional artist," said Rose again, with that proud little inflection of the voice. But all the effect which her communication had upon him was that he took it as an invitation, or at least as a warrant, for responsive confidences on his own part.

"I am a doctor," he announced. "I have been entitled to write myself one for the last two months. I have just passed my final exams, and got my degree—stiffish work for a fellow who does not take to sapping as easily as to the air he breathes."

"My father is a doctor," said Rose, brightly, with her tongue fairly loosened. "I forget whether he says examinations were easier or more difficult when he was young. He is Dr. Millar of Redcross."

"Millar!" exclaimed the tall young man so excitedly, that he stopped short for an instant, in the middle of the dismally lashing rain, and looked at her with a gleam of delight in his blue eyes. "I thought so, I saw it at the first glance. You have a sister among the lady probationers at St. Ebbe's."

"Yes—Annie," cried Rose, with equal ecstasy in the acquiescence; and she, too, stood still for a second in the rain. "Do you know St. Ebbe's? Have you seen Annie?"

"I should think I do, I should think I have," he answered her fervently. "St. Ebbe's is my hospital. I have been 'walking it' for a year past. I was there to-day, and Miss Millar is well known all over the place. She is a great favourite with the matron, Mrs. Hull, and the house surgeon, and especially with the operating surgeon. He is always asking to have Miss Millar in his cases since that boy had his leg cut off."

"I know, I know," chimed in Rose, "the little boy who begged you to wait till he had said his prayers, and when he could not do it for himself, Annie was able to do it for him. Now he is hopping about on his crutches quite actively and happily; and she has got him an engagement, to clean the knives and boots at Mrs. Jennings, the boarding-house in Welby Square where I stay. Isn't it too funny and nice that you should happen to have to do with St. Ebbe's and Annie?"

"It has been a great pleasure to me—well, these are not the right words," said the young fellow with sudden gravity and a shade of agitation in his manner. "I count it the greatest piece of good fortune which ever befell me that I took St. Ebbe's for my hospital. But I ought not to presume on my acquaintance with Miss Millar," he began again immediately, with an infusion of cautious reserve and something like vexation creeping into his tone; "it is purely professional. We are far too busy people at St. Ebbe's to know each other as private persons. Very likely if you ask her, she will deny all knowledge of me as an individual; she may not even be able to recall the fact of my existence apart from a circle of big uncouth medical students in the train of the doctors—all alike to her. At the same time I have drunk tea in her company both in the matron's room and in Dr. Moss's, and I have often sat near her in the services at the hospital chapel," he ended a little defiantly.

The speech, save for its ring of half-boyish mortification, was suspicious, as if he were providing a loophole for escape in case Annie refused to indorse his assertion of mutual acquaintance. But Rose, in spite of her spirit and quickness, was hardly more given to suspicion than her sister May showed herself, and saw nothing dubious in his remark. She was carried away with the agreeable surprise of having stumbled on somebody connected with St. Ebbe's who knew all about Annie. She chatted on in the frankest, friendliest way, plying him with girlish questions, and supplying free comments on his answers; and he was an auditor who was nothing loth to be so treated, and to be furnished with stores of information on points which had aroused his ardent curiosity. She forgot all about taking him out of his way, and when they reached Welby Square she crowned her unbounded faith in him by inviting him into the house. On his acceptance of her invitation, after a moment's hesitation, she presented him to Mrs. Jennings as a friend of Annie's from St. Ebbe's.

The young man had the grace to feel his ears tingle while Mrs. Jennings, looking a little astonished, took him on Rose's word, bowed her welcome, begged him to sit down with her usual gracious, languid good-breeding, and said she was glad to see any friend of Miss Annie Millar's.

He did his best, with a flushed face, to remedy his and Rose's rashness. He put down his card, with Harry Ironside, M.D., engraved on it, at Mrs. Jennings's elbow. He set himself with a strenuous and sincere effort to talk to her, and so to conduct himself as to do credit to Rose's voucher.

Mrs. Jennings was easily propitiated on receiving the attention which was due to her. She thought the young man's manners perfectly good; they had well-bred ease, and at the same time the modesty which ought to accompany youth, though his introduction to her had been somewhat informal.

Irregularity and singularity were among the fashions of the day. She would have been glad if her daughter Hester, in carrying out these fashions, had brought forward no rougher, or commoner-looking, or more eccentric satellites and proteges—secretaries of those horrid women's unions and clubs—than this friend of Rose and Annie Millar's.

Mrs. Jennings never forgot a name and its social connection. "Ironside?" she repeated tentatively, but with an air of agreeable expectation. "I am familiar with the name. One of my sons, Captain Lawrence Jennings, when his regiment was at Manchester, knew and received much kindness from a family named Ironside."

"It must have been the family of one of my uncles," said Dr. Harry Ironside, eagerly. "My Uncle John, and my Uncle Charles too, for that matter, stay in Manchester. Both are married men with families. My Uncle John was mayor a few years ago."

"The same," cried Mrs. Jennings with bland satisfaction. "Lawrie's Ironsides were the family of the mayor, I remember perfectly when you mention it;" and she added the mental note, "They were among the richest cotton-brokers in the place—well-nigh millionaires."

"Were you all named from Cromwell's Ironsides?" inquired Rose, lightly, inclined to laugh and colour at the absurd recollection that, though she had seemed to know all about him from the moment he spoke of St. Ebbe's and Annie, she had been ignorant of his very name till he put down his card. If he had not done so, she would have had to describe him to Annie as the big, fair-haired young doctor with the Roman nose, or by some other nonsensical item, such as the signet-ring on his left hand, or the trick of putting his hand to his chin.

Sarah Tytler

"I am sure I cannot tell"—he met her question with an answering laugh—"except that, so far as I know, we have had more to do with cotton than with cannon-balls. My father was a Manchester man, like my uncles. I have struck out a new line in handling—not to say a sword, but a lancet."

"Ah!" said Mrs. Jennings with mild superiority, "all my sons are in the services—I have given them to their Queen and country. Two of my sons-in-law are also in the army, and I often say of the third—a clergyman in a sadly heathen part of the Black Country—that, engaged as he is in the Church militant, he is as much a fighter as the rest of them." Having thus in the mildest, most ladylike manner, established her social supremacy, Mrs. Jennings was doubly gracious to the visitor. They made such progress in their acquaintance by means of the Manchester Ironsides and other members of her very large circle of friends, with regard to whom the two discovered the names at least of several were also known to Harry Ironside, that the lady made another marked concession. When he said he was in rooms in London, and had his only sister with him, she signified with a kind and graceful bend of the lace-enfolded shoulders and the bewigged head within the wonderful edifice of a cap, that she meant to have the pleasure of calling on Miss Ironside.

Rose could hardly believe her ears; and she did not wonder, though she was glad that he had the sense and good feeling to thank Mrs. Jennings with warmth, since Rose knew what a testimony it was to the genuine liking which the mistress of the house had taken to her chance guest. For Mrs. Jennings went very little out, and was exceedingly particular in adding to her visiting-list, as became the head of a select boarding-house, and the mother of so many officers and gentlemen, not to say gentlewomen.

But matters did not end even there. He managed to convey the impression that his sister and he were rather lonely in their rooms, while he alluded to the facts that he and she were orphans, and with the exception of each other had neither brother nor sister. They had looked forward to being together, and making a home as soon as Kate left school, and he had taken furnished lodgings at Campden Hill till he settled down somewhere. But somehow the lodgings were not very home-like. He should prize highly the friendship of Mrs. Jennings for his sister. At this point the slightest gleam of a business interest awoke in Mrs. Jennings's steel gray eyes, though she only told him softly that she had known it all—the loneliness of one or two members of a family in London, the comfortlessness of even the best of furnished apartments. It was such considerations, in a great measure, which had induced her to utilize her large house, much too large for herself and the only daughter left at home with her, to receive a few old friends as suitable boarders into her family. She had hoped to form a cheerful and refined little society round her, and so to be of a little use to her fellow-creatures. She might say she had succeeded in her humble mission, she finished with artless benevolence. He met her half-way with breathless alacrity. Had he and Kate but known in time Mrs. Jennings's generous idea, what a boon it would have been if she had let them avail themselves of it! Even yet if there ever occurred any change, any opening—but he was afraid, he added in disconsolate tones, there never would—the fortunate people would know too well when they were happy—it would be doing him and Kate the greatest favour, the utmost kindness to let them know. This was exactly the complimentary, beseeching, deprecatory mode in which Mrs. Jennings liked business to be conducted; whereas, if Hester had been present, she would have said in the clumsiest, coarsest manner, "Mamma, there are some rooms vacant, which any respectable person who cares to pay the rent may have."

But that was not Mrs. Jennings's plan. She said in her blandest voice—"Well, Dr. Ironside, we must see what we can do for you and your sister; I cannot bear to think of your feeling forlorn after what your cousins did for my son Lawrence. We must stretch a point with regard to accommodating you—that is, if you are not, both of you, dreadfully particular. No, you are not at all difficult to put up, you and your sister, you say? I am happy to hear it. It is such a good thing for young people to be easily pleased. I am not sure that something could not be contrived in the course of a week or two. I think I heard my old servant speak of rooms which were to have been kept for cousins of my friend Mr. Lyle, two charming ladies who were to have come up from the country for the season. But their dear old aunt died unexpectedly, and of course they are not inclined for any gaiety at present. I leave the details of arranging the sets of rooms and letting them to my Susan. I never interfere with her; she knows far better than I what is wanted, and she is a sensible, practical person to deal with. If you care to speak to Susan, I shall ring for her to see you in the dining-room, and she will tell you at once what she can do for you," Mrs. Jennings finished sweetly.

He did care; indeed he was so intent on benefiting by what Mrs. Jennings, in her ladylike way, made so great an obligation conferred by her on her fellow-creatures, that he caught at the hope held out to him. He had an interview with the potent Susan, and came back radiant to tell that the housekeeper had been nearly as kind to him as her mistress had shown herself. He and Susan had settled everything. He was free to give up the rooms which he and his sister were occupying the following week.

"What, without consulting Miss Ironside?" protested Mrs. Jennings in pretty alarm.

"Oh! Kate will like any arrangement I make," he cried confidently; and Rose came to the conclusion either that "Kate" was the simple school-girl he represented her, or that Dr. Harry Ironside was an autocrat in his domestic relations.

He insisted on furnishing references, because business was business, even in the light of the dawning friendship which he trusted Mrs. Jennings was going to extend to him and Kate, and they would come as soon as she would let them.

Oh! he must arrange it all with Susan. Mrs. Jennings put up

her still dainty hands, and waived him off playfully. She dared not interfere with Susan. All she would say was that she was delighted to look forward to such an agreeable addition to her pleasant little circle. She was fond of having young people about her, and was always ready to do what she could (which was no more than the truth) to make them happy.

Rose was driven to the conclusion that Dr. Harry Ironside must have found furnished lodgings such a pandemonium, that he was induced to believe a select boarding-house must be a paradise by comparison. It was comical how it had all come about. It did seem as if Rose's heedlessness, if she had been heedless in drifting without an introduction into an acquaintance with one of Annie's doctors, was likely to bear good fruits to Mrs. Jennings, among other people. Hester had been looking worried lately, and had not scrupled to give as the reason of her pre-occupation—family affairs not prosperous. The whole of the house was not let. Old Mr. and Mrs. Foljambe had actually been unreasonable enough to try to exchange the best rooms, which they had chosen for themselves in the winter for shabbier, cheaper quarters during the summer, when the husband and wife might be occasionally absent paying visits. Old Susan, in her black cap and gold-rimmed spectacles, was especially triumphant in seeing the scheme balked, and confided her mingled exultation and indignation to Rose, who had helped to balk the schemers. The confidential family servant even forgot some of her polite mannerliness in her excitement. "Now, Miss Millar, them Foljambes has done for themselves; serve them right for seeking to get a catch from a friend like Missus, as is that kind to her boarders, which you can testify, Miss; they might be her own flesh and blood. Bless you! she'll never make a rap by keeping boarders. She never grudges them anythink, and would sooner deny herself than that they should go without their fancies. But there, now, that fine young gentleman you brought," went on Susan with the slightest respectful significance, "I'm sure we're greatly indebted to you, Miss—speaks as if he meant to stay on here with his sister for the present. He has taken our largest rooms off our hands, so that we may be easy on that head, and I for one won't be sorry if Mr. and Mrs. Foljambe ain't able to shift back into them at their will and pleasure. The young gent, as is a gent, had no hargle-bargling about terms. He was satisfied to pay what we asked, because he knew that though it was not a common boarding-house, and though it was no more than right that he and his sister should pay for the privilege of being under the roof of a real lady like Missus, we were not the sort to ask more than our due."

The moment Rose got quit of Susan, she said to herself complacently, "It is very nice to have done such a service to Mrs. Jennings and Hester and everybody, instead of having got into a scrape and being scolded, as I almost feared at one moment. If only Miss Kate Ironside is not too much of a dumb belle and a mere school-girl," reflected Rose, with the supercilious consciousness of maturity in a girl who had been more than a year away from all teaching except what she had herself practised, and what she received as a grown-up woman at Mr. St. Foy's. "I wonder if Dr. Harry Ironside will have spoken of our encounter, and what came of it, to Annie before I can tell her. I should like to see her face when she learns that I know somebody who goes to St. Ebbe's," ended Rose, with persistent audacity.

Annie's face was a study when she heard of it. Rose had been guilty of a little wilful self-deception, still she received a shock.

The first time the sisters were able to meet and have a walk together, after Rose's encounter with Dr. Ironside, Rose broached the great piece of news, and witnessed the effect it produced. The girls had managed to reach the Marble Arch into Hyde Park, beyond which they found a seat for a few minutes. It was not too early in the season for them to take possession of it, and they were still sufficiently strangers in London to suppose that seats were placed for the accommo-dation of the weary of all ranks and both sexes, and not merely for the benefit of nurse-maids and their charges, or of able-bodied tramps. The sisters prepared to talk over their own concerns and Redcross with the *empressement* of girls, to forget all about the moving crowd around them, and the grinding of that great mill of London in the traffic that is never for an instant still.

"Oh! Annie, have you seen him lately?" began Rose—"Dr. Harry Ironside, I mean. Has he told you that he and his sister are coming to board at Mrs. Jennings's?"

"Seen him! Dr. Harry Ironside! What do you know about Dr. Harry Ironside? What are you saying, Rose?" cried Annie, sitting bolt upright, opening wide her dark eyes, and fixing them in the most amazed, displeased, discomfiting gaze on Rose. The rate at which the two had been walking and talking, the suspicion of east wind, the premature heat of the May sun, had converted the soft red in Annie's cheeks to a brilliant scarlet.

"What I am saying," answered Rose, nodding gaily, and trying hard not to flinch under the trying reception of her precious piece of information, "is that, by the funniest chance, I made the acquaintance of a friend of yours at St. Ebbe's. And the laughable coincidence of our meeting and happening to speak to each other, and then of my finding out that he knew all about you, is going to be a very good thing for poor dear Mrs. Jennings," Rose hastened to add, taking the first word in self-defence. "He is coming with his sister to board in Welby Square."

"He is not a friend of mine," said Annie, severely. "Is it possible that you are such a simpleton as to believe that all the doctors, medical students, and nurses—the whole staff of St. Ebbe's, in fact, are intimately acquainted with each other, are acquainted at all, for the most part, unless as doctors and nurses? Please, Rose, tell me at once what nonsense this is— what foolish thing you have been about."

When Annie said "please" to her sisters the situation was alarming.

On the other hand, Rose had not come up to London to be an artist, who was already getting orders for scroll-work and executing them successfully, to be put down by a sister not above four years her senior.

"What are you making such a fuss about, Annie?" protested Rose, "I am telling you as fast as you will let me. I came out this morning for the express purpose, and I thought—I was almost sure—you would be amused and interested, instead of 'getting into a wax'"—using one of Hester Jennings's slang words, which set Annie's fine little teeth on edge. "It is you who ought to explain and apologize to me," proceeded Rose, boldly; "I am surely at liberty to make the acquaintance of anybody you know without your looking annoyed, and accusing me of being foolish and nonsensical. It is very unjust and ungrateful of you besides, for he spoke very highly of you," Rose finished innocently.

"He spoke highly of me to my own sister!" repeated Annie, her lips curling with unutterable disdain, and her cheeks in a wilder flame than ever. "He had nothing to do speaking of me at all. And how did he come to speak to you? I insist upon your telling me, Rose. I am older than you, and we are alone in London. I am answerable for you to father and mother."

"Well, I always thought I was answerable for myself," said Rose, indignantly. "But I don't want to conceal anything from you; it is insulting me to suppose so," and Rose showed herself highly resentful in her turn. "As to how I met and spoke with Dr. Harry Ironside, I was just coming to that," she was going on deliberately, when she was stopped by Annie's irritable protest—

"I wish you would not bring forward that man's name and dwell upon it in the way you are doing."

"Why, Annie, what ails you?" cried Rose in her bewilderment at Annie's unreasonableness and excitement, forgetting any verdict that might be passed on her own neglect of the code of conduct imposed upon her.

"Well, if you only knew how I have been tried—and molested—and laughed at," Annie began wrathfully, saying the last words as if to be laughed at was equivalent to being burnt alive. Then she stopped short and turned again upon Rose. "What have you been doing? tell me this instant, Rose."

"I don't think you ought to speak to me in this manner," said Rose, rebelliously, holding her head high in the air, and forgetting in her soreness of spirit either to crumple her nose or wrinkle her forehead; "and I am not at all ashamed of myself. I have done nothing wrong; indeed, I believe I have conferred a real benefit on Mrs. Jennings, though she is apt to put it the other way, and indirectly on Hester. I *am* fond of Mrs. Jennings and Hester—*they* always treat me, even Hester does, like a rational creature. Oh! you need not fret and fume—I am not trying to avoid telling you, though you have no right, no sister has, to demand an account of my proceedings. Father and mother may have, but they would never brandish their rights in my face or refuse to trust me. I was coming home from Covent Garden on Saturday afternoon, carrying a little pot of tulips for my picture, if you must know, and I had also got a small parcel from 'Burnet's.' I was caught in the thunderstorm. I was standing in a doorway not knowing what to do when a gentleman passed—Dr. Harry Ironside, if I am to be allowed to say his name, though I did not know it then. He was good-natured and polite, like any other gentleman. He saw how I was encumbered, and he must have felt the pelting rain. He stopped and asked if he could do anything for me—call a cab or anything, and he wished to give me the use of his umbrella till we reached a cab-stand or till an omnibus came up. I thought I had better tell him why I was carrying things, for he might have thought me just a shop-girl, so I merely said I required them for a painting, and that I was learning to be an artist. He seemed to think he ought to tell me in return what he was, and he said he was a doctor. Then I said father was a doctor too, Dr. Millar of Redcross. He cried out at that something about a likeness which he had seen, and he asked had I a sister a nurse in St. Ebbe's, and oh! Annie, he looked so pleased, and he did say you were such a favourite with the matron and the doctors."

"Stop!" cried Annie, peremptorily, with an evident storm raging in her gentle breast, to which she was too proud and self-restrained to give free expression, "you are a greater baby than May is. You are not fit to be left to yourself—a girl who would speak to any man she might meet in the streets of London, and tell him all about herself and her family."

The accusation was too outrageous to be received with anything save indignant silence.

"And then, I suppose, the next thing was you took him to Mrs. Jennings and arranged between you that he and his sister should board there."

"I did not," Rose was goaded to speak. "When he had walked so far with me in the rain I could not do less than invite him into the house. Then I believe he gave his name, and Mrs. Jennings, who has a great deal of knowledge of the world and a great deal of discrimination," put in poor Rose with much emphasis, "seemed to like him immensely. She found that one of her sons knew relations of his in Manchester, and they had other friends in common. He spoke of his sister, who is with him, and of their not liking living in lodgings, and who glad he would be if there ever happened to be a vacancy in Mrs. Jennings's establishment which she would permit them to fill. She referred him to Susan to see if there were rooms which the Ironsides could have. It all came about quite naturally, and was settled in less time than I have taken to tell it, and I had nothing whatever to do with it. I should not dream of taking it upon me to interfere with Mrs. Jennings's or anybody else's domestic affairs."

"I do not know," said Annie, gloomily, "after the mess you have got yourself and other people into. But there is one thing I can tell you for your satisfaction, I shall not put my foot within Mrs. Jennings's door so long as he—as Dr. Ironside and his sister are staying there. You may keep your friends to yourself and do without your sister. You can take them instead of me; perhaps you will not miss me or care for the loss of an occasional hour or two of my society."

"Oh! Annie, how can you say so?" Rose was reduced to expostulation and pleading. "What has come over you? You must not stay away; it would be so unkind to me, so rude to everybody, and such a marked slight. We are all so happy when you come to Welby Square, and I am sure the change is good for you too. How can you be so cross?"

"No," said Annie with unbending decision, "it shall not be said of me that I went and struck up a friendship, apart from our intercourse in the wards, with any doctor at St. Ebbe's—one of the medical students, the other day! I am not going to make his sister's acquaintance and get up an intimacy with her, because you have chosen to introduce them to Mrs. Jennings. A fine story to be circulated, and tittered over, about a girl; a fine example to the working nurses, who are always seeking to evade the rules, to become on familiar terms with their patients and to gossip and philander with them, when they ought to have a great deal more to do. I call it disgusting trifling, and it was not for that I came up to London to be trained as a nurse."

Annie kept her word to Rose's and other people's deep chagrin. She made no further ferment about what had happened. She did not write home and complain of Rose's thoughtlessness, or take a single step to prevent Mrs. Jennings securing a profitable pair of boarders—as a matter of fact, she dropped the subject, perhaps she felt a little ashamed of the animus she had shown. But for nearly three months, if Rose wished to see her sister, the only plan was for her to go to St. Ebbe's, or to make an appointment with Annie at the Academy or the British Museum, or to eat their lunch together at some convenient restaurant.

In whatever manner Annie disposed of her few spare moments,

not one of them was now spent in Welby Square—just at the time, too, when the boarding-house was particularly social and cheerful (for the new-comers found special favour with the old, and promoted much good fellowship). At least Dr. Harry Ironside did. He was a young fellow born to be popular whether he would or not; handsome, with pleasant manners, kind-hearted, possessed of a respectable competence independent of his profession, to which he brought considerable abilities and great singleness of purpose. Everybody "took" to him, from crusty Mr. Foljambe to jaunty Mr. Lyle; from Miss Perkins, whose ear-trumpet he improved upon, to old Susan, into whose gold-rimmed spectacles he put new glasses which made her see like a girl again. The one drawback to his success in everything he aimed at was, that he was always tremendously in earnest, so that his very earnestness overweighted him, rendering him incapable of measuring obstacles, and marshalling his forces, as a more indifferent man might have done.

His sister Kate, apart from such importance as might be implied in her finding herself presently in the enjoyment of a very pretty little income for a young lady, was a simple, good-natured school-girl, in the echoing and imitative stage of school-girl life. She looked up to her brother in everything, and was disposed to regard whatever was by his decree as infallibly best.

Yes, Annie kept her word after the fashion of most of us, till she saw good reason to break it. She announced herself changeless till she changed, which, to do her justice, was when the interests of others, still more than her own, cried out against her maintaining her resolution.

CHAPTER XVII

MAY HAS TO FIGHT HER OWN BATTLE

All May's frantic efforts at resistance were useless; her destiny was too strong for her. She had to go away from her mother and father, Dora, and Tray, and face life all by herself as one of the girl-graduates at Thirlwall Hall, St. Ambrose's. Dr. Millar had learnt that she would just be in reasonable time for one of the earlier examinations at the close of the term. Having passed it without difficulty, she might compete for one of the Thirlwall scholarships. If she got that—as he allowed himself to think she had a fair chance of doing—it would greatly increase her status, as well as aid in defraying the expenses of her residence at St. Ambrose's. The little Doctor was feverishly anxious to compass both ends for his pet and scholar. In her own interest no notice must be taken of her heart-broken looks, though it wrung a manly heart, in addition to the tender hearts of Mrs. Millar and Dora, to witness May's desperate unwillingness to depart.

It will be better to throw a veil over the anguish of that leave-taking, including the final closeting with Tray and the torrents of tears shed on his irresponsive hairy coat. We shall draw up the curtain on a new scene—St. Ambrose's, in its classic glory and stately beauty, and Thirlwall Hall, in its youthful strong-mindedness.

Poor May felt horribly forlorn when her father left her behind, and she realized that she was for the first time in her life

Sarah Tytler

compelled to play her part without the support of kith or kin. Nobody was in the least unkind to her, any more than the conservative Miss Stones had been to Rose, unless in calling "little May" "Miss Millar," a promotion which somehow cut her to the heart.

The lady principal, Miss Lascelles, was an excellent intellectual woman, of mingled aristocratic and *spirituelle* antecedents. In another country and nation she might have been a distinguished *dame de salon*. As it was, she was sufficiently harassed and overworked in her double office of decorous, authoritative chaperon and qualified guide, philosopher, and friend to the girls under her charge. These might be vestal virgins or nymphs of Minerva, but they were also girls, so long as the world lasted—the most of them half curious, half friendly where May was concerned. This was true even of the wonderful young American who came and stayed with no other object in view than to say she had kept her terms at St. Ambrose's, according to what was the sum total of the ambition of many a young man at the great University. She *would* call the Atlantic "the herring pond," and speak of "fixing" her hair; still she was a girl like the rest of them. Miss Lascelles, with all the other ladies in residence at Thirlwall Hall, the American included, could not help wondering what the friends and guardians of a budding beauty and helpless baby like Miss Millar intended by sending her to live among a set of self-reliant, amply-occupied young women, who, as a rule, knew exactly what they wanted to do and did it.

The whole place and system overwhelmed May. The hoary dignity of the old colleges, receptacles of the concentrated learning of ages, the crowds of capped and gowned tutors and professors, potent representatives of the learning of the present, even the shoals of young men who were able to care for none of these things, and to carry their responsibilities lightly, all to be encountered in the course of a morning walk, struck May with a sense of inadjustable disproportion, and of intolerable presumption on her part in pretending to be a scholar. She was still one of a household largely composed of women, as she had been at home, but here the household was planted where it was an innovation, in the midst of a colony of men, which constantly threatened to sweep over it and submerge it.

The grown-up, independent, yet disciplined routine of Thirlwall Hall, founded as closely as possible on the venerable routine of the men's colleges, was widely, crushingly different from life in the Old Doctor's House at Redcross. Morning chapel, the steady business of individual reading, the attendance on the selected courses of lectures, with the new experience of being spoken to, and expected to take notes like men; the walks and talks, which even with the interruptions of tennis and boating were apt to be academically shoppy; the very afternoon tea after evening chapel had an impressively scholastic flavour utterly foreign to the desultory proceedings of an ordinary family circle. So had the further reading by one's self, for one's self, to get up a particular branch of study; the "swell dinner," as May persisted in calling it in her own mind, though it was simple and social enough—beyond certain indispensable forms and ceremonies—to the initiated; the withdrawal once more to the dreary retirement of her own room, since a new girl had neither the requisite familiarity nor the heart to go and tap at her neighbours' doors, where no substitute for "sporting the oak" had as yet been found, and drop in for a little purely human chatter.

May was so "hard hit," as people say—not with love, but with home-sickness—that she did not believe she could live to the end of the summer term. She felt as if she must die of strangeness, fright, and pining; and that was hard, for they would be very sorry at home, and so would Annie and Rose in London, though both of them had been able to go and stay away quite cheerfully like the girls at Thirlwall Hall. Perhaps May and Dora were not like other girls. There was something wanting or something in excess about them. Perhaps they were not fit to go through the world, as she had once heard somebody say of her—May. Perhaps they were meant to die young—like their Aunt Dolly—and not destined to live long and struggle helplessly with adverse circumstances. In that case,

Dora was the happy one to be left to spend her short life at home, though, save for father and mother, she too was all alone, and poor dear Dora would feel that, and was, perhaps, crying in another empty room as May was crying in hers at this very moment; but at least, Dora would pass her last days with father and mother in the old familiar places.

This isolated doom for herself and Dora fascinated May's imagination. She could not get it out of her head. She dreamt about it, and sat up in her bed crying and shivering in the silence and solitude of night, where even by day all was silent and solitary. She began to think that she would never see Redcross or her mother again. With the morbid sentimentality of early youth, and its lively capacity for self-torture, in which to be sure there is that underlying luxury of woe, she commenced to rehearse the loving farewells she would take on paper, and the harrowing last messages she would send to every member of her family.

Occasionally May's hallucination took the form of conjuring up a series of disasters which should suddenly descend on her absent friends. If she did not die herself, one or all of those she loved might die while she was separated from them. Her father might fall down in a fit; her mother might be seized with small-pox or typhoid fever; and what more likely than that Dora should catch the infection waiting on her mother?

This distempered frame of mind was hardly calculated for the rapid reception and assimilation of these particles, terminations, and cases of philological nicety in which May began to recognize that she was inaccurate and deficient.

If Tray could but have come to her, and laid his shining black nose in her lap, barked in her face, and invited her to take a turn in the grounds of Thirlwall Hall, he would have ceased to be the doleful, shadowy phantom of a Tray she was constantly seeing now, along with other phantoms. A game of romps with her four-footed friend would have done something to dissipate the mental sickness which was prostrating May's powers. But

Thirlwall Hall was moulded on the men's colleges, and there were no dogs for the girl any more than for the boy graduates.

Miss Lascelles was at once conscientious and kind, with considerable natural sagacity; but she led a busy, rather over-burdened life, and had little time to spare. Naturally she was tempted, in spite of the logical faculty which made her a capital principal of Thirlwall Hall, to leap at conclusions like many of her weaker-minded sisters. She had taken it for granted that Miss Millar was simply a spoilt child, without more ability and information than had just served her to surmount the preliminary test of admission to Thirlwall Hall, where, nevertheless, she had no business to be. Her time would be completely wasted; she would only be wretched, and serve to make other people uncomfortable. However, as she had stood the preliminary test, and was at Thirlwall Hall for the rest of the term, the most humane thing to do was to set some other girl who was not particularly engaged on her own account, who could be safely trusted with such a charge, who had plenty of acquaintances at St. Ambrose's to render the charge lighter, to make friends with the poor girl, take her about, cheer and entertain her, as far as possible, till the end of her stay.

Miss Lascelles, in default of better, fixed on Miss Vanhansen, the American young lady, as a friend for May. Miss Vanhansen had plenty of time on her hands, plenty of confidence, plenty of money. She had taken even exclusive St. Ambrose's by storm, for Athens itself would have found it difficult to resist her racy indifference, her shrewd mother-wit, her superb frocks, and her sublime heaps of dollars. At the same time she was perfectly good-natured and quite trustworthy in her own free and easy way. She had scandalized Miss Lascelles in the earlier days of their acquaintance by her energetic determi-nation to have "a good time of it." She had made the lady principal's hair stand on end by calmly suggesting nice rides and rows and luncheons at village inns, *tete-a-tete* with the "mooniest" young fellows who could be laid hold of and crammed with stories about America and the doings of

American girls.

But practically Miss Vanhansen had the good sense to do at Rome as the Romans did; she confined her independence to those sallies of the tongue, which were not without a rousing charm in a place grown partly languid, partly esoteric, by dint of a superabundance of culture and of college statutes elaborate, involved and irreversible as the laws of the Medes and the Persians.

Keturah Vanhansen rather liked the task imposed upon her. It appealed at once to her kindliness of nature and her love of creating a sensation; she would rouse this drooping young beauty who showed such a sinful disregard of her complexion and eyes. Miss Vanhansen was herself as sallow as a nabob, her small eyes, by an unkind perversity on the part of her fairy god-mother, were of a fishy paleness, yet she managed to her great satisfaction, by dint of dress and carriage, to be a striking-looking and all but a handsome girl, so that she had no overpowering reason to be jealous of her better-endowed neighbours. She would astonish Miss Millar's weak nerves, and give her "a wrinkle or two," before she had done with her.

At first May shrank back a good deal from the advances of the conquering princess from the Far West; but here the English girl's humility and good feeling stood her in better stead than her judgment. May was grateful to Miss Vanhansen, and went so far as to be flattered by her attentions even when they gave the recipient no pleasure. That frame of mind could not last at seventeen. May, the most unsophisticated and easily pleased of human beings, was won from her sad dreams of Redcross. She was deeply obliged, she was faintly amused. At last she was fairly launched on such a mild course of St. Ambrose gaieties as two girls in a college could with grace pursue. This included tennis parties, rowing parties, water-lily and fritillary hunts, "strawberries," concerts instead of lectures in the afternoons as well as in the evenings, afternoon teas—not *tete-a-tete*, not confined to a party of three, but under what even Miss Lascelles would have considered sufficient surveillance in the rooms of liberal heads of houses, hospitable young dons, social, idle undergraduates. These had no more business on their hands than could be summed up in cricket-matches or boat-races, and in meeting Miss Vanhansen and listening to her queer unconventional remarks.

At all these gatherings, May Millar in the budding beauty of seventeen and the simplicity of her youthful dress, with her modesty and *naivete*, was made very welcome. Soon she began to feel herself ashamed of the extent to which she was enjoying herself, as she was swept along by the stream.

She was able to write home now long letters full of girlish enthusiasm over the kindness of Miss Vanhansen, and the beauties and delights of St. Ambrose's. Dora, though greatly relieved in her ungrudging devotion to May, to find that Tom Robinson's words were fulfilled, was still a little puzzled to understand how May could find time for so many gay doings, and her studies into the bargain. But Dr. and Mrs. Millar could only be happy in the happiness of their child, and hug themselves on having thought more of her welfare than of her feelings at the moment of parting. It was right she should see all the charming sights which were to be seen, and enter a little into the special attractions of the great University town—*that* would not prevent her from settling down and doing her proper work presently. You might trust the lady principal and a studious young creature like May, who liked to be busy with her books far before any other occupation, with a great deal more license than that came to.

Then a new turn was given to the dissipation in which May was dipping. The longing in which she had indulged, ever since she had first heard of its possible fulfilment, was granted—a Greek play was to be acted by the young women who stood for the "Grecians" of the year at Thirlwall Hall, and May was there to see. From the moment the play was decided upon to the hour of the first rehearsal, May spoke, thought, and dreamed of nothing save "Alcestis."

Miss Vanhansen gave her up in disgust. "The ungrateful, soft-spoken wretch!" cried the forsaken fair one; "the hypocritical young blue-grass Penelope Blue! she has been bluer than the blue clouds all the time she has been imposing on me as a pining, bread-and-butter, home-sick miss among us Titanesses and daughters of the gods. Here I am ready to collapse with trotting her about among the few girls in St. Ambrose's who are sensible enough not to know the Empire of the East from the Empire of the West, and would not care which was which if they did know, and the still wiser young men who spend the long summer days lying on their backs in their own canoes, reading Mark Twain. Oh! she is a brazen-faced impostor. 'Molasses!' and 'Great Scott!' are not enough to say to her. I should like to try her with the final polite remarks of the last chief of the Dogs' Noses."

But contemporaneously with May's being thus dropped by her first friend, she was peremptorily claimed and appropriated by the actresses. They had not failed to notice her interest in their enterprise, and some of the cleverest of them had already mastered an astonishing problem.

They had been guilty of nicknaming Miss Millar "Baby," because she had been so lachrymose and shiftless when she came to Thirlwall Hall, and had never looked up till she was handed over to Miss Vanhansen, who had given her "airings" and "outings" all very well for a baby, and much to Baby's taste as it seemed, but not exactly severe study. Yet in spite of it all, and in spite of the halting inaccuracy of the training in a private ladies'-school, May Millar knew more by sheer instinct, as it sounded, of Alcestis, and felt more with her and for her, than the best of those who professed to be her interpreters.

It was therefore not with wisely repairing the breaches in her Latin and Greek, and laying these foundations afresh, as Rose was doing with her art under Mr. St. Foy in London, that May was engrossed. It was with becoming a bond-slave to those ambitious players. She lent herself to the minutest details of their attempt, coached herself in them day and night, till she could coach everybody in turn, and figured behind backs as universal prompter, dresser, stage-manager—the girl who had been so lifeless and incapable of looking after herself when she first came among them that they had styled her the baby of the establishment!

Miss Lascelles, who was deeply interested in the play, both in her highly-finished scholarship, and for the credit of Thirlwall Hall, was electrified when she discovered the efficient coadjutor whom the performers had found. "I am afraid there has been a mistake made, and time lost," she said to herself ruefully. "How could I be so shortsighted, when there is the making of the finest scholar in the Hall in Miss Millar, who threatened to hang so heavily on my hands that I was fain to send her to play with our generous 'Barbarian.' What discrimination, what taste and feeling with regard to the selection and fit declamation of these passages which we were doubtful whether to retain or reject, or what to do with them! With what pretty girlish shyness and timidity she made the suggestions! Nothing but her passionate love of the subject, and her jealousy for its honour, as it were, with her intense craving to have it fitly expressed, would have induced her to come forward. I should like to hear what Professor Hennessy," naming a great name among classical authorities, "thinks of this young girl's interpretation of several parts of the play when he comes to hear them. I should like to introduce Miss Millar to him if she were not so frightened, and if she had taken the place which she ought to have held to begin with. It is too late to rectify the mistake and set her to work this term, and she had much better not go in for the Markham scholarship which her father spoke of—that would be worse than useless. But we'll turn over a new leaf next term. After all, she is very young; and I suppose it is of no great consequence that she has wasted her first half. Her family are professional people, and these are generally well off." (Miss Lascelles was the portionless daughter of the impecunious younger son of a poor nobleman.)

When the play was performed nearly all the classical scholars of

St. Ambrose's—and what was a man doing at St. Ambrose's if he were not a classical scholar, unless, to be sure, he happened to be a philosopher of the first water, or a profound expounder of Anglo-Saxon, or a strangely and wonderfully informed pundit?—came with their wives and daughters, and graciously applauded the daring deed.

As for Keturah Vanhansen, she wore her *riviere* of diamonds, dripping, dancing, flashing like water that was perpetually flowing, and yet, by some enchantment, arrested in its flow in glorious suspension. Set in the middle of the enchanted water was such a breast-knot of rare, exquisite, uncannily grotesque orchids as no queen or princess had ever been seen to wear in St. Ambrose's. Indeed, it might have suited the Queen of Sheba.

Miss Vanhansen announced that she wore her war-paint to do honour to the Thirlwall Hall play, and to May Millar, whom she had forgiven, for rancour never yet dwelt in the Yankee breast. "Alcestis" was a little long, and "real right down funny," as her Aunt Sally would have said, though it was a tragedy, and she, Keturah Vanhansen, did not understand a word of it, notwithstanding this was her last year at Thirlwall Hall. One good joke was the man who was in cats' skins, and carried a kitchen poker for a club, and was half a head shorter than she was, and she was not big; they should see her Aunt Abe if they wanted to know what a big woman was like. Another joke was the sacks for the ladies' frocks, with holes for the head and feet, and holes for the arms, so nice and simple, and so graceful; Worth ought to get a hint of the costume. Only it was not very distinctive, when one regarded the corresponding sacks for the gentlemen. There was really nothing to mark out the ladies except the large towels which they wore hanging down their backs, while the gentlemen had Inverness capes over their sacks, fastened on the shoulders with Highland brooches. How came the Greeks, in the time of Euripides, to know about Inverness capes and Highland brooches? She, Keturah Vanhansen, had been so startled by what she feared might be a frightful anachronism that all her false hair had fallen off, and she had been left like one of her Aunt Abe's moulting fowls.

The truth was that, in the matter of hair, nature had favoured Miss Vanhansen with a peculiarly fine and luxuriant crop, so that she had no need to apply to art for its help.

But as for May, she saw nothing and heard nothing of the discrepancies which might mar the ancient story to far less ostentatiously matter-of-fact and mocking critics than the would-be barbarian from beyond the herring-pond. The piteous tragedy was enacted in all its terror and pathos to May. She forgot even to sigh for one of the original great open-air amphitheatres, with the cloudless blue sky of Greece overhead, which had been the fit setting to those old-world plays; while she appreciated, without being conscious of the appreciation, every scenic item—the double stage, the attendant chorus, the classic dress, that had awakened Miss Vanhansen's ridicule, from the sandal on the foot to the toque on the head—all which could lend verisimilitude to the spectacle. For the benefit of happy May, Alcestis lived again in modern St. Ambrose's. Once more she suffered and died willingly in the room of Admetus; once more the miserable husband's half-heroic, half-savage ally, Harakles, fought Death for his pale prey, and brought back the sacrificed wife from Hades, to restore her—a figure veiled and motionless, yet instinct with glad life, every vein throbbing with love and thankfulness—to the arms of her husband, more joyful, and at the same time, in the middle of his joy, more full of yearning sorrow and self-abasement than ever was happy bridegroom.

On the day after the play, Miss Lascelles casually mentioned to May that even if she went in for the coming examination, she, Miss Lascelles, thought May had better not try for the Markham scholarship.

"But I must, Miss Lascelles," protested May, starting up as if she were awakening from a dream, and opening great eyes of distress and apprehension—feelings which were only at that moment called into life. "My father would be so vexed and disappointed if I did not."

"If you will take my advice, my dear, you will wait till next year; there will be another scholarship falling in then. Very many of the Thirlwall Hall girls do much better the second year than they have done the first," Miss Lascelles continued to warn her girl-graduate, with the delicate consideration and tact which qualified the lady principal for her office. "It is bad policy to enter hastily into a competition with failure staring you in the face. It will only serve to dishearten you, and to mislead people with regard to what I am now certain—I can honestly congratulate you on my conviction—are your really exceptional gifts. You will do Thirlwall Hall credit, and we shall all be proud of you, if you will have patience. You are very young; you can afford to wait. It is a common occurrence for clever, studious girls, and lads too, to come up to St. Ambrose's from the country, from private schools or home-teaching, who are not sufficiently exact in their scholarship, and do nothing beyond remedying the defect in their first or even their second year. You don't grudge giving what is but a fraction of your life, after all, to thorough as opposed to superficial learning, do you, dear? Remember, the one is worthy and the other worthless—a mere pretentious waste."

"I cannot help it," said May, with a little gasp of despair. "To wait is just what I cannot afford to do. I am almost certain that my coming up next year depends on what I can do this term. We have grown quite poor. Father has lost a great deal of money lately. Even if he were content to send me back here, I do not think it would be right in me to come, unless I could do something to lessen the expense. My sister Annie is in London learning to be a nurse, and my sister Rose is coming out as an artist."

"I thought they were doing it from choice. Why did you not apply yourself before, Miss Millar? You knew what you could do, better than any of us here could possibly guess your talents and attainments. From your general behaviour until the play was started, I for one, I confess, fell into the grave error of supposing that you could do little or nothing, or that any progress you had made was entirely forced work." Miss Lascelles spoke sharply, for she was considerably discomfited, and full of unavailing regret for her share in the misadventure.

May could not tell her that she had been too miserable about coming away from home, and leaving her mother and father, Dora and Tray, to apply herself to learning; neither would there have been much use in her applying if she had been destined to fade away presently as she had imagined, and to die, bereft, among the lexicons, commentaries, and lecture-notes of Thirlwall Hall. She preferred to say with meek contriteness that she knew she had been very idle, but she would do her best to atone for her idleness by working every lawful moment of every hour of the few weeks which were left to her, if Miss Lascelles would but allow her to go in for the examination, preparatory to trying for the scholarship.

Miss Lascelles could not prevent her, she told May a little dryly, for the students of Thirlwall Hall, though some of them were no more than seventeen—May's age—were all regarded and treated as grown-up young women capable of judging and acting for themselves. What Miss Lascelles was bound to do was to see that Miss Millar did not run into the opposite extreme, and bring on a brain fever by over-study. "And you know, my dear," finished the kind, experienced woman, who was easily softened, who had always the greatest difficulty to keep from being sympathetic, "that would be a great deal worse than merely being turned back in your examinations, though Dr. Millar is not rich, and there may be obstacles—I sincerely trust they will not be insurmountable—to your coming back in the autumn, to work with a will and at the same time with moderation."

Poor May did not work herself into a brain fever, but she did in other respects exactly as Miss Lascelles—a woman who understood the position—had clearly foreseen. May succeeded in fretting, and worrying, and getting herself into a state of nervous agitation. Her brain, or that part of it which had to do with grammatical declensions, derivations, rules, and principles, became a complete muddle, so that in place of taking in new information, it seemed to be rapidly letting go the old which it had once held securely.

Before the eventful day of May's examination, she had lost the last shred of hope, and so had all who had heard her or formed a correct estimate of the contents of her papers, of her crossing the rubicon. Of her own accord she sorrowfully refrained from making any move to enter the lists for the scholarship.

It is the fashion at St. Ambrose's not to issue the result of the examinations for a considerable number of weeks, during which the unhappy candidates hang on the tenterhooks of expectation. A looker-on is inclined to consider this a refinement of cruelty till he or she has taken into consideration that the motive of the protracted suspense is to suit the convenience and lessen the arduous labours of the toil-worn professors and tutors who serve as examiners.

But in May Millar's case her failure was such a foregone conclusion, was so remedial by reason of her youth, and so qualified by the share she had taken in the Greek play, that a point was stretched for her, and she was privately put out of pain at once. Latterly May had not entertained the slightest expectation of any other sentence, yet the blow fell so heavily upon her that it was well it was the end of the term.

To do Thirlwall Hall no more than justice, everybody was sorry for their youngest, gentlest, prettiest, most inspired, and withal most inoffensive and obliging student. Miss Lascelles took May into her private sitting-room and recklessly lavished the few moments the lady principal had in which to rest and recruit from the fatigue of receiving company, and playing a becoming part in the academical gaieties with which the summer term at St. Ambrose's closes, in order to speak encouraging words to the poor crestfallen child. Miss Vanhansen implored May to cross the herring-pond at her expense, and have a good time among the Barbarian's relations in Ol' Virginny and Kentuck. The girl who had played Alcestis wanted to inaugurate a reading-party in which May should be coached all round every day. Failing this, the same adventurous spirit would get up a series of Greek plays in London drawing-rooms, with Miss Millar's assistance; and so far as she herself was concerned, she would never be contented till Miss Millar played Admetus to her Alcestis. A large deputation of blue-stockinged maidens from Thirlwall Hall escorted May to the railway station, and more than one was relieved to find that she was going first to join her sisters in London instead of carrying the mortification of her failure straight to her country-town home.

It might be the deferring of an ordeal, and yet it was with a white face, as abashed and well-nigh as scared as if she had committed a crime, that May awaited Annie in the drawing-room to which the probationers' friends were free at St. Ebbe's. The consciousness had come too late of having wasted the little money her father had to spare on sentimental self-indulgence and the gratification of her own feelings instead of employing it as it was meant to be employed, in controlling herself and doing her duty, so as to acquire fitting arms for the battle of life.

It was this horrible comprehension which made her wistful eyes grow distended and fixed in their sense of guilt and disgrace. She might have committed a forgery, and be come to tell Annie what she had done. May was essentially one-idea'd at this period of her life, and she had dwelt on the fact of her failure and exaggerated its importance, like the most egotistical of human beings, till it filled her imagination and blotted out every other consideration.

Annie, in the full career of a busy professional morning, snatched a moment between two important engagements to see her sister.

May looked with imploring, fascinated eyes at Annie in her nurse's gown and cap. The younger girl had some faint inkling

Sarah Tytler

of Annie's earlier experience in the life of an hospital; yet there she was as fresh and fair and bright as ever—a thousand times cooler and happier-looking than her visitor.

"Here you are, May," Annie was saying in glad greeting, as she held her sister by the two shoulders, after she had kissed her; "and I declare you have grown since you went to St. Ambrose's. Oh, you incorrigible girl, when you were so much the tallest of us before you went there."

May could only make one answer with parched lips, faltering tongue, and eyes dry under their heavy cloud of grief, "Annie, I have failed in my examination!"

Annie started in surprise, while her face fell for a second. "What a pity!" she could not help exclaiming. "Father will be—" She broke off in the middle of the sentence. "Don't fret about it," she added, quickly taking another look into May's face; "that will do no good, and it is not very much after all. I cannot stay another minute now, May," she went on to tell the bewildered girl in the most matter-of-fact tone, so that May was in danger of feeling half-offended at finding her tribulation taken so cavalierly—"just like Annie!"

"You must wait for me," Annie was saying further. "There is a poor fellow—a patient of mine—who is to have his arm amputated this morning, and I must be with him when it is done."

"Oh dear!" cried May, completely taken aback, "that is dreadful. Will he die, Annie? Will he die?" forgetting all her own high-strung woes, the product of an advanced stage of civilization, in heart-felt, human sympathy with the most primitive of all trials—bodily suffering and loss.

"Not if we can help it, please God," said Annie emphatically. Then an inspiration came to her as she gazed on the girl's white quivering face. "You have been working too hard, 'little May'; you shake your head like a tragedy queen. Then you've been worrying too much, which is a great deal worse. I shall take you in hand, but I can't stay to talk about it. Just you think how little my poor fellow would mind not passing an examination, in comparison with the loss of an arm— fortunately it is the left one. He is a printer who got his arm crushed under one of the great rollers, and he has a wife and five little children dependent on their bread-winner."

Annie was gone, leaving May suddenly transported out of herself, and plunged into the trials of her neighbours, the awfully near, common life-and-death trials, of which she had known so little. Her own seemed to sink into insignificance beside them. St. Ambrose's and its intellectual lists and wordy contests, even its lofty abstruse thoughts—excellent things in their way, without which the unlettered world would become rude, sordid and narrow—faded into the background. She forgot everything but the poor man passing through a mortal crisis, with Annie able to succour him in his need, and his wife and children waiting to hear whether the end were life or death.

May held her breath, and watched, prayed, and waited in her turn, with no thought left for the news she had brought to town, and was to carry to Redcross. What did it signify if only the poor man lived when May herself was well and strong, and all her dear friends were in health, and likely to be spared to her.

When Annie came in again with a cheerful face, and said, "He has stood it wonderfully; there is every prospect of his making a speedy recovery," May's face too cleared till for the moment it was almost radiant. She acquiesced, with responsive ani- mation, in Annie's arrangement that since she, Annie, had got leave of absence for the rest of the day she would put on her walking-dress, and she and May too would go and pick up Rose at Mr. St. Foy's class-rooms; and what was to hinder all the three from having an expedition together in the fine summer weather to Hampton Court, or Kew, or the Crystal Palace, thus celebrating May's visit to town, and making the most of Annie's holiday? It would be like dear old times of primrose hunting, blue-bell gathering, maying, and nutting down at Redcross before the cares and troubles of the world had taken hold of the girls. Annie had already sent on May's luggage to Welby Square, to which May would return with Rose. Annie excluded herself carefully from this part of the programme, with a kind of unapproachable haughtiness which had three strains of stubbornness and one strain of fiery youthful anger in its composition, while it was a complete enigma to May. But all she cared to know was that she was going with her own two sisters for an entire afternoon's delightful excursion. In the morning she had felt that she could never have the heart to be happy again. Even yet she would not be quite happy; she would be very much affronted when she was telling Annie and Rose the particulars of her, May's, silliness and selfishness; how she had given herself up to moping, and then how she had played herself—first with the St. Ambrose gaieties, and later with the Greek play, instead of setting about her work methodically and diligently. Annie would, perhaps, tell her a few home-truths, and Rose would crumple up her nose, shake her head, and look superhumanly wise—Rose who in the old days had been more thoughtless than May.

Still she deserved it all a thousand times over, and it would be a relief to have disburdened herself of the sorry tale.

Her own sisters would defend her from every other assailant. They would feel for her, seek to reassure her, even make much of her, as they were doing by taking her away with them this afternoon. May was very sensible that a burden was lifted off her back.

CHAPTER XVIII

DORA IS THE NEXT MESSENGER
WITH BAD TIDINGS

There is a curious feeling abroad in the world, that no two things happen alike on two days, or in two weeks, or months, running. If there has been a railway accident on Monday, there will certainly not be another of the same kind at the same place on Tuesday. Apart from the fresh precautions sure to be taken, it is not at all likely, in the chapter of accidents, that a facsimile will occur where the original has preceded it so recently. On a similar principle, if a man has been killed or badly injured by a fall from a horse, it goes against public opinion that his son or his brother should also be thus injured. If the singular repetition does take place, people will speak of it with bated breath, as of a fate or doom hanging over the family, and therefore bound to repeat itself again and again on the old lines. All this is in spite of the fact that there is such a word as "coincidence" in the language, and that there is hardly one of us who cannot remember several startling coincidences in the course of his or her history.

Annie Millar had an experience of the kind at this time. It was on the 20th of June that May arrived unannounced at St. Ebbe's to recount her lost battle. On the 21st Dora appeared, in a like unlooked-for manner, to divulge her sorrowful news.

Annie was much more troubled by the spectacle of Dora standing alone in the middle of the hospital drawing-room, pale and agitated, than she had been by the discovery of May in that very condition the day before. Annie's own colour died away while she ran forward and caught Dora's hand. "What is it, Dora? Has anything happened to father or mother?—yet if there had, you would not have left them and come up to town by yourself. Why are you here? Tell me quickly, for it is killing me to keep me in suspense."

"Don't be alarmed," entreated Dora's soft voice. "Father sent me up for the express purpose that you might not be alarmed when you heard. I must have managed badly to frighten you. I assure you nothing has happened, at least nothing very particular, only,—well, father is very rheumatic, and the warm weather has done him no good. He has not been out of the house for a month, though we did not mention it in our letters, always hoping that by the next time we wrote he would be better. But he has not left his room till he contrived to go in the cab yesterday. Oh! Annie, he has sold his business to Dr. Capes. He—father—said it was no use to protract the struggle, it was only doing more mischief; he would never be able, at his age, to go about again so as to act fairly by his patients. He has given up everything to the bank's creditors, and will pass through the bankruptcy court. He bade me tell you that he could see no other way, and he was afraid Rose or you might read his name in the *Gazette* without being prepared for it."

"Father ill, old, and a bankrupt!" Annie's cry was bitter. "It is hard after his long life of honourable industry. I can never forgive Mr. Carey."

"Hush! hush! Annie, you must not say that. Nothing would grieve father more. Nobody has suffered like the Careys. Besides, father always says that he alone was to blame for buying the bank shares. He did it of his own free-will, just that he might grow richer in the idlest manner possible for him to do so. Dr. Capes has taken our house, the Old Doctor's House too, and father and mother went into apartments—those over Robarts the book-seller's—yesterday, till they could look about them." Dora was crying quietly all the time she was speaking, and at the same time she was breaking off to say with pathetic resigned trust like her mother's, "But only think, Annie dear, how much worse it might have been! What a great deal we have to be thankful for. Look at poor Mr. Carey sitting paralyzed, and quite childish; and do you know the sad news arrived last night that poor poor Colonel Russell is dead? He had a sun-stroke, and died within twelve hours; he has not been three months at his new post. Dear father has all his senses, and he says himself he may live for years and years."

"I hope so," said Annie fervently; but it is doubtful whether she fully appreciated the blessings of her lot at that moment. She busied herself for a few minutes with Dora, her nurse's instinct as well as her affection telling her that Dora must be seen to first. Annie took off Dora's hat and jacket, seated her in the easiest chair, would hear nothing more till she— Annie—had learnt when Dora had breakfasted, and then rung for a basin of soup and made her swallow it. "Now, Dora," she said, sitting down by her sister, "tell me all there is to tell. What have father and mother to live upon? We must think and act for them now."

Dora explained as well as she was able, since, like her mother, she had no great head for business. In addition to the sum given for the good-will of Dr. Millar's practice, and for his house and furniture, which was to be paid over to the liquidators of the bank's debts, (in return for which the debtor would get a discharge from farther obligations,) a small percentage was to be allowed to him from his successor's fees.

"I am afraid it will be very small," Dora made the despondent remark, "because, though all his former patients are fond of father, they got to see he was breaking up, and did not like to send for him during the night, or at odd hours. Mother and I did what we could, going round for him and inquiring after his patients; but, as he said, such a make-shift could not last. We were always hearing of more families calling in Dr. Capes or Mr. Newton. Father declared he could not blame them; he would have done the same in their place, and that every dog must have his day."

"That was like father," said Annie, looking up with a fleeting sparkle in her eyes.

"Then we thought," went on Dora, "father and mother might have part of mother's money, since you have always said you did not need it, while Rose is getting paid for her work, and there is hardly any doubt" (brightening up,) "but that 'little May' will take the scholarship. She was working so hard to pass her examination when she wrote last, that she was quite out of spirits about her chances, which father says is always the way with the best men when they are going in for an examination that they are safe to win. He supposes it will be still more so with women. He tells mother that he will not mind taking help from her, where her money is concerned, when he can no longer stir from his chair—not to say to earn a fee, but to save his life. He has taken so much more help from her in other ways during all their married life, that this in addition will not count."

CHAPTER XIX

THE UNEMPLOYED—A FAMILIAR FACE

A lodging was found near the Hospital for Dora, who was to stay in town and look out for a situation; and for the next week, a week of hot summer weather, Annie, relieved from her hospital work, because it was her first holiday time, went to and fro, spending as little as possible on omnibus fares, with Dora and May in her train, in search of employment for them. People were beginning to leave town, and the time did not seem propitious. When was it ever propitious for such a pursuit where women are concerned? Even under Annie's able guidance, with the spirit which she could summon to her aid in all difficulties, the intentional and unintentional rebuffs which the two girl candidates, particularly Dora, got from agents and principals in connection with ladies in want of useful companions and nursery-governesses were innumerable. The swarms of needy, greedy applicants for similar situations whom the Millars were perpetually encountering in their rounds, were enough to cause the stoutest heart to quail, and to sink the most sanguine nature into the depths of despondency.

Dora Millar was not constitutionally sanguine, and she grew more and more nervous and dispirited as the fruitless efforts went on. Her little figure drooped, her eyes had a dejected expression, her lips quivered pathetically without any provocation. Annie was compelled to use strong language. "The idiots!" she exclaimed, *apropos* of the last persons who had found Dora too young or too old, not strong enough looking, or not lively enough looking ("not as if she could stand a large amount of bullying and worrying," Annie read between the lines). "What a chance they are letting slip through their fingers of getting the most unexacting, contented creature in the world to minister to their tiresome wants. They will never see her like again; serve them right for their blindness."

One particularly glaring, airless afternoon, the three sisters were toiling back to Dora's lodging, with the London pavement like heated iron under the feet of the crowds that trod it, and the cloudless sky, in which the sun blazed a ball of fire, like glowing brass over their heads. Then as the Millars turned a corner and looked longingly at the trees in a square with their leaves already yellowing and shrivelling, May uttered a little shriek of delight and darted forward to greet a familiar figure and face in the stream of strangers. What did it signify that the figure was insignificant by comparison, and the face with nothing distinguished in its pallor, under its red beard and moustache?—"a little foxy-headed fellow," any sharp-tongued bystander might have called him. It was a well-known face where all the others were drearily unknown, a Redcross face in London, the face of a man who might have shown himself an enemy, yet had proved a friend in need; and though there had been presented to the girls the bearing of a Jupiter and the lineaments of an Adonis, they could not have hailed him with greater gladness. If anybody hung back in the general acclamation it was Dora, for Annie did not say a word to rebuke May; she was too anxious to hear the last news of her father.

More than one man among the passers-by, glancing at Tom Robinson surrounded by a group of pretty girls, the two prettiest evidently making much of him and hanging on his words, called him in their minds "lucky dog," and speculated on the nature of the attraction.

"'*Prope'ty, prope'ty, prope'ty,*'" no doubt. It was disgraceful to see how mercenary even quite young women were getting.

Tom received the ovation, at which, by the bye, he was a little taken aback and puzzled, quietly and in a matter-of-fact way, as he received most things. He had had the pleasure of seeing Dr. and Mrs. Millar lately; indeed, he had availed himself of the privileges of an old friend to call on them at once in their new quarters, he told Annie, and he had found them, by their own account, fairly well and comfortable, though the Doctor was still dead lame.

Tom did not tell either Annie, or any one else interested in the information, that he had spent the last few days pushing the circulation of a subscription list, which he had headed with the promise of a handsome sum. It was to provide a testimonial not altogether inadequate to mark the esteem in which the townspeople held their old Doctor for his many virtues, and their sympathy with him in his misfortunes. A liberal offering on the town's part might do something to relieve the adversity which had befallen a fellow-townsman. The talk a little time ago had been of presenting Dr. Millar with a new brougham and horse, which, as they would have had to be maintained at the charge of a man who had just put down his old brougham as beyond his diminished income, was rather an illogical method of serving him. However, his complete breakdown, with the sale of his practice, had at once knocked that idea on the head, and had given its motive a much wider application. If the little Doctor were to submit to accept help, it must be commensurate with the dignity of Redcross and the county, and with his own professional status and merit.

Tom Robinson looked at the girls as two of them looked at him. "It is tiring weather," he suggested hesitatingly; "is it wise of you to walk out in the heat?"

"Oh! Mr. Robinson," cried May effusively, "we are so tired—just dead beat—though Annie there does not like me to talk slang—but it is so expressive, don't you think so? It is not to-day only, but yesterday and the day before, we have been hunting for situations, and have not found them yet. Do you know, Dora and I are going to take situations immediately if we can get them?"

His face changed, and he knit his brow involuntarily.

"What a magpie it is!" said Annie, impatiently. "But, of course, you have heard all about the turn father's affairs have taken since this bad rheumatic attack, which he does not believe he can shake off. It need not be any secret that my sisters are looking out for situations."

He did not answer; he was prevented by the painful conscious-ness that Dora appeared ready to sink into the ground.

"Won't you avail yourself of my arm, Miss Dora? Won't you let me see you home?" he proposed hurriedly.

She could not refuse; indeed, she was only too thankful for the offered support, though she murmured a protest against troub-ling him and taking him out of his way. And she could not altogether conceal how put out as well as weary she was, so that the little hand, which just touched his coat-sleeve, fluttered on its resting-place like a newly-caught bird.

He hailed a cab, and wished to put them all into it.

"I dare say it would be better," said Annie, glancing at Dora's white face, with the new trick of quivering which the lips had acquired. As the cab was driving up, she gave Tom Robinson their address—"17, Little St. Ebbe's Street," with the amount of the fare, looking at him almost fiercely while she took the money from her purse. "Will you be good enough to direct the man and pay him for us?" she said, and he dared not dispute her will.

But when he yielded, she seemed to think his friendliness and power of comprehension deserved something better than they had got. "Will you come with us?" Annie invited him; and when she softened, it was always in such a bright frank way that it was hard to resist her. "We'll be very pleased to give you a cup of tea at Dora's lodging—at least we can do that for you, and it may be acceptable on such an oppressive afternoon."

He, a guest at a lodging of Dora Millar's: it sounded odd enough!

"Do come, Mr. Robinson," his friend May was imploring, while Dora, sensible that something was due from her as the ostensible mistress of the lodging, echoed shyly, without raising her eyes to his face, "Yes, come, please."

Did she remember the last time she gave him tea in the drawing-room of the Old Doctor's House, where they were not likely to meet again? How awkward they found the *tete-a-tete*. How they shrank from their hands touching, while he reproached her for aiding and abetting May in trying to shirk going to St. Ambrose's; and she had borne his reproaches and admitted the reasonableness of his arguments, with all the meek candour of Dora, while still making a last stand for May.

He went with the girls as if he were in a dream; but he was not left to dream in Dora's very plain lodging, where Annie and not the mistress of the lodging poured out tea, and May insisted on helping him to bread and butter. He saw Rose, too, who had been awaiting the return of her sisters. It sent another pang to his brotherly heart to discover that Rose also was subdued and well-nigh careworn. She still wrinkled her forehead and crumpled up her nose, but it was no longer in the old saucy way; it was under her share of the heavy burden of trouble which had fallen on these dauntless girls and might end by crushing them.

May was not to be kept from the immense solace of making a clean breast to her former ally of her stupid dawdling and trifling, and the retribution which had at once befallen her. "Did father tell you, Mr. Robinson, that I have failed in my examination?" she began plaintively. "Yes, I have, and it was all my own fault. I was too silly; I would not pull myself together and work hard from the first. Now it will never be in my power to go back to St. Ambrose's. I'll not be able to atone for my folly by showing that everybody was not wrong when it was believed that I might be a fair scholar, win a scholarship, and rise to be classical mistress in a girls' school." At the announcement of the disastrous failure, by her own deed, of all the ambitious plans for her, May threatened to break down, springing up and turning away, her shoulders heaving in a paroxysm of mortification and grief.

Tom Robinson used to say, afterwards, that he never witnessed a prettier sight than the manner in which the three other girls rallied round their poor "little May," from Annie downwards. They took off her hat, pulled off her gloves, smoothed her ruffled hair, patted her tear-stained cheeks, seated her in an arm-chair, brought her tea, and made her drink it, bidding her not be too disheartened. They pledged themselves—even Dora pledged herself stoutly—that, if it rested with them, and they were young and strong, they would find work of one kind or another—May should go back to St. Ambrose's some day and vindicate her scholarliness. Father and mother and all of them would be proud of her.

It rendered the man doubly indignant from that day when he heard scoffers say that there could be no true friendship between women, and that the relation of sisters existed simply for the growth of rivalry and jealousy.

May was still shaking her head disconsolately, and reminding him, "Ah, Mr. Robinson, it would have been better if you had let me stay at home and go into your shop, like Phyllis Carey. I might have done some good there, though you may not believe it, and only feel glad that you got rid of me."

Then he took her in hand, and administered his consolation. "Nonsense, Miss May," he said, with sufficient peremptoriness for a man who had been rather accustomed to efface himself in these girls' presence, "you were not to be suffered to hide your light under a bushel. I wonder to hear you—I thought you had more pluck and perseverance. How many times do you think the young fellows at St. Ambrose's are turned back and have to try again? If I passed in my first exam, it was by the merest fluke, as three-fourths of the men will tell you they pass. As for my degree, I had the common sense and modesty to put off taking it to the last moment, and to stay up two different vacations, 'sapping' like a Scotchman, before I ventured to undergo the test. You don't mean to say you are too proud to do at Rome as the Romans do, that your genius will brook no rejection, and declines to grapple with an obstacle? I'll tell you what your father proposes for you, and let me say that I believe it would do him a world of good—now that he has been forced to give up his patients, and is confined to his chair. He has not lost heart and faith in your powers—of course not. He is thinking quite eagerly of brushing up his classics in his enforced leisure, and himself becoming your coach for the next six months. I need not say that any small assistance I can offer is heartily at your service also."

"Oh!" said May, with wistful brown eyes and a long-drawn sigh, "you are a great deal too good to me, all of you. I don't deserve it. It would only be too much happiness for me to have father and you to coach me—but I know we could not afford it."

"Wait and see," said Tom succinctly.

"If I got that situation," said Dora timidly, "I might do something to help May: I mean the one where the lady said she would take me into consideration, but we thought it would not do, because I should have to go out to Jamaica. On second thoughts, I am not sure that I'd mind so very much going. The lady seemed to consider I might be able to do what she required, and I should only be away for a year or two, since the family are coming back then. The salary was very good."

Dora go out to Jamaica to help May, or any one else! Not though he had to fling cheques in at the windows, and squeeze Bank of England notes through the keyholes, to prevent it.

"Hester Jennings says she would not be very much surprised if she heard of a buyer for my tulip picture; but I don't know," said Rose doubtfully, glancing at the picture, which was on an adjoining table.

"May I look at it?" asked Tom Robinson, jumping up with alacrity, probably to make a diversion in the conversation from the obnoxious topic of Dora's problematical voyage to Jamaica. He had seen Rose's work at Redcross, and he could give it as his honest opinion that she had made a great advance in her art, though he did not profess to be a judge. He said, however, that he had a friend, an old St. Ambrose crony, who was an artist. They had happened to be together in Rome at a later date, had been a good deal thrown on each other's company there, and had continued to keep up a friendly intercourse. He requested permission for his friend to call and look at the little picture. He might be of use to Rose in disposing of it; he was always ready to help a fellow-artist. Tom supposed the Millars had heard his friend's name, it was pretty well known; indeed they might have seen him, for Pemberton and Lady Mary, his wife, had spent a few days with Tom at Redcross, and had been in church on the Sunday during their visit, the summer before last.

In spite of the obligations of good breeding, the Millars looked at each other in open-mouthed astonishment. Certainly they had heard of Pemberton the distinguished landscape painter, and they had been told that he had married into the peerage, as Aunt Penny had married into the county. The girls also remembered perfectly the quiet-looking young couple who had been noticed walking about with Tom Robinson the July before last. People had wondered languidly who the strangers could be—whether they were cousins far removed on Tom's father's side of the house, since they did not quite answer to the style of his mother's yeomen kindred. But it was an effort to the provincial mind to identify the unobtrusive-looking pair with the Pembertons, to realize that Mr. Pemberton and his Lady Mary had actually come and stayed the better part of a week with Tom Robinson. They could hardly have been ignorant of "Robinson's," whose master was only received into the upper-class houses of the town on a species of sufferance.

The peerage must have unique rules by which to frame its standards. There was the Hon. Victoria, Mrs. Carey's niece by marriage, who, when Carey's Bank was in full bloom, would hardly be seen in the streets of Redcross, and scarcely deigned to acknowledge her own aunt-in-law. As to the familiarity of staying a night in the Bank House, she would never have dreamt of it. In this respect she did little credit to the teaching of her old governess, Miss Franklin, who had shown herself a philosopher in her own person. Perhaps, when it came to stooping at all, the peerage felt it might as soon, and with a still more gracious and graceful effect, bend low as bend slightly. Perhaps in the peerage, as in every other class, there are all sorts and conditions of mind and heart.

A little clue might have been supplied to account for the eccentricity of the Pembertons, and to lessen the shock of their conduct to the Millars, if the latter had been made acquainted with one circumstance. About the time of the stay of the artist and his wife in Rome, where he had been only too glad to run up against a favourite old college chum, when the three had been making a long excursion in company beyond the Campagna, Pemberton had been suddenly attacked in a remote little town with a violent illness.

His poor young wife would have been utterly frightened and forlorn had it not been for the moral courage and untiring good offices of the third person in the company—Tom Robinson.

Tom did not appear conscious of the sensation he had created by the mention of his friend. He arranged when Mr. Pemberton should come and view Rose's picture to suit Rose's convenience, and not that of the famous and courted artist. Then he explained in all sincerity, before he took his leave, that he, Tom Robinson, was very sorry he could not have the pleasure of bringing Pemberton and introducing him personally, because a business engagement called the master of "Robinson's" back to Redcross early next morning.

The party he left were quite silent and still for a moment after he had gone, till what she had heard of Mr. Pemberton went to Rose's head to such a degree that she rose, whirled round on tiptoe, and caused her spread-out frock to perform the feat which children call "making a cheese."

"Won't it be delicious to know Mr. Pemberton and get his advice—perhaps one day presume to ask him how he does his hay-fields and orchards? What will Hester Jennings say! I say, we'll have Hester to meet him; she will come for such a painter though the whole peerage would not get her to budge an inch. I wish we could tone her down a little bit, but he must just swallow her whole. She is good and clever enough to be permitted that rugged line of her own. Oh! but isn't Tom Robinson a trump? I *will* be slangy, Annie—as May says, it is so expressive."

"Yes, yes," chimed in May enthusiastically, in reference to the man and not to the slang. "I have known it ever since he came up like a lion—why do you laugh, Rose?—and rescued Tray— don't you remember, Dora?—from that horrid brute of a collie. Tray bit him—Mr. Robinson, I mean—not knowing that he was his best friend, and he only laughed. He was so kind about my wishing to go into his shop, like Phyllis Carey, though he would not take me. I think it must be a privilege, as Miss Franklin tells Phyllis, to serve him. She says all the nice people in the shop have the greatest regard for him."

"I am so sorry and ashamed that I ever drew caricatures of him," said Rose, in pensive penitence. "I think, whenever I am able, I must paint his portrait, as I see him now, to make up for it."

"And ask him to have it hung above the oak staircase in the shop," suggested Annie, a little satirically. But she added immediately, "Though it broke no bones to dwell on his lack of height and his foxy complexion, I am rather sorry now that I did it, because I have ceased to think that these objectionable details deserved to be made of any consequence. On the contrary, I own to the infatuation of beginning to see that there is something fine in them. I suppose I shall be calling Tom Robinson's hair golden, or tawny, or chestnut soon, and his inches the proper height for a man. It is true," broke off Annie, with sudden, unaccountable perversity, "I do hate great lumbering flaxen-haired giants." She blushed furiously after she had indulged in the last digression, and hastened to resume the main thread of the conversation. "As for Tom Robinson's having little to say, I declare that my present impression is that he says quite enough, and very much to the purpose too. It was so nice and like a gentleman of him not to propose immediately to buy Rose's picture when she talked rashly of her anxiety that it should find a purchaser."

"I don't think Cyril Carey, with all his airs, would have shown so much delicacy in the old days," said Rose.

"Or that Ned Hewett, though Ned has such a kind heart, would have been able to avoid blundering into some such offer," remarked May.

There was one person who remained absolutely silent while the others sang Tom Robinson's praises, and it might be her silence which called her sisters' attention to her.

"I wonder what you would have, Dora?" said Rose, with several shades of superciliousness in her voice and in her lifted-up nose.

"I cannot understand how you could be such a cruel, hard-hearted girl," May actually reproached her devoted slave.

"There is such a thing as being too particular," Annie had the coolness to say. "I am sure I do not go in for indiscriminate marriages or for falling in love," she added with lofty decision. "It has always been a mystery to me what poor Fanny Russell could see to care for, or to do anything save laugh at, in Cyril Carey. I hope the elderly 'competition wallah,' or commissioner, or whatever he is, whom she is going to marry, has more sense as well as more money. For her marriage was arranged, though the news had not reached England, mother writes, before the tidings of Colonel Russell's death came. But when a man who can act as Tom Robinson has acted crosses a woman's path and pays her the compliment of asking her to be his wife, I do think she should be careful what she answers."

Dora stared as if she were losing her senses. Were they laughing at her still? Could they be in earnest? If so, how was it possible for them to be so flagrantly inconsistent and unjust? She could only utter a single exclamation. But as the worm will turn, the exclamation was emphatic and indignant enough. "Well!" she cried, in utter amazement and incipient rebellion. "Well!" and she returned the challenging gaze of the circle with a counter-challenge, before which all eyes except Annie's fell.

Annie had the audacity to look Dora in the face and echo the "Well!" nay, to say further, "You never heard of anything so disgraceful as for us to turn upon you and find fault with you for refusing Tom Robinson, when all the time it was we who laughed at him, and scouted his shop, keeping you up to the point of dismissing him without delay? Quite true, Dora, dear; but then it was you, and not *us*, whom he was proposing to marry! and a girl old enough to receive such a proposal should have the wit to judge for herself—should she not? She ought to cultivate the penetration to look beneath the surface in so important a matter, and then fewer lamentable mistakes would be made. However, nobody could expect you to put force on your inclinations, and he does not bear you malice."

Annie did not regard her share in the matter so cheerfully and lightly when she was in the privacy of a ward of St. Ebbe's, where she had begged to sit up with an unconscious patient, just to keep her hand in and compose her feelings.

"What mischievous little wretches we were," she reflected, as she deftly changed the wet cloth on the sick woman's hot forehead. "How happy he might have made Dora, and how happy she might have made him! She is so single-minded and tender-hearted, that she could hardly have failed to see his merits, if we had given him the chance, let her alone, and left the pair to themselves. Then, if the worst were to come to the worst," and Annie frowned with anxiety and grief, as well as with wholesome humiliation, "if poor father and mother cannot get along, and none of us girls can help them effectually, his house might have been their home, where he would never have let them feel other than honoured guests. He would have been a son to them. But the mischief is done, and there is no help for it. If Dora and he were an ordinary couple, it might be mended; but now she will not look at him when we none of us have a penny, because she refused him when we were in comfortable circumstances; and he will not renew his suit with the thought in his mind that it would look and feel to her as if any favour he has magnanimously conferred on us, were a mere bribe to compel her to listen to him. So, Annie Millar, this is a pretty kettle of fish, of which you have been chief cook! There is the greater reason for you to make up your mind from this moment to devote yourself wholly to your family, and let nothing—*nothing*," she protested with suspicious vehemence, "come between you and them."

"What is it, you poor soul?" the young nurse responded quickly to a movement of the helpless ailing creature beside her. "Do you know there is somebody here? Will it ease you to have your head raised on my arm, do you think? You cannot hear or answer, but we'll try that, and then it is just possible you may drop asleep." And for the rest of the watch Annie was absorbed in care for her patient.

Sarah Tytler

CHAPTER XX

REDCROSS AGAIN

Tom Robinson's subscription list attained the respectable sum-total of two thousand pounds. Many of the subscribers were not only patients of Dr. Millar, but creditors of the bank whose claims he had striven with sturdy honesty to satisfy, till the task proved too hard for his years.

The little Doctor received the token of how greatly his courage and staunchness in the fulfilment of his obligations had been respected, with half pained, half pleased gratitude, and this was very much the attitude of mind of his daughter Annie. The rest of his womankind, from Mrs. Millar to May, only felt a glad surprise, and a soft, proud thankfulness.

The relief from present difficulties was great, but of course the gift did not obviate the necessity for the girls seeking work and wages. Even May, when she ventured to hope that she might stay at home for a month or two and be coached by her father and Tom Robinson in anticipation of a more successful campaign at St. Ambrose's, was eagerly speculating whether she might not become a coach in her turn. She was fain to earn a little money by helping the very youngest of the Grammar School boys to prepare their Latin grammar in the evenings, supposing she could get them to sit still, and give over wishing her to play with them.

Mr. Pemberton had not only himself called on the Miss Millar who was the artist, he had brought Lady Mary with him, and both husband and wife had turned out the refined, thoroughly unassuming, kindly disposed couple they had looked. They spoke warmly of Tom Robinson as their very good friend, and went so far as to express enthusiasm for his beautiful old shop. Mr. Pemberton did better than merely say a few words of languid, indiscriminating praise of Rose's picture, and then bow himself out. He examined the picture closely, and looked at her thoughtfully and attentively out of the dark gray eyes, the only good feature in his face. The next moment, to Hester Jennings's great edification, he addressed Rose seriously as a member of the Guild of St. Luke—not an amateur, "one of ourselves, so that you must not mind what I say to you, Miss Millar." He first displayed a generous capacity for discovering something good, whether it were to be found in the work of a tyro or of a veteran. Next he took the trouble of pointing out the faults, and urging their remedy, telling her the picture was worth the pains of making it as true as possible, until Rose hung her head in blended pride and humility.

What was more, he offered to enter into negotiations with a picture-dealer on her behalf, and brought them to a triumphant conclusion, making Rose happy with so fair a price as materially to lighten the millstone of her resigned office at the Misses Stone's hanging round her neck.

It was settled that May should go home and profit by the coaching which awaited her at Redcross, taking the chance of finding some little boys whose Latin grammar would be the better of her supervision.

Next Mr. Pemberton wrote that Lady Mary had been so charmed with the neighbourhood of Redcross, and had spoken so highly of it to one of her cousins, who had a great liking for English landscape, and was just refurnishing his town house, that he wished to commission a set of water-colour sketches of such and such spots for his morning-room. It was Mr. Pemberton's opinion that Miss Rose Millar could execute the commission to Sir John Neville's satisfaction, if she cared to

Sarah Tytler

accept of it.

"It is to help me," said Rose humbly, "for there are hundreds of good artists who would take the work and be thankful, and do it far better, though I will do my very best. Tom Robinson is at the bottom of it directly or indirectly, but he is like an old friend. I don't know a man to whom I would sooner be obliged."

In the third instance, a totally unforeseen application was made to Annie. A fever, in certain respects unfamiliar in its type, broke out at Stokeleigh, one of several suburban villages on the outskirts of Redcross. Some authorities called the fever Russian, and declared it had been imported—they did not pretend to say how—from that remote empire. Others insisted it was a slow fever, of English growth, with curious complications. It appeared doubtful whether it were infectious; but there was one thing which was unmistakable, that, whatever kind of malaria brooding in the summer air was at the root of the complaint, that malaria showed a disposition to spread extensively. It passed from Stokeleigh to the adjoining village of Woodleigh, whence it took a bend in the direction of the town, and proceeded to squat, as malarias can squat, and settle indefinitely on all the low-lying districts of Redcross. Neither did the epidemic improve in character with the change of locality. For, whereas on the higher, less encumbered ground the fever had been rarely fatal, the mortality increased with the transfer of the disease to the crowded, damp purlieus of the older part of the town, built more or less on the Dewes, and liable to be invaded by the river in flood.

A combined meeting of the Town Council and Vestry, with the Mayor, who happened to be a public-spirited man, and the Rector heading it, determined on taking prompt action to stop the mischief. The town had lately built a Corn Exchange in one of the highest, best-ventilated situations in Redcross. It was to be committed to the care of a town's officer and his wife, who were to have the adjoining rooms rent-free for a domicile, together with certain perquisites, in return for sweeping, scrubbing, and looking after the hall. But the place was just finished, and had not yet been occupied in the manner intended. It was proposed to convert it, in the absence of other accommodation, into a temporary ward for the sufferers from fever. The doctors consulted, pledged themselves that there was every probability of the unwelcome visitor being thus stamped out, while the chances of recovery for the patients would be multiplied. It was also agreed to bring a trained nurse from some nursing institution, to mould the raw nursing materials which Redcross supplied on the emergency. Dr. Millar's successor had a bright idea that it might be a graceful act on his part to mention the old Doctor's daughter, who had gone in for nursing as a profession. She had already served nearly a year in a great London hospital, and was no doubt competent to undertake the duties required. It would be a compliment to her and her father to try and get her for the occasion, and there would be a certain *eclat* in her coming to the help of her native town in its need. Dr. Capes was right as to the popularity of his motion. It was received with unanimous approval. Annie, the matron, and the directors of St. Ebbe's, were immediately applied to in proper form. Annie burned to go, if such a step were admissible at the present stage of her career. The favour she had won on all sides aided in the fulfilment of her wishes. She was promoted from the ranks of the probationers to those of the nurses while yet her year wanted a fraction of its complete round, and was officially sent down to represent the nurses of St. Ebbe's at Redcross.

"Of course, Dora, you cannot be left behind to go on by yourself hunting for a situation with three-fourths of the great world out of town. I am afraid you would make a poor job of it at the best, Dora dear, and at the worst it is not to be thought of; it would be a waste of nerve-tissue and muscle, as well as of pounds, shillings, and pence. You will come too; we'll be all together, or nearly together, again, for a holiday, after all."

Dora, who had been waiting patiently for Annie's decision, was nothing loth.

"Rose's expenses and mine are more than paid," calculated the practical Annie, "so that we shall be no drag on father and mother. I don't know if Robarts's accommodation will extend beyond the additional bedroom for Rose and May, but that can be easily managed. Oh! I have it, Dora, you will stay with me at the hospital—the Corn Exchange I mean—and save me from having a housekeeper for the short time one will be wanted. I'll take care that no infection, if there be infection, will come near you. Oh, 'won't it be jolly,' as Rose says, for you and me to keep house by ourselves at dear old Redcross, of all places in the world?"

It was arranged so, with only a little demur from Mrs. Millar, over-ruled by her husband.

There was another person, without right or power to enter his veto against the existing order of things, who nevertheless decidedly demurred at them. Tom Robinson showed that though he might be a humane man there were bounds to his humanity. "It is all very well for Annie Millar to come down and nurse the fever patients, it is in the way of her business, she does as much every day, she is well acquainted with all the precautions to take. But Dora is not a nurse, she never thinks of herself, she will forget to take the precautions if she has ever heard of them. She has not strong nerves, and she is used up with this preposterous stumping of London in July in search of a situation. What in the name of common sense and natural affection do they mean by lugging Dora into the risk!" he grumbled and worried. "Oh! yes, of course she would follow Annie or any of the rest of them fast enough if she had the opportunity, though she were to die at the end of it; but she ought never to have had the opportunity, it was preposterous to let her. The whole thing is monstrous. I never heard of such rashness. What can Dr. and Mrs. Millar be thinking of?"

It felt queer, to say the least of it, as well as "jolly," to be at Redcross and not at the Old Doctor's House, over which a bride of yesterday was presiding, for Dr. Capes's marriage had taken place simultaneously with his purchase of Dr. Millar's practice.

Annie used to look over from the opposite side of the street, as she was walking along, at the alterations which were being made in the garden, and the new arrangement of the window curtains, and try to criticize them impartially. Then she had to call and see Dr. Capes, and wait in the familiar consulting-room till he insisted on taking her to the drawing-room, in order to introduce her to his wife, who had come a stranger to Redcross. Annie felt as if she were a disembodied spirit, or a dreamer in a dream from which she could not awake, while she gazed on the changed yet well-known aspect of everything around her. But she had to think of Dr. and Mrs. Capes, in whose house she was, and talk civilly to them of their improvements(!). She had to emulate the submission of Dora, who had seen the transfer coming and taken part in it. She had to copy the mercurial spirits of Rose and May. They were so pleased to be with their father and mother again, and to take possession of Phyllis Carey's every free moment, that they declared the Robarts's apartments were the very nicest the girls had ever seen. They, the apartments, were delightfully cosy (which meant stuffy in July). They were more cheerful (noisier) than the Old Doctor's House. It was great fun for the pair to stow themselves and their belongings within such narrow compass.

A serious vexation to Annie at the commencement of her enterprise was the arrival of Dr. Harry Ironside to diagnose and make what he could of the fever.

"What is he doing here? His coming at all is most impertinent," cried Annie indignantly, sitting down on one of the still empty beds in the barrack-like hall, and as it were daring Rose and May, who had brought the news, and Dora who was listening to them, to contradict her.

"He is come in the pursuit of knowledge," said Rose, with full command of her countenance. "He does not understand

Russian fever, or whatever it is, and he thinks he had better make its acquaintance as a wind up to taking his degree. He is still a doctor at large; he has not fixed on where he is to go and what he is to do next, so his sister Kate writes to me."

"Then he and his sister Kate had better make up their minds to go away together, somewhere else, and not trouble other people," cried Annie quite illogically.

"Why, Annie, father thinks it is very praiseworthy of Dr. Ironside to seek to get all the information he can before settling down as a doctor," remonstrated May in the guileless-ness of her heart. "He has just been calling on father, who is delighted with him—so is mother; and, for *my* part," finished the speaker with unconscious emphasis, as if her opinion were of the utmost consequence, "I have thought him very nice since the first time I met him at Mrs. Jennings's. He is so big and handsome, without being stuck up, or a swell, like what Cyril Carey used to be—just frank and pleasant as a man should be. I cannot comprehend why you have such a dislike to him."

"Upon my word!" exclaimed Annie, with a gasp. "But I don't care," she added vehemently; "he shall not come and carry on his investigations here. Dr. Capes and I, with father to appeal to, and Mr. Newton to call in and consult, if necessary, are more than sufficient for all the patients we are likely to get. I tell you, if he forces his way into my hospital I'll have nothing more to do with it; I'll throw it all up and go back to St. Ebbe's at once."

"But it is not your hospital, Annie," said Rose with provoking matter-of-factness. "It is the town's, or if it is under the control of any private person, it is under Dr. Capes's orders. For the sake of his professional character, medical etiquette, and all that kind of thing, he will not refuse to allow a fellow-doctor to study the fever cases under his care. Dr. Harry was going to stay at the 'Crown,' but he met Tom Robinson, who said he should be his guest, and carried him off to his house."

"Just like Tom Robinson!" declared Annie with amazing asperity.

"Come along, May." Rose hurried away her sister and satellite, and then let loose her glee. "It is too funny, May; too preposterously funny. It is ever so much better than Dora and Tom Robinson. He was so easily rebuffed, and she was so reluctant to rebuff him. But here is Annie like one of the furies, and Harry Ironside is silly enough to mind her, so that he can hardly open his mouth before her, and looks as if he had lost his wits. Before Annie! What is our Annie, I should like to know, that she should daunt a clever, high-spirited young fellow such as he is? What strange glamour has she thrown over him? But he has plenty of mettle and determination for all that, and she will no more manage by her tirades to stop him from coming after her and laying siege to her ladyship, than she can keep the sun from shining or the rain from falling. For that matter, I believe the poor fellow cannot help himself; it is the case of the moth and the candle."

"But what is it all about?" demanded May, in an utter confusion of ideas. "She speaks as if she hated him, and I thought he had come to Redcross to trace the course of the Russian fever."

"To trace the course of his own fortunes. I beg your pardon, my dear, but you might have known enough of human nature to guess that there was a private personal motive at the bottom of his philanthropy."

"Then it is the worse for him and a great pity," said May, with the sweet seriousness into which one phase of her childishness was passing. "I wonder you can laugh, Rose. I am always affronted when I remember how we laughed at Tom Robinson and poor Dora, making game of what was no joke to them. And Dora was not half so much opposed to Tom as Annie is to this unfortunate, nice, pleasant young doctor. I could find it in my heart to be very sorry for him."

"Oh! you are a simpleton apart from Latin and Greek. Don't you see that Annie's wrath is neither more nor less than fright? She is frightened out of her senses at him, because she wants to keep her independence and share our fortunes. As I do not remember to have seen her in such a scare before, I should say that she is paying him a high compliment."

"I think it is rather a queer compliment," objected May in much perplexity.

"'Though you should choose to dissemble your love,
Why need you kick me down-stairs?'"

quoted Rose. "Oh! but the poet did not know the world, or pretended not to know it. I assure you there are many wise men who would much rather be kicked in this way than be civilly spoken to. Kate Ironside thought fit to confide to me how much interested she was in a suit which, if it ever succeeded, would make us all brothers and sisters. She was so good as to add that while she was aware Harry always knew best, and she had entire faith in his choice, still she was not entirely of his mind—I don't believe Annie has ever spoken to her, lest speech with the sister should be taken for encouragement to the brother. It is only natural perhaps that, as Kate ventured to admit, on the whole she would have preferred *me*."

"And what did you say to that?" asked the deeply-interested May.

"No, thanks, though I was much obliged, or something like it. I added with some dignity, I flatter myself, though really such dignity is thrown away on Kate, that for the present I was wedded to my art, like Queen Elizabeth to her kingdom, and to my sister Maisie. Besides, nothing could, would, or should ever induce me to meddle with my sister Annie's property, since, according to Kate's own account, it was for love of Annie, and not of me, that Harry Ironside took up his residence under Mrs. Jennings's roof."

But Annie had to give way to some extent. She was compelled to grant an interview to the aggressor. Dr. Ironside arrived on a special errand to the hospital, and he took up the position that Miss Millar was entitled to be consulted. Tom Robinson had been attacked with every symptom of the fever. He and Tom had agreed, in view of the public character of "Robinson's," and with the idea that the step might do good, by serving as an example, that the patient should come to the hospital and be laid up there, where Dr. Harry Ironside was ready to devote himself to the case.

"I believe Tom Robinson has taken the fever on purpose," said Annie to the shocked Dora. "But he shall not have much of my attendance; he may stick to his Dr. Ironside. Dr. Capes tells me he has induced a married woman, with a family, who has a brother and a nephew lodging with her, both of them down with fever, to send them here, so that I shall have them to look after. Now that there is a beginning made," Annie smoothed her ruffled plumes, and waxed cheerful, "if the hot weather does not change, and the disease is not checked, we are likely to have plenty of patients on our hands, with the opportunity of showing what service we can render them and the town."

Just as Annie predicted, the rows of beds began to fill, and she had no lack of occupation; but she changed her tale with regard to Tom Robinson when his case, among many which yielded readily to treatment, and proved triumphantly the gain to be got from a better locality and fresher air, was first grave, then dangerous, and at last verged on hopeless. Now she turned to the worst case on her list, and made it her chief care. She became totally unmindful of the fact that she was thus brought into constant contact with Harry Ironside, that it was he and she who were together fighting death, inch by inch, with desperate endeavour, for the prize which the last enemy threatened to snatch from their hands. Indeed, so entirely did Annie, like the excellent nurse and kind-hearted woman she was, lose sight of her own concerns in the interest of her patient, that she was heard to contradict herself, and record her sincere thankfulness for the strong support of Harry Ironside's presence in the light of the valuable aid he could afford at such a time.

"He was thought very clever at St. Ebbe's. He took his degree with high honours. He was held in much esteem by all the older doctors," she explained to all who cared to hear. "He is in possession of all the latest light on his profession. Now, I have heard father say, and what I have seen confirms it, that though Dr. Capes is most painstaking, and has had a good deal of experience as a general practitioner, he has no great natural ability, and he was not in circumstances to pursue his studies longer than was absolutely necessary to enable him to pass as a medical man. After all I take back my word. I am very glad for poor Tom Robinson's sake that Dr. Harry Ironside is here. No doubt we could have summoned a great specialist from London, but he would only have stayed a short time, and men like him have generally many critical cases on their minds. Now Dr. Harry Ironside is on the spot, and he can watch every turn of the disease which he came to master, and devote his whole attention to this example. I consider Tom Robinson is exceedingly fortunate in getting the chance of such scientific treatment."

But in spite of the good fortune and the devotion spent on him; it looked as if Tom were going to slip through the hands so bent on detaining him, and to die as quietly as he had lived.

When Redcross realized how even the balance was, and how heavily he was swimming for his life, the whole town woke up to his good qualities as a citizen, to what a useful life his comparatively short one had been, to how many benefits he had conferred without the slightest assumption of patronage or superiority of any kind.

It is unnecessary to say that "Robinson's" was figuratively in the deepest mourning, only rousing itself from its despair to proclaim his merits and those of his father before him, as masters. Men gravely pointed out the old servants he had pensioned; those in middle age whom he had kept on when their best days were past; the boys he had already taken in, fitted out, and launched on the world by judicious, unostentatious backing. Women tearfully reminded the listener how carefully he had provided for their comfort and well-being throughout his establishment, from the ample time allowed for their meals and the seats to which they could retire when not actually serving, to the early closing hours, which afforded them and the men who were their associates, some leisure for out-of-doors exercise and indoors recreation. As for mental and spiritual improvement, he was always ready to subscribe liberally to libraries, choral unions, friendly societies, Christian associations, missionary boxes—every conceivable means of rational pleasure, culture, and true human elevation of which his people would avail themselves.

Mrs. Carey called at the Corn Exchange and offered her unprofessional services as a nurse, if further aid were wanted.

Mr. Pemberton, acquainted with the fact of Tom Robinson's illness through communicating with Rose Millar on her commission, wrote that he could hardly keep Lady Mary from descending on Redcross to see after their friend, and if it would be the least good she would come down. It would be but a poor return for the aid Robinson had lent her when her husband lay desperately sick and she had nobody to appeal to, save the fat and fatuous *padrone* of a miserable little Italian inn.

May, who was at last prevented from coming to her sisters, presented herself when they went to their father's, her eyes swollen with weeping for her "coach."

Every time Annie left the transformed hall of the Exchange and repaired to the rooms which she and Dora occupied, she found a white face on the watch for her, and pale lips which could hardly form the syllables, "How is he now? Oh! Annie, must he die?" At least Dora was on the spot to hear each hour's report, as if she had been his nearest relative, and without asking herself the reason why, that was a little bit of comfort to her. In the same manner Tom Robinson derived a dim satisfaction from the fact that he was lying there under the same roof with Dora Millar, as he would have been supposing she had listened to his suit eighteen months ago, and he had fallen ill in the early days of their marriage. He was afraid it was pure selfishness which made him cease to resent her presence in close proximity to the fever ward, as he had resented it when he did not imagine he might be one of its patients. Sometimes he had a dim fancy that he heard her soft voice through the closed doors, and that it soothed him, though he might be only dreaming, or it was possible that there were tones in Annie's clear voice which under certain emotions of pity and tenderness answered to those of her sister.

Often Annie just shook her head sorrowfully as she warned Dora off till the nurse's dress could be changed. Occasionally she cried out petulantly, "If he would only be impatient, and fret and grumble like other people; if he would not take things so quietly; if he would resist and struggle, I believe he might fight the battle and win it yet. I think he will get over the crisis, but what of that if there is no rallying? He is letting life go because he will not grasp it hard, I suppose for the reason that he has no strong ties to bind him to it. He has either such a poor opinion of his deserts, or such a trust in Providence, that he considers whatever is is best, and does not exert himself to alter the course of events so far as it is in his power. It is beautiful in theory, but it does not always answer in practice. I am not certain whether it does not proceed, after all, from constitutional indolence, or the want of ambition, of which I used to accuse him, or whether he is really too good to live. Anyhow, skill and nursing are wasted upon him."

Dr. Hewett came to see Tom Robinson, and took the seat which Harry Ironside vacated for him, leaving the old friends together.

"Hallo, Rector! It is strange for me to meet you here," said Tom's feeble voice, while the ghost of his old shy smile passed over his haggard face.

"It is equally strange for me to meet you, Robinson," said the Rector, with an inconvenient lump in his throat.

"What a deal of trouble I'm giving," said Tom regretfully.

"Tut, man, nobody grudges the trouble, if you will but pick up and get well again," said the clergyman, almost roughly.

"I can see that Ironside thinks badly of me," said Tom in his quiet way, "and as far as feelings go, it seems to me I have reason to think badly of myself."

"We are all in good hands, Tom," said Dr. Hewett, seeing again the boy who used to play in the Rectory garden with Ned, and speaking to him in the old fashion.

"I know that," answered Tom. "I have known it all along, which has been a blessing to me," he added, a little as if he were speaking of a third person. Then he roused himself further. "I want to tell you where my will is. I don't like to hurt a woman's feelings by speaking of it to my kind, indefatigable nurse. Besides, the Millars will benefit by it."

"The old man," sighed the Rector, "always thinking of others before yourself."

"'I know that my Redeemer liveth,'" was Tom's testimony; "speak to me of Him, Rector, while I am able to hear," said the sick man, in the tone of one whose ears were growing dull to earthly sounds.

Sarah Tytler

CHAPTER XXI

MISS FRANKLIN'S MISTAKE

Tom Robinson went still deeper into the shadow of the valley, possibly as far as man ever went and returned. He grew as weak and helpless as an infant, until at last he lost consciousness, and lay prostrate and still, with closed eyes and sealed ears—nothing alive in him save the subtle principle which is compared to a vapour and a breath which no man can see or handle, yet whose presence or absence makes all the difference between an animated body still linked to both worlds and a mass of soulless clay hastening to corruption. All that skill and devotion could do—and Tom Robinson had them both—was to keep on without despairing, maintaining warmth against the growing chillness, and administering stimulants and nourishment by spoonfuls and drops.

On the night which it was feared would be Tom Robinson's last, Miss Franklin would no longer be denied her place among the watchers. She had been kept away in obedience to poor Tom's express orders, that in the attempt to minimize the fever no communication should be kept up on his account between the Corn Exchange where he lay and either his house or "Robinson's," notwithstanding the proofs that the disease did not spread by contagion or infection.

Miss Franklin did not desire to dispossess Annie of the post which, in spite of every remonstrance, she was holding latterly almost night and day. Miss Franklin had no faculty for nursing, and small experience to guide her. She was rather a nervous woman in her impulsiveness, and after one look at what was like the mask of Tom Robinson, utterly incapable of recognizing her or communicating with her, she was so much overcome that she was fain to retire to another room and submit to be gently ministered to by Dora.

Miss Franklin was only too thankful to be suffered to stay there in the background. It did not strike her as odd that nobody in the house except the other patients should go to sleep that night when her cousin was hovering between life and death—nearer death than life. Neither had the outspoken, kind-hearted gentlewoman any particular application of her speech in her mind when she said sorrowfully—"Dear! dear! how grieved he would be if he knew how worn out you were, Miss Dora. He thought that his coming to the hospital would not only serve as a precedent, it would be the simplest, safest, least troublesome plan where he himself was concerned, though if he would have let me, I should have been only too glad to have turned my back on 'Robinson's' for a time, and done what I could for him. There is enough difference in our ages, and I have known him all his life, in addition to our being connections if not near relations, so that nobody need have found fault. Not that I pretend for a moment that I could have done what your sister is doing—that is something quite wonderful in every respect" (and here Miss Franklin did draw up her bountiful figure, and fix the rather small eyes, sunk a little in her full cheeks, pointedly on Dora). "I dare say he liked to have her about him to the last, so long as he was sensible of her presence. Men are extraordinary creatures—that I should say that now, oh! my poor dear cousin Tom."

After she had recovered from her outburst of grief, and was sipping the tea which Dora had made for her, she turned again to her companion. "You look like a ghost yourself, Miss Dora. Will you not lie down in your bedroom and trust me? I shall sit here and bring you word the moment I hear that a change has come;" and at the ill-omened phrase poor Miss Franklin's well-bred, distinct enunciation got all blurred and faltering. In

Sarah Tytler

fact she shrank a good deal from the ordeal she was magnanimously proposing for herself. As it happened she had never undergone anything like it before, though she had reached middle age. It was not easy for her to contemplate sitting there all alone through the dreary small hours, knowing that Tom Robinson's spirit—the spirit of the best friend she had ever known—was passing away without word or sign in the adjoining room. It was a relief to her when Dora Millar, looking as if she had been sitting up in turn with every patient in the ward, as pale as a moonbeam and as weak as water, yet shook her head decisively against any suggestion of her retiring to rest.

There was a strong contrast between the couple who were to wait together for death or the morning. Miss Franklin herself might be on the eve of dying—but so long as she lived and went through the mundane process of dressing, she must dress exceedingly well. She was a good, kind woman all the same, and this night she bore a sore heart under her carefully contrived and nicely put on garments.

Poor young Dora, on the contrary, looked all limp and forlorn. The gingham morning-gown she had not changed was huddled on her, and crumpled about her. Her neglected hair was pushed back from her little white face. Annie in her nurse's spotless apron and cap looked a hundred times trimmer, and was altogether a more cheerful object. It was as if the whole world had come to an end for Dora, and she had ceased to notice trifles. Almost the first words Miss Franklin had said to her when the visitor began to recover from the shock she had undergone, were—

"Excuse me, Miss Dora, the lace at your throat is coming undone—let me put it right for you; and an end of your hair has fallen down. I may fasten it up, may I not?"

A delicate, exhausted girl was no great support for a woman under the circumstances, still she was better than nobody. She was company in one form, like the domestic cat, when no more available associate is to be found. Besides, in the middle of their dissimilarity, Miss Franklin had a natural liking for Dora Millar, and had always excepted her from the grudge which the elder woman was inclined to feel against one member of the Millar family. "A nice, well-meaning, gentle girl," Miss Franklin mentally classed Dora. "The most quiet and ladylike of them all." She was a great improvement, in Miss Franklin's estimation, on that too bright and restless Annie, whom everybody cried up as a beauty. She had found, Miss Franklin was creditably informed, a fine vent for her dictatorial imperious temper as a nurse. Yet she, Miss Franklin, ought not to find fault with Annie Millar at this time, when Dr. Capes had said her treatment of the fever patients, with dear Tom among them, was admirable; though, by one of the mysterious decrees of Providence, she might not be permitted to succeed in his case. And she was now ministering to his last wants as she, Barbara Franklin, arrived at mature age, with all the will, had neither the skill nor the courage to minister, much as she owed him, so long as he had other service. She was a captious, vindictive wretch to pick holes in Miss Millar's armour, when she was striving so hard to atone to him for any injury she had ever done him by delivering him from the jaws of death, or at least smoothing his path to the grave.

The seasons had gone on till the late summer was merging into the early autumn. It was the beginning of August, when the days are already not so long as they have been; but, to make up for it, the lengthening nights are balmier than they ever were, and the soft dusk remains full of summer scents and sounds.

It was on such a night that you might imagine a young man, dying long before his time, and yet after he has reached full manhood, and touched the crown of bodily and mental vigour, without ever feeling the tide on its turn.

The night was so warm that the windows of the room in which Dora and Miss Franklin sat were wide open. There was a lamp lit within, but it did not render the darkness without so great as to hide the outlines of trees in the nearest garden, and even

Sarah Tytler

the dim shape of a bed of late flowering, tall white lilies. Their heavy fragrance was on the air; and if ever there is a fragrance which is solemn and tender like the love of the dying and the memory of the dead, it is the all-pervading scent of lilies.

Annie Millar could never have been so good a listener as Dora was when Miss Franklin, constitutionally loquacious, relieved her distress, and got rid of the dragging hours, by indulging in a long and affectionate oration on Tom Robinson, the man who, not so many yards from them, was lying as indifferent to praise and blame as when he first entered this wonderful world, with all its joys and sorrows, from which he was ready to depart.

"You know, he is not really my cousin," the womanly confidence began; "the tie between us hardly counts—it is only that Mr. Robinson's first wife was my mother's sister. But I always called Mr. Charles Robinson and his second wife uncle and aunt. I might well do it, for they were a good uncle and aunt to me. I should have known few pleasures when I was growing up, and long afterwards, if it had not been for them. The Robinsons used to go away trips every summer to Devonshire and Derbyshire, the Yorkshire moors, the Cumberland lakes, Scotland, the Black Forest, Switzerland, and they always took me to see the world, and spend my summer holidays with them. How generous and kind they were in their friendliness! Tom was usually of the party—first as a child, then as a growing boy; but child or boy, such a nice manly little fellow, so much thought of, yet not at all spoilt. He was fond of reading, yet full of quiet fun, and in either light never in anybody's way. He was so considerate of his mother and me, and so helpful to us. The cows he has driven away! the horses going at large he has kept off! the bulls he has held at bay! I confess I am not brave in proportion to my size. I am very timid in such matters, and, strange to say, Aunt Robinson, though a country-woman born and bred, was as great a coward as I where farm animals were in question; but we always knew ourselves safe when Tom was at hand, and he never laughed at us more than we could stand."

"I can understand," said Dora faintly. "He once helped us—May and me—when a strange dog attacked Tray; and now Tray is running about with May full of life and health, while his champion is—" She could not say the words.

Miss Franklin looked at her approvingly, even went so far as to stroke one of the cold trembling hands lying nerveless in Dora's lap. "You will allow me to say that you are a dear, tender-hearted girl, Miss Dora. You could have appreciated my cousin Tom. What a tower of strength he was to me when I felt I was getting middle-aged, and my system of teaching was becoming old-fashioned. I had been in so many homes belonging to other people, with never a home of my own, for upwards of thirty years, since my poor father and mother both died before I was twenty. I do not say that I was not for the most part well enough treated, because I hope I did my best, and I believe I generally gave satisfaction. I had my happy hours like other people. But it was all getting so stale, flat, and unprofitable—I suppose because I was growing weary of it all, and longing for a change. You see I had not quite come to the age when we cease to want changes, and are resigned just to go on as we are to the end. In reality I could see no end, except the poorest of poor lodgings and the most pinching straits, with the very little money I had saved. (My dear, even finishing governesses can save so little now-a-days.) Or perhaps there was the chance of my being taken into some charitable institution. You will admit it was not a cheerful prospect."

"No, it was not," said Dora, in dreary abstraction.

"As I said," resumed Miss Franklin, "I had been in so many schoolrooms; I had seen so many pupils grow up, go out into the world, and settle in life, leaving me behind, so that when they came back on visits to their old homes, they were prepared to pity and patronize me. I could not continue cudgelling my poor brains until I had not an original thought in my head, and all to keep up such acquirements as I had, and preserve a place among younger, better equipped girls, certain to outstrip me eventually."

"I suppose so," acquiesced Dora mechanically.

"Then poor dear Tom came to see me, and I told him what I was thinking. He got me to pay a visit to Redcross, and made a new opening for me. I may say without self-conceit that I was always considered to have a good taste in dress. I know it was a question which had never failed to interest me, to which I could not help giving a great deal of attention—making a study of it, as it were. Tom insisted that I could be of the greatest use to him, and was worth a liberal salary, which I was not likely to lose. And there was a comfortable refined nest, which I could line for myself, awaiting me in the pleasant rooms he had looked out for me."

"I know, Miss Franklin," said Dora, with a faint smile; "you told Phyllis Carey, and she told May, who repeated it to me. But I thought it might be a relief to you to speak of it again."

"Yes," cried the eager woman; "and it has all answered so well—the duties not too heavy, and really agreeable to me; the young women and men, under Tom's influence, no doubt, perfectly nice and respectful; and within the last six months, dear little Phyllis like a daughter or niece to me. I thought always I should be able to do something in return for him one day, yet with all the will in the world I have been able to do nothing until it has come to this;" and poor Miss Franklin sobbed bitterly under the burden of her unrequited obligations, and beneath the dove's neck cluster of feathers in her bonnet.

It was for Dora in her turn to seek to soothe and compose her companion. "I am sure you have been of the greatest service to him, and that he has enjoyed the near neighbourhood of an old friend—his mother's friend. Oh! think what a comfort it will be to you to have that to look back upon," finished Dora, in a voice trembling as much as Miss Franklin's.

Miss Franklin sat up, instinctively put her bonnet straight, wiped her eyes with her embroidered handkerchief, and gazed pensively into the empty air.

"God's ways are not as our ways," she said; "and certainly we are told that we are not to look for our reward in this world. Still one would have expected—one would have liked that it had not been so hard all through for Tom—not merely to have been denied the desire of his heart, but to have had to endure in his last moments to be set aside, to lie still and look on at what is going to happen."

Dora sat mystified; but she had not the spirit left to seek an explanation.

Miss Franklin was not aware that an explanation was needed. "I know," she added, "how kind and attentive your sister has been to Tom, and I understand nothing can exceed the interest Dr. Ironside has taken in my cousin, while he has made the most unremitting efforts to save him; still you will grant that so long as my poor Tom was conscious, it must have been very, very trying for him to see the terms these two were on. I don't listen much to gossip"—the speaker declared, in a parenthesis, with a little air of dignity and reserve even at that moment—"but it is the talk of the town that he has followed her down from London, and that they are to be married as soon as the epidemic is past. Nobody can say anything against it. They are well matched. They will be a fine-looking couple," she struggled to acknowledge with becoming politeness and impartiality.

"This is the first time I have heard of it, I can say with truth," said Dora wearily, without so much as a smile at the characteristic report. She thought the mention of it most unsuitable at such a season. The very word marriage smote her. "And even if it were so, what could it have signified to Mr. Tom Robinson?" she was about to add naively, when a light flashed upon her. She had often wondered how much Miss Franklin, "Robinson's," the whole town, knew of what had taken place eighteen months ago. She saw now that however little the lady might care for gossip, a distorted version of the truth in which she was interested had reached her. Either there had been a very natural mistake on the part of some of the local news-mongers, or Miss Franklin herself had fallen into the error. The belle of the Millar family and not Dora had been believed to be the object of Tom Robinson's pursuit. The blunder had been perpetuated in Miss Franklin's case by the good feeling and good breeding which would keep her from discussing Tom Robinson's affairs with her neighbours more than she could help, and would prevent her attempting such a cross-examination of the man himself as might have elicited the truth.

"Oh! I know now what you mean," cried Dora, on the impulse of the moment, "and you were altogether wrong. He has been spared such misery —nobody could have been so barbarous as to inflict it on him, if it had been as you suppose."

Miss Franklin was sensitive and imaginative on dress, but she was not imaginative or even very observant with regard to anything else. She understood Dora's protest to refer to an actual engagement between Dr. Harry Ironside and Miss Millar.

"Well, well," she said a little dryly, "people do exaggerate. Matters may not have gone quite so far, and I can only trust that he, Tom, has not been sensible of what is in the air, though I have always understood love, while it is said to be blind in one sense, is very sharp-sighted in another. I believe every one else sees where the land lies. I saw it myself so far as the gentleman was concerned—he could not keep his eyes off her, though I was not five minutes in their company, and I was full of my poor cousin Tom. I am sure I hope they may be happy," gulping down the hope. "Tom would have wished it, quite apart from her having done her duty by him, at the cost of some pain to herself, no doubt; while Dr. Ironside has been more than kind, which nobody had any call to expect. He must be a very fine young man, likely to win what he fancies. Every woman is entitled to her choice, and most people would applaud your sister's choice. The thing that puzzles me—you will forgive me for mentioning it just this once, for where is the good of discussion now?—is that as, I have been told, she did not meet Dr. Ironside till she went to her London hospital, how, when she had got no opportunity of contrasting the two men, when she had not even seen one of them, she could yet be so set against Tom's proposal, knowing him to be the man he is—was, alas! I should say. Why was she so very hard to poor Tom?"

"Oh, don't say that," besought Dora, in much agitation. "Don't bring that forward at this moment."

But Miss Franklin, in the strength of her family affections, felt that she owed it to the manes of Tom Robinson to express to the disdainful damsel's sister a candid opinion that he had been summarily and severely dealt with. "I was not in his confidence, but I could tell that something was going to happen, and that he was very much cut up when it all came to nothing."

"Oh, don't say that," repeated Dora, clasping her hands over her eyes, and weeping behind them. "What good can it do except to inflict needless torture?"

"I don't mean to reproach *you*," said Miss Franklin, a little bewildered, but still very hot and sore. "You had nothing to do with it, and I am sure you could not have been so heartless. Forgive me for the reflection on your sister, who is so much thought of, whom everybody is praising, with reason, for what she has done in nursing the sick and poor. But young girls ought to be more careful. I don't mean to say that she trifled with my cousin Tom—I have no right to say that—simply that she never gave him a thought. Tom was surely deserving of a thought," cried Miss Franklin indignantly. "Dr. Ironside may be all very well—I have nothing to say against him—quite the reverse. Tom is not to be compared to him in personal appearance, and the one is a professional man, while the other thought fit to continue a linen-draper like his good father before him; but that is by no means to infer that Miss Millar has chosen the better husband of the two. Girls are so foolish —they play with fire, and never look or take it into account where and whom it may burn. Tom Robinson deserved more respectful treatment in Redcross. He has never been like himself since. I used to hear him whistling and humming tunes to himself as he worked in the office—there is no more of that, or of his hearty interest in everything."

"Miss Franklin, it is you who are pitiless to say this to me to-night," panted Dora, rising against the inhumanity, and totally forgetting that the speaker did not hold the clue which would have told her how her words scourged her listener.

"I am not blaming *you*, Miss Dora," said the accuser again, more bitterly than she had yet spoken. For she was in her heart accusing Dora Millar of affectation in pretending not to be able to hear a word against her sister, and in declining to listen to the pardonable utterance of a reproach directed against what Miss Franklin called in her heart Annie Millar's arrogance and callousness. Tom Robinson's cousin was provoked, not pacified.

"I dare say Tom would never have had this wretched fever but for the blow he got then," she was tempted to persist; "or if he had caught it, he would have thrown it off without any harm done. I can bear witness to his sound constitution to begin with. Everybody knows how disappointment and mortification lower the system, and he was never over careful of himself. I cannot quite understand why he took the cool rebuff he received so much to heart; but he did so, and you see the consequence."

"Spare me! spare me!" cried Dora passionately. "Don't say I have killed him, or I shall die myself, perhaps it is the best thing I can do."

Before Miss Franklin could do more than stare aghast, with a horrified inkling of the real facts of the case, and the tremendous mess she had got into, there was the sound of the soft opening of a door in the near distance, and a step rapidly approaching.

The two women who had been upbraiding each other were mute in an instant, first held their breaths, then sprang up and clung to each other, partners in sorrow, with teeth beginning to chatter, and eyes to grow large and wild. What had they been doing in the name of a gentle and manly soul, in the face of the awful news on its way, the majesty of Death investing the house?

It was only Annie, looking perfectly collected, nay, a trifle elated. "He is the least shade better—we both think so; and the slightest improvement means so much at this stage—the right crisis, I believe. He has been really sleeping. He swallows with less difficulty. He has roused himself ever so little, but he is fearfully faint and weak. We cannot get him to take more stimulants than we have been giving him. I am afraid there is no toilet-vinegar in the house. I came to see if either of you had a smelling-bottle, which might revive him."

All that Miss Franklin could do was to shake her head. She was so thankful, yet she felt so guilty, so ashamed of herself.

Dora fumbled nervously in her pocket and gave Annie something, which she carried off in triumph. Miss Franklin sat down again and cried afresh between trembling joy and lively vexation. "Oh, won't it be a mercy, for which we can never praise our Maker too much, if dear Tom gets over his illness after all?" she managed to say; but she could do no more— even that lame speech was made awkwardly. To apologize for the heinous offence she had committed would be a greater enormity than the offence itself.

But when Miss Franklin had time to think it over afterwards, she was under the impression that Dora Millar had forgotten all about their altercation. She sat there with hands clasped, lips parted, and brimming eyes half raised to Heaven, as if in instinctive acknowledgment of a thousand piteous prayers in the act of being answered by Him who counts the stars and calls them by name, and heals the broken in heart. Miss Franklin's account of Dora's look was that, for a moment, she was positively frightened at the dear girl, Dora seemed so near another world at that moment, and as likely as not to be holding communication with it. Even Tom Robinson could not have been nearer when he was more than half way across the border-land.

CHAPTER XXII

A SHRED OF HOPE

Tom Robinson's recovery continued a matter of fear and trembling for a week longer before it became merely a process of time. But no sooner was it clearly established to the initiated, and only likely to be endangered by some unforeseen accident, than Annie Millar, in her delight, lost sight of her former tactics, and called on Dr. Harry Ironside to rejoice with her on their success.

"We have been permitted to pull him through. Oh, isn't it glorious? I know we ought, as we are miserable sinners, to go down on our knees and give God the thanks, and I hope we do with all my heart; but I also want to sing and dance—don't you, Dr. Ironside?"

Nobody could imagine that Dr. Harry Ironside was indifferent to the wonderful recovery, which was such a credit to his skill, of the man whom he had nursed as if Tom Robinson had been his brother; but Dr. Harry forgot all about his patient at that moment when he saw his opportunity and seized it.

He had never had a faint heart, young as he was, but he had been dealing with an exceedingly coy and high-spirited mistress. However, even she had not been able to defy the effect of the last month of incessant intercourse, of being engrossed in common with one object of interest, when both had hung, as it were, on a man's failing breath, and were indissolubly linked while it lasted. In the light of its fitful rising and falling, its feeble fluttering, the terrible moments when it appeared to stop and die away, how small and vain was every other consideration! But their joint work was done by God's help, as they had hardly dared to hope for a time, and now it was Harry's innings.

"I have something to say to you, Miss Millar. I have wished to say it for a long time. You will not refuse to hear me?"

They were alone together in the little side-room, empty but for its hospital stores, where they had so often consulted, with and without Dr. Capes, on the condition of the ward. There was no longer any fluster of doubt and hesitation in his manner. He stood there in his young comely manhood, prepared to put his fate to the test, claiming his right to do so, and challenging her to deny his claim.

In a moment Annie saw what Rose had seen some time ago, but had not taken it upon her to put in so many words for Annie's benefit. It was of this moment she had, by an unerring instinct, stood in mortal terror, from the first dawn of her acquaintance with Harry Ironside, to the afternoon when he had succeeded in getting an introduction to her in the matron's room at St. Ebbe's, soon after the scene in the operating theatre. Then he had bowed low, muttered a few words in confused greeting, and looked at her with all his man's heart in his eyes; and she had felt by a sure, swift intuition, that, as she valued her dearly held personal freedom and her allegiance to her family, there must be war to the knife between her and this self-willed young man. She must, as discretion is the better part of valour, flee from him, while refusing to own, even to herself, any more humiliating reason for the flight than her duty, the honour of St. Ebbe's, and the folly of Rose in playing into his hands.

Now Annie was caught, and had to listen to him whether she would or not, while she and not he quaked with fright and agitation. For he stood before her, like a conqueror already, in the little room with its shelves of phials, which they had all to themselves, where burly farmers and iron-gray corn-factors would soon be thronging in the course of transacting their every-day business.

But presently she forgot all about herself in the interest of the tale he had to tell, and told well in his newly-found courage and coolness, in his personal modesty and professional enthusiasm. He had just taken his degree as she knew. He and his sister Kate had inherited a competence from their parents. He might look about him till he found a lucrative and agreeable country practice in a choice neighbourhood, where he could command good society and a little hunting, shooting, and fishing in their seasons. Or he might be on the watch for a West End London practice, which, while affording him all the interests and amusements of town, ought to bring him speedily into notice, and raise him, step by step, to the height of his profession. He had begun his medical career by thinking of both these eventualities as desirable, each in its kind, and had gone on cherishing a leaning to the first, till—he must say it— her example and influence had inspired him with greater ardour in the cause of science and of humanity. He had made inquiries and had heard of a post—in fact he had got the refusing of it—in connection with a new settlement, a fresh attempt to plant a colony where the climate was favourable on one of the great African rivers. His income at first would be small, and he must take his share of the hardships and labours of those who aimed at being more than gold-diggers or miners in the diamond-fields—that is, pioneers of civilization. The prospect, so far as it referred to scientific investigations, and to a large increase to accredited stores of knowledge, was simply splendid. Farther, he was assured of the sympathy and support of the leading men among the colonists, since they had already, to their credit, sought his co-operation. Those of them who were in the van—on the spot—had gone so far as to lay the foundation of an hospital, in addition to a church, to deal alike with black men and white, to labour for their spiritual and physical healing in common. He had almost made up his mind to take the post, but he wished to ask her opinion and advice first.

She was tempted to say she was no authority, but her truthfulness forbade the subterfuge. She could not meet his grave blue eyes and put him off with an evasive answer. She spoke bravely and wisely.

"I think it would be most right and honourable for you to go. With your ability and training you might furnish invaluable aid to a young colony; while it would be like another college course for you, with nature for your teacher. Any young man of spirit and philanthropy, with love for his calling, might well covet the chance. If the colony flourish, you and your profession, and the hospital you speak of, will flourish with it, and have as fine a future before you as you can desire. If the scheme fail, you can but return to England; and you will not have lost the time which a young man can well spare. For you will bring back all you have gained from a far wider sphere of usefulness, and from a fresher experience than you could ever hope to secure by staying at home. But if what you really want," Annie corrected herself, with a twinkle in her eyes and a curl of her lips, in the midst of her earnestness, "is the shortest and safest road to growing well-to-do within the briefest space of time, you had better adopt the latter alternative. If I had been a man and a doctor, I should have tried the former."

"That is enough," he said with conviction.

"But what will your sister say?" she hastened to inquire, in order to turn the conversation from ominous personalities.

"Oh! it will be a blow to poor little Kate," he owned regretfully, "because she is too young to go out with me at once, and set about keeping house for me as she has always proposed—a rough, primitive style of housekeeping it will be out there for many a day. But she is not without pluck, and she is as true as steel, though I say it. She must learn some of your fearlessness and faith, and make the best of things. She must go to one of our aunts in the meantime, and when matters are smoother and easier, and the fate of the colony is decided, perhaps she may join me. I do not believe that there is any danger to speak of from the native tribes, only it will not be drawing-room work for some time to come. You see it is not the same with a girl like Kate as it would be with a woman like you," he had the boldness to insinuate. "You would be a tower of strength in yourself from the beginning; you might be the making of a newly-founded hospital."

"Poor Kate!" said Annie, hastily apostrophizing the girl she had been said to ignore, and speaking in accents of far deeper pity than she had any idea of.

"And what do you say?" he turned upon her.

"I?" she cried in much confusion. "I have said my say."

"No," he answered; "unless you mean to send me away to the ends of the earth without a shred of hope. You cannot do that."

"I think you are taking advantage of me," she protested, but quite meekly and diffidently for Annie. "I have never been even civil to you till Tom Robinson was in danger, and then I had to put all my private feelings aside on his account. Before that I was more than rude."

"And you are a little sorry now? Confess it, Annie, when I am going off all alone, so far as old friends are concerned, to Central Africa, at your bidding."

"Not at my bidding," she declared hastily; "it is too bad of you to say so."

"And you are going to be far kinder in the end than in the beginning," he persisted. "You are going to say, 'Harry Ironside, if you ever come back, whether it is to stay or to go out again to your colony, you will find me waiting for you as your earthly reward.'"

"Of course you will come back," she exclaimed vehemently, thrown off her guard; "but *you* had much better wait and look out for some more gracious person to welcome you."

"I don't care for gracious persons," said the foolish fellow scornfully; "that is, for persons who are always gracious whether they like or dislike their company. But I say," he went on, in an eager boyish way, which was not unbecoming or inharmonious where his young manhood was concerned, only natural and pleasant, "I should care for the best and brightest and bonniest woman in the world being gracious to me; I would give much to make her like me, though I know I am far behind her in cleverness and goodness."

"Nonsense," cried Annie, quite testily. "I shall be used up in hospital service by that time," she remonstrated, keeping to the far future. "A faded woman with a sharp tongue would not be a great reward."

"I ask nothing better than a woman whom I could love, and who might love me."

"But you deserve something better," she said, in a softer, lower tone.

"Never mind what I deserve, if I get what I have wished, longed, and prayed for since the first moment I saw you— think of that, Annie."

"I can't," she said, almost piteously, while she suffered him to take her hand. "I meant it all to be so different. I was so proud of my independence; and I never, never will forfeit it, remember, Harry Ironside, till all my sisters are started in the world, and father and mother are made more comfortable. Oh! it would be doubly a shame in me to fail them."

"I am content to wait for my prize," he said, daring to kiss her lovely cheek, and he was content—for the moment.

"And you must not breathe a word of what has happened," she charged him.

But here he grew restive. "I must, dearest. Why, it would be doubly dishonourable not to speak at once to Dr. Millar, confined as he is to his chair; you cannot fail to see that."

"They will all laugh at me," sighed the subdued Annie, with comical ruefulness. "Rose will laugh, and May. I believe even Dora and mother will laugh."

"Let them." He gave the permission with cheerful insensibility to the ordeal, even though Annie's feelings were so much involved in it. "It may be a warning to some of them." Then he was so callous as to add, "Who cares though the whole world, including Tom Robinson, were to join in the guffaw."

"Oh!" she exclaimed, looking up with bright sweetness, "I think I could bear it if I heard Tom's voice in the chorus. He used to have rather a foolish, nervous laugh, for so sensible and brave a man. But I am sure I should not think it foolish, or anything save delightful, if I heard it again."

Sarah Tytler

CHAPTER XXIII

SECOND THOUGHTS AND LAST WORDS

Dr. and Mrs. Millar could make no objection to Dr. Harry Ironside as a suitor for their daughter. It was all the other way. They were highly satisfied with the young man's antecedents and credentials, and yet Dr. Millar was a good deal taken aback. He had grown to look on nursing as a career for Annie, and to take pride in her excellence in it, as he would have done had she been his son and a young doctor. He could not help feeling as if marriage interfered a little with his views for her. He had to recall that Ironside was a very fine young fellow, with a commendable spirit of inquiry in medical matters. He would do credit to his profession, and Annie, especially if she went with him to a new colony, might work in his company, and be his right hand.

Mrs. Millar had too much good sense and womanly experience to approve of long engagements, and she did not like the chance of Annie's going to Africa—still she would fulfil what Mrs. Millar considered the highest and happiest destiny for a woman, that of becoming the wife of a worthy man. As to Africa, the little Doctor, a fixture in his chair, told her, "My dear Maria, we shall simply be giving hostages to Providence, for man was told to occupy the earth, and carry civilization and redemption to its utmost bounds."

To spare Annie's feelings, her relations kept her engagement and their laughter well in the background, while Dr. Harry

Ironside, having probed the Russian fever to the bottom, and seen nearly the last of it, returned in triumph to London, to make arrangements for his medical mission.

As for Annie, in her eagerness to escape from the rallying she had provoked, she talked incessantly about going back to St. Ebbe's, where, however, she was not yet due. A longer leave of absence had been granted to her, in consideration of the fact that her holiday had been mainly spent in hard work in the impromptu hospital at Redcross. She would not have accepted the additional grant apart from the circumstance that Harry Ironside was in London. Annie admitted to herself, in the secret recesses of her heart, that now it had come to this, she would fain have passed these last precious weeks near her young lover. But she would not consent to give occasion to Rose, or any other person—not even to Harry Ironside himself—to think or say that she, Annie Millar, was already not able to live without him. Annie's wings might be clipped, but she would be Annie proud and "plucky" to the last; and her lover, instinctively knowing her to be true as steel, loved her the better because of her regard for what she considered his credit as well as her own. The pride was only skin deep; the pluck was part of the heroic element in Annie.

Rose had been delayed in her work. She had not found it in her heart to walk about taking sketches when the good friend who had so much to do with the commission was little likely to see its completion. But when Tom Robinson could sit up, walk into the next room, and go back to his own house, she felt at liberty to set about her delightful business, in which her father took so keen an interest. She lost no time in starting every fine day in pursuit of the selected views, to put them on canvas while their autumnal hues were still but tinges of red, russet, and gold.

Rose was mostly waited on by May, who took much satisfaction in helping to carry and set up the artist's apparatus, feeling, as she said, that she was part of a painter when she did so.

Sarah Tytler

Dora had been with Rose, May, and Tray at a pretty reach of the Dewes. The elder sister was returning alone, along the path between the elms by the river, near the place where Tom Robinson had come to Tray's rescue, when she met him face to face. He was taking what "constitutional" he was able for, and enjoying the light breeze which was rippling the river, just as it rippled the ripe corn and fanned the hot brows of the men who were working the corn machine in the field beyond.

Dora had seen and spoken to him several times since his illness, but there had been other people present, and now the old shy dread of a *tete-a-tete* again took possession of her. She would have contented herself with a fluttered inquiry after his health, and a faltering remark that she ought not to detain him. She would have hurried on, as if the errand on which she was bound demanded the utmost speed, supremely wretched while she did so, to notice how pale and worn he still looked when she saw him in the broad sunshine. She would have mourned over the circumstance that he wore no wrap, though there was always some damp by the river, and speculated in despondency whether it could be right for him, while he still looked so ill, to be walking thus by himself? What would happen if faintness overtook him, and he could not accomplish the distance between him and the town?

Tom Robinson, delicate though he looked, quiet as he was, would not let Dora have her way. He turned and walked back with her, which ought to have set one of her fears at rest. And his appearance must have belied him, for he was clearly in excellent spirits, with not the most distant intention of being overcome by faintness.

"This is very pleasant," he said, with a smile, and his smile was a peculiarly agreeable one.

Dora could not tell whether he meant the day, or the road, or her company, or even her summer dress, which was fresher and better cared for than when he had encountered the family group "place-hunting" in London. Dora had owned more leisure lately, and, absurd as it might sound, her heart had been singing with joy, so that she could not resist making her dress in keeping with the gladness of her spirit. Her little fingers had been cleverer than they had ever shown themselves before in the manufacture of a frock and the trimming of a hat which would not have disgraced the taste and execution of Miss Franklin. Yet the materials were simple and inexpensive to the last degree—a brown holland and a shady brown hat, and about the frock and the hat some old Indian silk which in its mellowed gorgeousness of red and maize colours softly reflected the hues of Rose's parrot tulips.

Dora did not dare to ask her companion what he thought so pleasant. It seemed right to take it for granted that it was the weather, so she answered quickly, Yes, it was a fine day for the harvest, which she believed was going to be a good one this year.

"Our present encounter is more tranquil than our last, near this very spot," he went on, still smiling. "Perhaps it is as well that there are no disturbing elements of collies and terriers on the scene, for though I am getting on famously, I am not sure that I am up to the mark of dragging Tray and a giant assailant to the edge of the bank, and pitching them head-foremost into the water."

"I should think not," said Dora briefly.

"How 'little May' screamed, and you stood, as white as a sheet, valorously aiming your stone."

"We were great cowards, both of us," admitted Dora, smiling too; "and I am thankful to say Tray has been much better behaved since he was at the veterinary surgeon's."

"There was room for improvement," Tom Robinson said, with the gravity of a judge.

"I left him on in front, begging to May for a bit of chalk."

"It is as well that it was not for a bit of beef," he said. Then he suddenly changed the subject. "Do you know that I have something of yours which has come into my hands that I have been wishing to give back to you ever since I was a responsible being again?"

As he spoke, he unfastened for the second time in their acquaintance the tiny vinaigrette case from his watch-chain, and handed it to her.

Dora flushed scarlet, and took it without a word.

"I got it one night in the course of that fever, when I was at the worst, and I know you will like to hear that I am sure it did me good. The first thing that I recollect after a long blank, which lasted for days, I believe, was feebly fingering and sniffing at the little box, with a curious agreeable sense of old association. Then I was able to look at it, and recognize it as my mother's vinaigrette. She had let me play with it when I was a child; and when I was a boy, subject to headache from staying too long in the hot sunshine in the cricket-field, she used to lend me her vinaigrette for a cure. But I knew that I had asked you to have it, and that you had done me the favour to accept it. The fascinating puzzle was, how had it come back to me? At last I questioned Barbara Franklin. She could not tell any more than myself at first, and was equally puzzled, until she remembered your sister Annie's running into the room on the night when you were listening for news of my death, and asking for a smelling-bottle, and your fumbling for an instant in your pocket, and giving her something. That made it perfectly plain."

Too plain, Dora reflected in horror, for what might not Miss Franklin have suspected and communicated in addition to her cousin?

"I was glad I had it in my pocket," said Dora, stammering. "I took it up to London with me, and—and found it often refreshing in the middle of the heat and fatigue. I am thankful to hear it was of use to you, who have the best right to it."

"No," he said emphatically, "though it was of the greatest use. My cousin Barbara said also that you were very sorry for me. Dora, was that so?" Tom himself blushed a little in asking the question, as if he had a guilty consciousness of having taken rather a mean advantage of Dora Millar, first by coming so near to death without actually dying, and then by listening to what his kinswoman had to say of Miss Dora Millar's state of mind at the crisis.

On Dora's part there was no denying such a manifest truth; she could only utter a tremulous "yes," and turn her head aside.

"That was good of you, though I do not know that I am repaying the goodness properly," he said, with another smile, very wistful this time. "For I must add, that hearing of it tempted me to wonder once again whether you could ever learn to think of me? If you cannot, just say no, and I'll cease from this moment to tease you" (as if he had been doing nothing else save besiege and pester her for the last year and a half!).

Dora could not say "no" any more than she could say "yes" straight out, though she was certain that to be kept any longer than was absolutely necessary in a state of acute suspense was very bad for him in his weakened health. By a great effort she brought herself to say in little breaks and gasps, "I do not need to learn, Mr. Tom, because I have thought of you for a long time now—long before you were so good and generous to all of us—almost ever since you wished—you asked—what I was so silly and so ungrateful as to refuse."

He drew her hand through his arm and held it tightly; he could not trust himself to say or do more. He was almost as shy as she was in the revulsion of his great happiness.

She struggled conscientiously to continue her confession. "I had thought hardly at all of you before then. Girls are so full of themselves, and I did not know that you wished me to think of you. I seem to see now that if you had given me more time, and let me grow familiar with the idea, even though we were 'donkeys,' as Annie and Rose say, and though we were choke-full of youthful folly—" She stopped short without finishing her sentence, or going farther into the nature of what she seemed to see.

"But I besought you to take time, Dora, love," he remonstrated. "You forget, I urged you to let me wait for the chance of your answer's being different." He could not help, even in the hour of the attainment of the dearest wish of his heart, being just to his old modest, reasonable self.

"Yes," she said, with the prettiest, faintest, arch smile hovering about the corners of her mouth. "But men ought to be wiser than to take simple girls at their first word, which the girls can never, never unsay, unless the men bid them. Now I'll tell you how malicious people will view the present situation. They will say that I refused you point blank when I thought we were well off, then got you to propose again, and graciously accepted the proposal, when I knew we had not a penny in the world. I own it looks very like it, and it is partly your fault; you should not have let me go the first time. But I don't care what people say, so long as there is not a word of truth in it."

"Nor I," said Tom undauntedly. "They may also say that I was able to make myself useful to your family, and like a very tradesman, traded on the usefulness, buying a reluctant bride with it. But what do we care when we love each other, and God has given us to each other? 'They say,'—what do they say? Let them say."

There was not the shadow of a cloud the size of a man's hand on Dr. and Mrs. Millar's pleasure in their daughter Dora's marriage to Tom Robinson. For instead of going with Annie to Africa, or starting on a mission of her own to bring May's college fees from Jamaica, Dora remained at Redcross to be

Tom Robinson's dear wife and cherished darling. Mrs. Millar had long seen, in her turn, that Dora could not do better. The fine old shop, and the fantastic shade of poor Aunt Penny, had both become of no account. The single thing which troubled Mrs. Millar was that the instant Lady Mary Pemberton heard of the wedding in prospect, she invited herself to come down to it.

Dora's sisters, with the charming inconsistency of young women, were not only acquiescent in her undignified fate— they were jubilant over it.

It did not arrest, though it subdued the general congratulations, when it was discovered that the event made Harry Ironside all at once both envious and aggressive. He could not see why, if Dora Millar were marrying a rich man, and he himself had a sufficient income not merely to make a satisfactory settlement on his wife, but to do his part in helping her relatives, who would also be his from the day he married her, that his marriage should not take place as soon as Dora and Tom Robinson's. In place of an indefinite engagement, with thousands of miles of land and sea, and all the uncertainties of life into the bargain, between him, Harry Ironside, and Annie Millar, would it not be much better that he should carry away with him the brightest, bravest woman who ever asked little from a new colony; who, in place of asking, would give full measure and running over? For Annie was not like poor dear little Kate—Annie would be a godsend, even though she had to go the length of learning to fire a revolver as a defence against lions and hostile natives. It would be nothing else than savage pride in Dr. Millar, Harry continued to argue, to decline to let Tom Robinson defray May's small expenses at St. Ambrose's, whether she won a scholarship or not. He was a man with an ample fortune, as well as the nicest fellow in the world, who was going to be not only May's coach, but her brother-in-law. In like manner it would be downright churlish and positively unkind to Dora if her parents refused to occupy the pleasant small house with the large garden belonging to Tom Robinson, and close to what

Sarah Tytler

would be their daughter's house. It was conveniently vacant, and looked as if it had been made for a couple of elderly gentle-folks, who were not rich, but were comfortably provided for. In fact, it had been fitted up by the late Mr. Charles Robinson for just such a pair, who had in the course of nature left the house empty.

With regard to Rose, she would have to submit to be more or less Harry Ironside's charge till she painted and sold such 'stunning' pictures that she could afford to look down on his paltry aid. What, not allow him to assist his own sister-in-law, when he was so thankful to think that she might be like a sister in the meantime for his poor little Kate to fall back upon? Why, the girls could go on making a home together at his good friend Mrs. Jennings's, till it was right for Kate, after she was old enough to choose, to cast in her lot with him and Annie, supposing the colony prospered. His heart was already in that strange, far-away region, which, with all its mysteries and wonders—ay, and its terrors—has such an attraction for the young and high-spirited, the typical pilgrims to a later New England.

And what did Annie think of this march stolen upon her, this attempt to extort a yard where she had only granted an inch of favour? Perhaps she was dazzled by what would have repelled many another woman, in the primitive, precarious, exciting details of the life of a young colony. Perhaps her heart and imagination were alike taken by storm when she thought of the untenanted hospital wards and the patients calling for her to go over and help them. Perhaps she was simply beginning so to identify herself with Harry Ironside that what he did seemed her doing. Anyhow Annie did not say no.

The Miss Dyers remarked oracularly, when the double marriage was announced in Redcross, that it was just what they had expected. The observation was somewhat vague, like other oracles' speeches. The general public of Redcross, including the Careys and Hewetts, were less indefinite and more cordial in their expression of satisfaction at the suitable settlement in life of the little Doctor's elder daughters.

Miss Franklin could not be too thankful and pleased that, after all, she had done no mischief to her cousin Tom by her blunder, and by what had been her only too personal reproaches and revelations addressed to his future wife on the night when he was believed to be lying dying. In fact, if she, Barbara Franklin, had not been conscious of a huge mistake, with all the deplorable consequences it might have carried in its train, if she had not thus been kept shamefacedly humble and silent as to her share in the business, she might have taken credit to herself, with greater reason than Mrs. Jennings could boast, of having united a supremely happy couple who were drifting apart. Even if Miss Franklin's part in it had been played voluntarily and advisedly, she would never have cause to regret that night's work. For Dora Robinson had no scruple in being the fast friend and affectionate cousin of her husband's forewoman. She had no more qualm than she would have felt if Miss Franklin had never condescended to trade, but had remained within the bounds of poor gentility by laboriously keeping up her halting classical music and waning foreign languages, and by continuing a finishing governess to the day of her death—or rather till she was superannuated, and had to retire to a too literal garret.

"Oh! Jonathan"—Mrs. Millar could not resist a long-drawn sob on the great day of the double marriage—"it is all very well to say Annie has got a good husband—a fine disinterested young man, certain to be distinguished in his profession, you tell me. I believe that, and am very thankful for it. How could I bear the parting otherwise? But to let our eldest, our prettiest, and wittiest, with her warm heart and untiring energy—'the flower of the flock,' as people used to call her when the children were young—go out to Africa, it may be to meet unheard-of trials, like your poor Aunt Penny, it may be never to see our faces again—" Mrs. Millar could say no more.

"Hush! hush! Maria; you must be reasonable—you must take the bad with the good," enjoined the little Doctor from his arm-chair. "Why, you are making as much commotion as you did when Annie said she would be a nurse. Is an hospital ward at home so preferable to an hospital ward in the dark continent, which is ceasing to be dark? Its sun is only too blazingly bright, its river plains too teemingly fertile, its mountains too grand even in the grander monotony of its deserts. There is gold in its dust, and its rocks are glittering with diamonds. But, thank God, that is not all. It is the great country for which Livingstone was content to spend his life, where the Moffats made the wilderness blossom like the rose, and Colenso won the wild heart of the Zulu to trust him as a brother. You will have Dora and Tom next door to you, and Rose and 'little May' will be constantly coming and going. As for Annie and Harry, how can you tell that their special gifts would not be wasted here, as I have often thought hers would have been if she had continued only a pretty, sprightly young lady, and not grown up into an hospital nurse!"

"Perhaps you are right, Jonathan," answered his wife meekly, coming round, as she did now more than ever, to his side of the question.

"Do you think Sir John Richardson's daughter, Bishop Selwyn's wife, missed the highest calling she was capable of when, instead of presiding over a pleasant country-house or a fine London drawing-room, she consented with all her heart to be landed on an island in Melanesia, and left among the native converts to help to prepare the Malay girls for confirmation? Her husband was away in the meantime in his missionary yacht on his noble enterprise, ready to take her off the island on his return, and not fearing to trust her in the interval to their God whose work she was doing," argued the old man, with a note of something like exultation in his voice. "Annie and Harry are not going out to Africa, as my Aunt Penny and poor Beauchamp of Waylands went to Australia in the days of the earlier squatters, entirely for their own hand, and because they cannot help themselves, since there is nothing left for them to do here. Our children are going to render gallant service on which their talents are well bestowed, of which we shall always be proud to hear. They are, as I told you before, our hostages in the carrying out of the great purpose of the Almighty Ruler of the universe, by which light is to take the place of darkness, and good of evil, from the rivers even to the ends of the earth."

Choose from Thousands of 1stWorldLibrary Classics By

A. M. Barnard
Ada Leverson
Adolphus William Ward
Aesop
Agatha Christie
Alexander Aaronsohn
Alexander Kielland
Alexandre Dumas
Alfred Gatty
Alfred Ollivant
Alice Duer Miller
Alice Turner Curtis
Alice Dunbar
Allen Chapman
Alleyne Ireland
Ambrose Bierce
Amelia E. Barr
Amory H. Bradford
Andrew Lang
Andrew McFarland Davis
Andy Adams
Angela Brazil
Anna Alice Chapin
Anna Sewell
Annie Besant
Annie Hamilton Donnell
Annie Payson Call
Annie Roe Carr
Annonaymous
Anton Chekhov
Archibald Lee Fletcher
Arnold Bennett
Arthur C. Benson
Arthur Conan Doyle
Arthur M. Winfield
Arthur Ransome
Arthur Schnitzler
Arthur Train
Atticus
B.H. Baden-Powell
B. M. Bower
B. C. Chatterjee
Baroness Emmuska Orczy
Baroness Orczy
Basil King
Bayard Taylor
Ben Macomber
Bertha Muzzy Bower
Bjornstjerne Bjornson

Booth Tarkington
Boyd Cable
Bram Stoker
C. Collodi
C. E. Orr
C. M. Ingleby
Carolyn Wells
Catherine Parr Traill
Charles A. Eastman
Charles Amory Beach
Charles Dickens
Charles Dudley Warner
Charles Farrar Browne
Charles Ives
Charles Kingsley
Charles Klein
Charles Hanson Towne
Charles Lathrop Pack
Charles Romyn Dake
Charles Whibley
Charles Willing Beale
Charlotte M. Braeme
Charlotte M. Yonge
Charlotte Perkins Stetson
Clair W. Hayes
Clarence Day Jr.
Clarence E. Mulford
Clemence Housman
Confucius
Coningsby Dawson
Cornelis DeWitt Wilcox
Cyril Burleigh
D. H. Lawrence
Daniel Defoe
David Garnett
Dinah Craik
Don Carlos Janes
Donald Keyhoe
Dorothy Kilner
Dougan Clark
Douglas Fairbanks
E. Nesbit
E. P. Roe
E. Phillips Oppenheim
E. S. Brooks
Earl Barnes
Edgar Rice Burroughs
Edith Van Dyne
Edith Wharton

Edward Everett Hale
Edward J. O'Biren
Edward S. Ellis
Edwin L. Arnold
Eleanor Atkins
Eleanor Hallowell Abbott
Eliot Gregory
Elizabeth Gaskell
Elizabeth McCracken
Elizabeth Von Arnim
Ellem Key
Emerson Hough
Emilie F. Carlen
Emily Bronte
Emily Dickinson
Enid Bagnold
Enilor Macartney Lane
Erasmus W. Jones
Ernie Howard Pie
Ethel May Dell
Ethel Turner
Ethel Watts Mumford
Eugene Sue
Eugenie Foa
Eugene Wood
Eustace Hale Ball
Evelyn Everett-green
Everard Cotes
F. H. Cheley
F. J. Cross
F. Marion Crawford
Fannie E. Newberry
Federick Austin Ogg
Ferdinand Ossendowski
Fergus Hume
Florence A. Kilpatrick
Fremont B. Deering
Francis Bacon
Francis Darwin
Frances Hodgson Burnett
Frances Parkinson Keyes
Frank Gee Patchin
Frank Harris
Frank Jewett Mather
Frank L. Packard
Frank V. Webster
Frederic Stewart Isham
Frederick Trevor Hill
Frederick Winslow Taylor

Friedrich Kerst
Friedrich Nietzsche
Fyodor Dostoyevsky
G.A. Henty
G.K. Chesterton
Gabrielle E. Jackson
Garrett P. Serviss
Gaston Leroux
George A. Warren
George Ade
Geroge Bernard Shaw
George Cary Eggleston
George Durston
George Ebers
George Eliot
George Gissing
George MacDonald
George Meredith
George Orwell
George Sylvester Viereck
George Tucker
George W. Cable
George Wharton James
Gertrude Atherton
Gordon Casserly
Grace E. King
Grace Gallatin
Grace Greenwood
Grant Allen
Guillermo A. Sherwell
Gulielma Zollinger
Gustav Flaubert
H. A. Cody
H. B. Irving
H.C. Bailey
H. G. Wells
H. H. Munro
H. Irving Hancock
H. R. Naylor
H. Rider Haggard
H. W. C. Davis
Haldeman Julius
Hall Caine
Hamilton Wright Mabie
Hans Christian Andersen
Harold Avery
Harold McGrath
Harriet Beecher Stowe
Harry Castlemon
Harry Coghill
Harry Houidini

Hayden Carruth
Helent Hunt Jackson
Helen Nicolay
Hendrik Conscience
Hendy David Thoreau
Henri Barbusse
Henrik Ibsen
Henry Adams
Henry Ford
Henry Frost
Henry James
Henry Jones Ford
Henry Seton Merriman
Henry W Longfellow
Herbert A. Giles
Herbert Carter
Herbert N. Casson
Herman Hesse
Hildegard G. Frey
Homer
Honore De Balzac
Horace B. Day
Horace Walpole
Horatio Alger Jr.
Howard Pyle
Howard R. Garis
Hugh Lofting
Hugh Walpole
Humphry Ward
Ian Maclaren
Inez Haynes Gillmore
Irving Bacheller
Isabel Cecilia Williams
Isabel Hornibrook
Israel Abrahams
Ivan Turgenev
J.G.Austin
J. Henri Fabre
J. M. Barrie
J. M. Walsh
J. Macdonald Oxley
J. R. Miller
J. S. Fletcher
J. S. Knowles
J. Storer Clouston
J. W. Duffield
Jack London
Jacob Abbott
James Allen
James Andrews
James Baldwin

James Branch Cabell
James DeMille
James Joyce
James Lane Allen
James Lane Allen
James Oliver Curwood
James Oppenheim
James Otis
James R. Driscoll
Jane Abbott
Jane Austen
Jane L. Stewart
Janet Aldridge
Jens Peter Jacobsen
Jerome K. Jerome
Jessie Graham Flower
John Buchan
John Burroughs
John Cournos
John F. Kennedy
John Gay
John Glasworthy
John Habberton
John Joy Bell
John Kendrick Bangs
John Milton
John Philip Sousa
John Taintor Foote
Jonas Lauritz Idemil Lie
Jonathan Swift
Joseph A. Altsheler
Joseph Carey
Joseph Conrad
Joseph E. Badger Jr
Joseph Hergesheimer
Joseph Jacobs
Jules Vernes
Julian Hawthrone
Julie A Lippmann
Justin Huntly McCarthy
Kakuzo Okakura
Karle Wilson Baker
Kate Chopin
Kenneth Grahame
Kenneth McGaffey
Kate Langley Bosher
Kate Langley Bosher
Katherine Cecil Thurston
Katherine Stokes
L. A. Abbot
L. T. Meade

L. Frank Baum
Latta Griswold
Laura Dent Crane
Laura Lee Hope
Laurence Housman
Lawrence Beasley
Leo Tolstoy
Leonid Andreyev
Lewis Carroll
Lewis Sperry Chafer
Lilian Bell
Lloyd Osbourne
Louis Hughes
Louis Joseph Vance
Louis Tracy
Louisa May Alcott
Lucy Fitch Perkins
Lucy Maud Montgomery
Luther Benson
Lydia Miller Middleton
Lyndon Orr
M. Corvus
M. H. Adams
Margaret E. Sangster
Margret Howth
Margaret Vandercook
Margaret W. Hungerford
Margret Penrose
Maria Edgeworth
Maria Thompson Daviess
Mariano Azuela
Marion Polk Angellotti
Mark Overton
Mark Twain
Mary Austin
Mary Catherine Crowley
Mary Cole
Mary Hastings Bradley
Mary Roberts Rinehart
Mary Rowlandson
M. Wollstonecraft Shelley
Maud Lindsay
Max Beerbohm
Myra Kelly
Nathaniel Hawthrone
Nicolo Machiavelli
O. F. Walton
Oscar Wilde

Owen Johnson
P.G. Wodehouse
Paul and Mabel Thorne
Paul G. Tomlinson
Paul Severing
Percy Brebner
Percy Keese Fitzhugh
Peter B. Kyne
Plato
Quincy Allen
R. Derby Holmes
R. L. Stevenson
R. S. Ball
Rabindranath Tagore
Rahul Alvares
Ralph Bonehill
Ralph Henry Barbour
Ralph Victor
Ralph Waldo Emmerson
Rene Descartes
Ray Cummings
Rex Beach
Rex E. Beach
Richard Harding Davis
Richard Jefferies
Richard Le Gallienne
Robert Barr
Robert Frost
Robert Gordon Anderson
Robert L. Drake
Robert Lansing
Robert Lynd
Robert Michael Ballantyne
Robert W. Chambers
Rosa Nouchette Carey
Rudyard Kipling
Saint Augustine
Samuel B. Allison
Samuel Hopkins Adams
Sarah Bernhardt
Sarah C. Hallowell
Selma Lagerlof
Sherwood Anderson
Sigmund Freud
Standish O'Grady
Stanley Weyman
Stella Benson
Stella M. Francis

Stephen Crane
Stewart Edward White
Stijn Streuvels
Swami Abhedananda
Swami Parmananda
T. S. Ackland
T. S. Arthur
The Princess Der Ling
Thomas A. Janvier
Thomas A Kempis
Thomas Anderton
Thomas Bailey Aldrich
Thomas Bulfinch
Thomas De Quincey
Thomas Dixon
Thomas H. Huxley
Thomas Hardy
Thomas More
Thornton W. Burgess
U. S. Grant
Upton Sinclair
Valentine Williams
Various Authors
Vaughan Kester
Victor Appleton
Victor G. Durham
Victoria Cross
Virginia Woolf
Wadsworth Camp
Walter Camp
Walter Scott
Washington Irving
Wilbur Lawton
Wilkie Collins
Willa Cather
Willard F. Baker
William Dean Howells
William le Queux
W. Makepeace Thackeray
William W. Walter
William Shakespeare
Winston Churchill
Yei Theodora Ozaki
Yogi Ramacharaka
Young E. Allison
Zane Grey

www.ingramcontent.com/pod-product-compliance
Lightning Source LLC
Chambersburg PA
CBHW030113180626
46812CB00002B/404